With a suppressed shudder, he set her quickly away from him, grinding his teeth against the violent stab of passion that had hit him unawares, like a sledgehammer blow to his middle . . . He shut his eyes, breathing deeply.

"Jamie, what's wrong? What did I *say*?" Her bewildered voice sliced across the battle Jamie was waging with his body, and he opened his eyes to see her face inches from his.

With a muted groan, he pulled her back into his arms. "No, sweet, nothing's wrong! You haven't—" He shifted his weight as the words tore from his throat, and then he was meeting her gaze, telling her with his eyes, of the sudden, terrible need inside him.

Her mouth opened with a small cry as Jamie claimed it with his. Lips parted, she felt his tongue graze her teeth; his lips were firm, his mouth, hot and demanding. The kiss deepened, tongue meeting tongue, and they let their hunger rage. . . .

HIGHLAND FIRE

VERONICA SATTLER

ST. MARTIN'S PAPERBACKS

To the memory of Major Acres Lacey and Champion
Sciota's Mor Dubh Fionn
Beloved companions, sorely missed.

HIGHLAND FIRE

Copyright © 1993 by Veronica Sattler.

Cover photograph by Nancy Palubniak.

ISBN: 0-312-92983-8

Printed in the United States of America

St. Martin's Paperbacks edition/July 1993

10 9 8 7 6 5 4 3 2 1

⊹Chapter 1:
London England⊹

Late June 1815

Lady Christina St. John sat, dry-eyed, staring at the pair of miniatures on her dressing table. The news that her parents had been killed in the accident resulting from a faulty carriage axle had reached her less than twenty-four hours ago, yet she still hadn't shed a single tear.

Dimly, aware that the thought seemed to come from a great distance, she supposed she must be in shock. She knew this inability to cry, to evidence some outward display of grief, did not mean she hadn't loved her parents. Indeed, she had doted on them, and as the only child of the earl and countess of Marston's twenty-year marriage, she'd been the recipient of enormous parental love and affection in return.

But somehow it was hard to reconcile what she was gazing at, the pair of smiling images in their silver repoussé frames, with the fact that she would never see them again. Her eyes rested on the titian curls of the woman in the portrait, curls so like her own, and she couldn't quite make herself believe that Mama wouldn't be calling to her soon, from her bedchamber down the hall, asking Christina's opinion on the latest coiffure, or the design of a new gown.

Her gaze shifted to the image of the fair-haired man in its matching frame. Papa's large, widely spaced eyes were intelligent and not without a glint of deviltry in their brown depths. Christina knew she'd inherited their shape, if not their color. Hers were gray, like Mama's. A clear, translucent gray that often held a hint of violet, especially if she wore that color . . . as Mama did . . . in the portrait . . .

Christina took a deep breath and let it out slowly, but still the tears wouldn't come. Shock, then . . . it had to be shock . . .

A soft knock at the door intruded. Grateful for a diversion, even if it was one of the servants, Christina called out permission to enter, deliberately turning toward the door—and away from the miniatures.

A dark-haired woman about her mother's age, still pretty despite the telling touch of gray at her temples, came quietly into the chamber. Maire Fitzpatrick had been with the St. Johns since Christina was born. Surviving the transition from nursemaid, to companion, to personal ladies' maid and confidante, the Irishwoman was the closest thing to family Christina had left now. She suddenly found she welcomed the comfort of Maire's sensible, maternal presence; hugging it to her like a benediction, she gave Maire a soft smile.

"Ach, lass, 'tis relieved I am t' see ye able t' smile," said Maire, whose own face was red from weeping. She set aside the small tea tray she'd brought and peered worriedly at Christina's delicate features. "Though a few tears from yer lovely eyes would not be taken amiss. Have ye not yet wept, lass?"

Christina shook her head and reached for the tea things, anxious to change the subject. She felt sure she would find time to grieve, perhaps once the small, private funeral she planned was behind them; but for now there were even more pressing matters on her mind.

Such as how to avoid financial ruin.

She was well aware of where her parents had been traveling in that carriage, over rocky, dangerous roads, and why. They'd been on their way to her mother's ancestral home in the Scottish Highlands. MacKenzie Manor, it was called, and although the countess had spent her childhood there, Christina was unfamiliar with it, having gone to it herself only once, when she was a baby. In fact, Margaret MacKenzie St. John hadn't seen it in years, not since the deaths of her maternal grandparents. At that time the surviving MacKenzie heiress—there was an old entailment that the MacKenzie properties had to be passed down through the direct line of *female* descent— had decided to be an absentee owner and remain with her husband and daughter in England.

Why, I suppose I am the MacKenzie heiress now! Christina suddenly realized, startled by the thought.

Well, all to the better, considering the half-formed plan which had been hatched in the middle of a long, sleepless night. Since her parents' desperate bid to rescue them from bankruptcy had been tragically curtailed, Christina knew it now fell to her to perform that rescue. If a rescue were even possible.

It had all begun with that strange letter, followed eventually by Papa's devastating losses on 'Change. Only Papa, Christina thought with a wry inner smile, could have heedlessly risked his entire fortune on the premature news that Napoleon had been *victorious* at Waterloo . . . dear, financially unwise Papa, who'd been solvent enough, if she was to believe his solicitors, that he hadn't *needed* to invest so heavily in high-risk ventures in a wartime economy. And then, to panic, and dump everything for a pittance, simply on the *rumor* that Bonaparte had trounced Wellington's forces!

A *false* rumor, as it turned out, but by then it was too late, and they were in jeopardy. Christina remembered the two of them, Mama and Papa together, telling her about it, not a week ago. They'd always been close, the three of them, with her parents sharing more and more with her as she reached an age where she would be able to handle adult confidences.

And it was in such a spirit of confidence that they'd shown her the letter from Scotland. That Mama had received it in late December didn't signify because, at the time, she and Papa had laughed about it, deeming its contents a flight of fancy from a senile old man. "Imagine," they'd told each other, "the poor old soul has it in his head that we should drop everything and hare off to Scotland on the strength of some Banbury tale of buried treasure! Isn't that famous?"

But then their reverses had come, and suddenly they'd begun to look at the letter from this Angus MacIver in a new light . . . a desperate, wildly hopeful light. And that was when they'd shared it with Christina, at the same time telling her they were off to Scotland in the morning, hoping against hope that the old Highlander's tale was true.

"His lordship called again this mornin'," Maire told her, breaking into her reverie.

"Did he?" Christina responded absently, her mind still flirting with thoughts of buried treasure. The "Seadog's Treasure," the old man had called it . . .

Frowning, Maire clucked disapprovingly. "Did ye hear what I said, lass? Yer *intended*, Lord Aaron, came t' call, t' comfort ye in yer hour o' n—"

An airy gust of laughter cut her off, and the Irishwoman's frown deepened. "Christina, lass, I fail t' see how ye can *laugh* when—"

With a smile, Christina cut her off again. "I'm sorry, Maire, dear, but never say my fiancé came to *comfort* me. It is simply not in Lord Aaron Crenshawe's nature. Say he came out of a sense of proper form, perhaps. Say that his father, the marquis, and conduct befitting a member of the *haut ton* demanded it. Say, even, that he came to discover some substance to the rumors he might have heard, that Papa lost heavily on 'Change and I might therefore no longer be the heiress he desires—but never say his lordship came to comfort! It will not answer."

The older woman's frown became a scowl. " 'Tis a fine piece yer're blatherin', me lass, and yerself just new engaged this spring!"

"Blatherin'?" Christina inquired in a perfect imitation of Maire's brogue. She was an excellent mimic, had been since early childhood; she'd often driven the Irishwoman to distraction, then ultimately to fond chuckles, with her perfect renditions of everything from Maire's Gaelic inflections to a stable lad's East End cant.

But Maire wasn't chuckling now. "Aye, blatherin'! Or worse! 'Tis wicked, even, I'm thinkin', t' be sayin' such things about yer intended!"

"Dearest Maire," said Christina with exaggerated patience, "this is hardly something to put you into such a taking! And it is *not* wicked. It is simply the truth: His lordship has, I am persuaded, a great many sterling qualities, but a tender heart is not among them."

"Saints preserve us!" cried Maire. "Then, 'tis true! I thought as much on the day he offered fer ye, and ye accepted, but I held me tongue. 'Here's the wee colleen,' says I, 'the belle o' the Season, with offers pourin' inta her lap from a good dozen fine gentlemen. So why,' says I, 'is the lass fixin' t' wed that marquis's son with the cold eyes?' But I gave ye credit fer the good sense ye were raised with, *macushla*, and figured ye merely knew his lordship better'n me. And now, here ye be, confirmin' me worst fears! Ach, lass, I cannot understand ye choosin' the man, truly I cannot."

Christina arched a delicately shaped brow at her, but said nothing, taking a sip of tea. She knew *Maire* couldn't understand, but *she* knew *exactly* why she'd chosen the future marquis of Beckwith. She knew she was not in love with Aaron, despite his handsome face and title. But there was a practical streak in her nature that had led her to accept his offer: the cool, haughty Lord Aaron was well reputed to be a managerial wizard who, by the age of thirty, had tripled the worth of the family holdings through shrewd investments and clever estate management for his father.

Unlike dear Papa, Aaron would never have considered risking all he owned in a venture such as the one which threatened the St. Johns. That final, foolish set of investments and its attendant poor judgment was only the last of a great number of close calls which had kept Christina and poor Mama feeling financially insecure in recent years. The last thing she required was a husband who would chance going Papa's route!

And she was also perceptive enough to realize Aaron didn't love *her*. But the large St. John country estate in Surrey shared a boundary with one of the marquis's, and she knew Aaron had been eager to attach it through wedlock. It was, after all, her dowry, for she had no siblings, and it was not entailed with the earldom, which would go, with the country seat in Sussex, to some distant male cousin now.

Moreover, none of those other young swains who'd offered for her after her coming-out had stirred so much as a single passion in her. So why, she'd reasoned, shouldn't she accept a match purely for the financial security the man could provide? It had seemed like a wise decision, even when she could still be considered an heiress.

Of course, now the only thing she was heiress to was a pile of debts and liens, one on the deed to Marchmaine, in Surrey, among them. And she wasn't such a fool as to think Aaron would still wed her if she lost Marchmaine.

Moreover, Aaron had already called twice now, though she'd told Maire and the rest of the staff to plead her excuses and say she wasn't receiving visitors. But she had no doubt his lordship would return, and, as she'd told Maire, his call would have little to do with condolences.

He was sniffing after news of their losses.

Suddenly she was acutely aware of the need to act. And act quickly, while somehow managing to put Aaron off! She hurriedly set down her teacup and rose, heading for the large armoire across the room.

"Maire," she said briskly, "have any of the mourning clothes arrived from Madame Bouchard?"

"Only a pelisse she happened t' have on hand. 'Twas put by fer old Lord Pomfret's young wife a bit, ah, prematurely, when the poor man was taken with that inflammation o' the lungs a few weeks back. Unfortunately, fer the young wife, that is," Maire added wryly, "his lordship took it in his head t' recover."

But Christina barely heard the older woman's acerbic commentary. She was busy rifling through the contents of the armoire, rejecting one garment after another, all far too bright and frivolous for mourning. Despite a preference for cool blues, greens, and violets to offset her fiery hair, her current wardrobe had, after all, been selected to launch her Season; even the pewter satin tea gown, chosen to draw attention to her eyes, was out of the question. But there had to be *something* she could locate to—

"Sweet Holy Mary, child!" Maire exclaimed. "What is it ye're after findin' in there? I *told* ye, 'tis only that pelisse—"

"Maire," said Christina, turning to face her with a deep blue sarcenet gown in hand, "you've got to help me assemble something appropriate. Perhaps, with the pelisse covering—"

"What! *Now?*"

"Yes, of course, now. Whyever did you think I was rummaging?"

"But—but where are ye *goin'*, lass? Yer poor parents are—"

"*We* are going, Maire, to the offices of Carruthers and Higgins, Papa's solicitors. And, then, perhaps, on a treasure hunt!"

* * *

Less than an hour later the two women were seated in the late earl's barouche, being jostled by the afternoon traffic along Piccadilly. Maire's normally good-natured face was severe, for she'd made it clear she did not approve of this trek across the West End at such a time. Mourning was mourning, as she saw it, a time set aside for the private business of dealing with one's grief. There were rules set down by genteel society, governing behavior during a bereavement, rules that served a sensible purpose. And those rules did not countenance an orphan of twenty-four hours traipsing across half of London on a fool's errand!

Buried treasure, is it? she thought, eyeing askance Christina's profile, heavily veiled by a swathe of black lace they'd torn off an old ballgown and attached to the high-crowned black beaver riding hat she wore. *Ach, lass, we've not even buried yer poor, dead parents yet!*

But the Irishwoman knew it would be futile to voice these thoughts aloud now. She'd already used all her powers of persuasion back at the town house, but to no avail. The child was after pursuing this course of action, and nothing would change her mind. Scots stubbornness, that's what it was. She'd seen well enough of this trait the lass had inherited from her mother's side during the years she'd watched her grow up.

Of course, it wasn't that she didn't appreciate the urgency that drove the poor, wee thing to these desperate measures. Christina had confided in her completely before enlisting her aid. Ach, 'twas a pity the earl, her father, hadn't had a better head for business about him! But to throw all decorum to the wind like this, just in the hopes of laying hands on her poor dead mother's reticule, because she was certain it contained that foolish letter from a daft old Scot! 'Twas sheer foolishness! And suppose these solicitors did have the reticule stashed among the countess's effects? What then?

Maire heaved a heavy sigh, for she already knew the answer: another fool's errand, this one even more wanting in decency—and sense! A trip to MacKenzie Manor, in the Scottish Highlands, that was what! And heaven and all the saints preserve them from the very same dangers that had cost Christina's parents their lives!

If Christina was aware of the forebodings plaguing Maire's mind, she paid them small heed. Her own thoughts hovered about the edges of those things she could recall, of the contents of Angus MacIver's letter. She'd seen it only once, and briefly at that. So if Carruthers and Higgins didn't have Mama's reticule, or even if they did, and the letter was no longer in the inner pocket where she'd seen her secrete it, there would be a difficulty. She knew the letter, in addition to giving a brief history of the Seadog's Treasure, contained detailed travel directions for reaching Mr. MacIver's . . . croft, yes, that was what he'd called it. And if she didn't have those directions, she'd have to come by another means of discovering the location of the croft, and that would mean a loss of secrecy.

And secrecy was imperative.

As it was, she knew she'd have difficulty throwing Aaron off the scent. He must never dream she was bound for Scotland, on a route the *Morning Post* had recounted her parents taking, or he would suspect something afoot. Aaron was no lackwit. He'd piece together the suspicions she had no doubt he already entertained. About Papa's losses. With the news that his grieving fiancée had been soliciting directions to the neighborhood of MacKenzie Manor, shortly before she withdrew "into seclusion," as she'd written him in her letter a short while ago. And then she had no doubt he'd find it exceedingly strange that for her "seclusion," she'd chosen the very destination which had so tragically ended her loved ones' lives. Moreover, even if he didn't find it odd that she'd selected the Highlands, with a difficult itinerary, over rough terrain, instead of a sojourn at Marchmaine, or Sunnyfields (their other unentailed estate which was mortgaged to the hilt), he'd be certain to post letters to her. Or perhaps he'd even *follow* her there, full of unwanted questions which she would then be forced to answer—truthfully, for she would never lie to him directly.

She had to recover the letter, then, because inquiring of, say, some of the grooms or other family retainers, as to the direction of MacKenzie Manor, was to surrender all secrecy: servants could be pressed for information, and she had no reason to suspect Aaron wouldn't scruple to press, or even bribe them, to achieve his ends.

Of course, if she could somehow, miraculously, recall the details of the letter without seeing it again . . .

My Dear Lady St. John, it had begun. *You ken me not, for I was away when last you visited your Highland home, but we MacIvers have been loyal clansmen serving the Mac-Kenzies since long before the dark days of Culloden Moor . . . the last of my family . . . keepers of the Seadog's Treasure . . . come before it is too late . . .*

Christina's brow furrowed beneath the heavy veiling as she tried to recall more of the words. There was something about the MacKenzie ancestral home being razed to the ground during the Jacobite uprising of 1745— "the '45 Rising," he'd termed it. But he'd claimed this had happened without discovery of the treasure. The treasure . . . he'd said it had been captured from a Spanish galleon . . . It was very old, then—if it existed at all . . .

The barouche drew to a halt before the solicitors' offices near Lincoln's Inn Fields, and Christina briskly set her doubts aside. The treasure *had* to exist—it simply had to! For she had no idea what she was to do if it didn't.

❖Chapter 2❖

It had begun to rain shortly before they arrived and, despite Maire's protests, Christina left the Irishwoman waiting in the carriage. There was no sense in both of them getting wet, she told her. In truth, she wanted to be free of the older woman's presence for a while, of *her* ability to cast a pall on her aspirations for this endeavor; she knew Maire regarded this visit, indeed, her entire scheme, as foolish, and she felt she could best initiate it without such discouragement.

Ignoring Maire's grumblings, she accepted the aid of Coates, her driver, in alighting from the carriage. Moments later she found herself ducking through the doorway and into a dim antechamber that fronted the offices of Carruthers and Higgins. At least, it *seemed* dim, until she realized this owed more to the swathe of black lace obscuring her vision than any deficiency of lighting in the building's interior.

She paused a moment, intending to shake the rain droplets from her pelisse, when she heard a door open, then a low exchange of male voices before she heard it close again. Expecting to be greeted by Oliver Carruthers —she'd sent a footman ahead with word of her impending arrival—or perhaps his clerk, she strode forward, si-

lently condemning the veiling which prevented her from
seeing clearly who it was.

All at once she found herself colliding into a solid wall,
it seemed, but as she lost her footing and gasped, the wall
moved.

"I beg your—here, ma'am, I have you. Steady, now!"

Christina's face grew hot with embarrassment as she
felt the unmistakable solidity of a firm male body thrust—
there was no other way to describe it—*intimately* against
hers. A muscular arm pressed and flattened the contours
of her breasts beneath the thin summer pelisse as the
man's hand reached under her armpit to keep her from
slipping to the polished floor; warm breath, faintly redolent of tobacco as he spoke, had no trouble filtering
through her veil; and as his other arm closed around her
waist, she realized she was thigh to thigh with her res-
cuer!

My God! she thought, well aware by now that this was
not Carruthers or that mincing clerk of his, but an utter
stranger—*American*, by his accent— *If he doesn't release
me this instant, I shall disgrace myself further by fainting!*

Of course, she had never fainted in her life, being of a
healthy, robust constitution, despite her slender frame.
But there was something about the sheer size of this man,
coupled with a physical closeness not even her betrothed
had been allowed, that was causing her a multitude of
strangely disturbing reactions.

Almost as if he'd read her thoughts, the stranger set
her firmly on her feet and broke contact, saying, with a
distinctly American accent, "There you are, ma'am, all of
a piece . . . Ah, you're not going to faint on me now,
are you?"

Christina tried to ignore the rapid beating of her heart,
the dampness of the palms of her hands, even beneath the
black gloves she wore, as she got her first real look at him.
This was afforded by what she later supposed was her eyes
becoming adjusted to the reduced light behind her veil,

or perhaps the fact that their encounter had taken them near a wall where an elaborate sconce illumined his features.

My God, he's—he's magnificent, she found herself thinking, and then almost laughed at the absurdity of this notion. For the ruggedly hewn features of the American were nothing like the currently accepted standards dictating male beauty. His was not the finely molded cheek, the perfect aquiline nose, the pale, fair complexion that, like her fiancé's, had women sighing across the drawing rooms of London.

He was blond and blue-eyed, yes, but it was as if an artist had used a radically different palette to create *this* coloring: the dark blond curls that covered a slightly longish, well-shaped head were burnished with unfashionable streaks of flaxen, from the sun . . . deep, dark honey shot with light. The piercing blue of his eyes suggested the evening sky . . . indigo, lit with starfire; the straight, long nose was flanked by high, angular cheekbones; the strong, aggressive chin squared a stubborn jaw which was in no way softened by the slashed male dimples bracketing sensually molded lips. And that mouth! It smiled lazily down at her—and was it mocking her?

This final notion caught Christina quite off guard. Her cataloguing of his attributes had flashed through her brain in less time than it took her to draw breath to give him an answer, but the realization that he appeared *amused* by her—her what? Her discomfiture? Her embarrassment? It was hard to surmise, since he was a stranger, and American, besides.

So she found herself flushing with even more heat when her reply came out in a stammer. "I—I—no, I—sir, I *never* faint!"

The smile widened into a grin, and there was no question now of the mockery; it glinted in his eyes, flashed in the set of perfect white teeth that contrasted so sharply with the deep golden bronze of his face. "I'm glad to hear it, ma'am."

His voice was deep . . . resonant and well modulated —the words, polite. Then why was it that she bristled? Was it the *unspoken* message he delivered? She'd seen his eyes flick over her figure briefly, then come to rest above her shoulders, where they seemed to want to pierce the veiling that—thank God!—covered her face. But beneath the look, beneath the politely spoken words, she had the distinct impression he was remembering the way her body had felt against his—remembering every intimate detail and reminding her of it while he—while he *enjoyed* her discomfort!

In other words, *this was no gentleman*.

But before she had time to make further assessments, he was giving her a parting bow—again, ever so polite, and yet somehow mocking—and retreating toward the door to the street.

Christina stood as if frozen, her speechlessness as alien to her as the multitude of other reactions he'd aroused. And it was only when Oliver Carruthers's embarrassed cough told her she was being addressed that she realized, with relief, that the stranger was gone.

"Here it is!" Christina's excitement rang in her voice as she withdrew a folded piece of foolscap from her mother's blue velvet reticule.

"Hmph!" muttered Maire, still miffed at having been made to sit in the carriage and await Christina's return. And didn't the incident the lass had just described, of a collision with some wild American, point to the foolishness of going about unattended? *She'd* have given the heathen lout a thing or two to think about before he dared unsettle a young lady so!

Of course what Maire couldn't know was that Christina had never intended to relate the distasteful incident at all. But when she'd exited the building after her successful meeting with Carruthers, just as Coates was handing her up into the barouche, she'd glanced across the street and spied the American, lounging against a lamppost! In the rain, if you please! Then, seeing her glance his way, he'd had the temerity to offer her a cheeky, mocking salute!

So she'd stormed into her carriage in high dudgeon. And of course, then there'd been no help for it, but to explain her state of upset to Maire.

But now the odious stranger was forgotten as the carriage sped along the thoroughfare and she held Angus MacIver's letter in her hands.

"Listen to this, Maire! It says, 'in the Rising of Forty-five, those loyal to the Bonnie Prince, who were still left alive, were stripped of their rights as well as their possessions. But an ancestor of mine, one Duncan MacIver by name, happened to save the life of an English officer, and for this he was spared and given the piece of land where my poor croft still stands today. It was carved from lands taken from the proud MacKenzies themselves, the clan my family has always served—and loyally!' "

"Ach," Maire interrupted, "that, right there, shows the man is daft! If the 'proud MacKenzies' were stripped o' their lands, then how is it yer ma's family has continued t' live at—and *own*—MacKenzie Manor all these years?"

"He explains that, too," replied Christina as she ran her eyes down the page. "Here: 'As for the MacKenzies, your ancestors, they were brought down a wee bit, but were fortunate enough to keep a portion of their lands in spite of their part in the Rising. This was because The MacKenzie—the laird—had taken an English wife. Her family pleaded their case and won them the right to remain on, and own, Scottish soil. This also explains why your family's Highland estate has since passed down through the female line of descent. The only concession made to the laird was that—and this continued until the time of the Union—the females be allowed to retain the MacKenzie name.' "

"Hmph." Maire sniffed again. "Well, it hardly explains why we should believe there's a treasure buried—"

"In the old wine cellar!" Christina broke in. "Listen! 'The Seadog's Treasure, so called because it was taken from a Spanish galleon by a MacKenzie who sailed with Sir Francis Drake in Elizabeth's time, was hidden in the old wine cellar as a surety against hard times, if they should ever come.

" 'I ken this because it was Duncan MacIver who swore an oath to guard it for them, and the secret of the treasure has been in the safekeeping of loyal MacIvers all this time.' "

"Ach!" Maire exclaimed. "This is all as ye've told me already, child. Very well, then. Supposin' there *was* this treasure. 'Tis possible, I'll allow. But lass, who in his right mind would believe 'tis still there, where that—that Seadog buried it?"

"Angus MacIver believes it," Christina said adamantly, "and this letter hardly sounds like the ravings of a madman."

"Angus MacIver is a Scot!" retorted Maire, as if that explained everything.

Christina gave her a pert grin. "And so, on my mother's side, am *I!*"

Jacques Beaumonde studied the man who sat across from him at the Black Lion Inn. The lighting in the common room wasn't the best, but flames from the nearby hearth and an oil lamp set in a wall bracket shed just enough for Beaumonde to assess his subject through the smoky haze hovering about their corner table.

A handsome devil, the Frenchman found himself thinking as Jamie MacIver turned and gestured for a barmaid to refill their mugs with ale. But it was not MacIver's blond good looks that had Beaumonde running his eyes over his new friend's features. It was his mood—or, rather, what he hoped the American's face could tell him of it.

Captain James MacIver, late of General Andrew Jackson's artillery forces in New Orleans, was not an easy man to know. In fact, had they met under circumstances other than the neutral conditions of battle, he doubted he'd have come to know *le Americain* at all. Or even *wanted* to know him.

Jacques well recalled the day he'd ridden out to MacIver's plantation for the first time. The Big House, as the plantation's main residence was called, sat proudly atop a low rise at the end of a long avenue of live oaks dripping Spanish moss. Grand and imposing, the galleried, pink brick structure boasted a dozen heavy marble columns across its front, and he could still see them gleaming whitely in Louisiana's January sunshine. The plantation itself was called Thousand Oaks, and Jacques had no doubt there was a vast amount of acreage to support that *grande maison*.

Mon Dieu, but Laffite had not exaggerated when he'd called MacIver the richest officer in Jackson's command! And this was the very reason Jacques would have eschewed an introduction to the man, had not war and the exigencies of battle intervened.

In some ways, Jacques Beaumonde knew, he was a snob.

The Frenchman chuckled wickedly to himself with this assessment as he watched the buxom barmaid try to engage Jamie with a flirtatious glance. Of course, *le Americain*, it was a good bet, wouldn't have wanted to come to know *him*, either!

Born a bastard in one of the filthy back alleyways of Marseilles, Jacques had watched his mother die before his eyes of a wasting disease. It had happened when he was six or seven—he couldn't remember which and couldn't care less. But what he did remember were her constant, pitiful reminders that his father had been a nobleman, one of those arrogant, unfeeling aristocrats of *l'Ancien Regime:* a man Jacques had hated profoundly.

He'd hated the man whose name he bore from the day he was old enough to understand how his sire had slaked his lust on a poor, but comely, *jeune fille,* then cast her aside with no more thought for her than for the seed he'd carelessly planted in her belly. And from that day forward, Jacques Beaumonde had harbored a strong aversion toward the wealthy and privileged of the world, no matter what their national origins.

It was one of the reasons he'd sought out Jean Laffite after a brief and dissatisfying stint in Bonaparte's navy. Jumping ship in the Baratarian Bay, he'd made his way to the infamous privateer's island headquarters; then he'd offered his oath and his sword arm to the man who made a practice of plundering the fat merchant ships that brought riches to men like his sire.

Ah, bien, thought Beaumonde as he raised his refilled mug, *that was all a long time ago. And, now, perhaps, I am ready to try my rudder in different waters, eh?* He chuckled softly, satisfied with the nautical image.

"You're sounding smug and happy, Beaumonde." Jamie's voice snapped Jacques back to the present. "What's so damned amusing?"

Jacques's teeth gleamed beneath a black mustache. "Merely a speculation on where fate leads us, *mon ami.* Who'd 'ave dreamed, when Jackson accepted Laffite's offer to fight alongside you *Americains,* zat I would be sitting in a London inn, preparing to journey to Scotland, eh?"

Jamie returned the grin. "Not having second thoughts, are you, Beaumonde? Scotland's said to be a pretty rugged place—especially the Highlands."

Jacques gave a deprecating snort. "It would 'ave to be hell itself to make me change my mind, *mom ami. Vraiment,* but I 'ad grown weary of it . . . ze stealing about in ze night, sleeping with a pistol beneath my blanket, never 'aving a sense of . . . roots."

"What?!" exclaimed Jamie, a mocking gleam in his eyes. "No more midnight runs? No more thrilling to the clash of steel on steel? The smell of gunpowder? The lust for adventure?"

"Oui." Jacques's face grew deadly serious. "No more."

Sobered himself, Jamie nodded, remembering the war. The two men drank in silence for some time.

"Ah, it was a good enough life for a number of years," Jacques went on after a while. "When I was a young hotblood, with certain . . . goals to satisfy. But I am getting a bit, ah, long in ze tooth, as you say. Too old to be playing *le corsaire,* or, to put it bluntly, to be running smuggled goods, even under a man of Laffite's genius."

Jamie nodded. "He sanctioned your leaving?"

"Gave me his blessing ze same day you went to Jackson and told him you wanted out."

Jamie laughed. "And got my wish, although no one could interpret it as having Old Hickory's blessing!"

Jamie drew himself up in the familiar, stiff-shouldered posture Jacques couldn't fail to recognize as the Major-General's. " 'Whut you want t' go'n do that fer, boy?' " he mimicked in the well-known Tennessee twang. " 'Why, you been with me since Alabama! And a decent showin' afore that! Whar's yore commitment t' yore chosen duty, son?'"

Both men laughed at the excellent imitation, prompting Jacques to risk a gentle probe.

"One *could* wonder why a man would devote years to ze call of duty and, then, suddenly cast it aside. . . . Was it Sommers, *mon ami?*"

Jamie paused a moment, thinking of the young lieutenant they'd both liked, but who'd been Jamie's closest friend. He'd had the bitter task of taking the news of

Sommers's death to his widow. She'd been just twenty years old and pregnant with their first child.

Reaching for his ale, Jamie downed it all, then set the mug on the table with a soft thud and gazed into the fire on the hearth for several long seconds.

"I guess you could say that triggered it," he offered finally, turning back toward Beaumonde. "It certainly made a telling mockery of things I'd been wrestling with, but was too blind or stupid to deal with for some time. The 'call of duty,' as you put it, for one."

As Jacques attempted to reconcile his bitter tone with the words, Jamie's eyes strayed back to the fire. But they weren't focused on the cheerful spikes of flame that danced there. Rather, in his mind's eye he could see a yellowed piece of paper he'd stumbled on, on a rainy day when he was twelve. . . .

He was rummaging through an overflow of books shunted from the library, into an attic trunk, certain he'd locate the one with engravings of Michelangelo's sculpture. He'd been working on the final stage of "Horse Frolicking" and wasn't entirely satisfied with the hindquarters. And so he had started on this search for some help from the ultimate master. No one did horses better than Michelangelo!

But what he now held in trembling hands, what he was reading as silent tears streamed down his cheeks, wiped all thought of art, and Michelangelo, from his mind. It was as if the eagerness, the bright passion he'd felt moments ago as he climbed those attic stairs, had belonged to a different child. . . .

"MAJOR ANDREW MAC IVER COURT-MAR-TIALLED: VERDICT CITES COWARDICE IN FACE OF ENEMY." Not wanting to believe it, he scanned the headline again. Tears blurred his vision, and he swiped at them angrily, forcing himself to go on to read the article beneath the headline on the yellowed, half-crumbling sheet of newspaper. . . .

Minutes passed, or maybe hours, and he could feel his

stomach clench, feel himself fight back the nausea as he digested the wrenching truth about his dead father . . . Father, the man his mother always spoke of with reverence, praising him as a hero of the War for Independence! The man she said Washington himself singled out for honors the day he disbanded the troops!

Lies! It was all lies! The talk of upholding the family honor. Honor! The move from Charleston, where he'd been born, to this remote territory, to enable his ailing, "war-hero" father to "regain his health."

No! Not to regain his health! More likely to move them far away from wagging tongues and—and the truth! The truth they never told me!

Oh, how could they? How could they have made the life we led such a lie? Oh, God, I wish I were dead! I wish—

A gentle clearing of the Frenchman's throat brought Jamie back to the present. He blinked, and the leaping flames in the fireplace came back into focus as Beaumonde patiently repeated the question he'd just asked.

"Did your solicitors 'ave any idea when ze marble you ordered from Italy would arrive in Scotland, *mon ami?*"

Jamie nodded. "They said it's already on its way. With any luck, it should arrive at Angus MacIver's croft before we do."

Jacques grinned and raised his mug in Jamie's direction. "Ah, but it is *your* croft now!"

Finding his own mug empty, Jamie signalled for more ale, but his mind was on the letter from those solicitors which had reached him shortly after the Battle of New Orleans. In it Carruthers and Higgins had informed him that he was the sole surviving heir of his father's late uncle, one Angus MacIver of Inverness-shire, Scotland. And that he had inherited a farmstead of some sort—a few acres and a small dwelling, termed a croft—in the wilds of the Scottish Highlands.

"You know, Beaumonde," he said, ignoring the barmaid's coy glance as he accepted another ale from her, "it's odd about how things work out. If I'd gotten that letter at any other time in my life, I'd likely have told them to sell off the place and stayed put, right where I was."

Jacques's grin bordered on being wicked. *"Mais oui,* yet it arrived on ze very day you 'ad invited me to visit you at Thousand Oaks. And I, of course, 'ad ze audacity to suggest you not only keep ze croft, but *go* there!"

"Huh," Jamie groused, "if you hadn't seen that damned horse in the courtyard, I'd likely be sipping bourbon whiskey in the shade right now."

Jacques assumed a deliberately horrified expression. "Never say so! It is a damned shame to let such creative genius go to waste! Zat sculpture was created by someone with *talent, mon ami!"*

Jamie tossed him a wry grin. "Even if the someone was a snot-nosed twelve-year-old?"

"All ze more reason to pick up your sculpting tools again! You 'ave allowed this God-given gift to lie fallow for—'ow many years? Twenty?"

"Twenty-two, to be precise."

"Sacre bleu!" Jacques could still see the sculpture Jamie had called "Horse Frolicking" in the courtyard at Thousand Oaks. The half-life-size statue of a capering, playful young horse had stood on the bricks just outside the French windows in the library. This was where he and Jamie had been talking, and when he'd spied it and exclaimed on its excellence, he'd been astounded to learn a twelve-year-old Jamie had been the sculptor.

Then he'd been equally astounded to learn it had been the last piece his friend had ever done.

"But *why, mon ami?"* he'd asked. "Why throw such talent away?"

Jamie had given him one of those enigmatic looks that said there were things he wouldn't discuss. It was the very sort of thing that had him studying the man from time to time, trying to figure him out.

A very private man, Jacques found himself thinking, *who only lets so much show, then draws the curtains on the rest.*

Well, Jacques was happy enough to call him friend, despite such limitations. What man who'd seen something of life, he reflected, didn't keep secrets? Jacques himself had his share of private devils, personal demons in his past which he'd buried and would be loath to resurrect. Why should Jamie MacIver be any different?

But still, sometimes, this didn't keep him from wondering what MacIver was all about.

Take today, for example. Jamie had left Jacques to amuse himself while the American went to his solicitors to settle things regarding this inheritance. When he'd left the Black Lion, he'd been restless, his mood hovering somewhere between uncertainty over his decision to go to Scotland (something he'd agreed to only on the condition that the Frenchman go *with* him) and an eagerness to put London behind them and be on their way.

At various times during their overseas voyage, Jacques had seen Jamie take out his sculptor's tools and stare at them broodingly. And he'd done that again this morning, before leaving the inn. It left Jacques wondering if he'd done the right thing in urging his friend to go to the wilds of Scotland to sculpt.

The only thing Jamie had deigned to tell him about why he'd set his tools and clay aside over twenty years ago was that he'd no longer had the passion—the "fire," he'd called it—even if he did have the talent. "To be good, Beaumonde—really good," he'd said, "one needs both."

Jacques had hazarded, then, the notion that perhaps one needed something to encourage the passion—like some solitude, or perhaps a major change of scenery—hence his urging of Jamie to make this journey. Moods like Jamie's this morning, however, had him questioning the soundness of his own advice.

But then, later today, MacIver had made a complete reversal that left the Frenchman dumbfounded. He'd returned from his solicitors—a short ride across town in a hired carriage—and he'd been grinning from ear to ear. He'd also been soaking wet! Yet this had seemed to have no dampening effect on his humor. When Jacques had asked him about it, wondering how well the meeting at this Carruthers and Higgins could have gone, Jamie had laughed. Laughed! And then he'd actually *winked* at him, saying enigmatically, that there had been "more fascinating things at Carruthers and Higgins than either Carruthers or Higgins!"

Still wondering about the American's current mood as they sipped their ale, Jacques decided to feel him out. "Are you still eager to leave in ze morning, my young friend? After all, London is a big place. We could linger here awhile and—"

"Hell no, Beaumonde! Now that the papers have been signed and I've got good travel directions from the solicitors, I see no reason to wait."

In fact, although he wasn't sure why, Jamie had been champing at the bit, ever since that delightful run-in with the veiled little morsel in black. Maybe it was the mystery she represented, he mused. Something as simple as a serendipitous encounter with a luscious little female in a dim hallway to tell him there were still pleasant surprises in life. A future to latch onto, even look forward to.

Some hope. God knew he needed something! Hell, maybe it didn't make any sense; but he knew that, somehow, ever since he'd watched her retreat into that carriage—in high dudgeon, once she spied him eyeing her from across the street—he'd been in great, good spirits. After all, if staid old London could offer such small delights, just think of what the wilds of Scotland might hold in store.

Jamie's attention came back to Beaumonde. The older man was regarding him rather closely, and Jamie knew there were questions Jacques wanted to ask. But he also knew that he wouldn't. It was one of the reasons, he suspected, that they'd become friends in such a short time. Each respected the other's privacy and would never intrude, unless invited.

Jamie sighed. There were times, of course, when he wished he could confide in someone. The hell of Desiree was several years behind him now, yet it still invaded his darkest dreams, making him wish—Christ! Would it never let go?

With a muttered curse, Jamie turned and summoned the barmaid. "Two brandies," he growled, sending the poor girl scurrying.

Jacques regarded him even more carefully. "Is something wrong, *mon ami?*"

"Hell, no, Beaumonde!" Jamie laughed, but it sounded harsh, even to his own ears. "Just calling for a nightcap. We'll need to be getting upstairs for some rest if we're to have an early start. How does dawn strike you?"

A glance at the clock on the mantel told Beaumonde it was already approaching midnight, but to his credit, Jamie noted, he didn't blink an eye as he nodded.

The barmaid plunked two glasses of brandy on the table and retreated, clearly unwilling to pursue her interest in the handsome American when he was in this odd new humor.

Jamie raised his glass and gestured for the Frenchman to do the same.

"To the Scottish Highlands," he said, "and may we find what we seek when we get there!"

Jacques raised his glass. "To ze Highlands," he echoed. Then, remembering Jamie's word for the creative passion he sought for his art, he added, "and ze *fire, mon ami!* Let us not forget ze fire!"

❖Chapter 3❖

It was a good thing, Christina thought as her small traveling party lumbered along an almost nonexistent trail skirting Loch Ness, that she was not of a delicate constitution. The crude, high-sided cart they'd hired in Dores, along with the small, surefooted mountain pony which drew it, would surely have jounced a frailer soul to death.

She threw a quick, sidelong glance at Maire, seated in a tangle of skirts beside her. The Irishwoman had been silent throughout this part of their journey, and, to her credit, had complained little before that, though Christina knew she must be as exhausted as she was. It had been a long three weeks.

Perhaps they ought to have taken the sea route as far as the port of Leith, she mused, trying to ignore her rattling teeth as the two-wheeled cart hit a patch of stony ground. Then they could have picked up MacIver's directions from Edinburgh, northward. Except that the four days they'd traveled from London to the Firth of Forth, near Edinburgh, had been the easiest part of this hellish trip.

Traveling by post-chaise—she and Maire in one vehicle, Coates and a groom named Tuppers in another—they'd gone a hundred miles a day with frequent changes of horses, and had rested each night in a comfortable inn. She'd brought her driver and groom along for the male protection required on such a journey, although Maire had grumbled about the extravagance of hiring a second post chaise for stable help.

But she'd been glad of their presence once they'd left the tame pastoral countryside of the Borders, with its flocks of grazing sheep. The high moorlands of Northumbria had been spectacular—vast and brooding—but somewhat desolate as well, and there was always the danger of highwaymen, or whatever they called bandits in the lowlands of Scotland. And then they'd found they needed a driver of their own to cross the twenty-mile-wide peninsula from the Firth of Forth to Newport, on the Firth of Tay: a carriage to hire had been found, but the only available driver had been drunk!

The firths, of course, they'd crossed by ferry, and in Dundee they'd spent their last comfortable night in an inn. After that they had begun their long, arduous trek into the Highlands. Proceeding north-northwest, they'd ridden everything from wagons to skiffs without sails, with a good deal of shank's mare in between.

They'd crossed the Sidlaw Hills, with their woods and tucked-away glens teeming with wildlife: red deer and roe deer, wildcat and pine marten. Then had come the majestic Grampians and, finally, the Cairngorms—wild, rugged terrain of unbelievable beauty (although she'd long since noted the natives, the true Highlanders, always referred to these lofty mountains as "hills"). Here the land was all crag and moor, with fast, clear rivers full of salmon and trout; with sweeping seascapes and curving headlands where the gannet's cry was heard on the wind. Here the golden eagle reigned supreme, and human beings seemed reduced to insignificance beside the vast, towering peaks with their wild sweep of landscape as far as the eye could see.

They went days without seeing a soul besides themselves and whatever native guides Coates managed to find. Food was often procured from humble crofters' stores and eaten by the side of a cattle byre or in the saddle; places to sleep for the night ranged from hay-strewn lofts in humble dwellings (Angus MacIver had provided their owners' names—and therefore safe accommodation), to an occasional laird's own bedchamber, to —more frequently than not—a bed of cloaks under the stars. When there *were* any stars, because all too often it had clouded and rained.

As she recalled the unbelievable storminess of the country, and that she had intrepidly set out on such a journey without giving weather its due consideration—out of sheer ignorance, she now realized—she wondered if Coates had not been right to declare her mad when she'd informed him of where they were going, back in London. (Coates could take such liberties, for, like Maire, he'd been with the St. Johns for years; moreover, he'd traveled with them to MacKenzie Manor on that trip when she'd been a babe. So she ought to have conceded then that the man knew whereof he spoke.)

Oh, well, she thought, shifting in the cart to try to make herself more comfortable—a hopeless task—at least the weather appeared to have taken a turn for the better. The Scots they'd met had informed them June was usually the least inclement month in the Highlands, but the spring had been late in coming this year; perhaps they'd be lucky, and June's sunshine would be delayed into July . . .

They reached MacKenzie Manor shortly after dark. Maire had wanted to stop for the night in Kingussie, where they'd taken a light supper, but when Christina learned the manor was only a few miles beyond the village, she'd urged them on. Now, as she dragged her weary bones out of the cart in a stupefied, exhausted daze, she wasn't so sure this had been wise. Every muscle in her body felt as if it had been gripped in a vise for hours; her knees threatened to buckle under her as Tuppers and Coates helped her set her feet on the ground; and her eyes felt grainy and smarted from the dust on the trail, their lids nearly impossible to hold open.

Dimly, she realized there were lights in several windows of the two-story Georgian structure before them. Mrs. MacLeod, the housekeeper, had apparently gotten the message she'd sent from Kingussie, of their impending arrival, then. Almost as if thinking this thought had sapped the last of her remaining strength, Christina felt her legs give way. And Coates caught her, lifting her into his brawny arms, just as the door opened and a large woman with iron-gray hair appeared on the steps.

"Weelcome, milady! We were just— Och, mon! What's amiss wi'—"

" 'Er Ladyship's 'ad a bruisin'-long day, mum," Christina heard Coates answer. "Needs a bed 'n may'aps a nice, 'ot bath, I'd say."

"Och, the puir, wee lassie!" exclaimed the Scotswoman. "Weel, bring her in, mon, bring her in!"

Christina opened her eyes at the sound of these no-nonsense tones and found herself gazing up into an elderly female face which looked both gruff and kind at the same time. "Mrs. . . . Mrs. MacLeod?" she managed tiredly.

"Aye, lass, the same as weelcomed ye here as a wee bairn, though 'tis unlikely ye'd be rememberin' me. An' though I was merely the upstairs maid at the time, I recall ye weel, red hair an' all."

Burring her r's as she spoke, the housekeeper took a candlestick with burning taper from a chest inside the entry hall and moved toward the staircase at the far end. "And 'tis Maire, isn't it?" she continued as she lit their way up the stairs.

"It is," said the Irishwoman. Her voice was as weary as Christina's. "Ye've a good memory, Mrs. MacLeod."

"Tha' I'll nae argue wi' ye, Maire, but the years have

been kind t' ye as weel. Here, now, mon, mind ye dinna drop her!"

Christina thought she heard Coates reply in a tone indicating he took umbrage with this, but she couldn't be sure. She felt her body sink into the soft contours of a feather mattress, and a moment later she was asleep.

Sunlight, warm and lemony, spilled across the feather tick on Christina's four-poster as she blinked the last vestiges of sleep from her eyes. The clink of metal on porcelain drew her attention, and she saw Maire by a table at the other side of the bed, preparing a cup of tea.

"Maire, you're already up and dressed! What time is it?"

"And good mornin' t' ye, too, lass. 'Tis nigh on half past nine." She handed her her tea.

"Thank you, and good morning to you, too, of course," said Christina, blushing at her oversight. She always exercised good manners with the servants, and Maire was much more than a servant; she was *family*. But there was something about the events of last night which seemed to disturb her, and she felt herself thrown oddly out of sorts. What was it, now . . . ? Something about—

"Maire, Angus MacIver is dead!" she recalled aloud.

"So we learned last night, lass. Here, try one o' these. They're called bannock cakes."

Christina shook her head with a smile and sipped her tea as she tried to remember how they'd learned of Angus MacIver's death. She'd been so exhausted, they'd let her sleep, fully clothed, for a few hours. Maire, too. Then Mrs. MacLeod had awakened Maire, and together they'd heated water and prepared a bath for Christina before awakening her.

She'd been groggy with sleep, but as the warm water had done its work on her aching muscles, she'd roused enough to ask some casually phrased questions of the housekeeper. Such as, was there someone in the vicinity named MacIver?

"Och, auld Angus, d' ye mean?" It was clear Mrs. MacLeod knew him. "Aye, lassie, I knew him weel."

"Kn-*knew* him?" Christina had stammered.

"Aye, but the poor mon's been dead a good six months."

Christina had been devastated. Angus MacIver, *dead*? Now how were they to learn the treasure's hiding place?

"Aye," Mrs. MacLeod had gone on, "found dead up at his croft on New Year's Day. I sent one of the lads from the village—t' bring him the haggis I always made him, ye ken—an' he found him dead in his bed, puir mon."

Shaken by the news, yet forcing herself to sound casual, Christina had made up a tale about having heard his name mentioned at home and wanting to inform him, as someone who might have remembered her mother, of her parents' deaths.

Of course, this had then brought on a stream of condolences and reminiscences about her mother from the housekeeper. Christina had accepted this in what she hoped was a proper manner, but all the while, she remembered, she was casting about in her mind for an unobtrusive way of obtaining additional information. She'd had a shock and she needed to find out all she could, to refashion some kind of a plan.

Finally, she got her opening.

"Heavy news," murmured the housekeeper, "yer mam's passing so soon after auld Angus. Odd, in a way, as weel . . . we received a letter not three days ago, of yer parents' tragedy, fra' His Lordship's solicitors—"

"Carruthers and Higgins?"

"Aye, but wha' is odd is, those same solicitors appear t' have been handlin' auld Angus's estate matters. Mr. Carruthers mentioned it in his letter—said he trusted the new owner was weel settled in, an'—"

"But who *does* own it, now that the old man's dead?" Christina hadn't been able to keep from interrupting, but tried to keep her voice casual.

"Och, lassie!" the housekeeper had exclaimed. "Puir Angus went t' the kirkyard wi' nary a bairn left t' outli'e him, and his wee, auld Jeannie dead these many years as weel. 'Tis a stranger treads the MacIver lands now, I'm sad t' tell ye—an American, at that! But he's a MacIver, true enough, I've heard. An' though he's ainly been here scarce a sennight, they say he's fast dug himsel' in."

Now, feeling quite restored as she drank her breakfast tea, Christina's brain worked furiously. A bit of resourcefulness was what was needed. That, and a good bit of luck, of course. But, the more she thought about it, the more she thought it might be possible to locate the Seadog's Treasure, even without Angus's information.

"Maire," she said, "we've got to locate the wine cellar, and then hire some men to dig or—"

" 'Twould be useless, colleen," said the Irishwoman as she nibbled one of the flat, baked oatcakes, or bannocks, she'd brought on the tea tray.

"Useless?"

Maire nodded, swallowing the oatmeal concoction in her mouth. She followed this with a sip of tea, then explained. "After ye went back t' bed followin' yer bath last night, I could see how dispirited ye'd grown at learnin' this Angus was dead . . . so I thought I'd do what I could t' help—by askin' a few questions meself." Her dark eyes fairly twinkled at Christina.

"Maire, never say so!" Christina smiled, knowing full well what the Irishwoman's views were of this whole business of searching for a treasure they couldn't be sure existed. Yet, here she'd tried to help with it on her own. "Oh, Maire, you are, indeed, too good to me!"

Maire gave her a warm smile in return. "I niver could resist ye, even as a child, when ye were all full o' hope and bright spirits after gettin' a thing ye'd set yer heart on, *macushla.*" The smile became a frown. "But I fear it'll take more than bright spirits t' get yer wish this time."

"Why? You said it would be useless to—"

"T' locate the wine cellar, that I did. Because Janet— ah, Mrs. MacLeod—explained t' me how this house, MacKenzie Manor, was built around 1750, and it is not even on the *site* o' the one the English destroyed in the Risin' o' Forty-five. The original site, in fact, is no longer even a part o' yer lands."

Christina blinked, trying to digest what this meant. "Then where—"

"The Scot, Duncan MacIver—ancestor t' Angus Mac-Iver—was given that parcel, fer savin' the life o' that Red-coat officer, if ye'll recall the letter. He built a croft on it."

Maire leaned forward to make her final point. "Colleen, the Seadog's Treasure, if it exists, would be buried on the late Angus MacIver's land."

Christina blinked once again, then nodded. "I'll have one of those bannock cakes now, Maire. And finish your tea. Then find us some suitable clothes for traipsing about these moun—ah, *hills*. This expedition is proving a great deal more difficult than I thought, but I'm not finished yet. Not by a long shot, I'm not!"

❖Chapter 4❖

"Well, will it answer?" Christina directed the question to Maire's image, just visible behind her own, as they stood before a pier glass in the sewing room.

The Irishwoman eyed the image of the pair of them dressed like Scots villagers in brightly colored plaids—long, full woolen skirts, wide, triangular swathes of tartan draped across chest and shoulder—and grunted.

"It will," she said. "Ye look the very picture of a Scot, and so, God and Saint Patrick fergive me, do I."

Christina chuckled at the sour expression on her face. She'd long been aware of Maire's subtle nationalism, a quiet pride she took in being Irish, but had never made much of a fuss about, during the years they'd been together. But suddenly, now they were on Scottish soil, it seemed the Irishwoman's feelings were coming to the fore, even taking a chauvinistic bent.

It had become most evident when, just this morning, Mrs. MacLeod had produced a trio of young women from the village, for Christina's inspection; she said she wished to take them on as day help, now that the MacKenzie "laird" was in residence. Heretofore, in the years the St. Johns had remained in England, MacKenzie Manor had made do with a skeleton staff consisting of the housekeeper, a cook, a charwoman who came in once a week, and a stableman cum gardener. But it seemed this was no longer sufficient, and so Christina had agreed. But then Maire, who'd been present when Katherine, Annie, and Lorna made their curtsies to the new mistress, had grumbled irritably that they'd do well enough as sculleries, but "no cheeky, tartan-wrapped know-nothin'" was going to set her "heathen foot" in milady's chamber: *she* would tend to Lady Christina's personal needs, "and no one else, I'm after tellin' ye!"

Christina had barely been able to hide a smile at this; the Highlanders were Protestants, so if that made them "heathen" in Maire's Irish Catholic eyes, then where did that leave Christina, who was Anglican, and therefore Protestant as well?

But the most telling moment had come when Christina inquired of the housekeeper as to suitable garb for taking a long walk today. Mrs. MacLeod had suggested she and Maire borrow some of the villagers' clothing: Annie and Lorna were just about their sizes, and, she was certain, they wouldn't mind lending them their spare, "second-best," attire.

"Ach! Sure and ye're not serious?" Maire had exclaimed when Christina explained what they'd be wearing for a hike to Angus MacIver's croft. "Wrap meself in those heathen colors? And yerself as well? Why, with all that red and green, we'll be back t' callin' ye 'Christmas'!"

Christina had laughed, recalling her childhood sobriquet of "Christmas"—because she'd been born on Christmas Day. Of course, largely at her very proper English governess's insistence, none had called her by it since her years in the schoolroom; but she retained a certain fondness for the nickname nonetheless. And her laughter had coaxed Maire out of her Irish pique.

"You must own, Maire," she said to her companion now as they viewed themselves in the mirror, "that these tartans are far sturdier than anything we brought with us.

Far more suitable for traipsing through the heather and gorse we spied along the way, I should think."

"They're hardly the color o' mournin'," grumbled the Irishwoman in a last attempt at protest. But from her tone, Christina could tell she was weakening.

"Then we shall simply have to travel incognito, as they say in the novels."

"Incog—what?"

"Concealing our true identities," Christina said cheerfully as she bent to adjust one of the sturdy boots they both wore.

"Hmph! Pretendin' t' be Scots, ye mean!"

Christina laughed as she gestured them toward the door. "How's yer Scots burr these days, madam?" she asked as they headed for the stairs. Her accent had suddenly become a perfect imitation of Mrs. MacLeod's.

"Hmph!" Maire sniffed again, but a telltale twitching at the corners of her mouth told Christina she'd been won over. "As good as yer own, lassie!"

Christina exploded with laughter. "Maire Fitzpatrick, you've been practicing!" she accused as they reached the downstairs hall.

"I have not," Maire said staunchly. "I've merely learnt t' tie me tongue in knots and roll me ruddy *r*'s!"

Christina guffawed as the Irishwoman's words demonstrated amply what she'd said, and their mutual laughter accompanied them out the door.

The day was sunny, with only a few high-flung clouds blown by the wind. But the wind proved quite chilly, especially when it gusted, and they were soon glad of the protection provided by the serviceable tartans.

Originally, Christina had asked Mrs. MacLeod about mounts to be let, saying she and Maire wished to explore the countryside—and, since both were excellent equestriennes, preferably on horseback. But the housekeeper had laughed at the notion, explaining that any but the surefooted mountain ponies would "likely breek their necks in these hills," and, even then, the safest traveling was best done afoot.

Now, as Christina led Maire over rocks and into hollows, or corries, as they were called, making their way with difficulty across the heather-strewn, rough-and-tumble terrain, she could appreciate the Scotswoman's warning. Gorse and bracken snatched at their skirts; piles of stone and scree seemed to appear underfoot without warning, hidden by the coarse, unpredictable landscape. It was a landscape as wild as it was beautiful.

Both women considered themselves in good physical condition, having ridden regularly in Hyde Park while in London, and over field and meadow at one or another of the earl's country estates at other times. Moreover, Christina had always been an athletic child, and as the earl's only offspring, had been indulged by him in a way that perhaps might otherwise have fallen only to a son: she'd wheedled and cajoled the services of a fencing master out of him at the age of eight and, in the years since, had become quite adept with foil and rapier. She'd coaxed him to teach her how to swim early on, had spent long summer afternoons slicing through the spring-fed waters of a hidden pool at Sunnyfields. And while handling the ribbons of the new high-perch phaeton he'd purchased for her just this spring hadn't required extreme physical prowess, the athletic endeavors of her early years had, without a doubt, contributed to the quickness and deft coordination those high-steppers of hers had required, as they'd drawn it along London's busy thoroughfares.

So it came as some surprise that she and Maire had to rest frequently, as they made their way toward the late Angus MacIver's croft.

"Sweet, holy Mary," said the Irishwoman as they stopped for the fourth time in an hour while she fished a pebble out of her boot, " 'tis a cursed hard land, colleen, and no mistake! And cursed hard on me old, tired bones, as well, I'm thinkin'. Why—"

"Old, tired bones!" Christina's translucent eyes danced with laughter. "Maire, dear, I've never seen a woman of your age as fit and— Ah, how old *are* you by the way? I've never known, exactly."

Maire shot her a quelling glare. "That's because 'tis rude t' be after pryin' inta—"

"Prying! Why, Maire Fitzpatrick, I've known you my entire life, and if that makes—"

"Thirty-eight next month, and don't be blatherin' it about!" came the disgruntled reply. "Now, if I'm not mistaken, that's chimney smoke risin' beyond those pines. Is that where yer directions say we're headin'?"

Christina pulled Angus MacIver's letter from the folds of her tartan after glancing where Maire'd pointed. "'. . . a small stand of pines, once you have passed the large, flat-topped boulder with the lichen covering the near side of it . . .'" she read aloud. "Indeed, it is, Maire, for look—there's the boulder." She pointed toward the landmark.

"Well, if there's a fire on the hearth, 'twould appear the new Mr. MacIver is at home," said Maire. "What d'ye suggest we do now?"

Christina pondered this for a moment, for she hadn't actually thought out all the details beyond the point of locating the croft. A great deal depended on whether the new owner was about; since it now appeared he was, she debated going directly up to his door and introducing herself as his neighbor and making a friendly overture, that sort of thing.

But what if this stranger—this *American*, she reminded herself, recalling Mrs. MacLeod's words—didn't like being disturbed? What if he weren't at all friendly—or civilized? She suddenly recalled her most recent encounter with an American—at the solicitors' in London—and found herself blushing furiously. Good heavens, if he were anything like *that* one, she had every reason to take precautions!

Perhaps it would be prudent to continue incognito, at any rate. And, beyond that, perhaps the direct approach wasn't the best. Yes, the more she thought on it, it appeared wise to pretend to be the humble village lassies their attire proclaimed them. Two Scotswomen out for a . . . stroll? No, that wouldn't answer. No woman in her right mind, even a hardy Scot, she thought, would select *this* countryside for a pleasure jaunt—afoot! But what, then?

She appealed to Maire for help, explaining the conclusions she'd reached, and was immediately rewarded.

"We'll be after searchin' fer herbs and roots, if anyone asks," said the Irishwoman as she rose from where they'd been sitting and began casting about the vegetation growing nearby. While Christina watched, she plucked some grayish-green leaves from a half-hidden plant and tucked them in her tartan shawl, gesturing for Christina to do the same.

" 'Tis a common enough practice among women who live on the land," Maire went on. "Me own grandmother did it in Donegal when I was a child. She was a *seanbhean uasal,* that is, an old wisewoman, who collected such fer homemade medicines and simples."

"Really?" Christina murmured as she followed suit. As a child she'd found Maire to be a treasure house of information on a wealth of things; but as an adult she often forgot how interesting the older woman's conversation could be, peppered as it often was with enticing tidbits of arcane knowledge. "Well, I shan't call you a *seanbhean uasal,* Maire, for you're much too young for that epithet, but collectors of roots and herbs, we shall be. Lead on, MacDuff!"

They resumed walking and were almost through the pines when they heard something up ahead of them. Stealthily drawing nearer, they discerned the unmistakable sound of an axe biting into wood. Then, as they stood in the shadows under the rim of the pines, they saw the man. He was shirtless, the strain of his labor sending rivulets of sweat down the flexing muscles of his shoulders and back, even in the crisp, cool mountain air. And encasing his lean lower torso was a pair of clinging buckskin breeches that showed dark in patches, where the sweat had soaked through.

They couldn't see his face as he was turned away from them, but he was a fine figure of a man, Maire found herself thinking with a tingle she hadn't felt in years.

Then, just as she was pondering the advisability of remaining, given the half-naked state of the man and her responsibilities to her headstrong young mistress, the man straightened and turned to face them. Maire froze where she stood.

He was a good deal older than she'd supposed, given his muscular physique. Dark hair clung to a well-shaped head, but it was frosted with gray at the sides and temples. And there were glints of silver in his dark mustache, as well as lines of maturity etching his swarthy face. But it was an agreeable face, she found herself thinking, and when a slow grin began to form, showing white, healthy teeth against his bronzed skin, she suddenly found it— *handsome* . . . passing handsome, indeed!

Jacques ran his eyes over the two slender figures at the edge of the pines and couldn't help the grin that tugged the edges of his mustache upward. A pair of local beauties —and prime stuff, or he wasn't a Frenchman!

"Bonjour, mesdames!" he called out.

"That's no American," murmured Christina as Maire gestured her back a step, into the shadows.

"A Frenchman, and no mistake," Maire hissed, but her eyes never left the attractive stranger's body.

"Do you think we've found the wrong croft?" Christina whispered.

I hope not, Maire was shocked to find herself thinking as she watched the man bend low and reach for something; his movements offered her a splendid view of rippling muscles, and she was again aware of a strange sensation prickling her insides. Suddenly aware of her duty to Christina, however, she gave herself a mental shake and managed a scowl. "Remember yer in—incog— yer Scots flummery, lass!" she warned.

Sensing some hesitation in the women, Jacques had purposely bent to retrieve his shirt from a nearby log, and now he quickly drew it on. He and Jamie had met their share of locals since arriving, and they seemed a friendly lot, but extremely provincial; he didn't wish to offend the sensibilities of two such charming representatives of their number with his state of *déshabillé!* As an afterthought, however, he realized he'd automatically greeted them in his native tongue and that, too, might have put them off. Therefore, as well as hoping to distract from the awkward business of donning a piece of apparel in plain view of them, he added as he strode forward, "Greetings, mi'ladies. 'Ow may I be of service?"

"Let me do the talkin', colleen," Maire murmured under her breath as Christina began to urge the Irishwoman forward.

Christina glanced at her from the corner of her eye, hesitated, then gave a brief nod. They strode toward the advancing stranger.

"Good day t' ye, sorr!" called Maire.

"Psst!" Christina hissed under her breath, and Maire glanced at her. "Make that 'sirr,' not 'sorr,' or you'll give it away," she added, barely moving her lips.

Maire mumbled something unintelligible in Gaelic, but gave a jerky nod of her head.

"We're verra sorry t' disturb ye, sirr," she continued to Jacques in an excellent approximation of the Highland burr.

"No apologies required, madame," Jacques replied with his most winning smile. "But allow me to introduce myself. I am Jacques Beaumonde, at your service," he added, bowing graciously.

"Aye," Maire answered, thinking fast for an appropriate response. "Weel, sirr, m'name is Mary—Mary Cameron, and the young lady, here, is—"

"Christmas MacKenzie," Christina broke in. She added a humble curtsy, such as she'd witnessed the village girls make when presented to her.

Maire threw her a surreptitious scowl when Jacques wasn't looking, but followed suit with a curtsy of her own.

Jacques found himself grinning again as he viewed the women at close range. They were lovely, the pair of them, although the redhead, with her dewy complexion and clear gray eyes, seemed hardly more than an exquisite child. But this Mary, now . . .

"We dinna mean t' be trespassin', Mr. Beaumonde," the one called Christmas was saying, "but, ye see, we were acquainted wi' the late Mr. MacIver who owned this land, an' we'd hoped the new owner wouldna mind if we—"

"Are ye kin t' this new owner, Mr. Beaumonde?" Mary interrupted.

"No kin," Jacques replied with that charming smile that left Maire feeling oddly breathless, "but a friend. We 'ave traveled together from New Orleans, in America, and 'ave taken up residence here for a time. But, tell me, what brings two such lovely ladies—"

"Me—my young cousin an' I do some simple nursin' and healin' fer our clansmen i' the village, Mr. Beaumonde," Maire answered. "An' we were after—we were searchin' fer the roots an' herbs we put t' use in our homemade medicinals." She unfolded a length of her tartan and showed him the bits of greenery she'd gathered.

Watching Beaumonde nod comprehendingly, Christina's thoughts spun rapidly; if they were to gain access to MacIver's croft, to search for the treasure without arousing suspicion, they would require a better "cover" than posing as herb gatherers. They needed something which would take them here, and *inside* the old Highlander's cottage, on a daily basis. Glancing at Maire, she ventured a probe.

"It canna be all tha' easy, Mr. Beaumonde, fer two gentlemen on their own t' set up housekeepin' in sich a place. Or d'ye ha' servants ye've brought wi' ye fra' America?"

Jacques glanced at her in surprise. Just this morning Jamie had complained of the time wasted while seeing to the cooking and other domestic chores about the croft. "I came here to think, and, I'd hoped, to create something worthwhile with my hands from the clay," he'd groused, "not spend my time doing servants' chores. Be a good fellow, Beaumonde, and scout up some day help from the village, will you?"

Of course, Jacques had agreed, and now he gave the two women a speculative glance as he wondered if fate might not have stepped in to save him a trip to the village.

"*Mais, non,* Mademoiselle MacKenzie, we 'ave not sought to bring ze servants, and I will tell you, it 'as not been easy, doing for ourselves. Ah, *pardon, mesdames,* but would you know of someone from your village—"

"This is a verra fortunate encounter fer us, then, sirr," Christina broke in with a sunny smile. She ignored Maire's fleeting look of displeasure at again having her control of the conversation preempted.

"*Oui?*" Jacques returned the smile.

"Aye, sirr, fer ye see afore ye two lassies weel accustomed t' cookin' an' cleanin' aboot the village. We earn some saerly needed coin for our family wi' sich labor, an' it just sae happens, we're free t' hire oot at the moment."

Christina—or Christmas, as she consciously now began to call herself—barely kept from wincing as Maire's heel collided with her instep. Instead, she managed a satisfied smile as the Frenchman replied.

"Mesdames," he told them with a bold grin, "I believe we can strike ze bargain, *non?"*

❧Chapter 5❧

Early the following morning "Christmas" and "Mary" again dressed themselves in the borrowed attire and made their way toward the MacIver croft. They'd agreed, the night before, to account for such prolonged absences from the manor by telling Mrs. MacLeod the young mistress was fond of sketching and painting watercolors from nature, and these excursions were in pursuit of this pastime. Inasmuch as such pursuits were common among gently bred young ladies of the *ton* in England—and, indeed, Lady Christina had received instruction along these lines as part of her rearing—the housekeeper accepted this explanation with no trouble. Moreover, Maire had fortuitously packed a sketchpad and some charcoals among Christina's belongings, so they were handily supplied with props for their double masquerade.

In fact, things were going so smoothly, Christmas found herself humming as they drew near the cottage, despite the need to find their way through daunting patches of fog that hugged the mountainside like eerie wraiths.

Close by her side, lest she lose sight of her amid the eddying swirls of mist that frequently kept her from seeing her own two feet, her companion was less optimistic. "We'll be lucky not t' be breakin' our foolish necks in this heathen country," Mary grumbled as they stopped to get their bearings for perhaps the dozenth time. "Christina, lass, I—"

"*Christmas*, Mary! Do remember, or we shall be undone before we pick up our first broom."

"Hmph!" Mary snorted. " 'Tis amazed I'll be, if ye even know which end of a broom means business! Ye're a gently reared lady, Christina, and—ach! I know, I know —Christmas! But the fact is, colleen, ye're familiar with nary a bit o' the labor we've been hired t' perform, and ye know it! So, tell me, how d'ye propose t' pass yerself off as a servin' wench? Answer me that, if ye please!"

Christmas shrugged, unfazed by such details. "I have every confidence in you, Mary dear. I shall simply have to rely on *you* to show me! After all, how difficult can it be?"

A mumbled reply met her ears, but Christmas ignored it. The outlines of the cottage had suddenly come into view as the mist parted. With a cheerful cry, she grabbed the older woman's hand and hurried toward it.

Inside the humble, one-room dwelling, Jamie MacIver waited impatiently for the morning to clear. While the mists remained, there was damned little light for working the clay, even outside, where he'd been forced to sculpt, given the cottage's inadequate light. Who'd ever have thought the blasted Highlander's abode would lack windows? *One*, it had—if you could call it that! A minuscule aperture high on one wall, and even then—

The cottage door swung ajar, and Jacques's robust accents cut across his dissatisfied musings. *"Entrez, mesdames, s'il vous plaît!* Jamie, they 'ave arrived!"

Jamie paused amid his pacing before the huge fireplace that took up an entire wall. He watched the ex-pirate make a grand gesture of welcome in the open doorway. Sweeping his broad-brimmed hat before him like a courtier, Jacques ushered a pair of slender, tartan-wrapped figures into the cottage.

It was apparent the mists were evaporating now, for a

broad sunbeam bathed their figures in light. But Jamie's thoughts suddenly had nothing to do with sculpting.

He might have known the Frenchman would turn up something like this—even here, in the middle of a wilderness. He'd begun to suspect Beaumonde had a discerning eye for the ladies, and this morning's evidence confirmed it. The smaller woman, a brunette whose eyes darted assessingly over the interior of the cottage, was obviously well past the first blush of young womanhood. But for all her evident maturity, she was exceedingly handsome, with clean, evenly spaced features and an air of graceful dignity as she moved. He found himself smiling into her deep-set, intelligent eyes as he learned her name was Mary Cameron.

But in the next instant his glance swept the willowy figure behind her, and he felt his breath catch. He'd never seen a creature so *exquisite!*

He caught her in profile as she exchanged a quiet word with Jacques, the finely etched outline of her face thrown into relief by the juxtaposition of shadow and sunlight in the doorway. Her delicate features were perfection itself, from the smooth, creamy brow, to the finely boned nose, to a small, proudly held chin.

And that hair! Its titian radiance fairly dazzled him as sunlight danced on a wealth of curls tumbling down her back. He felt his fingers clench and knew this came of wanting to touch it. To run his hands through that fiery, silken abundance, savoring its texture, stroking the tangled luxuriance where he would. Quite suddenly, he felt his loins tighten, and he turned abruptly toward the fire, pretending it needed a jab with the poker he grabbed. The buckskins he wore were tight enough to reveal this unexpected stab of lust, and he had no wish to embarrass anyone, himself least of all!

Christmas froze a few steps into the room, where she'd advanced to meet the croft's new owner. She stifled a gasp. *Good God, it couldn't be!* She blinked once, then again, but the figure that had abruptly turned toward the fire didn't alter: it was the American from the solicitors' office!

Glancing wildly about, she met, first, Mary's puzzled gaze, then Beaumonde's. The Frenchman was eyeing, with utter bemusement, the tall figure now poking at a log on the hearth. What was going on? Had the American recognized *her,* as well? No, impossible! She'd been heavily veiled at the time, and—

"Jamie!" Jacques's voice scattered her thoughts. But Jacques was having scattered thoughts of his own. What had possessed MacIver? To turn his back in this offensive manner, just as Jacques had been about to introduce— Ah, but the man was exceedingly strange sometimes. Still, he'd become a true friend, and with friendship such as theirs, one didn't question; one accepted.

With a Gallic shrug, Jacques repeated Jamie's name, but his friend was already turning toward them.

"My pardon, ladies," he said with a disarming smile. "I don't usually behave so rudely, but I'd sensed that log was about to crash, and . . ."

Christmas listened to his smooth, articulate voice as introductions were completed, wondering if they gave prizes in America for telling Banbury tales. Doesn't "usually behave so rudely," indeed! Why, the man had been nothing but a bundle of cheek since she'd first set eyes on him!

And, now she had a moment to reflect on it, she felt no man had a right to look the way he did, either! It wasn't merely that he was handsome. Although he was. She'd already noted that in London. But she'd forgotten all about him in these intervening weeks. And now, here he was all over again, inserting his handsome, arrogant presence into her life! And the *way,* the *way* his male beauty came across! It unsettled her, somehow, and she wondered why. She reminded herself it wasn't as if she were unaccustomed to attractive males. Her father had been so handsome, Mama had once told her, that in his youth, women had reached for their vinaigrettes when he entered a room. And she'd met scores of good-looking men during the Season. Indeed, she was betrothed to quite the handsomest among them!

But she was again astounded by the way Jamie MacIver's beauty was vastly different from Lord Aaron's—or any other men of the *ton*. It was as if the artist who'd sculpted the graceful, noble lines of those faces had suddenly thrown away his chisel and decided to hammer out this man's features on an anvil. As one would forge iron. As if those first great blows had created a kind of elemental beauty so vital and raw in the power of its masculine symmetry, it had stayed his hand, forbidding him to refine it—or add an ounce of softness.

Primitive and male, that's what it was, and Lady Christina St. John didn't like it, didn't like it at all!

But, of course, Christmas MacKenzie had to *appear* to like it; that fact was abundantly clear in the few seconds all of this passed through her mind. So, summoning up all her fortitude, she cast the American her sweetest smile and focused on maintaining her Scots accent.

"Dinna ye mind our presence, now, Mr. MacIver. My cousin and I are here t' manage the wee matters fer ye, sae ye can just go aboot yer business an' leave the domestic trifles t' Mary an' me."

Jamie almost missed what she said because, for the first time, he was seeing her face-to-face and could discern the color and shape of her eyes. They were huge and thickly lashed, their pale, translucent gray touched with a hint of violet. They were eyes a man could get lost in, he realized, their clarity and depth at once innocent and beckoning, their—

Unbidden, an image formed in his mind, of another pair of eyes that had once drawn him . . . black as midnight and laden with secrets . . .. ugly secrets, as he'd learned all too late. Ah, Christ! Would he never be free of—

"Mr. MacIver?" It was the older woman speaking, and her quiet voice pulled him gently back to the moment at hand. "Mr. MacIver, is there aught amiss? Perhaps the lass spoke too soon, an' ye'd rather gie us more detailed instruc—"

"No, not at all, Miss Cameron," Jamie replied, but there was an underlying anger in his tone which belied his words. "I'm sure you and Miss MacKenzie will do whatever needs doing with no instruction from us." He gestured about the room, which bore ample evidence of being inhabited by a pair of bachelors without servants. "As you can see, Jacques and I are hardly authorities on domestic management."

As the women's eyes darted over the room, touching briefly on a stack of dirty dishes here, a rumpled piece of clothing there, Jamie stalked across the room. Passing Jacques at the door, he didn't even pause to turn to him, but said brusquely, "Come on, Beaumonde. I've decided to help you catch those fish for supper, now we've someone to fry them up decently!"

Jacques paused, threw the women a helpless look, and shrugged. *"Pardon, mesdames,"* he began, but at Jamie's impatient call, he made a hasty bow, adding they were welcome to join the men for a fish supper—after they'd prepared it.

"Well!" huffed Christmas, watching him bound out the door. "I certainly hope the man catches something! I mean, the world might come to an end if there are no fish for supper!"

"I take it ye're referrin' t' the American," Mary said dryly as she hung her tartan shawl, called a *tonnag*, on a peg near the door.

"Of *course*, the American! But Mary, do you know *who* that American *is*?"

The Irishwoman paused in the act of rolling up her

sleeves. "I do not, but I take it ye're about to enlighten me."

Coppery curls bounced as Christmas gave an emphatic nod. "He's the same American I told you about, that day we went to Carruthers's office—the one who almost—"

"The rude one?"

"Did I say rude? I—"

"From the sparks flyin' from yer eyes that day, colleen, I gathered such. That, and the way ye were reluctant t' pass along any *details* about the gentleman."

"Gentleman! If Jamie MacIver is America's notion of a gentleman, that fledgling nation has a great deal to learn of such matters!"

Mary passed her one of a pair of scarves she'd tucked in her sleeves, then began to tie the other about her dark hair. She gestured for Christmas to do the same and responded thoughtfully. "That young man has some divils botherin' him, and that's fer certain."

"I should say *he* is the devil, if anyone is!"

Mary eyed her shrewdly. "So that's the way of it, is it?"

Christmas avoided her eyes and turned abruptly, reaching for a broom she'd spied earlier. "I cannot imagine what you are referring to," she murmured with what she hoped was an insouciant air.

"Blarney!" said Mary, watching with some amusement as the earl's daughter swished the broom experimentally along the packed earthen floor.

"I beg your pardon?" Christmas tried to sound affronted, but the question came out somewhat absently as she tried readjusting her hold on the broom's handle.

Mary's loud gust of laughter brought her head up with a start.

"Tell me, colleen," the Irishwoman said on another gale of laughter, "are ye after workin' that broom or dancin' with it?"

Christmas stopped moving and stared at the object in her hands. "Oh, bother!" she finally muttered as she looked at Mary. "I cannot fathom the difficulty, but perhaps you'd better demonstrate. I'm sure I shall learn to do it properly, once I'm shown."

She handed the broom over amid the Irishwoman's soft chuckles.

But as Mary demonstrated the art of sweeping, Christmas was soon to regret the lack of a distraction because the older woman's conversation quickly returned to their former topic.

"So, ye see the American as a proper divil, do ye?" Mary questioned as she moved the broom expertly over the packed floor, being careful not to disturb the clay surface as she cleaned it of dust and debris.

"The—the man disturbs me," Christmas admitted reluctantly.

Mary laughed softly. "Aye, lass, as a prime stud disturbs an untried filly!"

Christmas froze in the act of taking the broom Mary held out to her. "I—I do not take your meaning," she stammered. But the scarlet flush she could feel creeping to the very roots of her hair said she did.

Mary withdrew the broom and set it aside, propping it against a chair. When she turned back to Christmas, her face was sober, her voice, earnest.

"I think ye do, *macushla*. And if I thought ye'd be takin' a wee bit of advice from an older and wiser soul, I'd be after urgin' ye t' give it up."

"Give . . . give it up?"

"Aye. This entire scheme, which was foolhardy enough t' begin with, and ye know it. But now ye've met the new master o' this croft, lass, and don't pretend ye didn't see the way his eyes fairly devoured ye where ye stood, or—"

"Maire, I—"

"Or that yer own eyes weren't lookin' their fill o' the handsome brute!" Maire stepped forward and clasped Christina gently by the shoulders, forcing her to meet her eyes. "Ye cannot pretend with me, lass. I've known ye since the cradle. What disturbed ye about Jamie MacIver is a thing as old as Adam and Eve, and I seriously doubt ye're prepared t' deal with it!"

"Maire . . . I'm betrothed to another man," Christina argued.

"Aye, and precious little that will matter, if what my eyes were tellin' me is true—and I believe it is. There were hidden sparks flyin' between the two o' ye, colleen, and if ye mean t' remain here fer any length o' time, I fear ye'll be playin' with fire!"

Christina met her eyes for a long moment, then slowly nodded. "Very well, Mary, you've made your point."

"Ye're leavin', then?" The Irishwoman's voice rose hopefully.

"Of course not, dear. But I do own that Mr. MacIver presents a certain . . . danger."

"But, then—"

"Forewarned is forearmed, Mary. Now that I know the lay of the land, I shall be able to take every precaution. And I certainly do not intend to let that—that *American* intimidate me! We'll hunt the treasure despite that man and whatever devils he brings to bear!"

❖Chapter 6❖

$\mathcal{T}$he two women set about putting the cottage in order. But it quickly became apparent to Mary that she had her work cut out for her on a more immediate level: not only did Christmas barely know which end of a broom was which; the young mistress was hopelessly lost when it came to any aspect of domestic chores, and Mary would need to instruct her before she could begin doing her own share of the work. Through the course of the day this became the source of a number of incidents which had the Irishwoman either muttering under her breath or clutching her sides, weak with laughter.

At first she thought Christmas got on very well, having taken the old cloth Mary'd handed her and then carefully wiped down dusty surfaces—not bad. But when she'd half finished and Mary absently told her she'd better shake out the cloth before completing her task—Mary was busily involved in scrubbing pots at the time—Christmas gave a bemused shrug, then cheerfully complied by flapping the dust-laden rag vigorously—right in the middle of the room! It was many long minutes before their coughing subsided enough for Mary to explain that dust cloths are taken *outside* for such an exercise.

Then there was her attempt at collecting rainwater for washing dishes. She was to dip a bucket into a huge barrel obviously set aside, just beneath the eaves, for such purposes. But a few moments after she'd disappeared out the door, oaken bucket swinging merrily in her hand, Mary was treated to a fierce shriek, followed by an oddly echoing shout for help. She arrived outside to find Christmas upside down in the barrel—it turned out to be nearly empty—with only her lower legs and feet visible as they thrashed and kicked helplessly amid a jumble of petticoats and tartan plaid.

"Christmas, lass!" Mary'd exclaimed as she rushed to extricate her, trying her mightiest not to laugh at the comical picture the younger woman presented. "Why didn't ye tell me the water was only—"

"Some imbecile used up most of the water and didn't replace it!" Christmas hollered as Mary grasped her waistband and gave a tug, while trying to explain that it was up to Mother Nature to do the refilling, since this was a *rain* barrel.

It was several seconds before, with joint efforts, they had her extricated, and Christmas looked a sight. The length of red hair not caught up in her scarf was soaked and dripping, and part of it had become entangled about the handle of the bucket, causing the oaken receptacle to dangle drunkenly over her right shoulder. Her sleeves, where they'd been rolled to the elbows, were also sodden, and water dripped from her nose and chin.

Mary's look of dismay was offset by a telltale twitching at the corners of her mouth, which Christmas caught.

"Don't you dare laugh, Maire Fitzpatrick! I was only doing what you instructed!"

"*Mary C-Cameron*, lass!" came the choked reply as the Irishwoman proceeded to do exactly what *she'd* been instructed *not* to. Then, amid increasing gales of laughter, she managed to apologize. Explaining she'd not realized the barrel would be nearly empty, she'd added that, in such a case, it might have been wiser to leave it and go the extra distance to the well they'd spied near the stable.

"Hmph!" Christmas muttered, still unamused. "There was every reason to suspect this miserable barrel *would* be full! They've had buckets of rain recently, and from the evidence, there was little to persuade me those—those *Americans* could have used it up with their *own* cleaning!"

But in the end, as they toweled her dry, Christmas began to appreciate the humor of the situation, and her laughter joined Mary's. Of course, the Irishwoman had rather suspected it would; the child had enjoyed that very special virtue—the ability to laugh at oneself—from an early age, and it was the rarest of occasions when she couldn't be coaxed out of a fit of pique by laughter.

On the other hand, Mary's own sense of humor was severely taxed during the course of the afternoon. In the space of a few short hours, Christmas managed to confuse the sugar with the salt in the biscuits she was set to making, cover herself with soot from the hearth she swept, and set one of the bed quilts on fire. This last disaster was a mystery in terms of how it came about, for by then Mary lacked the heart to inquire as to how she'd accomplished it.

Somehow, amid all this chaos, they found a little time to search about the croft for the treasure. Christmas hadn't actually expected to locate it immediately, but she'd hoped, perhaps, to detect some evidence somewhere. Since they knew the croft had been built upon the ruins of the MacKenzie clan's old holdings, they realized it was unlikely to be in the cottage as a proper wine cellar, like the ones found in great houses; after all, this was a humble man's dwelling. Nevertheless they went over every inch of the floor, searching for a hidden trap door, for example, to a cellar below. No luck. Then they turned their efforts to a search of the immediate grounds and yard. But in the brief time they had, they turned up only the expected: the stable with its—ugh!—manure pile behind; a small lean-to for storing firewood; and a storage

shed behind the stable containing some rusting farm im-
plements, a moldy feather tick half devoured by mice—
and a curious assortment of tools wrapped in flannel.
Also, two huge blocks of marble covered with canvas, and
an immense bag of red clay!

"What, in the name o' the saints, is all this?" Mary
questioned.

"Hmm." Christmas poked about the flannel cloths,
picking up one of a number of chisels of assorted sizes.
"Unless I'm mistaken— No, I'm *not!*" she added as her
glance fell on a hunk of the red clay in the opposite corner. It was the half-formed figure of a deer, head rising
out of a more nebulous mass below, barely begun, but
already suggesting a slope of shoulder, the graceful sweep
of back and haunches.

"One of our two employers," she said thoughtfully,
"has an interest in sculpting, it seems."

"The American," Mary said without hesitation.
"Jacques strikes me clearly as a man in motion—too busy
doin' t' sit still fer the time 'twould take t' fashion this
kind o' work."

"Jacques, is it?" Christmas questioned slyly, an amused
look lighting her eyes.

Mary flushed a distinct shade of pink, pausing to clear
her throat before replying. "He's a fine figure of a man,
and I'm not blind. And—and he *asked* me t' call him by
his Christian name!"

"Jacques." Christmas kept an absolutely straight expression on her face.

"Well, 'tis Jean-Jacques, t' tell the truth—the French
love these double names fer their—*I fail t' see what's so
amusin'!*"

Christmas could barely speak around her ear-to-ear
grin. "I see I'm not alone in succumbing to the, ah,
Adam and Eve malady, shall we say?"

"Blather!" exclaimed the Irishwoman as she began
busily rewrapping the sculpting tools. "Faith, and ye're a

divil, Christmas MacKenzie, t' be throwin' me own words back at me!'"

Christmas laughed and began helping her with the tools. Then her voice grew serious. "Maire . . . how is it you never came to wed?"

The Irishwoman gave the flannels a final pat and stood up, silent for a moment.

"There was someone, once," she said finally, in a subdued voice. "A tall lad, with laughter in his eyes and . . . he was from me home village, and I was but a lass—too young t' wed, me da said—and needed at home t' help out. We . . . intended t' wait . . ."

A bird called somewhere outside, but it was otherwise very quiet as Christmas waited for her to finish. Maire had a faraway look in her eyes, not sad, really . . . dreamy, perhaps, but still she didn't continue.

"What . . . what happened to him?" Christmas finally prompted in a whisper.

Maire met her eyes. "He wed anither. His ma suddenly died, ye see, leavin' him—the oldest, by far—and his da with nine little ones t' feed and care fer. Then his da was killed in a foolish tumble from a loft—nary a fortnight later. So then there was only Kevin fer all those wee ones. He . . . needed a wife—in a hurry."

"And you couldn't—"

"I couldn't." Maire shrugged. "I thought me heart would break at the time," she added as they left the shed and began to walk back to the cottage. "But since then, I've had years t' grow philosophical over it."

"Philosophical?"

Another shrug. "D'ye think, lass, that if I, at the age o' fourteen, had plunged inta the rearin' of a pack o' nine children—not t' mention the babes *I* might've borne along the way—d'ye think I'd *begin* t' be the same woman I am t'day? We were *poor*, colleen. Poor as church mice, and then some! Why, I recall women in that village looking old—really old . . . all bent and stooped with tired, weary faces—only t' learn, later on, o' course, that they couldn't have been out o' their *twenties!* Lass, the chances are, I'd not even be *alive* by now—the life I'd have led was that hard."

"Then you don't really regret—"

"Regrets are fer the fainthearted. Now, come along and help me set a table fer those fish they've been after catchin'. And, fer sweet Mary's sake, keep yer lovely mouth shut and watch me when they ask us t' cook 'em!"

❧ Chapter 7 ❧

Jamie stood among some rocks in the fast-moving stream Jacques had located and heaved an exasperated sigh. The icy currents had already yielded half a dozen good-sized mountain trout—easily enough for their supper—so his mind wasn't really on the fishing. Rather, he was recalling their ride over to this wooded glen where the fishing had been every bit as good as promised; they'd thrown back as many trout as they'd kept, none of them small, but as Beaumonde had explained, "with so many *grand* beauties biting, why trifle with ze mediocre, eh?"

But en route the Frenchman had been immersed in beauties of a different sort. Two-legged beauties, to be specific; one a brunette, Jamie suspected, and the other a redhead. Sitting atop his sturdy little mountain pony, Beaumonde had begun the expedition by humming jaunty little airs to himself. These had progressed into richly lyrical love songs—*chansons*, he'd termed them—entirely in French, of course. Finally he'd settled on half-quoted phrases from Shakespearean love sonnets—exclusively those about the English poet's "dark mistress"!

Jamie had remained silent and annoyed throughout this performance, his mood bordering on the sullen. Although, even now, he didn't care to examine why. Of course, it was true, he'd thought the Scotswomen attractive himself. The redhead, he had to admit, was stunning, but there was also something odd there. For some reason, she didn't strike him as a common villager. Perhaps it was the way she carried herself . . . almost as if she were accustomed to giving orders, instead of taking them . . . And then there were her hands. Why had they struck him as hands which hadn't done a single day's physical work?

But he'd quickly dismissed the chit from his thoughts, heartily resenting Beaumonde for making this difficult. He'd come out here to *think* and, if he was lucky, to *create,* dammit—*not* to chase a pair of skirts!

But if Beaumonde had noticed his mood, he'd not let on. "Mary . . . such a lovely, simple name, *n'est-ce pas?*" he'd murmured at one point. "Just like ze woman who bears it. Do you not agree, *mon ami?*"

Jamie thought he might have grunted by way of an answer, but that hadn't fazed the Frenchman.

"And *Christmas!*" he'd gone on blithely. "*Très unique,* eh? But this is no Scottish name, eh, Jamie?"

Another grunt. Yes, Jamie distinctly remembered grunting.

"*Non,* I think not. Per'aps ze *jeune fille* can tell us why she 'as this name, eh? Perhaps you will ask her, *oui,* Jamie?"

Jamie had finally grown irritated enough to break his silence with more than a monosyllabic grunt. "Christ, Beaumonde!" he'd snapped. "If you need to know the reason for the chit's idiotic name, *you* ask her! And leave me the hell out of it!"

But had that stopped the man? Had it even put a dent in that demeanor that put him in mind of a lovesick calf? Oh, no! The ex-pirate had merely quirked an eyebrow at him and gone on to recite some damned poem about a "Highland Mary"—in a Frenchified Scots dialect, yet!

And that's how the day had progressed. Even when

they'd settled down to do some serious fishing, when there'd come a need to remain quiet. Of course, here Beaumonde had been as silent as thought itself—but from the ridiculous little smile he wore, Jamie had had no doubt as to what *kind* of thoughts permeated his French brain! Hell, why hadn't he been aware Laffite's man was such a Romeo?

He remembered the various times they'd gone about New Orleans together, occasionally encountering the fair sex during their off-duty hours. Women hadn't been all that prominent on the streets and promenades then, given the state of a city nearly under siege; but there'd been those occasional dinner invitations from officers' wives which he'd attended, often bringing Beaumonde as his guest. Yet he hadn't noticed his companion do anything more overt than bow politely in that gallant way Frenchmen had—or those with manners, at least. And Beaumonde did have the full complement of courtly manners! The women at these gatherings had, of course, eaten it up. They no doubt found the combination of the Frenchman's dangerous reputation, plus all this civilized polish, irresistible.

Jamie himself had given these women little heed. His mind had been on the upcoming battle with the British. But he also knew there were other reasons. Reasons that came of bitter experience where women were concerned. Not that he'd eschewed the female sex entirely, of course. There'd been plenty of a particular sort of woman in New Orleans to satisfy his physical needs. That had never been a problem. But he'd scrupulously seen to it that they never intruded on a personal level. A night or two, at the most, in the bed of any one woman had been all he'd allowed himself. Then, when some time passed and he found his body's urges pressing again, he'd find a new receptacle for his lust. Half the time he never learned their names; their faces soon blended into some easily forgotten amalgam, and he was content to have it so.

Suddenly his mind tripped on an image . . . a softly curved, yet slender, woman clothed in black, her face anonymously veiled . . . Was that why he'd thrown caution to the wind and behaved so outrageously toward a female who was so obviously a lady that—

"Jamie!" Beaumonde's voice slashed across his reveries. Jamie glanced downstream and saw Jacques holding an enormous trout aloft.

"I think we call it a day now, eh?" called the Frenchman with a bold grin.

Jamie grinned back at him and began to reel in his line. No matter how irksome the man could be, he couldn't remain out of sorts with him for long. Beaumonde was the eternal optimist, he reflected, and perhaps that was one of the keys to their friendship. Jamie knew he had need of such optimism at this time in his life. God knew, he had little enough of his own to draw on.

Jacques gathered their catch from the place in the stream where they'd immersed the fish to keep them fresh, while Jamie saddled the ponies. It was late afternoon by this time, but the sky had grown cloudy; there was a decided coolness to the air. Summer in the Scottish Highlands, Jamie reflected, was a far cry from the moist, torpid heat of Louisiana at this time of year, and he welcomed it. It was perfect weather for working the clay—or the marble, if he ever got himself up to that stage. Of course, he hadn't felt the least bit ready to tackle the fine Carrara blocks he'd had shipped, at an enormous expense, from Italy, but that could wait. It was early yet, and he hadn't even found a subject worthy of it, let alone tested his long-dormant abilities to any degree. Clay would suffice for now.

As they rode back to the croft, it was clear the Frenchman's mood was still buoyant; he whistled gay tunes to himself, occasionally pausing to echo the song of a bird hidden among the trees. This time, with his own mood much improved, Jamie found he didn't mind the manifestations of cheer. He used the time to drink in the dramatic beauty of the countryside they passed. Its fierce, stark splendor never ceased to awe him, and at one point he said as much to Jacques.

"*Oui*," replied the Frenchman. "So it is with me. But, of course, a man would 'ave to be blind, or stupid, or both, not to be awed by all this, *mon ami*." He gestured grandly, his arm sweeping out to encompass the wild terrain.

Jamie nodded. "And the natives we've met, have you noticed? They're a lot like the land. There's an intense, freedom-loving quality to the Highlanders that seems spawned by the very ruggedness of these mountains."

"*Oui*. Zey seem to flourish in a way of life that would kill a softer people. I admire them . . . but, then, I place great value on individual *liberté*, myself. This is, perhaps, why I found my way to *américain* shores years ago."

"Yes, I suppose we Americans do prize personal freedom. It's what the War for Independence was all about, wasn't it?"

Jacques frowned briefly, averting his face before Jamie could see his reaction. There'd been that distinctive note of sadness in MacIver's tone again, a . . . bitterness, almost, which he was at a loss to explain. And before he could ponder it further, Jamie's words drove it home.

"Of course, not every one of us has had the luxury of being wholly free. Sometimes . . ."

Jacques waited in the pause that followed, vaguely hopeful that, this time, the American would choose to unburden himself of what was bothering him. In his time Beaumonde had been told he had the quality of being a good listener. Perhaps this was true; perhaps it wasn't. Jacques himself only knew he'd always tried to listen to a friend with an open mind, and, more importantly, never to judge. Friends didn't pass judgment on each other.

But Jamie's voice, when it resumed, didn't even appear

to be addressed to him. Its tone seemed to be directed inward, much as if Beaumonde weren't even there.

"Sometimes there are things that keep us from being what we want to be . . . family . . . family pressures can do that. And the exigencies of duty, by God! Above all, let's not forget *duty!*"

Jacques was silent, waiting to hear more. This had already been more than Jamie had ever uttered on such matters, and he hoped—

But Jamie's next words disabused him of these hopes. "Listen, Beaumonde, if we don't put some ginger in our pace, it'll be dark before we get back. And I don't know about you, but I'm starving! Let's ride!"

With a characteristic shrug, Jacques threw him a grin and urged his pony into a lively trot.

⚜Chapter 8⚜

They arrived at the croft as twilight was gathering. The deep purple shadows of hill and crag seemed to bring it on even before the sun actually set. While stabling and feeding the ponies, they caught an aroma of something freshly baked and tantalizing. Jacques waxed rhapsodic over the apparent culinary skills of a certain pair, and Jamie admitted his mouth was watering.

As they entered the cottage, it was clear the women had been busy. The floor looked freshly swept, dishes and glassware sparkled in the open hutch, and not a single stray article of apparel remained in sight. The first through the door, Jamie murmured a greeting as his glance took this all in. Then he was drawn to the slender figure arranging wildflowers in a chipped crock on the center of the rough-hewn table.

He was again struck by the beauty of the young woman with the titian hair. Even with her long tresses bound in a kerchief and a smudge of soot on her chin, she was incomparably lovely. Slender as a reed, yet gently rounded where a woman ought to be, she evinced a fragility that was at odds with her dramatic coloring. He was at once reminded of a quiet pool they'd spied downriver from where they'd fished, still and deep amid the shadowed ferns; it had, at the same time, reflected on its surface a lofty crag soaring against a vivid blue patch of sky—embodying the dynamic face of the Highlands in a single image. And so, it seemed, did this young slip of a girl. She was a Highland Scot, all right, this Christmas MacKenzie . . . MacKenzie? Wasn't that the laird's name around here?

"How was the fishing?" Christmas inquired.

Mary turned from the bake oven, where she'd extracted a crusty brown loaf of bread. "Aye, tell us. Was it good?"

"Magnifique!" Jacques hoisted high their string of trout as he followed Jamie in.

Jamie glanced at the soft, white hands of the redhead, each fingernail a perfect, manicured oval. "They'll need gutting and cleaning straightaway, if we're to eat at a reasonable hour." His gaze lifted to a pair of startled violet-gray eyes.

"Ah, tha' weel be my chore," Mary said hastily as she shoved the breadboard at Christmas. "Here, cousin, be aboot settin' oot the rest of our fare whilst I take those trout oot t' scale an' sich." She turned toward Jacques and held out her hand for the string of fish.

The Frenchman's grin was every bit as compelling as the look in his eyes as they met hers. *"Mais mon, chérie!* How can I allow you to do this alone?" He gestured toward the door. "Come, I help you, *oui*, Mary?"

Mary's grin fought with the beginnings of a protest. But Jacques merely shook his head and was already scooping up knives and utensils from the cupboard. Still wearing a grin, he ushered her out the door.

As the door closed after them, Jamie headed for the washstand near the bed, eyeing the redhead as she set the steaming bread, with its board, on the table. He was pouring water from a heavy pitcher into a bowl on the stand when he saw her turn to the cupboard and grasp a small knife. He smiled archly.

"Ah, Miss MacKenzie, is there something unique

about Scottish bread that it doesn't collapse if you try to slice it hot from the oven?"

Christmas jerked the knife away from the loaf as if it had bitten her. "Why—um, certainly it—it collapses, Mr. MacIver. I—I was merely testin' it, ye ken."

"Ah, I see. That explains why you were using the paring knife instead of a bread knife, then." Jamie turned from her and began unbuttoning his shirt, humming to himself. He seemed clearly intent on his ablutions.

Christmas realized these were to be more extensive than a mere washing of his hands when she saw him drop his shirt, and she felt her face flame. Whether the result of her errors with the bread or the sight of the American stripped to the waist, she couldn't be certain. He was all rippling muscle and exposed bronze flesh—more male flesh than she'd ever seen in her life! Half wanting to run and hide, half mesmerized by the display, she froze where she stood, uncertain what to do. Of course, she knew what *Christina St. John* ought to do—act offended and perhaps shriek her shock and outrage, like any self-respecting lady of the *ton*.

But what would a Highland village lass do? Was it common for young women here to stand about while a man stripped to his breeches? She recalled overhearing snatches of conversation from Mrs. MacLeod's hired villagers that morning, when they hadn't known she was near. Among their comments had been some less than flattering speculations as to what the new heiress from London might be like. Unperturbed, she'd merely smiled wryly to herself at these remarks. But what she also remembered now was a surprising number of coarse and earthy expressions peppering their speech.

That said it, then. She must not bat an eyelash at the American's uncircumspect behavior. And she certainly needn't be surprised by it. She'd known he was no gentleman at the outset!

Fighting the flush that was as much from anger as embarrassment, she whirled about and busied herself with gathering dishes from the cupboard.

When Jamie emerged from his ablutions, he found Christmas engrossed in setting the table. Pulling out one of a pair of unmatched chairs, he spun it around and straddled it, on the side opposite where she worked.

"We'll need to find seating for two more," he said.

Christmas glanced up to find him freshly shirted, with his damp hair neatly combed as he observed her, arms folded across the top of the chair's wooden back. The faint, woodsy scent of the soap he'd used drifted over to her before being eclipsed by the aroma of freshly baked bread.

"There was only that one chair"—he dipped his head in the direction of the chair in front of her apron—"when we arrived. I purchased this one in the village the next day, so Jacques and I might eat at the table at the same time."

Christmas forced her eyes away from him and scanned the cottage interior. Why did she have the feeling he'd been focusing on more than the chair when discussing it? Like the shape of her hips, behind the chair back, for instance?

Quickly chiding herself for allowing this less than civilized foreigner to intimidate her, she indicated a crude, heavy wooden bench by the fire with a nod of her head. "Mary and I can use that piece there, sirr." She went back to arranging the tableware.

"Good enough," he told her as he disentangled his long legs and rose to fetch the bench. There was nothing awkward in these movements, she noted. He was all lean grace—and power, she added as she saw him heft the solid oak piece of furniture as if it were a featherweight.

"But," he continued, "I'd have you drop the 'sirr' "— he pronounced this in a perfect imitation of *her* imitation of the Scots burr. "Just 'Jamie' will do. We aren't much

for formalities around here, and that 'sir' business re-
minds me too much of my stint in the military."

Now, why had he told her that? He hadn't intended
getting on too familiar a footing with these women. And
what in hell was taking Beaumonde so long, anyway? But,
on second thought, he could venture an easy guess on
that.

"Ye were in the military, si—ah, Jamie?" Christmas
forced the familiar name past her lips. Now, she supposed, there was nothing for it but to allow him to call
her by hers.

With a mental sigh, she resigned herself; it was all in
keeping with their masquerade, after all.

"For a time," he replied, setting himself back astride
the chair, now that the bench was in place. "And what of
yourself, Christmas Mac— Oh, I may call you Christmas,
may I not?"

I wonder what he'd do if I said no. Dismissing the
thought as a pointless exercise in errant mischief, she gave
him a quick nod.

"Excellent," he said. "Now, about the other half. Isn't
MacKenzie the name of the clan hereabouts? The laird's
name?"

She'd been well prepared for this. "Aye, but in this case
the 'laird' is a 'lady.' "

"I beg your pardon?"

Christmas set the last piece of cutlery in place and
looked up to see those incredibly deep blue eyes on her;
their puzzled look was enhanced by knitted brows that
bore a hint of gold, as did his disgracefully thick lashes as
they caught the glint of firelight.

"Because of an auld entailment, the line of inheritance,
of the laird's position, fer the MacKenzie clan passes t'
the auldest *female*, Mr. Mac—Jamie. In this case, my distant cousin, Lady Christina MacKenzie St. John, lately
arrived from London. 'Twas an *English* entailment forced
upon us—through the vagaries of history, ye ken."

Jamie blinked. *"Vagaries"*? *What Scots peasant uses a word like "vagaries"*? Stilling the grin that slowly threatened, he decided to pursue this.

"I see," he said, as she went to fetch the butter crock Mary had discovered in a springhouse out back. "And this distant relative of yours, has she come to take up residence now?"

Christmas set the crock on the table. "I dinna ken fer certain. They say in the village she's here on holiday, though."

"You've not met her yourself, then?"

Christina's brow knitted in a tiny frown. What were all these questions? Did the man suspect something? Then, all at once, a hint of mischief lit her eyes. He wanted information, did he? Well, perhaps she'd just provide him some—and drive home the impression of her assumed role, as well!

"Aye, I've met her." Arms akimbo, Christmas threw him an exasperated look. "A right proper English bitch, she is, too! All ice water in her veins, despite her claim t' guid Scots bluid, an' a bearin' sae stiff, ye'd swear she had a broom rammed up her—ah, *spine.*"

It was exactly what she'd overheard one of the villagers say, when speculating about *her*. She'd repeated it, word for word—*except* for the last, of course, which she simply hadn't been able to bring herself to utter. Even with this hasty substitution, she felt her face go hot.

And was treated to an explosion of laughter from Jamie.

"Oh, I would, would I?" he chortled.

Christmas found herself bending forward over the table, ostensibly concentrating hard on rearranging the wildflowers.

A mistake, as it turned out.

Jamie suddenly reached out and cupped her chin in his hand while, with the other, he grabbed one of the serviettes she'd fashioned out of a strip of old homespun she'd found.

"Here," he murmured, ignoring the startled gray eyes that widened with apprehension, "I think it's about time we cleaned that smudge off your chin."

And far more gently than she'd have imagined, he made good his words, smoothing the napkin along her skin like a caress. But when he'd done this and laid the cloth down, his other hand remained, tilting her chin upward with bronzed knuckles.

"Did you know," he said with his gaze meeting hers, "that your eyes change color from time to time?"

Christmas felt herself go hot and cold all over, the heat emanating from a deep, sensual awareness of his closeness, of the warm touch of his fingers on sensitive skin. And the cold—for an insane moment she felt so cold, it seemed no fire could ever warm her.

"Right now," he went on in a low voice that seemed to hold wonder, "they're the most incredible shade of violet."

There was a crackling pop as a log fell on the hearth, sending up a shower of sparks and breaking the spell. Jamie jerked his hand away with a sudden scowl while Christmas whirled away from the table, desperately hunting for something to occupy her.

She was saved from this by the sudden appearance of Jacques and Mary at the door, laughter in their voices as they entered the cottage with a platter of cleaned and gutted trout.

"I reek of fish like one of ze dockside peddlers of Marseilles!" the Frenchman cried in mock disgust.

"Serves ye right," Mary told him with smiling equanimity. "Ye had nae call t' be sharin' my chore. Ye did yer oon part wi' the fine catch ye brought back, an' ye ought t' hae let me do mine."

"Ah," Jacques replied as he set the platter on the crude table near the fire and turned toward her, "but then I would 'ave been denied your sweet company, *ma belle* Mary!"

"Eeek!" Mary screeched, jumping back as he made as if to clasp her face between his odiferous hands.

The Frenchman chuckled, then gestured helplessly to Christmas and Jamie. "She scorns me for ze very task I help her with," he said in a mock-offended tone.

"At least till ye gie those hands a guid an' proper wash, mon!" Mary grinned as she hurriedly washed her own.

Jacques shrugged good-naturedly and went to the washstand while Mary prepared a pan for frying the trout, enlisting Christmas's aid with quietly voiced instructions. No one seemed to notice Jamie's silence as he walked to the open doorway and gazed out at the deepening shadows in the yard.

They ate their meal together a short while later, amid murmured acknowledgments of the deliciousness of the fare. It was agreed, after some protestations from the women, that Jacques would see them back as far as the path to the village, since it would be dark when they returned. He'd have preferred to escort them all the way home, but they wouldn't hear of it, of course. In the end, Jacques capitulated, but only when they'd agreed to take along a lantern.

Jamie watched the three leave the croft after the last of the dishes and pans had been washed and returned to the cupboard. The lantern's yellow glow receded, then disappeared among the trees as he followed their progress from the doorway where he stood, but still he didn't move.

Relentless images of Christmas MacKenzie danced in his mind, even as he tried to quell them. He saw her quick smile at something Jacques had said at table, the brilliant luster of her hair in sunlight, or, later, when its coppery sheen caught the softer glow of candles and hearth fire. He saw her slender form moving like a dancer's, among the simple furnishings of the cottage, suggesting a grace at odds with the humble abode . . .

Suddenly Jamie's head jerked up as he seized on the image. There it was again, that distinct impression that she was something more than she seemed. Yes, the more he thought of it, the more he was certain. He ran other details of her movements through his mind, deliberately steering clear of one particularly disturbing scene, settling at last on a picture of Christmas eating at the table.

The chit displayed manners a mite too refined for a Highland village lass.

With a slow smile, Jamie eased away from the door and shut it behind him. He nodded to himself as he ambled ruminatively toward the fire, stopping to stare at the flames that continued to conjure up the redhead's fiery mane.

They'd be back tomorrow, of course. And when he had her here, Christmas MacKenzie, or whoever she was, he decided, was going to face some interesting queries. Queries he had all night long to plan.

☙Chapter 9❧

Maire was humming as the two women made their way along the trail to the croft the next morning. Christina—or Christmas, as she'd begun to think of herself now, even in private—endured this blatant indication of the older woman's blithe mood, but barely.

Because her own mood was anything but blithe. Apprehensive, yes, and maybe even—well, frightened was perhaps too strong a term. But the uncertainty running through her like a strong current was something alien to her nature, and this, as much as its cause, had greatly unsettled her.

As to the cause, she could sum it up in short order: Jamie MacIver. The American had invaded her thoughts through every waking moment since they'd left the croft last evening, and disturbed her sleep as well. She'd awakened several times during the night, unable to recall, exactly, the substance of the dream that roused her; but in each case she was left with an undeniable conviction that Jamie MacIver had been a part of it.

Even now, she was besieged with impressions of honey-dark hair glinting gold in firelight, of blue eyes deepening to indigo as he talked about the color of her own, of—*damn!*

"Must you *hum?"*

The Irishwoman blinked, stopping short on the path to peer cautiously at her. "Not at all, child, but perhaps ye'll be tellin' me what ails ye?"

The ingenuous look on Maire's face, not to mention the worry in her dark eyes, had Christmas feeling instantly ashamed. "Oh, I— Do forgive me, Maire, but it— it seems I am not quite myself this morning. I—I slept rather poorly, you see, and—"

"He's crept under yer skin already, has he?"

"Who?" Christmas shot back. But she knew exactly who.

Maire chuckled. "And who else would it be, but that American whose divilish fine looks ought t' have a law passed against their bein' seen in public by innocent young lasses!"

Christmas flushed, then smiled ruefully. "He—he's not precisely all that—that handsome, really."

Maire raised a brow archly. "He's not, is he? Aye, mayhaps, when ye're accustomed t' thinkin' o' the *ton*, o' men like his nibs, milord Aaron Crenshawe, or—"

"Maire, *please!* Need I remind you I am *engaged* to Lord Aaron?"

The Irishwoman gave a grunt and briskly resumed walking. "Ye are," she remarked as Christmas scurried to catch up, "but not yet wed!"

A tartly questioning response hung poised on the tip of Christmas's tongue, but she thought better of it. She was well aware of the older woman's feelings about her betrothal to Aaron. Ever since she'd confirmed Maire's suspicions about him, admitting theirs was a liaison based upon reasons other than affection, or love, the Irishwoman had made no bones about telling her she was making a mistake. And while Christmas had frequently allowed herself to be guided by Maire's good sense over the years, in this she was determined not to pay heed to her misgivings. A marriage to Aaron Crenshawe—*if* she could still bring it off—was her passage to a secure future, and she would steadfastly pursue it. Platitudes about marrying for love and the like were all well and good, but they did not serve when the wolf was at the door. Well, this was one wolf Christmas intended to send packing, and no obstacle—Irish *or* American—would bar the way!

When they reached the croft, there was no one about, but a note in Jacques's scrawling hand lay on the table. It explained that the men had left early for the village and would return soon; one of the ponies appeared to have a swollen tendon and Jamie wanted the blacksmith, who knew about such things, to have a look at it. Meanwhile Jacques was buying some provisions for their supper.

Seizing this as an ideal opportunity to do some treasure-hunting, Christmas left Maire to straighten and sweep (having been told she could best lend a hand by staying out of the Irishwoman's way) while she made a careful search of the outbuildings. Unfortunately, a thorough scouting of the yard and stable turned up nothing new. Christmas grew more hopeful when she approached the springhouse; almost hidden by some dense foliage, it had been overlooked yesterday. But here she found only a near empty butter crock and several bottles of wine chilling in the icy water—nothing suggesting a hidden wine cellar.

It was only when she reexamined the storage area housing the sculpting materials she'd nearly forgotten, that she came upon something different from what they'd spied previously. There, scattered in the dust motes stirred by a sunbeam, lay the broken pieces of what had been the unfinished sculpture of a deer.

Had it been broken by some unfortunate accident? Bending closer, Christmas didn't think so. A few shards of dried clay thrust sharply from a mass of pulverized dust, suggesting the piece had not merely toppled, but been smashed by a violent hand. But why?

She was inclined to think Maire's instincts had been right in identifying Jamie as the sculptor. And with instincts of her own, she felt, surely, the destructive hand could not have been Jacques's. But then, what had happened to cause Jamie to do this to his *own* work?

"Find something interesting?"

Christmas gasped and whirled about to find Jamie standing in the doorway. His indolent pose struck her at once as being at odds with the intense light in his eyes.

"I—ye frightened me." It was all she could think of to say as her mind cast about for reasons to explain why she was there. But it was also the truth. There was something about the way he looked at her that suggested a predator about to pounce, and she couldn't help feeling faintly intimidated by it.

Dismissing this as ridiculous, she met his eyes and forced a smile. "Ye really shouldna be stealin' across a body tha' way, Mr. MacIver."

"Jamie," he reminded, his eyes dropping to her lips as she wet them with a small glide of her tongue.

"A-aye. Jamie." She shifted her glance and it fell on the broken clay. "I didna ken ye were an artist, Jamie— ah, 'tis *yours*, the sculptin', is it n—"

"Just something I waste my time with," he broke in. But he said this with an insouciant air she somehow didn't quite believe. "It helps to pass the time, especially when I'm away from home and not involved in the daily business of running my plantation."

"Plantation? But I thought ye said ye were in the mili—"

"I was, but I resigned my commission last winter when the war ended." His tone seemed to indicate this was all he would say to enlighten her.

"I see." She took a step, as if to leave.

"And what about you, Christmas?"

"Me?"

"What do *you* do when you're not hiring on to help a couple of strangers who are in dire straits with their, ah, domestic affairs?" He remained in the doorway, one shoulder leaning negligently against its splintered post, but the deep blue of his eyes indicated a heightened interest.

"I . . . weel, I help aboot at home, mainly."

"At home. In the village?"

"A-aye."

"Do you live with your mother and father, then?"

A sharp twist of pain caught Christmas suddenly off guard, and she answered him with honest anguish in her eyes. "My parents are dead, sirr. They—they were both killed in—in an accident this winter past. I dwell wi'—wi' Mary."

"I'm sorry to hear it," he told her, and she heard a note of genuine sympathy in his voice. "It cannot have been an easy time for you. Still, I suppose you're glad to have had your cousin. She seems a decent, caring sort."

"Och, tha' she is! Mary's like a—a second mother t' me. We—we've always been close, ye ken."

Jamie nodded, his gaze pensive as it rested on her face. "And you've always lived in the Highlands? Spent your entire life here?"

"A-aye." She began to move toward the door, but for her to leave, he'd need to shift and give her room; yet he made no move to do so.

"What was it like," he questioned, "growing up in these mountains as a child?"

Christmas smiled. She'd been expecting questions to arise, concerning the background they'd invented, though perhaps not the barrage of queries he was pelting her with now. Nevertheless, she'd gleaned what she could, from memory, of those occasional conversations she'd had with her mother over the years, on what her parent's Scottish childhood had been like. She'd even coached Maire on them when they'd planned this masquerade, so she felt well prepared to respond.

" 'Twas wonderful. A simple life, some would call it, tuned t' the rhythms of the seasons . . . t' the verra heart an' life of these hills. I've memories of long summer days filled wi' birdcall whilst we boated on the loch or gathered berries fer the—fer my mother t' bake into cakes." *Devil take it! I almost said "for the cook to bake"! It won't serve if I paint a picture of an aristocratic Scottish childhood!*

"An' i' the winter," she went on a bit more cautiously, "there were frolics on the frozen streams wi' the other village bairns, an' long evenin's by the fire, crackin' nuts whilst my—my father'd tell us tales of Clan MacKenzie fra' days gone by."

Jamie nodded. "And holidays? *Christmas* must have been especially memorable."

"No' sae memorable as ye might suspect," she answered readily. If there was one thing she clearly recalled, it was the very different customs her Scots mother and her English father brought to the winter holiday season from their disparate backgrounds. At home in England she'd grown up with both traditions, so she launched her explanation with ease.

"Ye see, Jamie, we Scots dinna make sae much over Christmas as the English an' others do. In fact, if it were no' fer my birthday fallin' on tha' day, 'twould scarcely hae been celebrated by my family at all. Because, i' the Highlands, 'tis the New Year brings aboot the merrymakin'."

Jamie nodded again. "Ah, yes. 'Auld Lang Syne' and all that. And haggis! Um . . . what *is* haggis, actually?"

Christmas was feeling so relaxed by now, she missed the speculative look in his eye, a look that might have told her he already knew this, but was probing to see if *she* knew. She'd advanced closer to the doorway during her reminiscences and stood barely an arm's length away from him, but this too she seemed not to notice. Nor the sudden catch in Jamie's breath as he caught the scent of flowers from her hair, where the sunbeam shining through the open doorway warmed it.

"Haggis?" She laughed. "Are ye certain ye truly wish t' learn?"

Jamie thought he nodded, perhaps even smiled, but he wasn't sure. All he could be certain of was the melodic trill of her laughter, sunlight catching the fire of her hair, the intoxicating drift of wildflowers filling his senses.

"Pay heed, then, sirr," she said with a seriousness belied by twin dimples he'd never noticed before. " 'Tis the heart an' liver of a sheep, mixed wi' suet an' oats, then seasoned an' boiled t'gither i' the sheep's stomach. A verra tasty dish, but I fear ye maun no' appreciate it, unless ye've been raised a Scot!"

Jamie murmured something low and inaudible, but before Christmas could ask him to repeat it, she found his eyes locked with hers. Her question died on her lips. She felt herself drawn in and held by their blue depths while her heart began to hammer in her breast like a wild thing, and a sudden heat invaded her skin.

"Perhaps," she heard him murmur in a voice gone husky and strange, "that is only the beginning of things I've missed by not growing up in this place . . ."

Rooted where she stood, she felt her breathing go shallow as his hand moved slowly toward her and lifted a lock of her hair until it curled about his fingers.

". . . the myriad beauties of it"—he tugged gently on the lock and Christmas felt a pleasurable prickling at her scalp before he ran the silken end of it along her cheek and she felt her breath catch—"are something I find"—he let the silken strands slide through his fingers, then took his thumb and ran it lightly across her lower lip—"fascinating."

Her eyes were two deep pools of purest violet now, and Jamie had to steady himself with a hand against the doorpost as he leaned down to brush his lips across the path his thumb had traced.

A rushing sounded in her ears as Christmas felt the warmth of his lips grazing her own. She felt herself leaning toward that warmth with a strange dizziness that invaded her, making her limbs feel boneless and liquid under the spell of his nearness. Dimly, if she heard them at all, the sounds of the morning receded into the background, and—

"Jamie!" Jacques's voice cut across them like an icy wind, and they broke apart with a mutual intake of breath.

"Jamie," the Frenchman's voice came again, "come quickly! This cursed sack of flour 'as broken and I need your help or it will— *Sacrebleu*, man, where *are* you?"

Muttering an indelicate oath and something barely intelligible about hundred-pound sacks of flour, Jamie whirled abruptly and raced for the outer yard.

Leaving Christmas to press trembling fingers to her lips and wonder why Aaron had never made them tingle so.

✣Chapter 10✣

The sunny weather that had heralded the arrival of Christmas and Maire in the Highlands continued. Besides making their daily walks to the croft pleasant, especially once they became more accustomed to the terrain, it also helped provide them with a continuing excuse for leaving the manor for long periods of time. Armed with sketchbooks and charcoals (which they later stashed under a large rock well away from the croft, to avoid being questioned about them by Jamie or Jacques), they cheerfully made their farewells to Mrs. MacLeod early each morning. And if the housekeeper thought this preoccupation with sketching odd, she never said a word about it.

As for the time they spent at the croft, the results were mixed. As each day passed, Christmas became more adept at many of the household chores she'd taken for granted all her life. They'd always been done by well-trained staffs of servants, after all, and as she gained insight into the amount of hard work involved, she quickly assumed an enormous respect for those who must physically labor for a living. Moreover, she began to take pride in these accomplishments, beaming visibly when Maire pronounced perfect a loaf of bread she'd baked, or grinning broadly at the neat appearance of a bed she'd made.

On the other hand, their primary objective met with

no success at all. They searched the cottage and grounds again and again, diligently, for they were left alone from time to time, when the men went fishing and the like. But they gained not the slightest clue as to the whereabouts of Angus's old wine cellar. After a week of such fruitless effort, Maire was more certain than ever that the old Scot had been "daft, or at least wanderin' in his wits," as she put it, but Christmas refused to give up. And since Maire, for all her pessimism regarding the treasure, did not appear averse to continuing with their assumed identities, Christmas met no resistance there.

Of course, she had reasons to suspect the Irishwoman's acquiescence had less to do with their objective than with a certain Frenchman, but on this she held her peace. Maire was quite capable of minding her own affairs, she reasoned, and besides, if, at this stage in her life, she at last had a second chance at some personal happiness, Christmas could do nothing less than silently cheer her on. Also, Jacques Beaumonde was a charming scamp who gave occasional indications of having a deeper, more steadfast nature than he showed on the surface, and Christmas couldn't help liking him.

As for the croft's other occupant, Jamie MacIver had begun to take on the earmarks of a puzzle more complex than the history of the Seadog's Treasure. He was, by turns, both closemouthed and open, leaving her with no clearly identifiable understanding of just what made the man tick.

But then came the day she learned more about him than she ever wanted to know. And perhaps more about herself than she was ready to deal with.

It was one of those rare days when true summer reigned in the Highlands. That the season which had always been Christmas's favorite was able to strengthen its tenuous hold on a landscape more often subject to stormy skies and chill winds, even in July and August, was remarkable enough. But on this particular day that softest of all seasons seemed to have taken on the best parts of itself and wrapped them up in a single package. It was as if Nature had reserved, for this one day only, her loveliest face, consigning all the rest to chance.

Not a cloud broke the even expanse of blue sky overhead, and the sun shone warmly, neither too weak nor too hot. The gentlest of breezes moved like a sigh over corrie and glen, and wildflowers nodded their colorful heads as if in perfect agreement with the land and the day.

Indeed, Christmas thought as she ambled along a path to a high meadow where she'd heard a profusion of wildflowers grew, God had never made a more perfect day. But when she emerged from the wooded path lined with creeping azalea and dwarf willow, she had to pause for a long moment and drink in the sight before her.

Some of the flowers she knew by name, having come across them before or studied them from prints she used as models in her sketching. Others, she realized she'd never seen before, but it didn't matter. What mattered was the glorious riot of color that dazzled under the Highland sky.

There were yellows of every shade and description, from the familiar brilliance of buttercups, to the showy shapes of mountain avens, or the deep golden hue of poppylike flowers nodding on thin, graceful stems. She recognized the purple and rose-colored flowers of saxifrages, and here they were more abundant than the similarly colored heather. Heather did not flourish as greatly here as in other regions of Scotland, she'd learned from Mrs. MacLeod, because of the wet northwest climate. Yet heather there was, and the blue raylike flowerheads of mountain bluets, and a tiny red blossom she'd never seen before, and the fading hue of mountain pinks.

White, red, yellow, blue, purple, rose—a rainbow drifted before her eyes. It was like stumbling across God's own palette, and Christmas felt a moment of pure, untrammeled joy. It was a powerful feeling of high emotion, of wonder running through her veins, and she reacted in a way she couldn't recall doing since she was a child.

Catching her skirts up high, she laughed out loud and ran until she found herself knee-deep in color. Then she whirled about, laughter still erupting from her throat in joyous cadence. Oh, but wasn't this the most wondrous place to be? Wasn't she the happiest woman alive?

And that was how Jamie saw her when his hands stilled on the clay he was working and he looked up at her trill of laughter.

He'd come to the meadow at first light, having judged the coming perfection of the weather correctly and wanting to take advantage of the beauty of the landscape, as well as the privacy it afforded. Before him, on a pair of packing crates he'd assembled as a portable workbench, was the two-stone lump of clay he'd been sculpting, plus a pan of water he'd collected to keep it wet as he worked.

But now the sculpting knife beside the clay lay ignored. So did those hands pausing over the reddish mass of earth as he saw her, as he felt the ebullience of her laughter ripple the air and meet him at the level of flesh and bone. Christ, but she was lovely! Coppery mane flying, catching myriad beams of light as she whirled, the clear, pure lines of face and throat turned skyward, she was the essence of feminine grace, yet fraught with something of the child at play at the same time.

Jamie felt something tighten in his chest as he watched, something dangerously close to an emotion long denied. It had been years since he'd allowed himself an appreciation of feminine perfection when it was couched in such innocence. He'd almost forgotten there were such women as Christmas MacKenzie . . . beautiful . . . pure . . . unspoiled.

And dangerous, he told himself, deciding to break the spell.

"I wasn't aware I paid you to cavort in meadows, Miss

MacKenzie," he called out. "Perhaps you'd care to tell me how this endeavor qualifies as a domestic chore?"

Christmas nearly lost her balance and fell as his stern voice sliced across her laughter and caught her in mid-pirouette. Clutching her *tonnag* with one hand as it slid from her shoulders, she used the other to shield her eyes from the sun and peer across the carpet of wildflowers until she located the source of the startling interruption.

"Jamie—? Ah, Mr. MacIver?" she corrected, belatedly recalling his use of formal address in that less than pleasant voice.

"The same," he answered as she began to walk toward him. As she moved, he couldn't help noticing it was with that innate grace that seemed as much a part of her as breathing. Then his eyes traveled the length of her as she drew near. He noted her hair swirling about her arms and shoulders, shot with primitive fire. He met the clear, translucent brilliance of her eyes as they returned his gaze.

"Och, but 'tis verra sorry I am, t' hae disturbed ye, sirr," Christmas said, deciding it was too lovely a day to warrant the forbidding look on MacIver's face. Or the stern tones she'd caught in his voice. She would simply have to coax him into sharing her rare mood with her. "Ah, what was it ye were sayin' a moment ago, sirr?"

She gave him her sunniest smile.

Jamie did his best to ignore it, and the suggestion of dimples in her cheeks, and the merry glint in her eyes.

"I asked how time spent gamboling about this place qualifies as something we're paying you to do here," he reiterated.

Christmas remained undaunted. "Och, mon! I fear ye dinna hear Jacques inform us he'd luv a bouquet of wild-flowers fer the table agin. I'm here t' fetch some."

Another dazzling smile, and Jamie felt his chest constrict.

"I see," he said, trying his damnedest to remain gruff

—employer to employee—but feeling a losing battle approaching.

Christmas was eyeing the shape of the clay before him. "Och! 'Tis a bonnie form ye're moldin' there . . . er, wha' is it?"

Jamie sighed. "In point of fact, Miss MacKen—"

" 'Twas t' be Christmas, I thought?"

Jamie gave her a curt nod of acknowledgment. "In point of fact, Christmas, it is nothing at all at the moment. During the course of the morning it has alternately *begun* to be a kestrel, a red deer, a linnet, and a capercaillie."

"A *capercaillie?*"

"Surely you know the local term for an indigenous species of grouse?" The glint in his eye said he doubted it and would know why she didn't.

Flushing, (she'd never heard of the wretched thing!) Christmas sought to deflect this latest interrogatory advance.

" 'Twould seem ye're inspired by the faces of Nature, here in the Highlands, Jamie." She swept her gaze over the meadow, then beyond, to the rugged peaks rising above the trees in the near distance. "Och, but I fin' I canna blame ye! 'Tis glorious, is it no'?"

Following her gaze, Jamie had to agree. "Glorious, indeed."

"Aye," she sighed. Then she stooped to begin picking some flowers, continuing to address him while she did this. "Yer hands maun itch t' shape the clay i' this place."

She felt the truth of these words as she said them. It was what she felt herself in a way. There was something about the Highlands which inspired doing, even if it was so simple a thing as gathering wildflowers. She'd *done* things with her hands before, of course, in her life in England. But as she thought about it now, it seemed to her they had always been things carefully proscribed . . . shaped by the various rules and protocols of her life there.

Whether it was wielding a sketching pencil or handling the ribbons of her stylish perch phaeton in the Park, each act adhered to society's precepts for conduct befitting a daughter of the *ton*.

Ah, but here, in this remote country where the land was as wild and free and limitless as a new idea! Here, she felt she could do almost anything! She thought about the simple task of baking a loaf of bread, or polishing a copper pan with salt and vinegar and sand until it shone. Why had she never guessed at the pure joy, the satisfaction a person could take in such things?

"A man could do worse than lose himself in all this majesty," Jamie was saying.

Christmas laughed. "Aye, and a lassie, too!"

Jamie rose from the rock he'd been sitting on, wiping the clay from his hands with a wet rag beside the basin of water.

Christmas's eyebrows rose slightly as he ambled toward her and began helping her pick wildflowers. Until now he'd been working at the clay, shaping the side that faced him as they spoke. But with her laughter, he'd seemed to change his mind, and now—

"I dinna mean t' interfere wi' yer work," she said hastily. "If I'd been aware ye were here, I'd nae hae—"

"Here," he interrupted, handing her one of the exquisite, tiny carmine blossoms. "A few more of these red ones ought to do well."

Christmas merely nodded, accepting the flowers.

"You know, Christmas," he continued as they walked desultorily among the nodding heads of color, "I envy you."

"Envy . . . *me?*"

He nodded, pausing to gaze about them. "I envy you" —he made a sweeping gesture with his hand—"all this. After all, you're the native here, while I—I'm only an intruder. You've awakened to this glory every morning of your life, haven't you?"

Christmas bit the inside of her cheek, hoping to forestall the flush of color she felt coming to her face.

"What must it be like?" Jamie went on, watching her, "to be born to this freedom? To take in the changing face of all this wild, untrammeled beauty and feel it running like quicksilver through your veins?"

Christmas didn't reply. She couldn't. To do so would be to admit the lie she'd been living. But it went deeper than that. She was as much the intruder here as he. She was never more aware of it than in those times she went down into the village and encountered the real natives, those gruff-spoken Highlanders who were as much a part of the land as the mountains. They were the original free-born Scots, no matter what the English might have done to them at Culloden Moor and after. They had a certain integrity, a fierce pride and a sense of personal worth that sometimes, when she sensed it most strongly, had her trembling with a longing she couldn't put a name to. What must it be like, indeed?

Finding Jamie looking at her expectantly, she finally managed a softspoken reply. "The Highland Scots were ever a fiercely independent people. I've—I've nae a doubt they get it fra' the land. Even—even an intruder here maun feel it, Jamie. Even sic as yersel'."

"Oh, I feel it," he answered. "I just don't believe it's the same as being born to it."

She cocked a brow at him. "Aye, but wha' aboot yer America, now? There be freedoms there aplenty, sae I've heard. Ye fought th' English king and won, did ye no'?"

Jamie laughed, but there seemed to be no mirth in it. "We fought him twice and won, my dear. And, yes, there are freedoms there, hardwon, as you suggested. But in some ways my fledgling nation is still a great deal like the Old World. At least, where I come from. There are parts of New Orleans where the houses and the people—the culture—are more French than in France, more Spanish than in Spain, more English than in the country we fought to break away from. We have a genuine aristocracy there, for all its lack of titles. And with it, all the rules, snobberies, social hierarchies, and attendant injustices the Old World can boast of. You haven't met uncrossable lines of social rank until you've encountered the blue bloods of New Orleans's old aristocratic families."

Christmas heard the bitterness in his voice and wondered at it. Was he not from one of these families, then? But she knew he owned a great estate—a plantation, it was called—and was therefore a wealthy landowner. And in England this had always been the measure of things. The great landowners, the titled lords with their laws of primogeniture to keep the land in the hands of a select few, were the men of wealth and power. And if wealth and power did not confer a great deal of personal freedom upon a man, nothing did.

Or did it?

She looked around her, at the vast sky above the mountains, at the boundless expanse of untamed land—crag and corrie, meadow and glen—and knew that here, the soul of the individual reigned. Here, each man was king . . . Or queen? she amended, thinking of the longing in her soul.

"And . . . wha' of yer own family, Jamie MacIver?" she asked suddenly. "Did yer Highland roots gie ye a Celtic soul tha' longs fer the fierce independence of yer forebears? Or are ye tied more t' the seductions of wealth an' power?"

Jamie's face grew instantly shuttered and unrevealing. "My own family," he replied in hard, clipped syllables, "does not exist, except for me. My . . . parents are dead, and I had no brothers or sisters."

She heard the bitterness again, despite his attempt at giving nothing away. There were devils here, as Maire had termed them, and they surrounded Jamie, with a remoteness as cold as polar ice.

Suddenly Christmas found herself shivering. It came to

her all at once that this man, despite his attractions—and she could no longer deny them, the way she felt herself drawn to him—was capable of doing her great injury. He was a man determined to cloak himself in his remoteness, preferring the devils that dwelt there to a warm, flesh-and-blood relationship. Jamie MacIver was dangerous to her, to something in her that cried for warmth and joy and sharing, never felt more than on this glorious day. If she were wise, she would run. Run from him and never cross his path again, treasure or no treasure.

If she were wise . . .

"You're shivering." Jamie's voice, softer now, and low, came to her as if from a great distance, as he closed the gap between them. She could smell the masculine scent of him, redolent of leather and tobacco and the woodsy soap he used as he took the tartan *tonnag* that had slipped from her shoulders and raised it, wrapping it securely about her.

She felt his hands, capable and sensitive, a sculptor's hands, move reassuringly over her arms and shoulders, driving all notions of wisdom from her brain.

She felt her nose pressed against the clean linen of his shirt, felt the hard, lean length of his thighs, even through the layers of her skirts and petticoats, and she suddenly went weak all over. Her limbs all at once seemed boneless, and she felt her breathing go shallow, then catch in her throat.

He had taken his hand and tipped her chin up with the knuckles, forcing her to look at him, and she found herself staring into eyes that were deep, fathomless pools of darkest indigo.

"Better?" he murmured, but his voice had changed again. Low and husky, it sent a quiver racing along her spine, made her feel as if something were unraveling deep beneath the pit of her stomach.

"A-aye," she answered, barely trusting herself to speak.

Jamie looked down into her flushed, exquisitely

chiseled face, met the violet depths of her eyes, and felt himself drowning. *So lovely . . . so utterly lovely and beautiful with an innocence I can hardly remember existing . . .*

Christmas felt his hands slide along the planes of her jaw and cup her face, felt, more than saw, his head descend, and closed her eyes as his mouth covered hers in a slow, sensual blending that left her weaker than before.

Placing her hands against his chest to steady herself, she felt sun-warmed skin through the fine linen of his shirt, felt the crisp texture of hair covering hard muscle, and before she knew what was happening, her arms were moving to his shoulders, then encircling his neck.

There she clung to him as his lips, firm and warm, moved with hers in lazy, sensual circles, testing her, learning the feel of her as she did him.

She felt his arms tighten about her, pressing the wool of the tartan against her back and shoulders at the same time that his mouth increased its pressure on hers. Unaware of her response, she parted her lips and then realized what she'd done when she felt the first questing probe of his tongue.

The touch of it sent a sharp, electric thrill along her nerve endings and a pulsing heat somewhere below her belly.

Gasping, though whether from the boldness of this touch or surprise at her reaction she did not know, she parted her lips further and received the full, sweet intrusion of his tongue.

Dizzy now, with the strange lassitude stealing over her body, she wound her arms about his neck more tightly, rising on tiptoe to accommodate herself to Jamie's great height.

With this, she thought she heard him groan somewhere deep in his throat, and before she knew what was happening, she felt him shift and then there was the warmth of his hand covering her breast.

"J-Jamie—don't—" she began in shocked protest as she tore her lips free.

"Shh," he murmured against her ear, sending another shiver along her spine.

And then she felt his thumb graze her nipple, and she gasped as a jolt of pure pleasure sluiced through her and lodged in the place between her thighs.

"So warm . . . so responsive . . ." Jamie breathed when he felt her nipple harden into a tight, pulsing bud. "No, sweetheart, don't fight it. I swear, you were made for this."

"F-for wha'?" Christmas barely remembered to maintain her accent as his lips scorched a trail of fire along her throat. What was she thinking of? she asked herself. She was a betrothed woman with a mission to accomplish! But the touch of his lips—and his hands!—was making it impossible to keep anything straight in her brain right now. Dear God, if she didn't stop him soon, she would be—

Almost as if he'd read her mind, Jamie broke his hold and released her, his low laughter curling around the edges of her nerve endings as he stepped away.

"Why, all the things your ripe body was yearning for just now, lassie," he told her.

Christmas followed his gaze, glancing down to see the peaked flesh of her nipple thrusting against the cotton of her bodice, where his hand had been. Heat rose to her face as his laughter, low and vibrant, told her he knew what was making her blush.

"It's nothing to be embarrassed about, sweeting," Jamie told her. "Just a natural, honest response to a man's touch."

"I—I dinna ken—I've never—"

Jamie chuckled as he bent to retrieve the bouquet she'd dropped and handed it to her. "Better stick to things you know, then, lovely lassie. Like picking flowers, hmm?"

"A-aye," said Christmas, blushing furiously as his amused gaze found hers.

With a grin, Jamie leaned forward and gave her a light kiss on the mouth, then took her by the shoulders and gently turned her about.

"That way, darlin', or I'll lose my chivalry and decide to finish what we started!"

He topped this alarming admission with a swat on her rump, making Christmas blush all the harder as she hurried across the meadow toward the path.

As she ran, she told herself she was lucky to escape him. Hadn't she known from the outset that he was no gentleman? She ought to have listened to her own warnings as they'd buzzed about in her brain.

But as she reached the dappled shadows of the path and at last slowed her pace, all she could seem to remember was the warmth of his lips in the sun and the sweet, unholy ache his hands had brought to her flesh.

Jamie watched her go until she passed out of sight. He sighed, and there was regret in the sound. It was echoed in his eyes, in the slow movements of his body as he returned to the workbench where the clay waited.

But then a stunned look entered his eyes when he gazed down at the half-formed image his hands had wrought. As it began to emerge out of the reddish mass, it was the figure of a woman, and it had Christmas Mac-Kenzie's laughing face.

And it was perfect.

The days that followed the incident in the meadow were difficult ones for Christmas, underscored by a heightened awareness of Jamie and the undeniable undercurrent of something magnetic between them. But she did her utmost to set this aside. Telling herself it was nothing more than an unusual physical attraction on her part—the man *was* possessed of arresting good looks, after all, even if they weren't in the classic mode—Christmas was deter-

mined to dismiss it as insignificant. She felt it was something that would pass as she grew accustomed to seeing
Jamie about. She knew she had no room in her plans for
the disruptions even a mild flirtation could cause: she was
betrothed, wasn't she? But when she was honest with
herself—most often, late at night, when thoughts of the
American prevented sleep—she knew in her bones the
thing between them was capable of igniting something
far more consequential than a harmless flirtation.

As the days wore on, however, her determination to
play down her attention to him met with numerous chal-
lenges. There was that lull in the supper conversation
when she looked up to find Jamie's eyes on her before
they quickly shuttered and he glanced elsewhere. But not
before she felt her pulse race and her heart begin to
pound. Or the incident in the yard when she'd gone to
collect rainwater, caught her heel on a loose rock, and
stumbled, only to find Jamie suddenly at her side. Seeming to come out of nowhere, he'd steadied her with
strong hands while an electric charge coursed through
her body. And then there was the time his fingers had
brushed her sleeve as they inadvertently reached for
something at table at the same moment, and she'd felt
the shock clear to her toes.

But perhaps the worst of these incidents was what had
happened once when she was careless with a paring knife
and cut her finger. It happened at the beginning of their
second week at the croft, on a quiet morning when Maire
had left her to peel vegetables for a stew while the Irishwoman went to collect fresh herbs to enhance its flavor.

Christmas had thought she was alone in the cottage.
The men had disappeared upon their arrival, Jacques to
explore the loch and see if a skiff could be had to sail it,
Jamie to some undisclosed destination. She was aware he
did his sculpting out of doors in good weather and had
assumed this occupied him. Deeply absorbed in the business of peeling potatoes and delighted that Maire had

entrusted her with the task, she'd been about to attack the last spud in the batch when her finger slipped and she sliced it with her knife.

She could recall yelping aloud, more in surprise than pain, for the cut was minor; and then she'd chided herself for her carelessness. "Clumsy ninnyhammer! Now look what you've done!"

"You're hurt!" came a voice from the open doorway, and she'd whirled around to see Jamie striding toward her, a frown furrowing his brow.

"Och!" she'd exclaimed. " 'Tis naught t' be—"

"Let me see it." The command in his voice had cut off her protest as he reached her side, and she'd readily complied, picturing him ordering troops about in that exact tone.

"You need to be more careful," he'd murmured almost absently as he examined the cut.

Blood was trickling from the slight wound on her index finger, and before she realized what was happening, he was raising it to his mouth and gently—oh, ever so gently!—sucking away the blood.

Christmas had instantly frozen, her feet rooted to the floor as a hot liquid sensation washed through her body. His lips and tongue were warm as they laved her finger, and, except for his capable hands clasping her forearm near elbow and wrist, he'd touched her nowhere else. Yet she'd felt the heat and texture of him with every part of her body, which tingled and throbbed as if caressed by the most intimate hand.

And then suddenly she'd been freed, but only momentarily; all at once he'd perched atop the worktable, thighs widespread as he pulled her near with one hand, while with the other, he withdrew a square of white linen from his pocket.

Christmas had squirmed in his grasp, light as it was on her arm; all she could think of was the overpowering nearness of his big frame, the proximity of those long, muscular thighs on either side of her hips, and she'd wanted to run.

"Hold still," he'd ordered as he shook the handkerchief from its folds.

She remembered nodding, not trusting herself to speak. What was wrong with her? she recalled a frantic interior voice questioning. The man was competently ministering to a simple wound—nothing more!

But she knew she'd held her breath, her heart beating so loudly, she'd been certain he could hear it.

"There," he'd finally pronounced as he wrapped linen around the injured finger and tied the securing knot. Christmas's eyes had involuntarily lifted . . .

To find herself caught in the incredible blue depths of his gaze.

A bird had called somewhere outside, the warbling notes only half registering in her brain as the silence between them lengthened. Christmas recalled being aware of a sensation of falling, the room and its furnishings suddenly as remote as the distant Cairngorms in the mist.

"You're beautiful," he'd murmured at last, his voice a husky whisper.

She remembered voicing a half-formed response; what it had been, she could no more now recall than she could sprout wings and fly.

He'd sighed then, a long, weary expulsion of breath. "I wish—"

But whatever that wish had been, she was never to learn. Jacques's hearty laughter had cut into their awareness like a blade, and when a minute later he and Maire entered the cottage amid mutual laughter, they'd found Christmas back at her cutting board and Jamie heading toward the door.

❧Chapter 11❧

Jamie was silent and pensive during supper one evening. It was midway through the women's second week of service. Letting the other three carry the conversation, he quietly reflected on the scene which had taken place a couple of days before, when Christmas had cut her finger.

His ruminations began with the same things that had kept him lying awake for hours the following night, and last night as well. Over and over, he recaptured in his mind the feelings she'd aroused in him by her nearness. His senses had responded to her like the fingers of a master musician to a favorite song, coaxing forth the separate purity of each note until the blended melody of the piece flooded his awareness, leaving him breathless and reeling, yet utterly alive.

First, as always, there'd been the sight of her . . . those huge gray eyes dominating the delicately carved features of her face, their innocence in stark counterpoint to the fiery magnificence of her hair . . . the willowy grace of her body when it moved . . . the unconscious sensuality of a simple gesture, such as the habit she had of running her tongue along her lips when uncertain of a response she ought to make. Oh, yes, the visual had been the first to draw him in.

But it hadn't ended there. It never did. Her voice had a

soft, lyrical quality that was ever easy on the ear, yet he'd
detected a husky timbre hovering in the lower registers
when he drew her close. It had had the immediate effect
of making him wonder what it would sound like if he had
her beneath him in bed, a captive to the untapped passion
he sensed churning beneath that lovely surface.

And then there was the exquisite softness of her skin.
Its satiny warmth had led him to that moment when he'd
felt the need to taste as well as touch. He wondered, even
now, at the urge which had driven him to take the delicate finger into his mouth, to suck and savor that simple
taste of her which had only left him longing for a more
intimate exploration elsewhere. It had doubtless been entirely too bold a gesture, and he felt himself lucky she
hadn't fled, or worse, delivered a resounding slap to his
face.

Damn him! Christmas MacKenzie had him casting
prudence to the wind, and if he wasn't careful, he'd find
himself walking a path he'd sworn never again to tread.
Better, and infinitely safer, to slake his lust on whores
whenever the need arose. A quick tumble in a darkened
room, and he could be on his way, with nothing more
than the remnant of some cheap perfume to take away
with him.

But cheap perfumes were cloying; they sent him hurry-
ing to take a bath, to wash away reminders of an impersonal coupling in the night. They were to be discarded,
like the whores who wore them, not savored like that
other scent he'd come to know.

He caught it even now, the scent of her, a subtle
blending of the floral, perhaps from a soap she used, and
an essence he knew was entirely Christmas's own. Always
a part of her, it never overwhelmed, remaining delicate
and subtle as it teased his awareness; yet it had the power
to intoxicate him like no liquor ever brewed.

He tried to tell himself it was only lust that drove him;
they were miles from any city, where the need for a warm

female body could be easily met. Yet when he glanced briefly at the animated face of the woman across from him, chatting amiably with her cousin and Jacques, he was vaguely aware of other needs she stirred. Needs long held at bay, lest he foolishly grasp at something not only his body, but his heart, might be yearning for.

Christ, it was hard! But he had to let it go. Besides the risks, he had no right. No right at all. If he hadn't—

Beaumonde's voice intruded, and Jamie found himself nodding and accepting more wine. But a moment later he was back at that time, two days earlier. Now, however, his thoughts took a more practical turn.

He replayed the moment he'd entered the cottage and heard her vexed cry when the knife slipped. Then she'd chided herself, thinking she was alone: *"Clumsy ninny-hammer! Now look what you've done!"*

And those words had been uttered in *perfect, unaccented English!* No Scots burr, no curling of the tongue to accommodate the Highlander's rounding of vowels and clipping of consonants.

Just pure aristocratic English—the accents of London's *ton*, or he was a witless fool!

So she wasn't even a native, though she had the coloring for it. Well, he'd suspected she was lying. Too many things hadn't fit. The question was, why? And then, who the hell *was* she? He'd have some answers, and soon, by God! His gaze drifted upward from where it had been focused on his glass of wine, and he studied the women across the table. Odd, but he'd have sworn Mary, at least, was what she appeared. Yet the older woman had to be a part of this charade, too.

So, if they weren't Highland villagers, where had they come from? He had a feeling he'd be closer to the truth very shortly. Tonight, when he followed them home.

Jamie stood well within the shadows of some pines which flanked one end of the drive curving before the stately

Georgian manor house. He'd just seen his two female
employees walk directly up that drive and boldly enter the
mansion through the door beneath its imposing front
portico. And before that door had shut behind them,
he'd glimpsed an elderly man, obviously a servant by his
dress, *bowing* deferentially to the flame-haired nemesis of
his sleepless nights!

This was the MacKenzie place, unless he missed his
guess. None but the laird would own a place of such
grandeur in these mountains. An English, *female* laird.
Who was no more a Scots peasant than Jamie was a New
Year's haggis! Christmas MacKenzie was this Lady Christina St. John!

Unbidden, a smile tugged at the corners of his mouth
as a sudden recollection came to mind. Of his hired "lassie" characterizing the new MacKenzie heiress "a right
proper English bitch." With ice water in her veins! Was
this how she saw herself when she wasn't busy masquer-
ading as a simple villager? He found himself intrigued by
the possibility.

But this was the least of his questions. What in hell
were they doing at the croft? That was apparently their
target, since he doubted they had time to pursue their
sham elsewhere, with all the hours they spent there. Was
it Jacques and something, perhaps, from his past that mo-
tivated all this subterfuge? He could certainly think of
nothing to link them to himself.

But it simply didn't make sense! Why go to all this
trouble, spending days and weeks out of their lives—and
doing work that clearly had to be distasteful to a woman
of Lady Christina's background—to insinuate themselves
into the lives of total strangers? Was Beaumonde truly
much more than he seemed? Did he carry some risky
secret, maybe something attached to his service with Laffite, that made him prey to a pair of unlikely female spies?

By damn, he didn't like to think so! He considered

Jacques a close friend now, and the notion that he might hide something of that nature didn't sit well with him. Of course, they each had a private side. But hell, didn't every man?

He considered his own choice not to share with Beaumonde all the details of his personal history—*of betrayals which still left him too raw to talk about them, even to a friend*. There still wasn't anything there that might provoke this odd spy mission, if that's what it was. Yet, what else could it be? And somehow he didn't think the Frenchman lay at the root of it, either. Beaumonde was just too damned open and honest, despite his past.

Well, he would approach him on it anyway. And if Beaumonde had no answers, he'd have them from a certain redhead soon enough, by heaven!

Turning back toward the croft, Jamie set off at an easy lope.

But as it turned out, he had no opportunity to question Jacques when he reached the cottage. An exceptionally large and unfamiliar mountain pony stood in the yard, telling him they had a visitor. Wondering who it could be, especially at this time of night, Jamie approached the door, only to be further intrigued by the sound of canine yipping as he opened it.

"*Allons,* Jamie!" Jacques exclaimed as three dark, shaggy forms bounded for the doorway.

"What the devil—" Jamie braced his hand against the lintel beam; a trio of overgrown pups had launched themselves at his lower torso with excited yips and a furious wagging of tails.

"Beasties, *doon!*"

All three dogs immediately dropped to the floor while Jamie's eyes flew to the source of this bellowed command.

Sitting on the crude bench by the fire, opposite Beaumonde, was the largest man he'd ever seen. Clearly a

Scot by his tartans, including kilt and sporran, the giant sported a full, graying red beard on a face that looked amiable, despite the bushy red brows that had lowered when he scowled at the dogs.

Jacques stood and hauled a chair toward the fire, gesturing to Jamie to join them. The giant rose too, and Jamie sized him up as close to seven feet and well over twenty stone.

"Jamie, meet Robbie MacTavish," said Jacques. "This is my friend, James MacIver, Monsieur Mac—"

"Just Robbie'll do, mon." MacTavish thrust forward a huge, callused hand that reminded Jamie of a bear paw, and Jamie took it, trying not to wince with the enthusiastic grip.

"Pleased to meet you, Robbie, and call me Jamie."

"Good, good," murmured the Scot, settling himself back on the bench. "Never cuid bear formalities. Too much like th' bloody Sassanachs!"

"Ah, ze English," Jacques explained. As Jamie nodded and took a seat, Jacques poured some wine into a pewter mug and handed it to him.

"Nae doubt ye wonder who I be, laddie," said MacTavish, cradling his wine in hands that dwarfed his mug.

Jamie smiled, meeting the giant's keen hazel eyes. "That'll do for a start."

A rumble of laughter accompanied Robbie's nod. "Weel said, laddie, weel said! Now, t' begin, I met yer frien', here, early this mornin'!"

Jamie's eyes darted to Jacques. "This morning? I don't recall your mentioning—"

Jacques laughed. "But I did, at ze supper table! If you 'ad not been so busy dreaming over Mademoiselle Christmas, you would 'ave heard me, *mon ami!*"

Jamie scowled, but said nothing. Beaumonde had been teasing him good-naturedly for days about the redhead's charms, or more to the point, about how they might be affecting him; but he'd refused to rise to the bait, and he wasn't about to start now.

MacTavish said something in Gaelic, and the trio of canines rose from where they'd been lying and came toward him, tails wagging. " 'Twould appear yer frien's interested i' my hounds, Jamie. He met th' rest of my pack up by th' loch an' recognized them fer th' fine Scottish deerhounds they be."

"*Oui*, Jamie, and Robbie said he would come by and show me a pup from his last litter."

"Apparently he's decided to show you three." Jamie eyed the gangly forms of the young animals, now sprawled comfortably at MacTavish's feet. The two nearest him were of a size—about four stone each—but the third dwarfed them, hardly seeming to come from the same litter.

"*Alors,* I can now select ze one I wish to purchase, eh, Robbie?"

The Highlander shook his shaggy head in the negative, and Jamie caught a shrewd look in his eyes before they shifted to Jacques. "Ye'll no' be happy wi' merely one, mon, an' th' hound will no' be happy, either. Hounds work i' packs, sae if ye're interested i' buyin', ye'll be layin' oot silver fer a' three."

"Three? *Mon Dieu,* but I require only one—for a companion, *n'est-ce pas?*" Jacques reached down to stroke the nearest long, dark head, and the pup wagged his tail affectionately; then he rolled on his back to have his belly scratched.

A word from the Scot, again in the guttural Gaelic, had the other two suddenly advancing on Jacques. They proceeded to wash his face with their long pink tongues, and the Frenchman, obviously enjoying this display, laughed and stroked them affectionately.

Then another guttural command had them backing off

with a few regretful whines and dropping obediently to the floor again.

"They appear well trained," said Jacques.

"They ha' th' rudiments," replied the Scot, "but ye'll need t' work 'em a wee bit t' improve their huntin' skills. 'Tis th' reason I'm ainly chargin' ye fifty poonds."

"Fifty pounds!" Jacques looked stunned. He'd been told that morning that a well-trained youngster went for fifteen, and even that had seemed steep; but MacTavish had hinted he'd be amenable to bargaining on the price, so he'd told him to bring one around. Now, it seemed, he'd brought him three, and the price was even steeper!

"Aye," the Scot was saying, "fer a' three."

"But monsieur—Robbie—I require but one, and ze price—"

The giant was shaking his burly head. "I told ye, mon, th' beasties fare best i' packs. 'Tis three'r nae a one. Take it 'r no'."

Jacques was immediately skeptical. The Highlander struck him as a bit too shrewd, and he wondered if he hadn't been set up.

Jamie's thoughts were akin to Jacques's. He'd already discerned a crafty look in the Highlander's eyes; and now, as he listened to Beaumonde remonstrate, reminding the Scot about a fifteen-pound-per-pup pricetag, he waited, curious as to how the giant would respond.

"Weel, mon," MacTavish replied, scratching his beard, "tha' was fer any ordinary pup, an' I've brought ye twa of 'em." He gestured at the two smaller hounds at his feet. "But look at th' other laddie there, wi' th' braw bones 'neath his coat. Ye'll be gettin' a good bargain wi' *him* thrown i' th' lot!"

Jamie hid a smile as he witnessed a series of emotions pass across Jacques's face: doubt and skepticism came first, accompanied by a suspicious scowl; then came an adamant look, as if he'd made up his mind to reject the entire offer; but a downward glance as one of the pups whimpered and began to lick the Frenchman's boot had his face softening in the next second, showing the beginnings of a foolish grin.

As if catching himself, Jacques let his features go blank as he met the Highlander's eyes.

"Forty," he told him, "and not one penny more."

MacTavish grinned, hazel eyes crinkling in his weather-beaten face. "Forty-five."

"Done!" said the Frenchman and stuck out his hand to seal the bargain.

As they shook hands, Jamie turned and reached for the wine bottle, averting his face; it wouldn't do to let Beaumonde see the laughter lurking in his eyes, for poor Jacques obviously felt he'd driven a hard bargain.

But somehow, Jamie suspected as he poured them all some wine for a toast, the wily Scot had bested the former pirate in the deal.

Later, after MacTavish had departed, forty-five pounds richer, Jamie told Jacques what he'd learned when he followed the women home. Then he asked him, point-blank, whether there was anything in his background which would prompt such chicanery, especially if the women were using it to spy on him.

Beaumonde swore he knew of nothing, and Jamie believed him. They'd reached a point in their relationship where they could read each other like an open book; Jamie knew there was nothing covert in the Frenchman's direct gaze, and he told him so.

"C'est bien," Jacques replied with a nod, "but what do we do now, *mon ami? Nom de Dieu!* I cannot credit *la belle* Mary with this deception, even as I believe you saw what you saw!"

"She may have had little choice in the matter," said Jamie. "This has all the earmarks of something engineered by a person who's used to giving orders, and they say in the village that Lady Christina St. John is an earl's daughter. It may be that Mary is one of her servants and merely doing what she's been told.''

Jamie poured the last of the bottle of wine into their mugs. "Drink up, my friend," he told Beaumonde, "because tomorrow we'll have the truth!"

But the first truth to emerge the next morning had nothing to do with the women's false identities; it had to do with a hound's.

"Och!" exclaimed Maire when she and Christmas encountered the frolicking pups in the yard. "What's an *Irish* hound doin' wi' those twa skinny Scots runaboots?"

Jacques ceased his patting of one of the deerhounds and looked at her. *"Irish?"*

Maire was staring at the larger pup, an amazed expression on her face. "One of the legendary great wolfhounds of Ireland, an' nae mistake! An' here I'd heard they were extinct!"

Jamie, who'd just emerged from the cottage in time to hear this, threw Jacques a glance that held suppressed laughter. The Frenchman's expression said he realized he'd been hoodwinked, after all.

"Are you absolutely certain, *chérie?"* Jacques asked dolefully.

"As certain as heather grows purple. Why, look at 'im! He's th' spittin' image of th' hounds ye'll find i' th' auld books, barrin' th' ten stone or sae he'll take on when he matures!"

"Ten—! *Mon dieu!"* Jacques looked aghast.

"Och!" Maire continued. "I still canna *believe* it! An *Irish*—"

A surreptitious kick to Maire's shin silenced her. Christmas threw her a quelling glare. It was, of course, a signal for her to cease waxing enthusiastic over things Irish, when she was supposed to be a Scot.

Mary instantly left off, biting her lip, for it was difficult to avoid being peacock-proud of the young hound and his obvious merits.

And Jamie stifled another laugh. Because he'd seen the swiftly delivered reminder, and believed he knew exactly what it meant.

❖Chapter 12❖

With help from Maire, Jacques named the hounds MacDuff, MacRae, and O'Kelly. Following this, he decided to take them out for some training, and the women watched him take his leave. Muttering Gallic imprecations under his breath, darting severe glances at O'Kelly, the Frenchman soon disappeared among the trees.

Jamie too appeared to have gone for the day. They'd seen him wrap some bread and cheese in a cloth and head for the stable; minutes later they heard the sound of his pony leaving the yard.

"Excellent," said Christmas as she ran to the door in time to see Jamie trot out of sight. "We'll have a bit of time to do some searching."

"Ach!" exclaimed Maire. "Sure and I cannot think of a place we have not already searched. 'Tis weary I am, of all this skulkin' about. Will ye not give it up?"

Christmas bit her lip, her consternation evident. If the truth were known, she was tired of it, too. What had seemed almost like a game at first, despite her desperate need of its objective, had begun to chafe as time wore on. It was one thing to assume an accent and pretend for a few hours; it was quite another to be forced to return to it day after day, always on guard to avoid making a mistake, never knowing if a slip would undo everything.

And then there was the added difficulty of Jamie MacIver. Despite all her efforts to reduce his presence to something mundane, he still had the power to affect her in a host of ways that made her breathless and uncomfortable at the same time. Just this morning she had caught him gazing at her with an enigmatic, brooding look on his face; and if it hadn't been for the diversion of the incident with the hounds, she felt she might actually have gone up to him and made a clean breast of everything—just to put an end to this charade.

But of course she hadn't done that, and a good thing, too. There was no telling what this man, whom she still regarded as entirely too secretive himself—and no gentleman—would do with her information on the treasure. As the owner of the croft, he had every right to keep any property it contained for himself, didn't he? Every legal right, that was. Morally, as she saw it, he would be bound to turn the treasure over to her, as the MacKenzie heiress; but a man who was no gentleman could not be depended upon to subscribe to such honorable behavior, and that was that!

No, she must continue with things as they were, and she said as much to Maire. "But if it will make you feel any better," she added as the Irishwoman prepared to leave with a basket on her arm for gathering some roots and tubers, "today I intend to be more aggressive in my search."

"Aggressive?" Maire queried with mild sarcasm. "Faith, and what d'ye have in mind, child?" She glanced at an ancient blunderbuss Angus had left hanging above the fireplace. "D'ye mean t' shoot the secret out o' the walls?"

"Very amusing!" Christmas snapped, then became instantly contrite. The strain of pretense must be getting to her if she was taking it out on Maire! "Forgive me," she

said. "I only meant that I've decided to poke about with
a spade I saw in the shed yesterday, and I was hoping you
might approve."

Maire gave her a warm smile. "No apologies needed,
lass. The strain ye're under with the mission ye've set fer
yerself is considerable, and I tend t' ferget it meself."

She gave Christmas a kiss on the cheek and headed for
the door. "Dig about if ye must, *macushla*, but do take
some care with yer poor, wee hands. They're hardly accustomed t' such labor."

Christmas promised and watched her go. Then she
withdrew a pair of riding gloves she'd tucked in her waistband and concealed with her tartan. Drawing them on,
she headed for the stable shed with a determined thrust
of her small chin.

Minutes later, with spade in hand, she found her spot.
There was an odd-looking rise in the ground beside the
springhouse. She'd spied it yesterday and had given it
little thought at the time. But last night as she'd lain
abed, sleepless as usual, she'd turned this over in her
mind, deciding such an inexplicable interruption in the
levelness of the yard could mean something had been
buried there—or covered up. It was then the notion of
digging had come to her.

Unfortunately, the ease with which she'd conceived the
idea was to be greater than its execution. Upon reaching
the spot, she immediately realized she could not simply
dig, willy-nilly. How would she explain, to Jamie or
Jacques, the disturbed earth? A moment's reflection gave
her the solution: she must carefully carve out the turf
with the spade, so that it might be refilled—replaced exactly as it had been. She'd seen gardeners do this at the
family's country estates back home, so she knew it could
be done; but it wasn't until she'd made her first efforts
that she realized how difficult it would be.

Nevertheless, she set her mind to it, and minutes later

she was hard at work cutting the first square, her concentration intense.

It was so intense, in fact, that she never heard Jamie MacIver's approach.

The last thing Jamie had done before retiring was to tell Jacques they must both leave the croft early today, making it appear they'd be gone for hours. Then, he'd explained, he would circle back and arrive unexpectedly, pretending to have forgotten something if he interrupted the women at nothing unusual. If, on the other hand, he surprised them at something untoward—

But the last thing he'd expected was the scene which greeted him after he entered the cottage and found it empty.

"What in hell . . . ?" The unmistakable sounds of someone digging had drawn him to the scene of Christmas's labors, but he still couldn't credit what he saw.

There she was, her fiery mane shielding her face as she set a spade at a right angle to the earth and *hopped upon it with both feet!* Christmas used her full weight and the added thrust of a jump to force the spade's cutting edge into the ground. Even then, the combination was inadequate to drive the implement deep enough, so she was forced to step off and perform this ridiculous little hop again.

Jamie's lips twitched with laughter before he remembered the seriousness of his investigation, and his face grew stern. *What the hell was she doing, digging up his turf?*

Christmas withdrew the spade from the first careful cut she'd made and prepared to insert it at a right angle for the next. She was so engrossed in the task, it took a few seconds for it to register that a man's elongated shadow lay across the newly disturbed earth.

Jerking her head up, she met Jamie's frosty blue eyes.

"Now, why do you suppose," he queried in a tone which was too soft, by far, for the menace it implied, "that a man's hired maidservant would be interested in digging up a pile of buried trash on his property?"

"Trash?" Christmas recoiled a step, flinging the spade to the ground as she looked at him, aghast.

Jamie's smile was at once superior and mocking. "Trash," he reiterated. "Everything from moldy chicken bones to moth-eaten rags. There was so much of it when we arrived, Jacques suggested we dig a pit and bury it. Which we did . . . right"—he glanced at the fruits of her careful labors with a look of amused contempt—"here."

Reeling backward, as if the wind had been knocked out of her with this news, Christmas felt her face crumble. "Trash," she repeated on a strangled sob, and buried her face in her hands.

The superior look left Jamie's face the instant he observed her shaking shoulders, the despair written in every line of her slender frame. And what had begun as an angry compulsion to face her down and toy with her until she broke and admitted her deception, now became an overwhelming urge to soothe and protect. But protect from what? Himself?

Swearing softly, he closed the distance between them and reached for her.

With a choked gasp, Christmas withdrew from him. The face she raised to meet his eyes was tear-stained and wary.

Christ! Is she afraid of me? Jamie followed this thought with a violent oath as he saw her take another backward step, catch her heel on the handle of the spade, stumble—

"Devil take it!" Jamie swore as he scooped her up before she hit the ground.

"D-don't!" she protested weakly as he swung her into his arms and headed for the cottage. "There is no need—"

"There is every need," he countered brusquely, "beginning with calming you down so you can respond coherently to a few hundred questions I have—is that clear?"

Christmas was feeling light-headed, though how much from the shock of being discovered, and how much from his physical nearness, she couldn't tell. She only knew the uncharacteristic weakness she'd exhibited at being caught out by Jamie said a great deal about the strain under which she'd been operating, and she'd give anything to have her old fortitude back just then.

This last was a sobering notion, and she made the attempt. "I assure ye, sirr," she said, meeting his eyes with a look she hoped was resolute, "there's nae—"

"Give it up, Christmas," Jamie told her as he entered the cottage. He kicked the door shut behind them with the heel of his boot and headed for the double bed in the far corner. "Or should I say *Lady Christina?*"

Christmas gasped as he deposited her on the mattress. "You know!"

"That much, yes," he told her as he stalked to the cupboard and grabbed a tumbler and the flask of Scotch whisky he kept. "But only as of last night, when I followed you home."

She watched him pour the amber liquid into the glass and return with it to the bed.

"Drink," he instructed as he handed it to her. "Then —we talk!"

Christmas eyed the contents of the glass warily. Then, keenly aware of the commanding presence towering above her, she took a large swallow.

And collapsed into a paroxysm of coughing as the fiery liquid found its way down.

"I—I assure you," she gasped, "the—this thing I've— I've done was never so dast—dastardly that you should feel compelled to kill me!"

Jamie's lips quirked with the hint of a smile. "Good," he said as he took the tumbler from her limp fingers and set it aside. "At least you've kept your sense of humor in order."

He arranged the pair of pillows on the bed behind her, indicating she should make herself comfortable. This accomplished, he took a seat on the edge of the mattress.

"Begin at the beginning, m'lady," he told her. "And do try to include all the relevant details. I'm a fairly patient man when there's a need—especially when the need is to learn *what in hell is going on!*"

He saw her blanch and immediately regretted his loss of control. But, dammit, she'd been deceiving him for days on end, and where deceit figured in his life, there was little patience and even less forgiveness. He was actually amazed at the forbearance he'd exhibited thus far.

"Sorry, Christmas," he murmured, running a hand haphazardly through dark blond curls before meeting her eyes again. "Ah, Lady Christina, that is. I—"

"Oh, but you may certainly continue to call me Christmas," she replied hastily.

"That part, at least, is no lie. I—I find I actually prefer the name now."

Jamie nodded, adding an impatient gesture for her to go on.

She began by telling him of Angus's letter, glossing over the details of how it came into her hands, for she found she was not yet ready to confront too closely the fact of her parents' deaths. But she went on at length about the Seadog's Treasure, filling him in on all she knew, hoping desperately she could trust him, even as she felt she was being a fool to do so. She was also careful to describe Maire's reluctance to take part in their deception, explaining her lifelong relationship with the Irishwoman, blaming herself, and the desperate financial straits she'd found herself in, for the entire business. The only real omission concerned her fiancé. Of Aaron Crenshawe, she said not a word, though later she was to wonder at this, even as she rationalized it as having no vital importance to her plans.

Jamie listened with a mixture of fascination and analytical inquiry, sifting the details of the complicated story she told him for evidence of truth—or further lies. But long before she was done, he found he believed her. No one, he decided, could have made up such an incredible account on a moment's notice. And the anguish he'd caught in her eyes when she alluded to her father's financial embarrassment had the feel of truth: she found it painful to connect the desperate situation which had driven her here to the folly of a parent she'd obviously loved. There was something inside him he couldn't put a name to, but which had him following up on this when at last she'd finished and sat staring up at him with wide, expectant eyes.

"Your parents . . ." he said softly, "you loved them very much, didn't you?"

Mutely, Christmas nodded, dropping her eyes.

Jamie's next words came out in a voice that was oddly brittle. "Dear God, what a shock it must have been to have learned, hard on the heels of your loss, that a parent you loved and trusted had suddenly become the cause of—"

"*No!* Oh no, Jamie, never say so! It wasn't like that! Not at all! Papa was the dearest, most wonderful father on earth! Why, Mama and I—"

And all at once the dam broke. The grief she'd been holding in for days and weeks came rushing in on her, crushing in its awful weight. With a raw cry of pain, she brought her fist to her mouth, blindly trying to stifle the sound. It was as if hearing it would give vent to a need to howl her loss to the heavens, and if she could only stop it now, somehow she would be in control again, and she could go on.

But it was too late. Great, shuddering sobs racked her body as she gave in to it all at last. Jamie cursed himself for a fool, wondering how he could have been so insensitive. And Christmas wasn't even aware of it when he took her in his arms and held her like a child.

"Damn me to hell!" he swore again. Christmas had clearly loved her parents with an unqualified love that was as alien to his ken as it was sobering. To love someone, no matter what he was, no matter what he'd done . . . what must it take?

But in the next second he was dismissing this as the sounds of Christmas's grief drew him. It was apparent she'd kept it all bottled up inside, and from his battlefield experience, he knew that wasn't healthy. Better to mourn, and mourn deeply, then leave it behind. Only then could the living do what they had always done: go on.

He lost track of the time as he sat there, holding the grieving young woman in his arms. He knew only that he held her, saying not a word, as she cried out her pain. Until at last he felt the broken sobbing cease, the tears diminish into an occasional watery hiccough, and finally silence.

"Better?" he inquired softly.

He felt her head nod beneath his chin, where he'd tucked it when he wrapped his arms about her and drew her into his lap.

"You needed to release it, Christmas. The grief. How long has it been?"

She told him in a voice still tinged with sadness, but steadier than it had been before.

Jamie pulled away slightly, enough to assess her mood. Her cheeks were still wet and streaked with tears, and he wiped these gently away with his fingers, gauging her condition by the look in her eyes. *Christ, she's lovely!* he thought as he observed those gray eyes, enormous in her face now, their lashes spiked with tears.

He quickly forced his thoughts back to her needs,

however. There was something in those clear, translucent depths that needed more than just a shoulder to cry on.

"Tell me about them," he said gently. Jamie had been the bearer of death tidings all too often as an officer in the military, and he knew it helped the grieving process if the bereaved could share their memories of those they'd lost.

Slowly, in a voice that grew firmer as she spoke, Christmas told him of her parents. Some of this he'd heard before, when she'd repeated certain incidents in the guise of her "Scottish" childhood; but now that there were no longer any lies between them, they became personal revelations of the life she'd led, nurtured by parents she'd adored.

She spoke of her mother's soft, warm presence at the beginning and end of each day. Of how she had made it a point to be a part of her daughter's upbringing, despite the presence of servants whom most other women of her class relied upon to do this in their stead. She told of her father's open, handsome face, his beaming approval as he witnessed her developing skills in those boys' sports she'd always been able to coax him into. She spoke of walks in the country and quiet evenings by the fire, when there had been just the three of them . . . and laughter, and a life fully shared. She even told of their weaknesses, and the things many might see as shortcomings in this pair she'd loved; but as she did this, there was nothing of rancor, or bitterness, or regret in her words. It was clear to Jamie she was remembering them as flesh-and-blood human beings, neither adding to their strengths, nor taking away from them the faults which made them human.

He marveled at her capacity to do this . . . she was so very young, after all. And somewhere in the back of his consciousness, a sobering respect began to take hold in him, for this tender slip of a girl he was only beginning to know.

". . . and so you see, they weren't just parents to me,

Jamie. Although they were that, the best I could have wished for. But, like Maire, they became my . . . friends . . . good friends, deep and true.''

Christmas pulled away from his embrace and looked at him. "Does . . . does that sound strange, or perhaps . . . improper, somehow?''

Good friends, deep and true . . . Sweet Christ, how I could have wished for— The thought pierced Jamie's mind with a stabbing agony, but his eyes quickly shuttered as he answered her. "No, sweetheart, it doesn't . . . a bit unusual, perhaps . . . rare, but never . . . never improper.''

Christmas let out a sigh, then offered him a shy, tentative smile. "I'm glad. I had governesses who seemed to think so, although, of course, they never voiced their disapproval aloud. But Maire knew . . . and understood. And now you.''

Her final words were punctuated by a brilliant smile— open, innocent, and dazzling. Jamie felt something rip through his gut when he saw it. Something bittersweet and painful, yet—

With a suppressed shudder, he set her quickly away from him, grinding his teeth against the violent stab of passion that had hit him unawares, like a sledgehammer blow to his middle . . . He shut his eyes, breathing deeply.

"Jamie, what's wrong? What did I *say?*'' Christmas's bewildered voice sliced across the battle he was waging with his body, and he opened his eyes to see her face inches from his. The wide gray eyes held confusion, even hurt, and there were echoes of pain in her words.

With a muted groan, he pulled her back into his arms, his words a ragged whisper in her ear. "No, sweet, nothing's wrong! You haven't— Ah, *Christ!*''

He shifted his weight as the words tore from his throat, and then he was meeting her gaze, telling her with his eyes, of the sudden, terrible need inside him.

Christmas met his look and recognized, at once, his hunger. It matched her own. She had just come to terms with death—the final loss, the pain, the need to heal—and in this naked moment that lay throbbing between them, she knew a blind, pulsing urge to reaffirm *life*.

Her mouth opened with a small cry as Jamie claimed it with his. Lips parted, she felt his tongue graze her teeth; his lips were firm, his mouth, hot and demanding. The kiss deepened, tongue meeting tongue, and they let their hunger rage.

Without thought, Christmas wound her arms about his neck and pulled him down with her, onto the bed. And Jamie felt a roaring in his ears as he gave her what she sought, pressing his big body against the soft contours of hers. Twisting, straining, yearning for the moment that would take them out of themselves, they succumbed to their passion.

The clothes they wore were no barrier against the heat that drove them. Their open mouths clung, crisscrossed, as they tasted each other's heat again and again. Jamie tangled his hands in the skeins of her hair, pulling it free of its pins, and it fell about them like a fiery, silken curtain.

"Your hair . . ." Christmas heard him rasp as he clenched a mass of it in his fist, then let it slip through his open fingers. "God, how I've wanted to touch it like this!"

He buried his face in it while his hands began to course over her body, stroking it, preparing it for the pleasure he meant to give her, to give them both.

Christmas felt his lips trace a heated trail over the contours of her face and along her neck, felt him nuzzle the sensitive spot where neck joined shoulder. She arched against him, trying to bring him closer, her fingers threaded through the thick, blond curls at the nape of his neck.

Jamie murmured something low and unintelligible in

her ear, at the same time stilling her body with his hands. She opened her lips to question his intent, but he claimed them with a drugging kiss; and it was only when he finally released them that she realized he'd somehow removed her outer clothes and she was lying beneath him clad only in her shift.

But then there was no room for thought as she felt his hands move to her breasts and begin to cup and stroke them with slow, skillful movements. Christmas gasped as a tingle began where he grazed their tips, his work-roughened sculptor's thumbs raising them to swollen, pebbled buds beneath the thin batiste. A white-hot shaft of pure pleasure darted through her, traveling from where he touched to her woman's core, and Christmas cried out softly, the sound, an ecstatic surprise.

Then Jamie lowered his head and caught an aching peak lightly with his teeth, right through the thin material of the shift. Christmas moaned, feeling the intensity of her pleasure build, aware now of a strange wetness at the juncture of her thighs. And when he lowered the bodice of her shift and began to nibble and tease and suckle, she thought she would go mad from the sweet, aching pressure building below. Restlessly, she began to arch and writhe beneath his touch. In seconds the lower part of her shift became twisted about her waist, and she could feel the rough fabric of his breeches against her naked flesh.

Then, suddenly, Jamie was shifting away from her, and Christmas cried out at the loss of his warmth. She thought she heard him utter an oath, then recognized the sound of impatience as he tore off his clothing, finding the process too slow. In an agony of anticipation, she waited, wanting to feel his skin against hers.

A moment later he again held her in his arms, and where the anticipation of his naked flesh against hers had been almost enough to drive her mad, the reality was something close to madness itself.

"Jamie?" she cried. "Jamie, I can't—I want—"

"I know, sweet," he answered in a ragged whisper as his hand traced magical patterns across her belly. "I want it, too."

Deft fingers found the sweet, moist place between her thighs, and Christmas knew a moment's doubt. *No one* had ever touched her there! Her eyes flew open and she met Jamie's gaze. Its azure intensity made her suck in her breath.

"No, don't look away from me, sweetheart," he told her in a voice that was a husky command. "You're beautiful there too, and I want to see your face when I touch that beauty. When I give you pleasure."

His fingers found the slick opening beneath her nest of auburn curls, and he smiled into her eyes. "So ready for me . . ." he murmured throatily, "so damned wet and ready . . ."

And suddenly his thumb found the tiny bud above the aperture he stroked, passed across its swollen hardness, then again—

And Christmas gave a sharp cry as a jolt of inconceivable pleasure sliced through her. Again, his knowing fingers did their magic, and again, she cried out, arching against his touch, her muscles rigid as her body convulsed in helpless ecstasy.

And then, before she could digest the wonder of what had happened, his body closed on hers and she felt a muscled thigh wedge insistently between hers, which were trembling.

"Open to me, sweetheart," he urged, his breathing harsh now, his voice thick with the need that strained against knowledge that he must proceed slowly, and with care.

But Christmas was beyond knowing of his intent, of the control he exerted and what it was costing him. She only knew the fierce beauty of what he'd given her, a sweet, heady radiance that was still consuming her body in a spiraling vortex of pleasure. And something in her woman's place hungered for more. Hungered with an even greater need.

With a cry of total abandon, she felt his swollen hardness push against the slippery entrance where his fingers had done their work, and she arched against him.

"Don't!" Jamie groaned, even as her sharp cry of pain filled his ears. Sweat broke out on his brow as he summoned the strength to be perfectly still. Too late, he'd felt her move, felt the virgin's barrier give and tear as she'd arched against him. He'd wanted to make it easier for her than this, but she hadn't understood, and now the impossible tightness enclosing him in her velvety shaft was making it impossible for him to think, let alone respond to her pain-filled sobs.

"Shh, sweetheart," he coaxed as he smoothed back damp tendrils of hair from her face. "It's only for a moment."

Christmas raised wide, tear-filled eyes to his. "Wh-why?"

Jamie managed a smile. "Because this is your first time, darling. It won't ever hurt again . . . I promise."

She seemed to relax a little at this. Jamie saw the lines of tension leave her face, the shadow disappear from her eyes.

"Good girl," he murmured unsteadily and claimed her lips with a kiss so sweetly drugging, it erased all memory of pain. And in moments, when he felt her begin to move in a softly undulating rhythm beneath him, Jamie closed his eyes and gave in to the need hammering in his loins.

He withdrew and thrust, withdrew again, then caught them up in the pulsating rhythm of the age-old cadence. Thrust upon thrust, bodies straining, pleasure building, they rode the primal wave—until the candent furnace of their passion broke—and they fell together in a mutual spasm of mindless bliss that flung them to the heavens.

* * *

"M'lady, I do believe you're purring."

It was the first thing spoken between them as they lay on the bed in the aftermath of their lovemaking. Christmas raised her head from Jamie's chest to see him smiling down at her.

She blushed under the directness of his gaze, but managed to smile back at him.

"Perhaps I am," she told him. Then, shyly, "I—I had no idea . . ."

"Evidently." He grinned, planting a kiss on the tip of her nose. "Or it's certain you'd never have described yourself as someone with a broom in, ah, rather awkward contact with her anatomy!"

Christmas groaned and felt the heat rise to her cheeks. She ducked her head, burying her face in his shoulder.

Jamie's soft laughter ruffled the fine wisps of hair at her temples as he tightened his arms about her and drew her close.

"Ah, m'lady," he breathed, "you blush as prettily as you purr! How delightful to find myself the source of both"—he nuzzled the hair at her temple—"as well as a host of other sweetly unexpected reactions!"

"Jamie!" His name was a muffled groan against his shoulder.

He clasped her small chin with firm, yet gentle fingers, forcing her to look at him. "Jamie, *what?*" he queried with a wide grin.

Christmas met the merriment in his eyes and felt her heart lurch wildly while a giddy ripple of pleasure coursed along her spine. Acutely aware of all that had just passed between them, she sought for something to distract her from the deeper blush she felt building.

"I—I knew you from before, you know."

Jamie arched a questioning brow.

"In—in London. I was at my solicitors' offices, veiled —dressed in mourning garb . . ."

As her words trailed off and she peered up at him expectantly, Jamie stared at her blankly for a moment—then threw back his head with a bark of laughter. *"You?"* he questioned after a moment as laughter continued to dance in his eyes. *"You* were that delectable little morsel in—"

"I cannot fathom your finding it so amusing!" she retorted, clearly irked. "Surely, even Americans recognize mourning garb, and yet—Jamie MacIver, you were *no gentleman!"*

Another bark of laughter greeted this, and as far as Christmas was concerned, it merely confirmed that unfavorable opinion she'd held of him from the start. At once, her thoughts zeroed in on her mission and the fact that she'd shared confidences with him in that regard.

"Now that you know what brought me to Scotland, what do you intend to do about it?" she demanded. "What about the treasure, Jamie?"

"What *about* it?" he replied, instantly sobered by her tone. The amusement was gone from his eyes, his features carefully arranged, to give no indication of what he might be thinking. Christmas was immediately reminded that, despite what had so recently passed between them, she hardly knew this man. Keeping her eyes on his face, she chose her words with care.

"You—you have every right, I realize, to send us packing. The croft is your property now, and—"

A low growl of displeasure broke from his throat as he shifted his weight and she found herself pinned beneath him on the bed. His eyes were shards of blue ice. They bored into hers while he addressed her in syllables measured and clipped.

"And you wouldn't put it past me to throw you out on your ear and seize the treasure for myself, is that it? Dammit, is that what you take me for, Christmas? A robber of women and orphans?"

Trying not to shrink from the hostility blazing in his eyes, Christmas made herself answer. "I—I merely wished to point out that—that I'm aware that, legally, I have no right to be here, and—"

"Legally!" He spat the word at her. "What about the rest of it? Do you think me such a dishonorable bastard that I'd betray you on a legal quibble?"

Unable to bear the ferocity of his gaze, Christmas dropped her eyes. Her words, after a moment's pause, were soft and uncertain. "I—I hardly know you, Jamie. How was I to know what you would do, unless I asked?"

He seemed to consider this for a moment. Then, giving a nod as if he'd made up his mind to something, he released her and began reaching for his clothing.

"So it's assurances that are needed then?" he questioned as he began to dress. "Very well, m'lady. So be it. First: I have no interest whatsoever in this fabled treasure you seek, even if I were to be persuaded that it exists— which I *doubt.*" He finished drawing his breeches on.

"Second: I have all the wealth I'll ever require, both in landed property and other resources, and no need whatever to add to it, by fair means—or foul!" He pulled on his boots.

"Third: I came to this godforsaken wilderness in the hope of reviving a talent some thought I once had"—he thrust an arm into his shirt—"and that is the one thing, *the only thing,* I intend to occupy my time with here." He finished donning the shirt and jabbed its bottom edges into his waistband.

"And, finally, I expect to see you and your Irish friend up here, daily, as we agreed, taking care of the domestic chores that will free me to pursue my sculpting. What you do with the rest of your time is entirely up to you. After you've cooked and cleaned, you can dig up the whole goddamned parcel, if you wish. As long as my clothes are clean and my meals served on time, I couldn't care less!"

Without looking at her, he stalked to the door, opened it, then threw her a parting shot.

"I wish you well in your treasure hunt, Christina—but if you ever question my integrity again, I'll wring your lovely little neck!"

❖Chapter 13❖

"He's smashed anither," said Maire.

Jacques set down the pickaxe he'd been wielding and accepted, with a tired nod, the cup of water she handed him. *"Oui.* Ze second this week." He swiped at the sweat on his brow with his forearm and raised the cup to his lips, drinking deeply.

" 'Tis only Tuesday," Maire reminded him with a frown. "Last week, 'twas a total o' five lovely sculptures he destroyed, if ye count the one he'd scarcely begun before we heard it crash against the back o' the cottage."

Again, Jacques nodded, then heaved a frustrated sigh. "My poor friend . . . I wish I could help him." He handed the empty cup back to her with a soft smile. *"Merci, ma belle."*

Maire smiled warmly in return, but a moment later the frown was back. "Has he said naught, then, o' the divils chasin' him?"

Jacques shook his head—a gesture of chagrin. *"Non,* and I fear we cannot expect it of him. Jamie is *très*—'ow you say?—private . . . *oui,* a very private man: He is not in ze habit of sharing his deeper feelings with anyone, not even a friend."

"Hmph! 'Tis a wonder he has any, with that attitude!"

"Ah, but he has me, *chérie,* and perhaps he values me

precisely because I accept him exactly as he is. I do not pry and prod him with questions he is not ready to answer."

"Hah! It appears t' me a wee bit o' proddin' wouldn't hurt, especially at a time like this—when *he's* clearly hurtin'! Has he done this sort o' thing before, do ye know?"

Jacques shrugged. "Our acquaintance is fairly recent, despite ze bond we seem to 'ave formed. But I tell you this, *chérie:* Jamie was not without his private demons before, yet I believe he had learned to live with them. But *now* . . . Something has happened—recently, I believe—"

"About ten days ago, would ye say?"

"Oui . . ."

"At about the time he uncovered the lass's scheme?"

Jacques was thoughtful for a moment. He recalled the night Jamie had followed the women home, telling him, after MacTavish left, what he'd discovered. There'd been a sense of anticipation, of smug satisfaction, even, in having uncovered their secret doings. But nothing untoward, nothing in his manner to indicate the kind of mood that was driving him lately. That had come afterward, after—

"What does Christmas have to say about the discussion she and Jamie—"

"Hmph!" interjected Maire. "Precious little, I'm thinkin'! She's been as close-mouthed as I've iver seen her. Beyond the basic facts—that she told Jamie who we are and what we're after findin'—nary a comment. I even had t' pry it out o' her, that he'd given his assurances, he'd not stand in the way of our search!

"I tell ye, Jacques, she's not actin' herself. At first I thought it must be the strain of all that pretendin', not t' mention the pressure she's under t'—"

Maire broke off as she noted the broad grin spreading across Jacques's face.

"I love your excitement when you become caught up

in your role of mother hen, *chérie!*" Jacques's grin wasn't half so bold as the look she caught in his eyes.

"Mother hen!"

Jacques chuckled, catching her by the hand and drawing her toward him. "*Vraiment!* But that is not all of it, *ma petite*, as you know. There are many things I love about you. Shall I tell you of them, *chérie?*"

Maire flushed, murmuring a weak protest about being seen in broad daylight; but the brush of Jacques's hand on her breast as he pulled her into his arms had her breathless. And then she went altogether silent when his mouth found hers.

Christmas rounded the corner of the cottage, and Maire's name froze on her lips. Blushing furiously, she whirled about and retraced her steps, thankful the embracing couple hadn't seen her.

Maire and Jacques . . . how *right* they seemed together! Ah, but she was glad at least one good thing had come out of this sorry business! From all indications, the older pair were deeply involved with each other—in love, unless she missed her guess. All the signs were there, from the look of quiet adoration in the Frenchman's eyes as they followed Maire across the room, to the warm glow on her friend's face whenever she spoke Jacques's name.

Without warning, the acrid sting of tears assailed her eyes, and Christmas muttered a stringent oath, blinking them back. Now, what had brought that on? she asked herself crossly.

Grabbing the handle of the broom that stood outside the cottage door, she set her small jaw at a pugnacious angle and went inside. The two deerhound pups raised their heads and wagged their tails in greeting as they lay by the hearth, but O'Kelly rose and came forward eagerly. The wolfhound pup had taken a particular liking to her, and she stroked his head fondly, feeling, at the moment, an unusual need for the balm his affections provided.

After a while a quiet word to the young hound sent him back to the hearth, and Christmas began to sweep. She kept the movements slow and controlled, the way Maire had taught her. They seemed an odd counterpoint to her inner rhythms, which were racing in disjointed leaps and bounds.

How *dare* he ignore her this way after what had passed between them! It made her feel like some kind of—of trollop! Someone who'd been cast aside after being used and—

Damn him! She was no *lightskirt!* She was—

A betrothed woman. *Betrothed to a man I fear I cannot abide!*

And Aaron was arriving in a few days. She'd received his letter last night, from Mrs. MacLeod; the housekeeper had been given it by a private courier who'd ridden direct from London.

"My Dear Christina," it had begun. *"What a naughty puss you are to have made it so inconvenient for me to track you down . . ."*

Track her down! As if she were some unfortunate quarry who—

But the unvarnished truth of the matter was, *he* was the quarry, not she! Lord Aaron Crenshawe, future marquis of Beckwith, was the prize catch she must land, using all the wit and skill she possessed before m'lord realized he could not possibly allow himself to be caught by someone in her circumstances.

But she was no further along in her search than she'd been when she escaped Aaron in London. Despite her cards being turned up on the table, here at the croft, ten days ago.

And Jamie MacIver went about saying nothing of greater import to her than "pass the salt"! Though they'd been lovers who'd shared passion so shattering she still trembled when she allowed herself to think about it. Which was all too often.

No, better *not* to think about it! It was bad enough she had to endure his brooding presence in the aftermath of what had happened. Bad enough she had to see his face in her sleep at night. When she could sleep at all.

And what had she done to provoke him, after all? Wouldn't anyone have wished to learn where things stood, given the complications the treasure involved? She had a duty to perform, damn it! She was the last of the MacKenzie line—the last in direct succession to the St. Johns, as well. She *had* to make a financially secure marriage! She owed it to Mama and Papa!

Christina ceased sweeping, her eyes falling on a broken fragment of clay that lay before her broom on the floor. It was the talons and lower torso of what had been a passingly lifelike eagle, clinging to a crag, but poised for flight. She'd glimpsed the nearly completed sculpture last week, after coming upon it unexpectedly while taking some carrots to the ponies in the stable.

And then she'd learned, the following day, from Maire, that it had been smashed—by the man who'd made it. The older woman had carried this piece and a couple of other shards into the cottage in her apron, as if she'd needed Christmas to reaffirm that Jamie had actually done such a thing. "To his own lovely creation," Maire had muttered softly. "A bird so real, ye'd swear it could fly. Is the man daft? He's after destroyin' the very beauty he created!"

Slowly, Christmas bent to pick up the fragment. Turning it over in her hand, she marveled at its perfect proportions, the lifelike textures: scaly birdskin meeting airy feathers . . . lethal claw clinging cruelly to primal rock . . .

Beyond the open doorway, a bird called, and was answered by its mate. She turned, half fancying she heard her name . . . Christmas . . . spoken as Jamie had whispered it in her ear in the heat of passion . . .

And then she remembered that he'd only been addressing her, if at all, as "m'lady," or "Lady Christina," since that day, and never again as Christmas.

With a broken cry, she hurled the eagle fragment to the floor and watched it shatter into dust.

❖Chapter 14❖

Days passed, with Jacques continuing to lend a hand with the search, despite his serious doubts that a treasure still existed, if it ever had. He was, as he explained to the women, well acquainted with rumors of buried treasure from his years with Laffite. Unfortunately, this experience had convinced him there were dozens of dead ends for every hunt that resulted in a find.

Nevertheless, the Frenchman was happy to do what he could to help, especially after seeing the disappointment in Christmas's face at his skeptical words. Moreover, he felt he had to do at least that much to offset the sting of Jamie's refusal to help the women. Jacques was puzzled by his friend's attitude and longed to question him on his reasons. But Christmas had insisted, with a look in her eyes that had Jacques wondering about *her* reasons, that Jamie was to be left out of it. "We'll leave Mr. MacIver to his art," she'd pronounced in a tone indicating the discussion was not to be pursued.

Maire, however, who knew her better, had noted the brief flash of bewildered hurt lurking beneath Christmas's pretended indifference. She had witnessed the same thing more than once during her charge's years of growing up and recognized it for what it was: the lass's pride, and perhaps something more, had been hurt. Yet the Irishwoman also knew that when this was so, nothing could force Christmas to admit it. The child would need to be left alone to work the problem out for herself. So Maire gritted her teeth and helped with the search, as did Jacques.

While Jamie MacIver continued to sculpt—and then destroy—one piece of clay after another.

Then one day, as Christmas dug at something her spade had struck beneath the dung heap that lay behind the stable, Maire came riding hard into the yard on one of the ponies. The other pony, riderless, ran behind on a tether. The Irishwoman had been persuaded by Jacques to accompany him to the loch to work with the hounds around midday. Since the women had finished their morning chores, Christmas had urged Maire to go, insisting she could dig on her own for a change. (Jamie had long before disappeared into the shed to sculpt.)

Wrinkling her nose at the odor of manure she'd shoveled, Christmas was glad for the interruption. When she heard the sound of hooves, she flung her spade aside, then frowned when she perceived Maire's haste, as well as the fact that Jacques and the hounds weren't with her.

"Maire, what's wrong? Where—?"

" 'Tis the hounds!" Maire called as she dismounted. "They've run off and disappeared—we've *lost* 'em! Where's Jamie?"

"Why, I suppose he's— *Lost the hounds?* Maire, how is that possible when they've been trained to—"

"Ach, lass, 'tis the storm that's brewin'. They bolted with that clap o' thunder a while back. Now, where's Jamie? Jacques wants his help in findin' the pups."

Christmas gestured toward the shed while, for the first time, she noticed the sky. She realized, with a start, that it had grown quite dark, and a wind was building from the west. She supposed she'd been so intent on her digging, she hadn't been aware of the weather which, in the Highlands, was likely to change at a moment's notice.

Maire had tethered the ponies to a pair of posts in the yard and was running for the shed. Thunder rumbled in the distance as she shouted for Jamie.

Christmas retrieved her spade and was heading for the shed to put it away as Jamie emerged, meeting Maire outside the entrance. She saw him wiping clay from his hands on a damp towel as Maire gesticulated wildly in the direction of the loch. The Irishwoman was shouting something as well, but Christmas couldn't make out her words over the howling wind.

Suddenly Christmas was seized by an image of the young hounds, frightened and running about in panic, as the storm crashed over their heads. In the short time she'd known them, she'd come to love the gangly pups, especially O'Kelly who'd attached himself to her in an inordinate bond of affection. Could she wait out the storm, safe and dry in the cottage, while she let someone else try to find those poor dogs?

"Here," she said to a surprised Maire as she thrust the spade into her hand. Without waiting for a response, she ran after Jamie, who was sprinting toward the ponies.

Jamie noticed her as she came up beside him while he untethered the first pony. "What are you—?"

"I'm coming with you!" she shouted over the wind. She made for the second animal.

"Like hell, you are!"

Christmas continued as if she hadn't heard him.

"Dammit, Christina!" he shouted. "I said—"

"I know what you said!" came the response. Christmas untied the second pony. "And I know what needs to be done. I have a means of summoning—"

"You have a means of behaving like a *fool!*" Jamie led his pony over to her, his face an angry mask. "Jacques is expecting *me* to join him *with his mount*, woman! How in hell is he to use it, if you're *on* it?"

Christmas paused in the act of tightening the saddle girth. She frowned, then replaced the frown with an obdurate look that settled her mouth in a straight, stubborn line.

"Two will just have to ride double for the return," she told him. The wind was whipping her hair loose from its pins and had set her skirts flying.

Jamie looked as if he would throttle her on the spot. "Hand over those reins, Lady Christina!" he yelled. "You may be accustomed to giving the orders at the manor, but around here—"

He got no further. Angered by his repeated use of her formal name, she held his gaze, raised two fingers to her lips, and produced an earsplitting whistle that cut him off in mid-sentence.

"That," she told him as she hitched up her flailing skirts, preparing to mount the pony astride, "is the reason I *must* come with you. It's louder than anything you men can produce in the storm, and the hounds will come when they hear it—because *I* taught it to them!" She saw Jamie open his mouth to respond and made a deliberate show of ignoring him by turning her back and mounting. Then she turned the pony's head toward the loch and urged it forward.

Jamie swore a violent oath and followed suit, pausing only briefly as Maire came running up to him from the cottage with a bundle in her arms.

"I wish ye'd told her t' wait here with me!" the Irishwoman exclaimed as she shoved a pair of cloaks into his hands.

Jamie glared at her, biting back a scathing response, and gave a curt nod. Jaws clenched, he eyed the departing rider in the distance, kicking his mount into a gallop.

They arrived at the edge of the loch amid great rumblings of thunder and flashes of lightning. Despite the fact that Jamie led them to the exact spot where Maire had said Jacques would be waiting, they saw no sign of the Frenchman—or the hounds.

"Well, Lady Whistle?" Jamie made the sarcasm evident, even over the roar of the wind. "Have at it!"

Christmas threw him a deprecating look but raised the two fingers to her lips and whistled, just as the first huge, splattering drops of rain began to fall.

The only response was a loud crack of thunder overhead, and the rain quickly became a wicked downpour.

"Again!" shouted Jamie, fighting to keep control of his frightened pony.

Christmas took a moment to comply, needing both hands to handle her own mount. The downpour became a deluge as her second whistle competed with the wind and rose above it. She saw Jamie gesturing at her, but barely; he was hardly visible through what appeared a solid curtain of water. Rain sluiced over him, plastering his hair to his head, and she could feel the sodden mass of her own hair clinging heavily about her neck and shoulders.

Finally she realized he was indicating a return to the croft. Christina hesitated, afraid he might be right. How could they locate anyone or anything in this torrent? Pity for the hounds and fear for Jacques warred with a practical streak that said they were doing none of them any good by standing about, exposing themselves to the danger. It threatened with every flash of blue-white light that illumined the landscape.

But she had to give it one more try—she simply had to! Ignoring Jamie's furious urgings, she stood in her stirrups and repeated the whistle as loudly as she could.

Jamie's displeasure was obvious, despite the poor visibility. He seized her pony's reins near the bit, clearly intending to force her to go back with him. Christina was about to tell him to desist when she saw him freeze—

As a distinctive baying of hounds carried over the noise of the storm.

The pair of them looked at each other in amazement, then shared a grin. Christina needed no urgings to repeat the whistle. A louder baying answered it, and they turned their ponies' heads in that direction.

"There!" cried Jamie. "I see them!"

Christina's gaze followed his pointing finger. Bounding toward them were three dark shapes. O'Kelly was ahead of the two deerhounds, and he gave an eager bark of recognition when Christmas called out to him.

But then the oddest thing happened. As she and Jamie ordered the hounds "home," and turned their mounts' heads for the croft, the dogs seemed reluctant to follow. Instead, they circled the riders a couple of times, barking frantically.

"What do they want?" Jamie shouted as O'Kelly cut him off from their destination for the third time.

"I—I don't know! They seem—" Christmas's reply was lost in a peal of thunder, and she had all she could do to control her pony. The terrified animal was prancing nervously as the two deerhounds dodged about its hindquarters.

"I'm not sure, but I believe they want us to follow them!" she cried.

Jamie eyed the wolfhound as he bounded off to their right again, barking fiercely at them when he returned. "Perhaps they're leading us to Jacques!" he shouted as a jagged dart of lightning revealed the churning waters of the loch. "Let's go!"

But it wasn't Jacques they found when they finally reached the place where the dogs led them. It was shelter. The hounds bounded eagerly toward a large pile of rocks and boulders, and when they followed, Christmas and Jamie found themselves entering a huge cave.

It was large enough to accommodate all of them, including the ponies, with room to spare. Moreover, it quickly became evident that the dogs had been there before. Amid flashes of lightning that illuminated the interior, they saw the remains of several cookfires and a huge pallet covered with a MacTavish tartan. Clearly, the big

Highlander had used the cave, perhaps as just such a refuge from the weather, and the hounds, also; as soon as
they entered, all three canines went to a pile of clean
straw at the rear and lay down on it. They looked utterly
at home.

Jamie found a lantern and tinderbox near the entrance.
It contained ample oil, and once he had it lit, there was
adequate light for their needs. Jamie built a fire, using dry
tinder and logs he found stored against one wall of the
cave. Christmas saw to the ponies, unsaddling them and
rubbing them down with handfuls of straw. At last, with a
warm fire burning and the animals comfortable, all that
remained was for them to deal with their own sodden
state.

Jamie seemed to have no problem on this score; he
erected a primitive drying frame near the fire, using some
of the remaining logs, and proceeded to remove his
clothing and drape it over the structure to dry.

It was when he was down to only his breeches that he
paused, suddenly noting Christina standing silently across
the fire from him. She was fully clothed and hugging her
sides in an obvious effort to keep warm.

"I suggest you remove those dripping garments,
m'lady. They'll hardly dry sufficiently while you're wearing them, and unless you wish a bout of—"

He was cut off in this admonition by a rumble of thunder and a sustained flicker of lightning, which illumined
her face more than the firelight. What he saw had him
swearing under his breath as he circled the fire and came
toward her: Christmas's lips were blue with cold, and she
shivered violently beneath the dripping folds of her cloak.

She seemed not to have heard him, merely gazing
straight ahead of her with blank eyes and chattering teeth
as Jamie rushed to her side.

"Idiot!" he shouted over a rumble of thunder. "Do
you want a lung fever?"

This at last roused her, or perhaps it was the movements of his hands as he untied the cloak and threw it down.

"D-don't!" she cried as he went to work on the next layer of clothing. She took a long backward step, intent on pulling out of his reach. "I have no intention of disrob—"

The words faltered, in tune with her feet as her heel caught on the hem of the skirt he'd loosened. Christmas yelped as she careened precariously toward the ground.

Jamie scooped her up into his arms before she hit, muttering furious imprecations between clenched teeth. He strode toward the tartan-covered pallet, set her down upon it with a glare that dared her to object, and began stripping away the remainder of her garments with ruthless efficiency.

Christmas made ineffectual blocking movements with her hands, but soon gave them up. She was shivering more than ever now, and was no match for Jamie's strength.

Soon she found herself wrapped, chin to feet, in the tartan while Jamie took her clothes and spread them to dry beside his own. She eyed him warily, but said not a word when he returned with his shirt, which appeared nearly dry, and knelt down beside her. She had but a moment to be thankful he hadn't divested himself of his damp breeches before Jamie began to use the shirt to towel moisture from her hair.

"I—I can do that for myself!" Christmas protested. She actually felt he was doing a creditable job of it, but felt it necessary to say something to keep her mind off the all too acute memory of his hands on her naked flesh when he'd unclothed her. It was not that his touch had been sexual. It hadn't. But what she had to fight was the memory it stirred of the time it *had* been thus—and the burning doubts engendered by his rejection of her ever since.

"Don't be a fool!" Jamie snapped. "Your lips haven't

yet regained their color and— Dammit! You're *still* shivering!"

With a growl of exasperation, he flung aside the shirt, stretched out beside her on the pallet, and pulled her into his arms.

"Th-that's the second t-time you've used th-that word with me," Christmas told him as she felt him run his big hands up and down her cocooned body to warm her. "It's th-threatening to b-become an annoying habit!"

"What is?" He paused in his ministrations to study her face with this bemused inquiry.

"Calling me a fool," she told him, meeting his eyes. She shifted her gaze, looked away toward the fire, and added, half under her breath, "Although I'm beginning to believe I may just be the biggest kind of one after all."

Jamie froze at the softly delivered rebuke, then let out his breath on a lengthy sigh. "I guess I deserved that," he told her.

Christmas shook her head and bit her lower lip in an effort to stem the trembling that was not from being cold. "Y-you've got it all wrong, Jamie. I—I said that *I* was the one—"

A fierce growl cut her off as Jamie caught her chin and forced her to look at him. "Dammit, Christina, I . . ."

The words faded as he caught the shimmer of tears in her eyes. "Ah, Christmas . . ." he whispered, "please don't—"

"Why?" Christmas questioned brokenly. She struggled up on one elbow and succeeded in loosening her arms from the tartan, but her eyes never left his face. *"Why, Jamie?"*

Jamie's eyes took in her face with the firelight on it. The golden light danced on the damp tendrils of hair that framed those perfect contours. It caught the brilliance of unshed tears that brimmed in eyes gone huge and sad. He had never seen a woman look more beautiful—or more lost—and he was suddenly seized with an overwhelming stab of guilt. He knew he was the cause. He knew, too, that he owed her at least an explanation, but the words died on his tongue. How could he explain when the older guilt, not to mention the rage, had him tied up inside like an iron knot?

The silence lengthened, and Christmas realized he wasn't going to answer. But she'd had all she could stand of unanswered doubts. Such feelings were alien to her, and, besides, she'd already broached the silence he'd imposed on them since that time in the cottage. She might as well continue.

"Do you know what I've been feeling?" she asked him. "I keep asking myself how it is that I should be made to feel like a trollop, a wh-whore who's been used and tossed aside, despite the fact that I was clearly a virgin when you—"

"Stop it!" Jamie cried. The words rang with anguish, and he pulled her into his arms, which were shaking with the remorse that crashed over him.

"Ah, Christmas . . . darling, for God's sake, *don't!* I couldn't bear it if you thought *you* were to blame!" He pulled back to look into her face, which was very pale.

"Don't *ever* use those words in connection with yourself again," he pleaded in a raw whisper. "Sweet Christ! If anything, it's *because* of your innocence I've stayed away!"

"B-*because* of . . . ?" Christmas's voice registered bewilderment. "I—I don't understand."

"Sweetheart, *I'm* the one—"

"Or then again, perhaps I do," she broke in bitterly. "Was I so unknowledgeable—such a failure in—in bed, that you—"

A growl of denial cut her off, and Christmas's eyes widened when Jamie caught her head between his hands, his gaze boring into hers.

"I've never *had* such pleasure in bed," he told her. "Never!"

Christmas looked stunned. "Ohh . . ." she breathed. She blinked, and then a shy smile curved her lips before she met his eyes with open candor. "I . . . I felt it, too, Jamie . . . the—the pleasure. I—I even felt it begin all —all over again," she whispered, "every time you—you even *looked* at me! That's why I—"

A ragged groan tore from Jamie's throat, and he pulled her fiercely into his arms. His mouth covered hers with insistent hunger, while, outside, the storm rumbled and cracked. It seemed to echo the violence of his need, but Christmas paid it no mind. Her arms wound eagerly about his neck, the blood rushing in her ears as she returned his kiss with equal force. She was back in Jamie's arms again, and he *wanted* her! And now she couldn't think beyond the fact that she wanted him, too—wanted him with a force as elemental as the storm.

Greedily, they tasted of each other, mouth on mouth, hot, open, and sweet. Arms entwined, they rolled upon the pallet, the tartan twisting about their limbs. Again and again, their lips met, clinging together as if they could never have enough.

Suddenly, a peal of thunder boomed, and they broke apart, gasping for breath. Jamie was above her now, the hard planes of his face etched with desire as they were caught by firelight. He met her eyes.

"Christmas . . ." he breathed, "sweet, merciful heaven, how lovely you are! Ah, woman—"

He eased aside the last folds of the tangled tartan. Then, beginning with her face, he traced his fingertips over every part of her body. Much as if he would memorize it, he savored each sculpted line, each curve. His eyes followed his fingers' path, drinking in the perfection that had haunted his dreams for nights on end. "Beautiful . . ." he murmured, "so very . . . very . . . beautiful . . ."

Christmas began to tremble under his touch, which was gentle and light as swansdown. But when his lips began to follow the trail of finger and eye, lingering on sensitive spots like that below her ear, or the place where neck and shoulder joined, she felt her arousal grow. And when his lips and teeth began to tease and nibble the tips of her breasts, when his palm cupped the downy mound above the juncture of her thighs, she moaned helplessly. Pleasure coursed wildly through her body, settling relentlessly in the woman's place at her core. She began to move beneath the skillful touch of those hands, the heat of his mouth, uttering sharp little ecstatic cries with each teasing nibble and stroke.

"Oh, Jamie—Jamie!" she cried when his fingers found the slick, throbbing wetness below. "Please! I need—"

"I know, love, I know," he murmured against her lips. "But don't rush it. I only want to make it better for— *Ah, Christmas!*"

Her name was a hoarse cry on his lips as he felt her hand on him, stroking the hard shaft that strained against the damp fabric of his breeches.

On a harsh intake of breath, he rolled away from her and, with a few deft movements, shed this last barrier between them.

Breathless with anticipation, Christmas watched, feasting her eyes on his naked flesh. Firelight gilded muscle and sinew, playing across the broad expanse of his chest, catching the ripple of movement as iron-hard thighs bent and flexed. Then he was facing her again, and her eyes traveled from the golden whorls of hair on his chest, to where they narrowed along the flat, hard plane of abdomen, to—

"Oh!" she cried, and her eyes flew to his face, her own reddening at that last, proud image.

Jamie laughed softly as he came to her. Catching her chin to hold her gaze, he whispered, "See what you do to me, little one? No—don't be shy. I love what your eagerness— Here . . ." He took her hand and kissed the inside of her palm, then moved it downward, between them. "Touch me," he urged. Christmas found the long, hard heat of him and, with a shy murmur of exclamation, began to stroke as he taught her.

"That's it, sweetheart . . . yes . . ." Jamie breathed, and then the breathing became a harsh intake of breath, her name a ragged exhalation. With a groan, he broke her hold and moved quickly, until she lay beneath him.

"You minx!" he accused with a shaky laugh. "An instant more of that, and it would all be over."

Christmas's eyes were puzzled. Her lips parted to question him, but he caught them with his own in a kiss that drove her senseless. His hands roamed freely, pausing now and again in delicious sport: cupping rounded flesh and grazing straining peak; stroking, parting, dipping, and gaining entrance; finding her, learning her, bringing her to the very brink—until she began to thrash and arch beneath him in a mindless frenzy.

"All right, little one, all right," he told her when he felt her nails bite into the flesh of his shoulders and heard her sob his name. In truth he knew that he, too, could wait no longer. The sweetness of her flesh was a brand that lit a fire in his veins, the very urgency of her cries, a threat to the teetering edge of his control.

With a softly murmured endearment, he coaxed her thighs apart, bracing himself above her, seeking entry. Outside, a roll of thunder tore across the heavens, and their eyes met . . . held . . .

"*Now*," he murmured thickly, and Christmas heard herself moan his name as he filled her with his sweet, turgid strength.

Then they were moving as the thunder rolled again, drowning their ecstatic cries, closing them off from the world outside themselves. Reaching, straining, caught in the fierce, joyous rhythm of their bodies, they traveled toward the peak—

And found it as one. Christmas cried her pleasure while Jamie shuddered with a spasm that flung her name past lips gone taut with rapture, felt his seed spewing hotly into her welcoming flesh.

Outside, the storm began to ebb, its fury spent, while, within the cave, the hushed murmurs of repletion drifted on the quiet air. Minutes passed . . .

"Are you cold, love?" Jamie questioned lazily, his lips against her hair as Christmas nestled within his arms.

Christmas felt it impossible that she should ever again feel less than warm, given the memory of what they'd just shared. She managed a negative murmur and burrowed in closer. The murmur became a hum of satisfaction, vibrating low in her throat.

Jamie chuckled softly and planted a kiss atop her head. "You still purr like a kitten, m'lady." He disengaged enough to catch her chin and tilt it so that he could see her face. "But I recall the kitten's claws," he added with a teasing grin, "and am hard put deciding which I relish more."

Christmas felt her face flame as she recalled the moment her nails had raked his flesh. "I—I cannot imagine how—how I—"

Low laughter interrupted this stammering reply, and Jamie lightly kissed the tip of her nose and then, more leisurely, her mouth.

"Never," he breathed when he was finished, "attempt to make apology for the passion that is in you, sweetheart . . . the passion you just shared with me. I count it rare and priceless—believe me." He grinned again.

"I'll have to temper my teasing, too, I can see—until I've taught you more about"—the grin widened—"lots of things."

Christmas felt herself flush again, but couldn't be certain if it was from the "things" he alluded to, or pleasure —because he implied there would be something to share in the future.

The future . . . Her mind tripped on the word, and she felt a sharp stab of guilt. The future meant Aaron and a marriage offering financial security. It meant rescuing herself and her family name from ruin and—

" 'Alloo! Jamie! Christmas! 'Allooo!"

They both started as the unmistakable sounds of a French accent echoed from outside.

"Good heavens, it's Jacques!" Christmas's voice almost squeaked with alarm. "Jamie, if he sees—"

But Jamie was already moving. He quickly retrieved their garments—nearly dry now—and handed hers to her, then wordlessly began to don his own.

Christmas needed no urging. Hurriedly, she began to dress while Jacques's calls grew closer. She prayed he wouldn't locate the cave.

Unfortunately, the hounds had also heard the Frenchman, and before Jamie or Christmas could stop them, they bounded toward the mouth of the cave.

"Oh, nooo!" Christmas wailed. "They'll lead him right to us!" She glanced down helplessly at a torso clad only in a thin shift and stockings.

Jamie stepped to her side, and she felt his arms go around her for a warm hug. With a start, she realized he was completely dressed.

"I'll go out and delay him," he told her, "and you can repair your toilette. Don't worry. Jacques will learn nothing of how we've spent this time." He gave her a soft kiss on the ear, then added, "Though for me, I account what has passed between us as nothing we need be ashamed of."

The last thing Christmas remembered was the promise in his smile before he left the cave.

❧Chapter 15❧

They learned, as they prepared to leave the cave, that Jacques had made it back to the croft after the storm broke, when he ran into Robbie MacTavish. Apparently MacTavish had been in the cave when the hounds sought shelter there. Realizing he might be of help to the new master they'd deserted, Robbie had ordered the hounds to stay, then taken his pony to rescue Jacques, whom he'd heard calling the pups. Assuring the Frenchman the hounds would be safe, he'd taken him, riding double, back to the croft.

"But where is Mr. MacTavish now?" Christmas questioned as she eyed the Highlander's pony, which Jacques was preparing to mount.

"Oh, that one!" Jacques complained as the three of them started back toward the croft. "I tell you, I 'ave not figured him out. Just when I think I know him for the cheating *canaille*, he behaves honorably and with complete courtesy."

"These Highlanders are not without a code of honor," Jamie put in. "In fact, they have a rather stringent one."

A snort of disbelief from Jacques punctuated the rhythm of the ponies' hooves.

Jamie grinned. "Of course they do sometimes appear

to have a separate set of standards for those outside the clan . . ."

Another snort, this time accompanied by a contemptuous Gallic imprecation.

"And that isn't to say," Jamie went on, "that they haven't a reputation for, ah, shrewdness in business, even—"

"Shrewdness!" Beaumonde exploded. "That rogue—"

Jamie's laughter cut him off. "Come now, my friend," he added with a wink for Christmas, who rode between them and was following this banter with a grin, "you cannot claim to be unacquainted with rogues yourself. In fact, I thought you once enjoyed quite an affinity for them."

"Bah!" Jacques exclaimed. But his dark eyes twinkled, and a roguish grin quickly followed.

"But you still haven't told us how you wound up with the man's pony," Christmas reminded him.

"Ah," Jacques began, "you would not believe it! After we reach ze croft and learn only Mary is there—that you two 'ave gone to search for me and ze hounds—*alors,* that crazy Scot!— He leaves us ze pony and says he wishes to *walk* to ze village—*in ze storm!*—and off he goes!" He finished with a shrug that said he'd never understand such behavior.

"Hmm," Jamie mused, "so he left you and Maire to wait out the storm together, snug and warm, at the croft?" He eyed his friend archly.

Christmas thought she saw Jacques flush a deeper color under his tan before he replied.

"*Oui,* but—"

Jamie was grinning again as he cut him off. "Perhaps, Beaumonde, instead of 'rogue,' you ought to be naming him the 'Celtic Cupid'!"

The Frenchman colored for certain this time and cloaked his reaction with a theatrical cough. But Christmas sent Jamie a quelling glance. She deemed it the height of temerity for him to be teasing and insinuating about the possibility of an intimate interlude between Jacques and Maire when it was just such a private matter *they* were trying to conceal from Jacques!

Seeking to divert the conversation, Christmas ignored Jamie's grin and addressed the Frenchman. "I wonder why we didn't see you and Mr. MacTavish on our way to the loch. You must have passed right by—"

"Mais non, chérie," said Jacques. "That madman took a different route, despite my desperate urgings. He—"

"A different route?" queried Jamie. "As far as I'm aware, there's only this one path through the—"

"Exactement!" Jacques groaned. "That idiot did not use a path! And when we reach ze croft, I can produce ze apparel he ruined with that insane trek. *Sacrebleu!* I 'ave never seen such wilderness! Briars! Brambles! I tell you, *mes amis,* I wonder that I am here to tell of it!"

Jacques regaled them with a running commentary along these lines for the duration of the ride. Waxing, by turns, indignant, incredulous, annoyed, and flamboyantly disgusted, Jacques spared no pains to delineate the extent of the outrages perpetrated on him by the Highlander. He had a dramatic flair with words—and an absolute genius for comic exaggeration—Christmas decided amid fits of laughter, which suggested he'd missed his calling and should have been on the stage. She told him as much when they reached the croft in what seemed no time at all, owing to his entertaining monologue.

Jacques merely winked at her as they dismounted. Then, when Mary came running out across the yard to meet him, he flung his reins at Jamie and ran to meet the Irishwoman.

Mary's laughter rang like a young girl's as Jacques enveloped her in a hug. And when he picked her up and whirled her about, she gave a squeal of delight, sounding even younger.

Christmas and Jamie paused in open surprise, beside the ponies, as they witnessed this enthusiastic display. Mouth open, Christmas viewed the antics of her normally staid, older companion, then glanced at Jamie as if to question him as to what they were seeing.

A slow grin emerged on Jamie's face, but before she could respond, the older couple were running toward them, hand in hand—and explaining all.

"She 'as consented, *mes amis!*" Jacques announced, laughing like a boy. "This beautiful creature will be my wife!"

Christmas's eyes flew to Maire and the flushed countenance. The happiness lighting the dark eyes told her this was true. "Oh, Maire!" she cried, running to embrace her. "I am so happy for you! So very glad!"

Jamie's sentiments echoed hers, and for the next few minutes there were hugs all around and a congratulatory slap on the back for the Frenchman as the younger pair shared the others' joy. Amid smiles and laughter, the four of them went to stable the ponies, and Christmas suddenly realized that the ex-pirate's humorous monologue had very likely been concocted to divert the conversation from him and Maire—and their surprise.

Evidently Jamie thought so, too. "You're a sly rogue," he told the Frenchman with a grin. Jacques laughed aloud, pausing to give Maire a squeeze while, over her shoulder, he threw Christmas another wink.

Maire informed them that MacTavish had sent word he'd be along that evening to collect his mount. This produced an observation by her fiancé that he had every expectation the timing would be gauged to coincide with the supper hour. There was knowing laughter, but Maire gestured excitedly, indicating she had something else to tell them.

"I nearly fergot!" exclaimed the Irishwoman. "Whilst ye were all gone, after it stopped rainin' and the sun came out, I decided t' take a turn about the yard, and—" Her eyes sparkled as she took a deep breath.

"And . . . ?" Christmas prompted.

"And 'twould appear that torrent we had up and washed away a good part o' that manure pile ye were diggin' in, Christmas—and guess what I saw!"

Three faces regarded her expectantly.

"There looks t' be the beginnin's of a set o' stone steps beneath that manure, *macushla*. They look, fer all the world, I'm thinkin', like they could well lead to an old wine cellar!"

Spades and shovels in hand, they all hurried out of the stable and around to the back, where they saw that Maire hadn't exaggerated. There, amid manure-redolent runoff washed aside by the downpour, were the contours of a couple of ancient stone steps. Jamie quickly began to dispose of the remaining manure, and Jacques threw Christmas a sharp glance, but no one said a word.

When Jamie had finished, they attacked the packed earth in which the steps were buried. They were careful, avoiding one another's tools and working in shifts for the most part, but it was hard to contain their eagerness. Slowly, more steps appeared as the hours passed.

Unfortunately, they were not to achieve their end that day. The digging went too slowly, for there was a great deal of debris embedded in the packed soil, and more steps than they'd expected: at least a dozen, they concluded, when darkness and their hunger forced them to call a halt.

But they also realized the morning should bring success. Exhausted, but exhilarated, they repaired to the cottage to wash and then devour the excellent supper Maire had prepared.

Deciding to begin digging again as early as possible the following morning, all four were in excellent spirits as they prepared to leave for the manor. The men were to escort the women home. But just when they reached the door and opened it, Robbie MacTavish's huge frame filled the entry.

"*Merde,*" Jacques muttered under his breath. He'd forgotten all about the cursed Highlander. So had Jamie, apparently; it was evident in his tone as he murmured a hesitant greeting. Meanwhile, Christmas gaped, speechless at the immense size and rough appearance of the Scot. Only Maire had the grace to smile and remember to bid the man welcome, this amid the excited yips and tail-thumpings of the hounds.

MacTavish, undaunted by the fact that they'd obviously already eaten, accepted Maire's tentative invitation to enjoy the leftover stew that remained in an iron pot on the hearth.

"Aye, lassie," he replied as he drew a chair up to the table, "fer I've a fierce hunger aboot me fra' the walkin' I've done. A few tasty bites wouldna gang amiss—an' I maun enjoy a wee drop of ale, too, if ye dinna mind. 'Tis thirsty work, wanderin' these hills afoot!"

Maire drew on her apron, throwing an anxious glance at the clock on the mantel as she prepared to serve the Scot. Meanwhile, the others' glances showed they shared her concern. It was clear the old Highlander was making himself at home and would likely remain at the cottage for a good while. But the women had to get back to the manor, and soon, Christmas whispered to Jamie and Jacques, or risk the chance of alarming her staff; this would bring questions she didn't wish to deal with.

But someone had to remain with their guest. Not only would it be inhospitable to leave him alone; it would be imprudent to leave the croft, or more specifically, the evidence of their digging, unguarded while MacTavish lurked about.

Christmas and the two men discussed all of this in furtive whispers while the Scot enjoyed Maire's attentions as she served him. Quickly, it was decided that Jacques would have the dubious pleasure of entertaining the Highlander while Jamie saw the women home. Jamie had volunteered to stay, but the Frenchman insisted, saying that there was still a certain matter of an Irish hound on which he wished to question their guest, and this would afford him the perfect opportunity. He had been hoodwinked, he reminded them, and he wasn't about to suffer this in silence and "allow ze *canaille* to get off Scot free!"

Murmuring apologies to MacTavish, Jamie and the two women set off for the manor house, taking the ponies to make better time. (MacTavish had cheerfully volunteered his mount again, after expressing some dismay at losing the company of the "twa bonnie lassies.")

As they rode, Maire and Jamie fell into a discussion of what the morning might bring. But Christmas remained silent, immersed deep in thought. This was the first opportunity she'd had to reflect on the day's events, especially on what had occurred between her and Jamie in the cave. The subsequent hours had simply been too crowded with other business to allow time for this, but now her mind was filled with questions and a sudden need to sort things out.

She knew she felt relieved that the afternoon had brought an end to the estrangement Jamie had imposed on them. No, it was more than relief—it was . . . *wonderful!*

But she still didn't know why he'd erected those barriers recently. Dimly, she recalled his anger at being questioned about her rights to the treasure . . . something about his honor . . . And in the cave he'd taken pains to assure her of his honorable regard for *her* . . . *It's* because *of your innocence,* he'd said . . . But what did that signify? Where did his feelings about honor tie in to what had transpired between them? The concept of honor suggested perhaps something related to his military background, and, yet, his comments had arisen entirely out of some very personal exchanges between them. It was clear

Jamie had some deep-rooted private feelings, memories from his past, no doubt, that affected him with regard to their relationship, but what were they?

Oh, but she wished he weren't in the habit of being so closemouthed! For how was *she* to know how to regard their relationship if—

Christmas hesitated, concentrating for a moment on the trail and the feel of her mount's movements as she rode. Beside her, Jamie murmured agreement to something Maire said as Christmas reviewed her own words in her mind . . .

Their relationship . . . what did that signify?

Just what do you mean by such an assessment, Christmas MacKenzie? she asked herself. *Think! You came here, an engaged woman, with a serious mission. Then, somehow, you lost sight of both those things when a handsome foreigner entered the picture, and you fell into his arms! Without a thought for either your status or your future—not to mention your reputation! Think of your betrothal! Think of restoring what poor Papa lost! Jamie MacIver has no place in any of it!*

Beside her, in the dark, she heard Jamie laugh at something Maire said, and the deep resonance of his voice sent a ripple of pleasure through her. She was instantly back in the cave with him, recalling not only his voice, but his eyes as they'd held hers, his hands . . .

She almost gasped aloud as she felt the tips of her breasts tighten and contract, the sweet jolt of pleasure below . . .

So much for Jamie having no place in her life!

But what was she to do? Cast all her plans aside in hopes of seeing where this would lead? And what was *he* thinking about? Where, exactly, did she fit in with *his* plans? Did he even have any, regarding her?

She clearly had to learn more about this enigmatic man who, with his wondrous touch, could turn her life upside down. But she suspected it would take time, and time was the one thing she lacked. Tomorrow might bring her treasure hunt to an end—a favorable one, God willing! And if she found the Seadog's Treasure, then there was Aaron to deal with, and—

This time she did gasp. She'd been so intent on her ruminations, she'd failed to realize they'd reached the manor drive. And there, standing beside Mrs. MacLeod and some footmen bearing lanterns, was the tall, impeccably tailored figure of her fiancé, Lord Aaron Crenshawe!

"Ach!" she heard Maire exclaim in dismay as the three of them approached the group with the lanterns.

Jamie said nothing, but Christmas saw his eyes were focused on the aristocratic Englishman.

"Och! There they are!" Mrs. Macleod grabbed a lantern from one of the footmen and hastened toward them. "We were aboot t' begin a search! Are ye all right, m'lady?"

"I—I'm fine, Mrs. MacLeod." Christmas scrambled in her mind for some explanation to account for their lateness—and the presence of Jamie and the ponies!—while she dismounted. She saw Maire throw her an anxious glance as she slid off her mount. *Aaron! Why didn't I consider Aaron? I might have guessed he'd turn up at an awkward moment!*

"M'dear, you've given us all quite a turn," said her fiancé as he drew near. "It was already dark when I arrived, and your housekeeper had begun to grow quite frantic. Couldn't imagine where you'd gone to for so long with your . . . sketching?"

He caught her hand and brought it to his lips—his habitual greeting—but tonight, somehow, Christmas couldn't help sensing a proprietary air to the gesture.

"Good—good evening, m'lord," Christmas managed. Out of the corner of her eye she noticed that Jamie, still atop his mount, was eyeing Aaron in utter silence.

"If—if I'd known you were about to turn up so—so

unexpectedly, I'd have been less careless," she went on as Maire quietly came to her side and handed her her sketching materials. *Thank heaven for Maire! I didn't even think of them when we left the croft!* "Maire and I quite lost track of the time, you see. And then, somehow, we took a wrong turn and had every expectation of becoming quite lost. In fact, we should have, were it not for the happy occasion of"—for the first time she turned toward Jamie, indicating his tall presence on MacTavish's pony with an airy gesture—"of running into my neighbor, Mr. MacIver, here. He was gracious, indeed, to escort us home, and he even provided these sturdy little mounts."

Aaron ran his eyes over the shaggy Highland ponies, and then her tartan garb, with a look of utter disdain. It was all too clear what he thought of her trafficking in things native.

Finally, she saw his eyes move to the mounted figure beside her. "It seems we owe you a debt of gratitude, sir." Aaron's gaze was cool, assessing. "I hope my fiancée's rescue hasn't proved too great an inconvenience."

Christmas felt, rather than saw, Jamie stiffen in the saddle before he replied with all formality. "There was no inconvenience, Lord—ah, m'lord, I fear you have the advantage . . ."

"Crenshawe," Aaron supplied, then glanced at Christmas. "Really, Christina, I fear you've been in this wilderness retreat too long. Your manners are slipping!"

Christmas's face was awash with heat as she stammered an apology. "I—I beg your pardons, gentlemen." She glanced at Jamie, nearly wincing at the frozen profile, the hooded eyes that revealed nothing in the lantern light. *Oh, Jamie, I never intended any deceit!* "Mr. James MacIver . . ." she went on, "allow me to present Lord Aaron Crenshawe."

Aaron sketched a bow and was answered with a curt nod. Then, before Christmas could think what to say or do next, Jamie murmured something about the lateness of the hour, gathered the reins of his mount and the two riderless ponies, and, giving another wordless nod, rode off.

❖Chapter 16❖

With Jamie's departure, Mrs. MacLeod ushered everyone briskly into the manor house. There were inquiries as to whether the two women had eaten, there being a light supper under way for his lordship. Christmas gave her standard reply when arriving home from a day of "sketching": "No, thank you, Mrs. MacLeod. Maire and I had sufficient victuals from the kitchen when we left this morning."

But then Aaron took it upon himself to dismiss the hovering housekeeper, who was clucking like a mother hen, inquiring after having baths drawn and the like. And just as Christmas was about to object to this peremptory handling of her staff, he dismissed Maire as well.

Maire threw Christmas a sympathetic glance, curtsied, and retired, leaving her alone in the drawing room with Aaron.

Aaron eyed her creased tartans, the skirts stained with mud and manure, and sniffed disdainfully. "Really, m'dear, I confess I cannot like your attire. Perhaps I ought to have allowed you time to bathe and change. But there are things I should like to discuss with you, and after that arduous trek to this backwater, I find my patience worn a bit thin . . . Sherry?"

Christmas ran her eyes over him as he helped himself to

the contents of one of several decanters she kept on a
sideboard. He was impeccably groomed, as always, despite the "arduous" journey . . . not a hair out of place
among his fashionable *à la Titus* curls, not a smudge on
his gleaming Hessians, not even a trace of stubble on the
aristocratic face with its aquiline nose and pale blue eyes.
She glanced at the glass of sherry he now poured for her
without waiting for her reply. *My own sherry* . . . She
fastened on his choice of words regarding her appearance,
the need to bathe and change . . . "Perhaps I ought to
allow you . . ." *Allow me* . . .

And she felt resentment grow.

Clamping down on an urge to remind him who was
the host and who the guest—the *uninvited* guest—she
accepted the glass of sherry and moved toward the fireplace. She saw, as he came to join her by the fire, that
Aaron's choice of libation was brandy.

He raised his glass and smiled, but she noted the smile
didn't quite reach his eyes. "A toast," he said. "To one
journey's end and . . . new beginnings."

Christmas nodded and took a sip from her glass.
Aaron's eyes did not leave her face as he raised his snifter
and swallowed.

"Your housekeeper tells me you spend precious little
time here, m'dear," he told her. "I had no idea you were
so fond of . . . sketching."

Christmas stifled the urge to voice her irritation. This
was the second time he'd alluded to her invented pastime
with innuendo. That it *was* invented didn't signify;
clearly, he suspected the deception, but she resented the
manner in which he slyly implied his suspicions; why the
devil couldn't he deal with her more directly? Jamie
would—

Catching herself before she could complete the
thought, Christmas hastily took another sip of sherry,
then shrugged.

"It has served to while away the time and take my mind off other things, m'lord."

"Things?" he questioned snidely. "Like your American, ah, *neighbor*, perhaps?"

"I was referring to my grief at the loss of my parents!" she replied with more asperity than she'd intended.

"Ah . . . of course. And with regard to that, allow me to express in person the condolences I offered in my letter of several weeks ago. It goes without saying, my dear Christina, that I would much prefer to have been allowed to voice them then . . . *to your person*, that is."

There was the innuendo again! Of course, she'd been expecting him to inquire as to her reasons for leaving London without seeing him. He'd hardly have followed her to Scotland if he weren't curious about her reasons . . . suspicious of them, actually. But, dammit, this cat-and-mouse game was the outside of enough! She would put an end to it—at once!

"Why did you come to Scotland?" she asked abruptly.

He raised an eyebrow—coolly: an affected gesture. "Why, to ask you the very same thing, m'dear. Not the thing, to go haring off to some wilderness after a bereavement, y'know . . . not the thing at all. Makes a man wonder . . . Could there have been other, ah . . . more pressing concerns?"

"More pressing concerns, m'lord? And what might be more pressing than a daughter's grief, the need to deal with it in seclusion?"

Aaron took another slow sip of brandy. The shrewd, pale eyes studied her face for a moment before he replied. "I own, I cannot think of too many . . . perhaps not even one—*unless* it were another kind of grief. One associated *with* those losses. You see, I had occasion to be privy to some very disturbing rumors going about 'Change at the time you left, m'lady . . . rumors which—"

"The Exchange!" she exclaimed, hastily seeking to deflect the attack she'd been expecting. *"Rumors?* Come, m'lord, surely you cannot expect me to believe you journeyed hundreds of miles—on some fool's errand! On the strength of some market gossip! Why, the Exchange is always rife with rumor—and most of it rubbish, I might point out!"

"Most, yes—but not all!" he snapped. "And as to the fool's errand, as you so acerbically put it—that is precisely what I traveled to these barbaric mountains to avoid. Because the fool's errand I have no intention of running is one which leads me to the altar with a betrothed who is not what she seems!"

Christmas decided to bluff it out. "Not what she seems, m'lord? And what, pray tell, have I seemed to be?"

The coolness was back after the momentary outburst. Aaron smiled, then took his finger and ran it over the contours of her cheek.

His touch was impersonal, a cold, mechanical gesture. Christmas forced herself to endure it while, unbidden, the memory of Jamie's warmth intruded. Gritting her teeth, she made herself listen to what Aaron was saying.

"Why, the Prime Beauty of the Season, m'dear . . . as well as . . . one whose inheritance will compound well with mine, when I come into it . . . *if* there *is* an inheritance, that is."

Suddenly his eyes went hard. "You cannot expect me to disregard my responsibilities, Christina. Therefore, let us have done playing with words: are you, or are you not, yet an heiress?"

Christmas froze in the act of taking another sip of sherry. Here it was. She couldn't say she hadn't been expecting it. Now the question was, how should she answer?

She considered lying to him, outright, to put him off until she had time to think. But she had never been very good at lying, probably because she had an aversion to it. Damn him for pressing her this way! But putting him off, at least until tomorrow, would allow her to put her original plan into action—*if* the treasure turned up, of course.

It would also allow you time to deal with Jamie, said a small voice in the back of her mind. *He didn't look too pleased to learn you have a fiancé, and if you decide to break with Aaron, you'll need to—*

Break with Aaron? Was she really even considering such a thing? What of her family's honor? What about saving poor Papa's name? Didn't she have obligations that were more important than the heated embraces of a man who'd committed himself to nothing with her?

But Aaron Crenshawe . . . Could she really spend a lifetime with this cold and haughty man? This overbearing peacock? Oh, she needed some time to think!

But since she had no skill in prevaricating, he'd likely see she was lying if she denied Papa's losses. On the other hand, so much depended upon tomorrow! Perhaps a tiny *bending of* the truth could be contrived, then . . .

Managing to look her betrothed directly in the eye, Christmas bought herself some time. "Very well, Aaron, since you were presumptuous enough to inquire, I shall tell you: my . . . circumstances have altered somewhat, yes."

Aaron's eyes were like frost. "You mean your father left you penniless," he said boldly.

"No, that is *not* what I said, my lord. I said *altered.* And, in fact, the extent of that alteration is what I have come to my mother's ancestral home to learn."

"Learn? Learn what, pray tell?"

"The size of my *maternal* inheritance, my lord."

There was silence as he surveyed her with canny eyes. Christmas met his look with as much serenity as she could muster.

"How much?" he queried curtly.

"A fortune, by any standards, Aaron—even yours."

"When?"

"When?" she echoed bemusedly.

"If it were already in your hands, I doubt you'd be hanging about these wretched mountains, Christina. Therefore, I suspect problems. What are they? A difficulty in the entailment, perhaps? A Scottish legalism that—"

"Tomorrow evening, m'lord."

"Eh?" For the first time, Aaron looked off balance, and Christmas was quick to follow up on her advantage.

"You shall have your answer by tomorrow evening, Aaron, and not a moment sooner."

She set her glass on the mantel and strode quickly toward the double doors that led to the hall. "And now, if you'll excuse me, m'lord, I believe I shall have that bath . . ."

Before he could summon a reply, she left the room.

"Mon Dieu!" Jacques exclaimed as he saw Jamie's face when the younger man entered the cottage. "You look like a man who 'as seen ze devil!"

"I may have, I just may have!" Jamie snarled as he tore off the wide-brimmed hat he wore and threw it on the table. He began to strip off his leather riding gloves with short, jerky movements.

"Ze Scot?" Jacques inquired, for he knew Jamie had run into MacTavish in the yard. The Highlander had been anxious to get home, and he left the cottage as soon as they'd heard Jamie returning with the ponies.

"No, Beaumonde," Jamie replied in clipped, furious syllables. "This devil doesn't have horns or a tam-o'shanter. This devil"—he finished removing the gloves and flung them after the hat—"wears *skirts!*"

Jacques frowned. "Christmas?"

Jamie jerked his head in the direction from which he'd ridden. "I just had the pleasure of meeting her *fiancé!*"

Jacques blinked, then swore softly in French. He reached for the whisky bottle he'd been sharing with Robbie MacTavish. "Here," he said, gesturing for Jamie to sit, "you look as if you could use this, and, fortunately, that greedy Scot left us some."

Jamie strode to the chairs by the fire, and Jacques handed him the Scotch.

"Now, tell me about it, if you will, *mon ami,*" said the Frenchman as he poured himself a drink.

Jamie downed his Scotch and slammed the tumbler down on the bench between them. Then he described the scene outside the manor house while Jacques listened sympathetically. Jamie was reaching for a refill of Scotch as he finished: ". . . a genuine blue-blooded English dandy, if I've ever seen one, Beaumonde. Christ! The smell of his cologne was enough to make me puke!"

Jacques nodded, feeling a stirring of his own aversion to useless aristocrats who polluted the lives of others. Yet he knew Jamie's fury had less to do with the English lord than with the woman he was betrothed to . . . a woman who had never given them a single indication she was thusly committed. In fact, even Maire—

As if he'd read his mind, Jamie queried, "Did Maire ever mention—"

"*Non.*" Jacques sighed. "But, then, we never discussed Christmas's personal life, *mon ami.* Maire 'as too much respect for—"

"*Respect!*" Jamie spat. "Now, *there's* a word! Tell me, what else comes to mind when you hear it?"

Jacques gave him a penetrating look. Jamie was in a strange mood, perhaps even a dangerous one. He'd never seen him like this, and it worried him. He decided to go along with whatever game he was playing, in hopes of drawing him out; then, perhaps he could help. "Ah, 'esteem,' *mon ami?*"

Jamie barked a sardonic laugh. "Not bad, Beaumonde, but I'll give you something better: 'honor'!" The dark laughter erupted again, and Jacques winced at what he saw in Jamie's eyes.

"Respect . . . esteem . . . honor," Jamie echoed

bitterly. "Brave words to live by, Beaumonde! And there you have it. Among them—those simple-sounding, innocuous words—they form a catechism that has tied my life in knots!" He reached for the tumbler of Scotch and raised it in a toast.

"But here's to the final word that gives me my religion," he went on, and the tone was mocking. " 'Betrayal'!"

Jacques's eyes were compassionate as he watched him down the Scotch. "Talk about it, *mon ami*," he said quietly, setting the whisky bottle out of reach. "It may help, and it will certainly leave you with a clearer head in ze morning."

Jamie frowned, eyeing his empty tumbler and then the Frenchman's face. At last he nodded, a look of defeat about his hunched shoulders as he stared into the fire and began to speak.

He told him then of the father he'd been brought up to believe was a war hero—only to discover the truth in that attic when he was twelve. He talked about the sense of betrayal he'd felt, the shame and the need to redeem the honor of his family name, culminating in his decision to join the military.

Jacques listened, nodding thoughtfully as the story unfolded. He could well understand the childhood betrayal's driving force. Hadn't his own choices been shaped by what he'd experienced as a boy in France?

But what disturbed him as well was a significant difference between them. With himself, the years with Laffite had exorcised the demons; he had left Barataria with a past he could put behind him, ready to move on to a more mature phase in his life—to put down roots, as he'd told Jamie in London. And now, with Maire, he knew this would come to fruition. But Jamie, it seemed, had merely brought his devils with him. Was the parental betrayal to haunt him forever, then? And what of his art?

Was the passion he'd talked about losing all too tangled up in the childhood pain?

Cautiously, not wanting to intrude where he wasn't welcome, he decided to try a gentle probe.

"Jamie . . ." he began, "this newspaper clipping . . . did you ever confront your fa—"

"He was already dead when I found it," came the terse reply.

"And your mo—"

"She was too frail—unstable, really, after—after my father died. She lived only a few years more. I could never have talked to her about it. It wasn't possible."

Jacques nodded. "And so you kept it all inside yourself, eh?"

There was a brief nod as Jamie stared at the empty glass cradled loosely between his hands.

"But Jamie, did you never consider that ze newspaper story did not tell ze *real* story—perhaps not even ze truth?"

Jamie frowned. "What in hell are you talking about, Beaumonde? Newspapers—"

"Allow me to tell you a story of my own," Jacques cut in hastily. "Or, to give credit, it is a story I 'ave from Maire . . .

"Once, many centuries ago, there was a prince who owned one of ze great Irish hounds." Jacques paused and bent to stroke the head of O'Kelly, who was lying beside his chair.

"One day," he went on, "this prince went hunting, but without his hound, who was unaccountably absent. On ze prince's return, ze truant, stained and smeared with blood, joyfully sprang to meet his master. Ze prince, alarmed, ran to find his son, and saw ze *enfant's* cot empty, ze bedclothes and floor covered with blood. Ze frantic prince plunged his sword into ze dog's side, thinking it 'ad killed his son. Ze dog's dying yell was answered by a child's cry. Ze prince searched and discovered his boy, *unharmed*. But nearby lay ze body of a mighty wolf. *Ze dog 'ad slain it.* Ze prince, filled with remorse, is said never to 'ave smiled again."

Jamie drew a long, shuddering breath and met Jacques's gaze with a bleak look. "Beaumonde . . . are you trying to tell me—"

"I am only pointing out possibilities," said Jacques. "Ze poor hound in ze tale 'ad no way to tell ze prince what 'ad 'appened. It was merely circumstance that allowed ze prince to learn ze truth—*too late!* But, of course, ze man was in great pain when he saw ze damaging evidence. *Quel dommage!* . . . That pain—that sense of betrayal—led him to destroy all ze joy in his life—forever!"

Jamie heaved a sigh and closed his eyes, as if to shut out something painful. "Beaumonde . . ." he began in a choked voice, "you don't understand. There's more I haven't—"

"Bah! Listen to me, Jamie. I can well believe I do not understand all of it. *I* am not *you!* A man does not live in another man's skin."

He reached across the bench and clasped Jamie's shoulder. "I am merely trying to help with what I can, *mon ami.* I know you came here with hope of putting ze past behind you. *To discover ze passion again, oui?* Jamie, you 'ave a real talent! Yet we 'ave watched you destroy one piece of clay after another. Why? Because an ancient betrayal saps your creative drive? Are you going to allow this—this old pain to keep you from—"

"*Old* pain!" Jamie's eyes darted to a chest across the room. He rose abruptly and stalked toward it. "Don't you know anything yet, Beaumonde?" he questioned acidly.

Reaching the chest, he flung open the lid and withdrew something. Jacques couldn't see what it was because Jamie's large frame blocked his view, but as he turned and held it up, the Frenchman caught his breath.

In Jamie's hands, catching the light of the fire as he carried it forward, was an exquisitely rendered clay sculpture of a woman. The figure was wearing Highland dress, and its feminine proportions were the very essence of grace and beauty. Although Jacques couldn't yet see the face, which was turned away, the willowy lines and magnificent tumble of unbound hair could only belong to one woman—Christmas MacKenzie.

"Ahh . . ." Jacques breathed. "And here we assumed you 'ad smashed every—"

"This is the one piece," Jamie interrupted in a hollow voice, "that I haven't wanted to destroy completely, though I've worked on it continually, late at night, since the moment I saw her this way. I *still* see her there"—he gestured toward the window—"standing in the meadow while the sunlight caught her hair and turned it to living fire. She was—*is*, in my mind's eye—the loveliest thing I have ever seen or imagined, Beaumonde. And my hands *itched* for the clay!"

Jacques nodded. He was no artist, but he remembered in vivid detail the magic of the moment when he first saw Maire. He would remember it till he died.

"Yet when I began to sculpt," Jamie went on, "she was already becoming more than just the beautiful image I saw when I beheld her in the meadow that day. She was becoming a person—a flesh-and-blood woman with habits and quirks, laughter and tears . . .

"Did you ever notice the funny way her nose wrinkles when she doesn't like something? The way she chews her lower lip when she's not sure of what she's going to say? Or the way her eyes—"

Jamie broke off with a laugh that held no mirth. Then he sighed and ran the tips of his fingers lightly over the face of the sculpture. It was a gesture that was infinitely sad, as sad as anything Jacques had ever seen.

"I wanted to capture those things, Beaumonde—all of them. Not just the outer beauty, the physical grace and perfection. I wanted to re-create the *life* I saw there! The heart and soul and essence of Christmas MacKenzie!"

Jamie's eyes moved from the statue to Jacques's face, and he smiled ruefully. "But I guess you can imagine what else began to happen then. One doesn't delve beneath the surface of a creature like Christmas MacKenzie —young as she is—without sensing the complexities and currents, the . . ."

"Passions?" Jacques supplied softly.

Jamie took a deep breath, closed his eyes, and nodded.

Jacques said nothing, sensing there was more, and at length Jamie continued.

"But I fought it, Beaumonde. I fought it because—" Here his eyes darkened, and he shuddered, leaving Jacques with the certainty that there were still things he didn't wish to share, secrets, perhaps, that comprised more ancient wounds.

"And then today," Jamie was saying, "today, as we were riding back here after the storm, I finally thought that maybe there was a way to—"

Again, he stopped himself, laughed. And Jacques winced at the jarring note of self-mockery he heard.

"You are thinking of this English lord," Jacques said. "You are thinking of betrayal again." The statements were casually uttered, as if he were announcing the weather, and Jamie sent him a deprecating glare.

"And you're saying I shouldn't be—is that it?"

Jacques sighed. "I am saying, *mon ami,* that you 'ave one powerful advantage over a *pathétique* prince in a legend: you do not 'ave to wish—in vain—that a dog could speak!"

Jamie gave an incredulous snort. "Oh? And what do you suppose I'll learn from Lady Oracle, hmm? That her fine English fiancé is not her intended at all? That I somehow *imagined* him?"

"Stranger things 'ave 'appened," Jacques replied. "I am only suggesting that you give Christmas—and yourself—and your passion!—a better chance than that poor bastard of a prince gave a dog, *n'est-ce pas?*"

The look Jamie gave him was doubtful, but he nodded, and Jacques rushed in before he could change his mind.

"*Très bien,* and now sit down and share a nightcap with me while I try to explain how I allowed that Scot to convince me I require two more hounds!"

There was a split second of silence, followed by Jamie's bark of laughter as Jacques reached for the Scotch.

Jamie joined him and a smile emerged, the first of any genuine warmth since they'd first sat down together, Jacques realized.

"You know, Beaumonde," he told the Frenchman, "you may make a lousy dog trader, but you sure make one hell of a friend!"

❧Chapter 17❧

It was barely light outside the following morning when
Christmas and Maire crept stealthily out of the manor
house. Rising before dawn, they'd dressed warmly—again
in the borrowed tartans, which Mrs. MacLeod had had
cleaned and aired the night before. Then Christmas had
left a hasty note for the housekeeper, asking her to see to
his lordship's comfort while she and Maire were away.
The note said she needed to "attend to some private
MacKenzie business," and she knew this would insure
Mrs. MacLeod's cooperation. The Scotswoman had
made no secret of her dislike for the haughty English lord
who ordered the MacKenzie staff about so peremptorily;
and by implying that Aaron was to be distracted while she
attended to private *clan* matters he was not privy to,
Christmas knew she had also appealed to the woman's
strong sense of loyalty: Aaron would be kept safely out of
her hair until she returned.

"Did ye leave a note fer his lordship as well?" Maire
asked as the two women hurried along the trail to the
croft.

"Indeed, I did," said Christmas. She chuckled and
slanted Maire an arch glance. "Although it did not contain all it *ought* to have said!"

Maire eyed her with cautious curiosity. Christmas's

mood, since the evening before, had shifted dramatically. Upon retiring to her chambers, where Maire had helped her bathe and prepare for bed, the colleen had been solemnly pensive. She'd resisted all Maire's efforts to draw her into conversation, submitting absently to her ministrations while her mind seemed miles away. Maire had hoped this had to do with her being tired and said nothing about it, although she'd have loved to ask Christmas a few questions: what had transpired between the lass and his lordship, for instance? And what might be the reason for Jamie MacIver's apparent change in attitude, that he'd suddenly begun to help them dig for the treasure? Oh, she had questions, she did, indeed!

And now, with the night behind them, she had a new one: why did Christmas all at once appear so . . . *happy?* The child had gone to bed deeply troubled. Yet, upon rising, she'd been as light of heart as Maire had ever seen her! This was far more than a simple night of rest should have produced, and now she said as much to Christmas.

"Do I really seem so happy, Maire?" Christmas replied. "Well, then, I suppose I must have made the right decision."

"Decision? And what decision might that be?"

Christmas laughed, her bright hair catching a beam of sunlight as she turned to face Maire on the path. "Why, to break with Aaron, Maire! To end my engagement to wed that strutting ice-lord."

"Break with— Holy Mother o' God! And what o' the treasure and all yer plannin'?"

Again, Christmas laughed. "They simply do not signify. Treasure or no treasure, Maire, I have found I cannot abide the thought of a lifetime with Lord Aaron Crenshawe!"

"Saints preserve us!" Maire breathed, stopping dead in her tracks. Then a slow smile of dawning comprehension crossed her face. "And would a certain *ither* gentleman be havin' anything t' do with this decision, lass?"

A look of uncertainty shadowed the gray eyes, and Christmas turned to resume walking on the path.

Maire joined her, wondering what she was thinking. There was no doubt in the older woman's mind that something significant had happened between Christmas and the American the day before. Surely the decision to break with his lordship was tied in with it.

It was disappointing, therefore, when Christmas's response was an airy change of subject. "Maire, dear, have I told you how happy it makes me to know you've at last found someone to love? And I've no doubt Jacques is exactly the right man for you. Why, he practically worships you with his eyes! And you should see *your* face when you're with him! You've truly—"

"Christmas . . ."

The patter ceased, and Christmas glanced uneasily at Maire, then studied the ground as they walked. "Yes?" she replied almost inaudibly after they'd gone a few yards.

Maire put a hand on her shoulder, and they both stopped. Overhead, a bird called, and sunlight dappled their tartans as they looked at each other.

"Christmas, darlin'," said Maire in a gentle voice, "what is it? Am I pryin' where I oughtn't? If that's the case, ye need only say so, but—"

"Oh, Maire, don't be silly!" Christmas tried to smile, but didn't quite succeed. "Of course you're not prying! I simply—simply couldn't contain my good feelings about —about you and Jacques, that's all. Why, Maire, you mustn't look so solemn. Now that you've found your own heart's love—"

"And haven't ye found yers, *macushla?*" Maire's eyes were tender as they searched hers. " 'Tis yer Jamie, I'm meanin', lass."

Christmas met her gaze in silence for a moment, the open honesty they'd always shared an almost palpable thing between them. At length, she nodded and heaved a forlorn sigh.

"Well, then," said Maire. "Now that's settled. So would ye mind tellin' me why ye're so troubled of a sudden?"

Christmas swallowed the emotion that clogged her throat. "B-because," she replied with difficulty, "it is not at all the same as with you and Jacques. Maire, *Jamie hasn't asked me to marry him!*"

"Ach!" cried Maire. "Is *that* all that's fashin' ye? Why, 'tis easily solved, child!"

Christmas threw her a look that was skeptical and wary. "It is? How?"

"Why, *ye'll* simply have t' ask *him!*"

Now the look was pure shock. "Maire," she began in a low voice, "I knew you Irish were a bit fey—"

Maire laughed. "Fey, is it?" It sounded like a challenge.

"All right, *mad*, then!"

The laughter died, but the warmth was still in the Irishwoman's eyes. "D'ye love him, lass?" she queried gently.

Christmas grew very still. In her mind's eye she saw Jamie in a dozen different moments . . . Now he was meeting her eyes, telling her how their color changed . . . now he held her as she sobbed out her grief for her lost parents . . . now he was above her in firelight, his face taut with longing . . . and, finally, she fastened on the days they'd spent estranged, that terrible time, when she'd felt as if something had been uprooted inside her, the aching sense of loss that only went away when he'd taken her in his arms again, in the cave.

Finally, she focused again on Maire's face. "Yes," she said simply, "I love him."

Maire grinned at her. "Then ye'd better ask him t' wed ye, I'm thinkin'."

"Maire, I don't know whether—"

"Whether he loves ye?"

Swallowing the lump that had suddenly lodged in her

throat, Christmas nodded, not meeting the Irishwoman's eyes.

But Maire was undaunted. "Ach, but Christmas, lass, tell me ye've not seen the way the man looks at ye when ye enter a room! And I can tell ye how he looks at ye when he knows ye're not watchin'—like a starvin' man set before a feast! Aye! Don't look at me as if ye think me daft again! 'Tis true, I'm tellin' ye!"

"But—"

"No buts! Consider anither kind o' madness we've been witnessin', lass. D'ye recall Jamie's own madness, his smashin' one fine piece o' sculpture after anither? And didn't it reach its peak when the two o' ye had a fallin' out recently?" she added shrewdly.

There was a sudden alertness in the gray eyes.

"Aye, I can see ye do recall it. None of us could understand what possessed the man. But now 'tis all beginnin' t' come t'gither, I'm thinkin'. I've heard tell, a man's passion fer his art can sometimes be a reflection o' his deeper emotions. There was an old poet I knew as a child, in Ulster—"

"Maire!" Christmas broke in excitedly. "Are you saying that Jamie—"

"I'm sayin' 'tis a likelihood, *macushla* . . . a likelihood—that's all. But how are ye t' know, if ye don't pursue it?"

Slowly, Christmas nodded, but still looked uncertain, producing a deep sigh from Maire.

"Ach, lass, I've known ye all yer life, and the love I bear ye couldn't be greater if I'd birthed ye meself. Yet, I cannot tell ye what t' do. 'Tis glad I am, ye've decided t' break with Lord Aaron, though ye'll recall I niver urged ye to it. Ye had t' come to it yerself.

"Well, darlin'," she went on, " 'tis the same in this matter. I cannot *tell* ye what t' do, but I can say what *I'd* do in yer place—I'd *ask* him!"

Christmas looked into the dark, honest eyes and felt all

protests die. Slowly a smile began to form. "Maire," she whispered, "you're as fey as a leprechaun, but I love you."

Maire's response was a grumpily muttered imprecation —in Gaelic—and Christmas giggled. When the giggle became a bubbling eruption of laughter, Christmas put her arm about the older woman's waist and gave her a squeeze.

"You know, Maire," she teased as they hugged, "perhaps I shall take you up on your fey suggestion—but I've never so much as asked a man to go for a walk before. I daresay the concept of proposing marriage, by comparison, seems a bit . . . daunting!"

Maire chuckled and gave her a final squeeze before they resumed walking. Then she said, "Before ye begin composin' some dauntin' proposal, lass, I suggest ye first consider mendin' a fence that's been broken. I didn't like the look on yer Jamie's face when he learned who his lordship was!"

When they reached the croft, Jamie and Jacques were already digging, and Christmas breathed a sigh of relief. If Jamie was still this energetically involved in helping her search for the treasure, he couldn't have been too put off by Aaron's suddenly turning up, she reasoned.

But Maire's cautioning words on the path still weighed heavily in her mind. She realized she hadn't given Jamie's reaction adequate thought the night before, what with having to deal with Aaron and the like—not to mention her decision to break her engagement.

But now, as the two women rounded the corner of the stable and Jacques laughed and swept Maire off her feet in a welcoming embrace, Christmas's concern grew: Jamie didn't even pause to look at her; he just kept digging.

Maire seemed aware of this as well; after her exchange with Jacques, she glanced thoughtfully at Jamie's back as he worked. Then she gave Christmas's arm an encouraging squeeze.

"Jacques, darlin'," she said to the Frenchman, " 'tis pleased I am, ye're after diggin' so early, but ye cannot have had a proper breakfast, just the two o' ye. Come with me t' the cottage and I'll fix a bite fer ye t' help me carry back here."

A momentary look of bemusement crossed Beaumonde's face at her suggestion of this odd arrangement. But then he caught Christmas's troubled glance darting in Jamie's direction; he nodded, touched Christmas lightly on the shoulder with an encouraging smile, and joined Maire, who was already heading for the cottage.

Christmas chewed her bottom lip as she watched Jamie exchange the spade he'd been using for a pickaxe. He still hadn't said a word or even turned to acknowledge her presence.

Wondering how to begin, she watched the flexing and contracting of muscles across his broad back and shoulders, easily visible beneath the thin muslin shirt he wore. Then her eyes focused on the brown, muscular forearms revealed by sleeves he'd rolled to his elbows; she saw their corded strength, watched the glint of sunlight on the blond hairs covering the bronzed skin. She shivered, remembering the feel of them as he'd held her in passion.

Closing her eyes in wordless prayer, she forced words out of a throat suddenly gone dry. "Good—good morning, Jamie."

Jamie paused, pickaxe suspended; then he lowered it to the pile of rubble beside him. "Is it?" He still hadn't turned to look at her.

Christmas swallowed around a knot that seemed to be constricting her throat. "I—yes . . . a good morning . . . for—for apologizing and—and rearranging my future. You see"—she took a deep breath—"I've decided to break my engagement to Aaron—that man you met last—"

"Why tell me?" The words were uttered stiffly as he turned to face her.

Christmas nearly flinched at the remoteness in his eyes. "Well, I—because—"

"You really needn't trouble yourself with explanations, m'lady. You certainly don't owe me any for—"

At that instant the sound of heavy hooves resounded, and a loud voice bellowed from the yard. *"Beaumonde! Are ye aboot? Hoot, mon, I've fetched the hounds I promised!"*

"Christ!" Jamie swore, throwing aside the pickaxe. "It's MacTavish! Quick, run out and try to keep him where he is while I try to camouflage these stairs!"

Christmas hesitated, her mind still caught up in the words that had been passing between the two of them.

"Dammit, woman, don't just stand there!" Jamie growled as he reached for the huge swathe of canvas that had once draped a block of marble in the shed and began dragging it across the digging site. "That Scot has a nose for opportunity that's bigger than he is! Do you want to provide him with a chance to claim part of any treasure that may be here?"

This and a renewed bellow from MacTavish seemed to jar Christmas out of her indecision. She whirled and ran toward the yard where the voices of several baying hounds had joined the Scot's.

An hour later Maire was declaring it a miracle that the big Highlander had come and gone without discovering what had been taking place behind the stable. And Jacques was declaring it a miracle that the Scot had left him with a "sou to call my own"; pounds poorer, he was now the owner of two more hounds—both female and characterized by MacTavish as "the two bonniest bruid bitches a mon cuid wish fer."

Then the excavation resumed, with the men wielding pickaxe and shovel while Maire and Christmas did what they could to assist. This was not much in the way of physical labor, for the stairwell had grown quite deep, and even the process of heaving the excavated soil and rocks out of the pit required strength which was beyond them.

But the two women kept busy all the same; such digging was "thirsty work," as Maire termed it, and they made numerous trips between the site and the cottage, supplying the men with water and, when they paused for the midday meal, a picnic luncheon of bannocks, cheese, and ale.

As the hours wore on, there was only occasional conversation, and this was supplied almost entirely by Maire and Jacques. The older couple exchanged affectionate banter over cups of water ladled out during work breaks; and during the luncheon shared beneath a pine tree in the yard, they discussed their plans for settling in America once they were wed.

Jamie spoke little beyond an occasional word to Jacques regarding the digging, and this had the effect of silencing Christmas as well. Mutely damning MacTavish's interruption of her exchange with Jamie, she found no renewed opportunity to pursue that conversation, and yet she could think of nothing else. *He's been so distant toward me!*

In fact, his mood could still only be described as distant, although once or twice she caught him looking at her before his eyes quickly shifted elsewhere, and then their look was as enigmatic as his silence. Each time she forced herself to continue the task at hand, with a reminder that a successful conclusion to the treasure hunt ought to be her chief priority at the moment. The wolf was still at the door, after all; without the marriage to Aaron, she would require good financial resources more than ever if she was to get on.

But the final thought that got her through the long afternoon was that Jamie hadn't quit on her; he seemed to work harder than any of them, sweat pouring off his brow and soaking his shirt as he dug and shoveled. Surely, she reasoned, these gargantuan efforts on her behalf were an indication he cared. Weren't they?

Consoling herself with this—and the promise that she would find a time to make things right between them—Christmas managed to endure the day. But it was with no small relief that, late in the afternoon, as she prepared them some tea in the cottage, she heard Maire come dashing in with the news. "They're through!" she exclaimed. "Ach, Christmas, 'tis the most amazin' thing! A door—under all that *dirt!* Hurry! Ye must come out—"

But she got no further as Christmas went flying past her, the teakettle forgotten on the hearth. Maire grumbled something under her breath and took the time to remove it safely from the fire before following her. But secretly she allowed herself a smile; it was the first excitement the lass had shown all day, and she could easily forgive a lapse in the kitchen procedures she'd been preaching to her all these weeks.

The old door was worm-eaten and heavily rusted at its lock and hinges, but it still held; they had a quarter hour's work of prying and hammering at the rusted metal before they succeeded in opening it. But when at last they did, they knew they'd reached the end of their search.

Late afternoon sunlight slanted directly into the aperture, revealing a long, stone-walled chamber lined with row after row of casks, most of them still full of wine. Jacques produced a lantern from the stable, and it didn't take them long to discover, at the rear of the chamber, the large chest secreted behind a false wall of wine bottles —also still full.

After Jacques used a hammer to smash the rusted lock, he stood back and gestured to Christmas with a grin and a sweeping bow. "Ze honor must be yours alone, *ma petite*—and may there be enough to ransom five hundred seadogs and their queens!"

Christmas thanked him in a less than steady voice, then took a deep breath and raised the lid—

There, in an abundance almost too vast to comprehend, lay a glittering array of riches. The first impression was gold, in myriad shapes and sizes, from jewel-encrusted arm bands and rings, to filigreed Renaissance collars, to old coins that had to be ancient doubloons; there were chalices made of it, as well as heavy plate and other tableware, candlesticks and ornate statuary. And everywhere, there were the rainbow hues of precious gemstones; rubies and sapphires, emeralds and pearls, they reflected the light in a symphony of color, now marching along a necklace, now sparkling in a pendant, all winking from a hundred crevasses at once. Brooches, buckles, bracelets—the variety was endless—and it was several minutes before the four who stood there could do anything more than mutely gape in wonder.

Jamie was the first to break the silence. "It looks too heavy for just the two of us to carry as a single load, Jacques. But we'll need to secure it in a safer place."

"*Oui*, if only to keep it out of ze path of *le grand* Scot! Christmas, 'ave you given any thought to how you will transport this treasure?"

Dazedly fingering an octagonal gold coin which she vaguely surmised might be one of those pieces of eight she'd read about somewhere, Christmas didn't hear him, and Jacques had to repeat the question, touching her on the arm to gain her attention.

"*What?*" she replied with a start. "Oh . . . transport it . . . yes, I suppose we shall have to, won't we?"

Maire laughed and gave her shoulder a squeeze. "She's a tad moonstruck at the moment, *macushla*—and small wonder! Come, colleen, we'll allow the lads t' determine what's t' be done here, whilst we repair t' the hearth fer some o' that tea ye were after fixin'."

Still dazed, Christmas allowed herself to be led out of

the cellar while Jacques and Jamie set about following Maire's suggestion.

An hour later found them all gathered about the hearth, enjoying a light supper. Having come out of her stupor in the Irishwoman's sensible presence, Christmas had even helped Maire with the cooking. The men had decided to leave the treasure where they found it for the time being, except for a sapphire ring Jacques had thought to bring Christmas "so you will 'ave something to hold in your hand, to prove to yourself it is real." Using Jamie's canvas, they'd constructed a temporary camouflage of the stairwell by dropping the cloth across the pit, securing it with rocks to hold it in place, and then masking the entire affair with a layer of dead leaves and some of the discarded manure.

"It'll do for tonight," said Jamie when Maire questioned him about the effectiveness of this, "but I'd get some reliable help from the manor to remove it in the morning."

He glanced at Christmas with this, and she nodded, absently accepting from Jacques a refill of the fine madeira they'd taken from the springhouse to celebrate. Sipping the wine without really tasting it, her hand absently fingering the sapphire ring in her pocket, Christmas found her thoughts entirely absorbed with Jamie.

What was in his mind? Was he as conscious of her as she was of him? Although she'd gone through the motions of celebrating—eating and drinking, laughing, even joining in a song Jacques introduced at one point—her entire awareness centered on Jamie. How his hair curled damply over his collar after the swim he'd taken before supper in the nearby stream. How he moved with an easy, almost effortless grace, despite his size. The way his teeth gleamed whitely in the tanned face when he grinned at one of Jacques's jokes.

The remoteness of that morning seemed to have gone, as if crowded out by the near overwhelming event of the treasure's discovery. But she still hadn't a clue as to the nature of the mood that had replaced it. He seemed congenial enough; it was hard not to be in the wake of the euphoria that had claimed all of them this evening. But he had yet to give her any personal signals that went beyond this. And, suddenly, she felt as if she would scream if she went another minute without knowing his mind. She loved him, and even if she learned he didn't care for her in the same way, *she had to know!* It was imperative that she get him to resume their aborted conversation of the morning. But to do that, she had to get him alone. Now, if Maire and Jacques could be persuaded to cooperate . . .

Ten minutes later she had her wish. Maire had seen Christmas's glance and correctly interpreted the plea in her eyes. The older couple had gone for a stroll outside, "enjoyin' the beauty o' the evenin'," as the Irishwoman had put it, and Christmas finally had Jamie to herself.

She glanced at him as the sounds of Maire's and Jacques's voices faded beyond the yard. He had been standing beside the fireplace, sipping his wine, but now he'd set it aside and was adjusting the fire with the poker and a pair of ember tongs.

His back was to her—again.

"Jamie . . ."

She saw him tense, the muscles in his arms and shoulders thrown into rigid relief by the firelight.

"What is it?" he responded all too casually as he set the fireplace tools aside and rose slowly to his feet.

Oh, Jamie, you know what it is! Don't pretend you don't know! "I . . . please, Jamie, we have to talk."

He turned slowly to face her as she stood beside her chair. Only a few feet separated them, and she could see the texture of his skin, the fine, pale lines radiating from the corners of his eyes, where he'd squinted in the sun.

"Do we?" he replied—as offhandedly as if she'd suggested taking tea. And suddenly Christmas couldn't bear it any longer. Her face crumpled, and she swallowed a sob.

"Oh, Jamie . . . please don't shut me out! I don't think I can bear it if you shut me out again!"

Then she did start to cry, and remorse shadowed Jamie's eyes as he closed the distance between them.

"Christmas, don't," he pleaded as he pulled her against him. "Ah, sweetheart, don't cry."

Like a benediction, she felt his arms go around her, but her sobs continued nonetheless. It was as if all the events of the recent weeks and months were crashing in upon her at once . . . the loss of her parents . . . the urgent trip to Scotland with its uncertain goal . . . the chaotic surgings of her emotions since Jamie had entered her life, climaxing with the frightening discovery that she had fallen in love with him—and fast on the heels of that, which still had her reeling, the appearance of the treasure —at the very moment, almost, when it had ceased to be the most important thing in her life.

She began to tell him these things, but the words became incoherent, choked by her sobs. Jamie did what he could to soothe her, murmuring her name and wordless reassurances as he stroked her hair and pressed tender kisses along her brow.

At length she quieted, her sobs dwindling to breathless little gasps and hiccoughs, and finally, a long, watery sigh.

"Better?" Jamie questioned softly as he caught her chin and gently tilted it up to see her face.

His breath caught as she opened her eyes. Huge and brilliant with tears, they shimmered like amethyst pools.

"I love you," she whispered, her eyes more eloquent than her words.

A look of pain flashed across Jamie's face, and he seemed, almost, to wince with it. He took a deep breath, closing his eyes as he released her and stepped away.

"Oh, Christmas . . ." Wearily, he shook his head. "Don't," he went on. "You mustn't love me. I'm not—"

"Mustn't? Don't?" Christmas echoed his words in stunned disbelief. "But, *why?* Is it that you don't—don't care for me? Very well, then, *say* so! And never say I mustn't love you, because even if you don't love me, that doesn't mean—"

"I love you," he broke in raggedly. "I love you more than I've ever loved anyone or anything!"

Christmas hesitated, confused. His words, which should have meant more to her than anything in the world, were accompanied by a look of such anguish, she nearly flinched. Joy fought with doubt in her eyes as she tried to assimilate the contradictory message, but she clung to her only hope and forced a smile.

"Very—very well, then," she offered in a shaky voice. Then, taking a deep, quavery breath, "Will you marry me, Jamie?"

He did wince then, and there was torment in his eyes as he slowly shook his head. "I cannot marry you, Christmas." And then he destroyed her world with a few simple words: "You see, I am already wed."

❖Chapter 18❖

"**A**lready wed?" Christmas's voice was a whisper. She felt her hand tremble as she raised it to swipe at the tears that had hardly begun to dry on her cheeks. "You're . . . *married*?"

Closing his eyes against the raw shock and pain gathering in her face, Jamie nodded stiffly. He began to say something then, but Christmas cut him off.

"And when did you plan to let me know about this, if I hadn't so foolishly precipitated it with my"—she gave a short, brittle laugh—"my silly little proposal? *After* we made love again? Surely not *before*? Or were you simply relieved, last night, to learn of my engagement to Aaron, only to find that relief short-lived because I told you I'd decided—"

"Christmas, *stop* it!" The anguish in his eyes was underscored by the taut lines about his mouth as the words cut across the rising bitterness in her voice. "I know you have every reason to be angry, even to hate me, but—"

"*Hate* you? Oh, I haven't *begun* to hate you—yet! For now, I'm just trying to *understand* you! Trying—trying to understand how you could have led me to believe— *how you could have made love to me*, while all along, you—"

"And how is it so difficult to understand?" he cut in

defensively. "Didn't the same thing happen to you, when you had a *fiancé* waiting back in England?"

Christmas flinched as if she'd been struck, but managed to meet his eyes. *"Touché,"* she murmured in a broken whisper.

"Oh, Christ! Christmas, I—"

She whirled as he reached for her; tears streaming down her face, blurring her vision, she headed for the door. Blindly, she groped for the latch, pushing the door ajar just as Maire and Jacques were returning to the yard. But she was sobbing convulsively by now and didn't see them or hear Maire call to her as she ran from the cottage.

"Christmas!" Maire called again. "What is it, child? What's—?"

"Go after her, *ma chère*," Jacques said to her but his eyes were focused on Jamie, who looked like all the demons of hell had descended on him as he stood in the lighted doorway.

Jacques handed Maire the lantern they'd taken, for it had begun to grow dark, then murmured some words of caution about the trail.

Maire followed his glance, saw Jamie turn and stumble blindly back into the cottage, and nodded, urging Jacques to see to him while she went to Christmas.

Jacques kissed her cheek, murmuring *"Bonne chance, ma chère."* Then he took a deep breath and strode to the cottage.

Jamie was sitting, staring into the fire when he entered. He said nothing when the Frenchman closed the door behind him, nor did he acknowledge Beaumonde's presence when he crossed the room to stand beside Jamie's chair.

Wordlessly, Jacques glanced at the open bottle of madeira, noted it was nearly empty, then strode to the chest where he kept his personal belongings. Opening it, he withdrew the bottle of Scotch whisky he'd coaxed out of

MacTavish with the purchase of the brood bitches and carried it to the bench by the fire.

Only when it was open and two glasses had been generously filled, did he sit down.

"Here, *mon ami,*" he said, handing Jamie one of the tumblers full of Scotch. "And do not talk if you do not wish to, but know I am here to listen if you do."

Mutely, Jamie nodded, accepting the Scotch. He took a deep swallow, ignoring the burning sensation as it found its way down. Then he glanced at the glass, raised it again, and drained it. This time he welcomed the burn, wishing it could blot out the pain of what he'd done. He gestured to Jacques for a refill; if the burn couldn't help, maybe the whisky's numbing propensities could.

Downing the second Scotch, he glanced at the Frenchman's anxious face and sighed. "Are you sure you want to hear this, Beaumonde?"

"If—"

"I know, I know—only if I want to talk about it." Another sigh. "Well, I'm not at all sure I do, my friend."

Jacques nodded, sipping his drink while he watched Jamie pour a third for himself.

"On the other hand," Jamie went on, "you and Maire were just subjected to a scene you shouldn't have had to— No, Beaumonde, no protests! I never meant to inflict my personal problems on anyone, not on good friends like you and Maire, and least of all . . . least of all on Christmas!"

There was silence as Jacques waited for him to continue. Jamie took a sip of his Scotch.

"Tonight," he said with a bitter twist to his lips, "I told Christmas I was married."

"Mon Dieu . . ." It was an incredulous whisper. "I 'ad *no idea* you—"

"Don't trouble yourself over it, Beaumonde. I said I *told* her I was wed . . . I am *not.*"

Jacques gazed at him, speechless, and Jamie gave a bitter laugh before taking another hefty swallow of Scotch.

"Don't you see, Beaumonde? It was the only way I
could think of to force a decent end to it . . . a sharp,
clean break. Painful at first, maybe, but a damn sight
more decent than—than letting her get hooked up with
the likes of me!"

It was Jacques's turn to drain his glass. He was reaching for a refill when Jamie went on.

"Maybe I'd better start from the beginning. You see,
the lie I gave Christmas is only a skewing of the truth
. . . because I *was* married . . ."

Jacques looked up from his drink at this, but Jamie
didn't see him. His gaze was back on the fire.

"Because Desirée—my wife—is dead. I'm a widower . . ."

He went on then to explain, his voice a dull, toneless
rasp.

He'd married, five years before, the daughter of a
wealthy Creole family in New Orleans. Desirée had appeared to be all a man could wish for in a wife: she was
beautiful, graceful, seemed biddable and mild, as were all
young women schooled in the tradition of that elitist,
aristocratic society. In fact, she was such a prize, he'd
wondered at her family's being amenable to a marriage
with an Anglo husband; for the proud Creoles were a
virtually closed society, regarding themselves far above
their American neighbors.

Then, shortly after the wedding, he discovered why
they'd let him have Desirée: she was given to violent fits
of temper that went far beyond what some might call
childish tantrums, which would have been bad enough;
he was afraid Desirée's denoted a mental instability.

To confirm his fears of her mental instability, he angrily
confronted her father. After initial evasions, the man admitted it. Desirée had begun having these rages in her
childhood, but, the father had argued, they'd been infre-

quent and, if she was "handled gently," of short duration. Unfortunately, as Jamie was to learn soon enough, the family's idea of gentle handling had been to pamper and cosset her, doing anything to placate her, at the slightest sign of a disturbance. She became a vain, entirely spoiled creature whom no Creole would accept in marriage.

Jacques nodded agreement. *"Oui.* They could 'ave passed her off to some unsuspecting Creole *gentilhomme,* as they did with you—but after ze truth emerged, they would 'ave 'ad ze man's *famille* to deal with!"

Jamie smiled, but without humor. "As I said, theirs is a very closed society. The deception would have ruined them socially."

He went on to explain how he'd said as much to Desirée's father, and more, with angry words flying back and forth between them. But in the end, Jamie knew he was trapped in an impossible marriage that he would somehow have to live with.

But this soon became even more impossible, because the second difficult truth to come out of their marriage was that Jamie soon realized he'd never loved her. He had been attracted to her, of course, but he suspected his chief motivation had been to cultivate deeper roots at Thousand Oaks and provide himself with heirs from a wife of impeccable background.

Beaumonde nodded again. "It is not unusual, *mon ami.* In fact, most men of property wed for this reason. And for ze fortunate ones, love does come later."

Jamie took another swallow of Scotch and shook his head. "But it did *not* come for me. How *could* it? Desirée was a spoiled, selfish child at the best of times, and at the worst—" He shuddered. "She once took a riding whip to a house slave—her personal maid who came with her as part of her dowry—for failing to do her hair to her liking. The girl was half dead before my overseer stepped in and stopped it—I was away on campaign at the time—and before he did, she lay *his* face open to the bone . . . When I returned and learned about it, I emancipated all my slaves and retained only those who knew the score and wished to stay on for pay."

"*Sacrebleu!* It must 'ave cost you—"

"It did. But I could afford it. What I couldn't afford was the terrible responsibility for—the guilt, I should say —for the kinds of things she— Christ, Beaumonde! That poor slave was permanently crippled from that whipping!"

Jacques closed his eyes, shuddering.

"But the worst of—the real guilt," Jamie went on, "was yet to come . . ."

He went on to explain that Desirée quickly began to realize her husband didn't love her, and that this became the source of more rages. He had, early on, become an infrequent visitor to her bed, where she'd been cold and unresponsive from the outset, on the wedding night. This had prompted the first of the accusations that he didn't love her, the rages that made his stays at home a living hell. He began to spend more and more time away with the militia, even when he didn't need to.

"And then one night, on one of my rare appearances at Thousand Oaks, I'm afraid I got very drunk . . ."

Involuntarily, Jacques glanced at the glass in Jamie's hand; Jamie caught the glance, nodded with a rueful smile, and set the glass away from him. Then he went on to describe how another violent scene ensued, with Desirée continuing to accuse him of not bedding her as proof that he didn't love her.

". . . and largely because I'd been drinking, and partly because I was willing to do almost anything to shut her up," Jamie explained in a tone of self-disgust, "I took her, and none too gently."

Jacques nodded, sadly, this time. "And so ze guilt you spoke of."

"Part of it, yes. But by no means all of it, Beaumonde. *Oh, no.* The worst guilt came *after!*"

And as Jacques listened with increasing horror, Jamie went on to tell him of the child that was conceived that night—a child he hadn't wanted, not only because he couldn't love its mother, but because, from the moment Desirée told him she was pregnant, all he could think of was how it had been conceived.

"And neither did Desirée want it," Jamie said. "She raged against our poor, unborn child as much as she raged against me. She loathed being pregnant—hated the thought of losing her figure, swore she was too delicate to endure the rigors of childbirth.

"And then, Beaumonde—then one night at headquarters, a message came . . ." Jamie's eyes were bleak as they moved from the fire to Jacques. "Desirée was dead —of a self-inflicted abortion."

"Mon Dieu," Jacques breathed in a strained whisper. *"Mon Dieu!"*

Maire's eyes were troubled as she scanned Christmas's pinched, tired-looking face. "Are ye certain this is what ye wish, *macushla?*"

Christmas cast a final glance at the portmanteau they'd packed, closed it, and nodded.

They were in her bedchamber at MacKenzie Manor, and this was goodbye. She was sending Maire back to Jacques, and to the croft, to oversee the handling of the treasure and its transfer to London. Coates and Tuppers and a pair of trustworthy footmen would accompany her and manage the physical work as well as provide security; she'd already spoken to Coates, and he and Tuppers were armed, as they had been for the trip from England (although she hadn't known about that until a blushing Coates had informed her of it this morning, when she'd explained the need for guards on this journey). But Christmas knew it wasn't the treasure Maire was asking about, nor even the fact that they were parting—a separation, difficult as it was, had been inevitable from the moment Maire had decided to marry Jacques. So Christmas knew Maire had been asking about her decision to leave immediately for England—and to marry Aaron.

"You'll say goodbye to Jacques for me?" Christmas asked, fighting back tears that threatened in this preamble to their own parting. "And explain why—why I couldn't—"

"Sure and there's naught to explain, lass. Haven't ye written it all in this fine letter?" Maire's eyes glistened as she patted a pocket of her pelisse. It held a letter which not only begged Jacques to understand Christmas's reasons for not returning to the croft to say goodbye, but which instructed him to retain a quarter of the treasure (she told him she thought a man who'd served Laffite would be able to calculate this) as her wedding gift to him and Maire.

"How can we iver thank ye, colleen?" The Irishwoman tried to blink back her tears, then gave up, mumbling a watery imprecation in Gaelic as she caught the younger woman to her breast in a fierce hug.

"It's I who should be thanking you, darling Maire. You've been like a second mother to me, and I thank God I've had you this long. But I—I'm a big girl now, and we —we always knew this time would come, didn't we?"

Christmas tried desperately not to cry, fearing that once the floodgates opened, there'd be no stopping her tears. She'd fought valiantly against the sobs that had claimed her last night and had ultimately succeeded, with Maire's help, before they'd reached the manor house— and Aaron. Not only had his lordship informed her—ages ago, it seemed now, back in London—that he despised tears in a woman and was glad she was "so sensible as not to indulge in such histrionics"; but she had been determined that Aaron should learn nothing of what had transpired to cause those tears. *And what will you do on the wedding night, to conceal the fact that you're no longer an innocent?* a small voice niggled, but she thrust it aside. *Time enough to deal with that when I must.*

The practical nature of this final thought served to strengthen her resolve not to bend to her emotions now, and she even managed a smile when the two women disengaged and she patted Maire's hand. "Just write to me as often as you can, dear Maire—sheets and sheets—and be sure to include every detail of your wedding! And I—I shall do the same, of course."

Maire nodded, wondering if they would ever correspond about the things Christmas *hadn't* shared last night. By this Maire did not mean the shocking news that Jamie MacIver was married; the lass had told her that much—sobbed it out on Maire's bosom when she'd caught up with her on the path. But the lass had refused to elaborate beyond the basic details of what he'd told her, on what she surely regarded as a betrayal.

Maire sighed.

"Never think you must worry about my wedding plans, Maire," Christmas chided. "It won't occur all that soon, given the fact that I am in mourning, so perhaps you and Jacques can attend."

Maire had her doubts about his lordship wanting the likes of a former servant and an ex-pirate at his high *ton* wedding, but she held her tongue. The lass was doing a brave job of trying to master the hurt that was likely threatening to tear her apart inside, although she couldn't succeed in keeping an old hand like Maire from seeing the shadows in her eyes. For Maire felt the least she could do was refrain from adding to her burden by citing the shortcomings of her future husband.

And pray to all the saints that the lass would come to see them for herself—in time to cry off the frosty Sassenach for good!

They finally parted, outside on the drive. They were dry-eyed and formal, since Aaron was present. His lordship, who was noticeably quiet, had a smug look of satisfaction on his face; Christmas had handed him the antique sapphire ring earlier that morning, as evidence of the treasure that constituted her maternal inheritance and she knew this had gone a long way toward producing that look—she was once again, in his eyes, a desirable heiress.

Then Maire left for the croft, accompanied by Coates and his capable escort. And Lady Christina St. John, still dry-eyed and formal, left for her life as the future marchioness of Beckwith.

There was a time, Jacques thought, when he wouldn't have been able to read Jamie MacIver at all. It was Jamie's long practice at hiding his feelings from the world, of course. He did this so well, even now, that Jacques had to force himself past his hangover from last night to recall the quiet clues that gave MacIver away.

The clues were things he'd manifested in subtle ways when he'd opened up to Jacques last night. And thank *le bon Dieu* he'd at last opened up! Now Jacques understood what was behind all those shadowed looks he'd noticed in his friend since he'd begun to know him. Jamie was a man haunted by guilt. And betrayal. And if someone didn't help him free himself, Jacques feared the worst.

He feared Jamie would destroy himself.

Jacques gritted his teeth against the throbbing pain in his head and forced himself to concentrate on Jamie's movements as he went about the cottage, packing his belongings. He noted the grim face, blue eyes shuttered to reveal nothing. But he also saw how Jamie's fists clenched and unclenched from time to time; he saw the way he ran his hand haphazardly through his hair now and again; he saw the telltale tic of facial muscles along the square jaw. All these signs, he'd shown last night, and the night before, when he'd spoken of the father he believed to be a coward; all were indications of pain he worked desperately to conceal.

Jacques cleared his throat and winced at the increased throbbing in his skull, but he went on to address Jamie. "Are you certain you wish to leave, *mon ami*? You might achieve something with your sculpting if you 'ave ze croft to yourself."

Jamie paused in the act of gathering some toiletries. "I'm done with the sculpting, Beaumonde." The muscle along his jaw jumped as he went back to packing.

Jacques nodded, then groaned when his skull rebelled with greater force.

Jamie glanced at him, amusement warring with sympathy in the look. "Believe it or not, there's a little *aqua vitae* left in that bottle. You might try some 'hair o' the dog.' "

Jacques held his head with one hand and waved off the suggestion with the other. "Is that what you used? *Your* head appears to be intact, and you consumed ze lion's share, *vraiment.*"

Jamie gave him a sardonic grin. "My ancestors *invented* Scotch whisky, Beaumonde. And I suspect we Scots simply have harder heads than the rest of the world."

And hard hearts? Jacques was thinking of the sobbing figure running from the croft the evening before.

"But in truth," Jamie went on as he resumed packing, "I got up before dawn and took a curative plunge in the creek."

"Sacrebleu! That creek, she is liquid ice!"

Jamie chuckled. "It got the blood going. And I have some hard traveling ahead of me today."

Jacques sighed. "I wish you did not, *mon ami.* I fear it is a mistake, as I tried to tell you last night."

Jamie had grown very still, his back to the Frenchman, hands frozen on the razor strop he held.

"Sometimes it is a mistake to run from our demons, Jamie. They 'ave a way of . . . following."

Jamie slowly turned to face him. "Is that what you see me doing? Running?" The blue eyes were glacial, and Jacques dropped his glance, noting the whiteness of Jamie's knuckles as he clenched his hands into fists. His eyes went back to Jamie's and met them for a long assessing moment before he replied.

"I will not lie to you, Jamie. *Oui*, I believe you are, because— *Non*, do not ask me this, believing me your friend, if you do not wish to hear ze truth."

Jamie looked as if he wanted to argue, then gave a jerky nod of assent.

"*C'est bien*," Jacques murmured, "for I regard you as a friend as well, as you must know." He started to rise from the bed where he'd been sitting, grimaced, and reached for a glass of water on a stand beside the bed instead. When he'd drained it, he went on.

"I 'ave thought about this, *mon ami*, and here is what I concluded: you joined ze *militaire*, where you performed with valor—*where you never ran from any danger*—because you thought to escape—to *run* from, *oui*—ze demon of your youth. And this demon 'ad two heads—ze first was ze betrayal you saw in your father's weakness; ze second, ze guilt you felt for it yourself . . ."

Jacques waited, thinking to hear a denial, but Jamie said nothing, merely gazing at the Frenchman in stony-faced silence. Jacques went on.

"I do not know if you were successful in outrunning that beast, but I suspect not. Ze night you discovered Christmas was betrothed, ze beast was there, between us and ze whisky bottle, rearing its ugly head."

Jacques poured himself another glass of water from the pitcher beside the glass he'd emptied, took a swallow, and continued. "But no matter. Because a second devil 'ad entered your life, and it 'ad ze same two heads. Here ze betrayal came in ze form of a wife you could never love—

who was not what you 'ad supposed her to be—and ze guilt . . .''

He threw a sharp glance at Jamie, who speared him with one of his own.

"I told you how the child was conceived, Beaumonde." Jamie's voice was bitterly accusing, although Jacques wasn't sure if the accusation was directed at him or Jamie himself. Both, he suspected. "So now you can give yourself a pat on the back, Beaumonde. Your neat little allegory of two-headed demons fits. My congratulations."

Jacques ignored the biting sarcasm and went on as if he hadn't heard it. "Perhaps," he said, "but I suspect it goes deeper."

"Really? *Do* tell! I am all ears!"

Jacques ignored this, too. "I suspect your real guilt comes of not wanting zat child any more than you wanted Desirée. You feared an attachment to any—"

"You're crazy, Beaumonde! I told you how she was! How *could* I form an attach—"

"*C'est vrai.* Desirée was beyond loving." Here Jacques leaned forward, his dark eyes penetrating, but not unkind. "But Christmas is not. Yet you run from an attachment with this woman, too—even resorting to a monumental untruth, which is so totally unlike you, it is absurd, to make sure she will not try to follow you when you do your running!"

Jamie continued to face him, white-lipped and silent, but there was denial in his eyes.

"Ah, *mon ami*, listen to me, for I know something of running from demons . . ."

He went on then to tell him of the father he'd never known, and of the rage that had driven him much of his life because of this, until the final escape he'd sought with Laffite's band.

". . . I was fairly certain I 'ad outrun my demon-rage on Barataria, Jamie. Until one night, shortly before you and I met. It was during a boarding—ze last act of piracy I took part in, as it turned out. An effete-looking Frenchman was somewhat reluctant to part with his valuables. He looked ze part of an aristocrat . . . ze kind of creature I 'ad always pictured my sire to be . . . accoutered in velvet and fine lace . . . disdain in every look and movement . . .

"And so, in a violent surge of rage, I killed ze man." Jacques sighed. "It was ze only time I ever killed while I was with Laffite. Ze poor *bâtard* was unarmed and totally defenseless."

Jacques shook his head, a sad, rueful gesture. "But zat was not ze final triumph of my demon before I found ze courage to face it. Zat came later that night, when I 'ad to face Jean and try to explain my wanton act. I learned from Laffite that ze man I killed was no aristocrat at all, but an *actor!* A poor traveling player who liked to act and dress ze part of ze roles he portrayed—no more. Not an aristocrat, but a poor man, like myself . . ." Jacques shook his head again, the gesture still sad, but with a look of tired wisdom to it.

"Like the prince who killed his hound," Jamie murmured.

Jacques shook his head. "Not quite, for you see, I am 'ere to smile again.

"That was ze day I made my decision to leave," he went on. "Ze war with ze British merely postponed it, for I owed Jean that much. But I 'ad met my beast and recognized him. I was done with running. I was done with my rage, as well. Once I faced how it nearly destroyed me, it no longer 'ad power over me."

There was a heavy silence while Jamie digested his words. "You think my . . . demons will destroy me in the same way—is that it?"

Jacques held his gaze without flinching. "I fear it . . . *oui.*"

Jamie started to say something, then gave a curt, dismissive gesture. "How the hell can you be so sure you exorcised your own demon, Beaumonde? For all you know, it could be crouched there on your shoulder, ready to make you shoot one of your hounds—whatever!"

Jacques smiled, shaking his head in absolute denial. "You are wrong, Jamie. For if it still lurked, I could never 'ave come to love Maire as I do. *Never.*"

Jamie looked at him for a silent moment, then pivoted and, without a word, left the cottage.

But Jacques saw the regret in his eyes as he passed.

❖Chapter 19❖

Lady Christina St. John paced the length of the Aubusson carpet in her sitting room and back again. Betty, the new ladies' maid, dropped a quick curtsy, which was ignored. Bewilderment on her freckled face, the maid beat a hasty retreat from the chamber. Christina was aware of her unseemly display of agitation, yet she was too irked to try to control it. In one hand she held the folded letter the maid had just handed her; it was, in part, responsible for her irritation. She tapped it furiously against the open palm of her other hand as she continued to pace.

It was bad enough that, in the fortnight since her return to London, she'd had to fob off Aaron's constant urgings to attend various social functions. She'd thought her reminder that she was in mourning quite enough to relieve such pressure. But he'd merely tailored his urgings to suit: they really must attend Lady Melbourne's ball, where she needn't actually dance, for example; or they would naturally avoid the theatre, but she ought to accept the Prince Regent's invitation to dine at Carlton House.

It was really the outside of enough! Attend a ball when she couldn't dance? Dine with the Prince Regent in his glittering private palace, where the very limits of excess were stretched? When she could wear only unadorned black and must not be seen to laugh or even smile too often? It would not answer!

But Aaron simply wouldn't quit. Now that he was assured her dowry would come to him intact, m'lord had begun to assume he had total control over how she conducted her affairs.

He was beginning to act like a husband.

And the latest addition to this behavior was this—this insufferable missive which had just arrived by the morning post! In it, his lordship not only reiterated an objection, which he'd first voiced days ago, to her current way of life: "It is not proper for an unwed young woman to live alone, Christina!" But he also now informed her of steps he'd taken to remedy that impropriety: "I have therefore engaged to have my mother's cousin, a maiden lady of mature years, join you as a live-in companion until the wedding. Lady Arabella Arbuthnot will be arriving in London in a few days, from her home in Bath. I shall apprise you of the particulars regarding exact day and time of arrival, when I am able, and escort her to your home shortly thereafter."

Christina mouthed an indelicate oath and crushed the letter in her fist. Install some withered old drybones in her home, would he? She'd see about that! Aaron had much to learn about her willingness to be led by the nose in these matters. He was not her husband yet! And even when he was, she could not allow him such autocratic control over her.

Somehow, she must make him see she was not some brainless young twit—the sort of empty-headed female she'd observed paraded about London's drawing rooms and assemblies when she'd come out for her Season.

To begin, dear Mama and Papa had raised her to use the brains she'd been born with. But beyond that, the weeks she'd spent in Scotland had given her a feeling of independence far in excess of anything she'd heretofore experienced. Even those painstakingly acquired domestic skills she'd learned from Maire had contributed to this, and—

Christina paused in her pacing, a bittersweet smile on her lips. An image came, of being stuck upside down in a rain barrel while Maire pulled her out, of Maire's laughter, and then her own joining in . . . *Maire* . . .

For the hundredth time since leaving the Highlands, Christina swallowed tears that threatened when she thought of the Irishwoman. Maire, who'd always been there for her . . . Where was she now? Were she and Jacques married yet? Most likely they were, although a fortnight was too soon to have received word, the mails being what they were.

She knew, too, that the couple had discussed traveling to Ireland to visit some of Maire's family before taking ship for America. Were they there now? Were they happy?

This last question brought the tears she'd been trying to avoid. Christina blinked hard to stem the flow, then forced her attention back to the crumpled letter in her fist. Anger, she knew, was a safer emotion at times like this; it could be used as a bulwark against pain.

She took a deep, settling breath, exhaled slowly, and marched to the delicate marquetry escritoire near the windows. One of the pair of double windows was partly ajar, and she could hear birdsong outside. Her eyes went to the lush foliage of early autumn in the garden below before she tore them away and sat at the writing desk. A contemptuous glance fell on the wad of crinkled foolscap in her hand, and she pitched it into the dustbin beside the desk. Then she reached for the feathered quill beside a porcelain inkstand to her right.

But before she could dip the quill in the ink, she paused, biting her lower lip in thought. Was she making a mistake not to accede to Aaron's wishes in this case? Instead of avoiding society, should she be encouraging it? Her period of mourning notwithstanding, she knew she could immerse herself in other people's company if she so chose. Yet her return home had been marked by a self-imposed seclusion. She had, in fact, enjoyed being alone. Welcomed it.

Or had she?

Aaron had been fastidiously careful of her reputation while escorting her home to England. When they'd stayed in inns and other lodgings, he'd always taken a room far from hers, setting Coates or Tuppers outside her door to guard it all night as well. Or, when public lodgings hadn't been available, he'd deliberately slept with the servants, in haylofts or the like, to safeguard her against any possibility of rumors that they'd had access to each other, since she traveled without a female companion.

And yet, she'd caught him looking at her now and then, with something less than decorous intent: Aaron was not above lusting for her. She knew, as well as she knew what those glances implied, that he would not hesitate to compromise her virtue before the wedding, as long as her reputation were not compromised as well. If he could contrive, here on his home turf, to get her alone with him in such a way that there would be no risk of impropriety, she had not doubt that he would do so.

Therefore, she made herself admit now, she'd been avoiding him. Because the slightest thought of intimacy with M'lord Ice had become distinctly unpleasant to her. Yet she knew she had to overcome this aversion somehow. *They were to be wed as quickly as the protocol for mourners would allow!*

Unbidden, an image of Jamie MacIver came to her, his eyes ablaze with passion. Christina gasped at the sweet stab of pleasure this sent to the place below her belly. This was the first time it had happened in daylight, where she'd thought she was free of the tyranny of her dreams.

For dream of him, she had, almost nightly since her abrupt departure from MacKenzie Manor. The first time it had happened, in a narrow bed belonging to a crofter's

daughter, she'd awakened to a shaft of longing so piercing in its intensity, she'd cried aloud with it. The girl
whose bed she occupied slept in the chamber, sharing a
bed with a younger sister, and had awakened to ask her
what was amiss. Though Christmas had managed to pretend sleep, she'd lain awake for hours afterward, her face
wet with tears.

Oh, Jamie, why can't I let you go?

The pain of his betrayal was, in fact, still as raw as the
night she'd run from the croft. It was merely that this
marked the first time Christina was forced to admit it.

Unwillingly, she found her gaze drawn to the garden
outside the windows. The sun shone brightly on her
mother's late-blooming roses, from a sky remarkably free
of the soot that normally poured from London's chimney
pots. *Brightly and cruelly,* she thought. She didn't want
to be there, gazing at those roses that were so heart-
stoppingly lovely, while, far away in a country church-
yard, the woman who'd planted them lay buried. She
didn't want to contemplate such loveliness while, somewhere, a man walked—perhaps embraced his wife—who
still had the power to haunt her dreams.

And now, her waking hours as well.

Damnation! There must be some way to rid her mind
of him! And her heart!

Setting her small jaw at a stubborn tilt, Christina
quickly grabbed a sheet of blank foolscap from a pile on
the desktop. She would write to Aaron, telling him she
would accept certain carefully chosen invitations for the
two of them. Of course it meant giving up her solitude,
but if she filled her days and nights with the company of
others, perhaps she would be too busy, too tired even, to
succumb to traitorous thoughts.

She dipped her quill in the ink, raised it, then had to
clamp a hand over the foolscap when a breeze from the
window threatened to carry it aloft.

The breeze carried the scent of roses.

With a broken cry, Christina flung the quill across the room.

In the end, Christina never penned the letter to Aaron. But she spent several difficult days and nights questioning whether she should or shouldn't capitulate; giving in to Aaron's wishes would, after all, make it ever so much easier to get on with him. It was only the advent, three days later, of a fortuitous arrival at her town house which saved her from giving in to these urgings.

It happened in the late afternoon when she was taking tea. Alone. The elderly Lady Arabella had not yet made an appearance, for which Christina thanked Providence; albeit she had begun to blame Providence, as well, for not providing her with an adequate excuse for refusing that unwanted guest entirely.

She was sitting in the smaller drawing room downstairs when she heard a commotion in the hall, beyond the closed doors. A moment later, Townsend, the unflappable majordomo who'd served the family for over a dozen years, appeared in the doorway. He did not look unflappable.

"Good heavens, Townsend, what is it?" She hastily set down the teapot, taking in his disheveled clothing and the wild look in his eyes.

Townsend gathered himself into a semblance of dignity with obvious effort. "A highly irregular, ah, a most unusual . . . delivery for you, milady."

He glanced apprehensively over his shoulder as he spoke, all the while clutching both doors as if he were guarding them.

"A delivery?" Christina tried to think of something she'd ordered, beyond the usual household necessities, for these were her housekeeper's domain. She hardly thought Townsend would trouble her about such. But she'd done no shopping since returning to London, nor had she ordered anything that would necessitate a delivery. "A gift, do you mean?" she questioned more carefully.

Townsend turned suddenly at a renewed commotion in the hall behind him. When he turned back to face her, she saw that the wild look had returned to his eyes. "It—it would seem so, milady."

With this, a loud male voice called out from behind him: "Faith, sorr, if ye could be after hurryin' a bit, we'd be iver so grateful. The lad, here, is a youngster and lacks the patience t' wait, ye understand."

Christina's eyes widened at these accents which reminded her instantly of Maire. But a loud, familiar bark had her jumping to her feet.

"O'Kelly?" she cried, running toward the doors.

There was an answering bark, and Townsend had just enough presence of mind to leap aside as the doors swung wide, and a huge, shaggy form bounded up to her.

"O'Kelly! Oh, O'Kelly, it *is* you!" Christina's voice rang with laughter and tears as she bent to embrace the great hound. And "great" was exactly the word that came to mind as the wolfhound licked her cheek in joyous greeting; O'Kelly, she realized, was now larger than she was!

In fact, she thought as she straightened to see Townsend approach hesitantly, he was nearly as large as the majordomo, who was not a small man!

"It's quite all right, Townsend," she said. "This dog is welcome. He's infinitely gentle."

The look on Townsend's face as he made a pass at brushing dog hair from his sleeve suggested he might argue with her. Instead, he nodded deferentially while the figure who'd come up behind him claimed Christina's attention.

"A thousand pardons fer intrudin' on ye this way without warnin', me lady, but as yer man discovered, there was no holdin' the lad back, once he had the scent o' ye."

Christina blinked at the figure who now executed a

gracious bow, her stab of disappointment that the hound had not been accompanied by Maire or Jacques giving way to open curiosity. He was tall and lanky, with a full head of silver hair and a neatly trimmed beard to match. As he straightened, she had time to note merry blue eyes in a tanned, weather-beaten face before the full impact of his sober black attire hit: the man was a priest!

"Father Liam Killeen, me lady, at yer service." He smiled, handing her a sealed letter. "Although 'Father Liam' will do well enough. Maire said ye weren't one fer great formalities."

"Maire!" Christina exclaimed, recognizing the familiar handwriting on the outside of the letter.

"Me cousin," said the priest.

Christina's eyes flew to his face. "Your *cousin?* Maire's *your cousin?*"

"She is." His eyes twinkled and he gestured at the letter in her hand. "Her very *senior* cousin, as I suspect she's explained in there."

Christina glanced at the letter, anxious to read every line, but courtesy demanded its deferment. "Father Liam, I was about to take tea. Won't you join me?"

The priest accepted with a smile. And while Townsend was sent for tea sandwiches and another cup and saucer, they repaired to the settee where she'd been sitting before he arrived. O'Kelly joined them, stretching contentedly at Christina's feet.

As they sat, Father Liam noted her third quick, but telltale, glance at the letter and chuckled. "Go ahead and read it, lass—oh, me lady. I'd find it difficult t' wait, meself."

Christina gave him a bright, appreciative smile. "Thank you, Father—and 'lass' will answer very nicely. Both it and your brogue remind me fondly of your cousin."

By the time Townsend had replenished the tea tray, she was done reading Maire's letter, which was long, having been crossed over, front and back. Father Liam had waited patiently while she read, responding in kind when she interrupted once, with a chuckle, to comment, "You were right about the explanation that you're older."

But now, having digested it all, she was brimming with added comments—and questions. *"You* married them?"

"I did, on Inishowen. That's a peninsula in the north."

"But Maire never mentioned— How did she know where to find you? Have you a church there?"

"Ach, lass, would that it were possible! But Catholic churches on the Auld Sod are nearly as scarce as snakes, which, as ye may be aware, our good Saint Patrick banished from Erin centuries ago. Truth t' tell, I've spent most o' me adult life in France, where I trained fer me vocation. I ran a home fer orphans there until recently, but the troubles . . ." He shook his head sadly, then paused to sip his tea.

"Troubles?"

"The war, lass. Boney's madness. 'Tis what created most o' the orphans we had, but a year ago we decided the wee ones themselves were no longer safe anywhere on the Continent. So me three assistants—two nuns and a younger priest, and all Irish, by the way—and I managed t' spirit the children out o' the country—"

"You must have had to *smuggle* them out!"

The blue eyes twinkled. "We did. Faith, and ye're a quick one, lass. The only ither person t' pick up on that point so fast was Maire's new husband, and I understand I needn't explain why."

Christina chuckled, recalling the day Maire had, rather hesitantly, told her of Jacques's background. "But do tell me what became of your orphans, Father."

"We each brought a handful home t' live with us— with our obligin' relatives, that is. In my case, 'twas with Maire's two sisters and their families. On Inishowen, d'ye see."

Christina nodded. "So Maire knew you'd gone there and—"

"She'd *hoped* t' find me still there, and as luck would have it, I was, although 'twas close. I was two days away from leavin', but two days was time and enough t' see t' me favorite *young* cousin's weddin'."

"But why would you leave if—"

"I was afraid ye'd be after askin' that." His eyes shifted to O'Kelly at her feet. "I don't suppose 'twould answer t' say 'twas t' deliver himself, there, t' London as their, ah, weddin' gift t' ye?"

"No, because you said you were already planning to leave when they— Their *gift?*"

Father Liam grinned at her while Christina stared, openmouthed, at the wolfhound. "Ye see, Maire knew ye'd grown attached t' the lad, here, and Jacques swore O'Kelly was after missin' ye, as well. And I understand ye're plannin' a weddin' o' yer own?"

Christina paused while embracing the wolfhound and scanned the priest's face. There had been an odd, questioning note in his voice when he mentioned her own wedding plans. She wondered just how much he knew— how much Maire had told him.

She met his gaze. Its canny directness did nothing to dispel her suspicions. Feeling acutely uncomfortable, she shifted the conversation back to safer ground. "You never did say *why* you were leaving, Father Liam."

The priest sighed. "Faith, and ye're a persistent minx, I'm after thinkin'! Very well, then, but ye must promise t' keep it t' yerself, lass."

He leaned forward conspiratorially. Christina's eyes widened with curiosity, and she quickly gave him her promise.

" 'Tis t' fetch more orphans," he said in a low voice.

"Fetch more—"

"Shh! Softly, lass, softly."

She lowered her voice to a stage whisper. "Fetch more orphans! But the war is over now."

"It is, but its devastation is not. Me bishop and I have

been in touch, and we agree that war-torn Europe is not the best place fer the children if a better one can be had."

"But . . ."—she remembered Maire's tales of Irish poverty—"Ireland?"

The cleric shook his head and whispered, "America."

"America? But surely, the cost of—"

"We have certain benefactors, includin' some wealthy Americans." He eyed her archly. "In fact, even a certain newly rich Irishwoman and her bridegroom wish t' help."

Christina smiled. It was just like Maire to use some of her share of the Seadog's Treasure to help others.

"The main problem," said the priest, "will be gettin' the poor children out. Governments, especially shaky new ones such as Talleyrand and his fat Bourbon king have strung t'gither, have a way of impedin' things with piles of official nonsense."

Christina grinned. "So you're going to 'spirit' them out?"

The priest returned the grin. "Ach, lass, as I told ye, ye're a quick one!"

That evening, as she retired to her chamber, Christina had more than one reason to be grateful for Father Liam's visit. The news from the Beaumondes and their gift of the wolfhound headed the list, of course. And in her letter Maire had promised that she and Jacques would be paying Christina a visit before they sailed for America. Welcome news, indeed!

But the unlooked-for bonus had come late in the afternoon, following the priest's departure. To her dismay, a footman arrived bearing a hastily written note from Aaron: the elderly cousin had arrived, it said, and he would be escorting her to Christina's home a couple of hours hence, before it grew dark.

Christina had silently cursed her misfortune, desperately searching for a last-minute way out, even as she penned a brief response to Aaron, telling him she had prepared a guest chamber for the cousin.

But in the end, all this had proved unnecessary. Lady Arabella Arbuthnot had taken one look at O'Kelly and fallen into a paroxysm of sneezing and coughing so fierce, Christina had thought to see her expire on the spot. Aaron had offered to see the hound exiled to the stable (which did nothing to endear him to his betrothed), but Lady Arabella had assured him this would be useless. Her health could not abide her being so much as *near* a room where a canine had been, and even a single dog hair could endanger her. Coughing and wheezing her regrets to Lady Christina, she'd begged Aaron to return her to the marquis's house at once.

Christina smiled now, giving O'Kelly an affectionate pat on the head as she prepared for bed. It had been all she could do to contain her delight at that serendipitous turn of events. Aaron had been quite irritated, of course, and this had delighted her, as well. Send O'Kelly to the stable, would he?

She giggled as she rang for Betty to come and help her undress, then instantly sobered. What would she do if Aaron objected to the hound's presence in the house, once they were wed? O'Kelly had been raised to live with people, and she knew it would be cruel to relegate him to an outside existence. Moreover, she had become inordinately attached to this particular hound, not realizing how attached until Father Liam had arrived with him this afternoon. Aaron would simply have to accept him, and that was that!

Ignoring a small voice that questioned whether it would be that easy, Christina used Betty's arrival as an excuse to put Aaron from her mind. Instead, as the maid helped her prepare for bed, she allowed her thoughts to drift back to Father Liam. She'd found herself liking the priest immensely. Even when her offer of a generous donation to his orphanage had produced a baldfaced, "I was countin' on yer bein' as bighearted as ye are quick-witted, lass!''

Christina closed her eyes while Betty unpinned her hair and began to brush it with slow, soothing strokes. The priest's visit had, indeed, been the brightest light in the weeks since her return. He'd been merry and witty, making her laugh for the first time since—

Her mind shied away from completing the thought, but she found herself dwelling on Father Liam's leave-taking, which had also been disquieting. He'd jotted down an address to which she was to direct her solicitors to send the cheque for her donation; but as he pressed it into her hand, he'd added the following: "I'll be away for at least a fortnight, lass. But if iver ye should need help, ye've but t' send word t' this address. If I cannot come, they will know t' send someone, and whoiver 'tis, 'twill be a friend."

❖Chapter 20❖

In the weeks that followed, Christina found herself deeply grateful for the wolfhound's company. Knowing the young animal required exercise, she made a habit of rising very early in the morning to take a turn about Hyde Park with O'Kelly. The dog ran beside her mare, with Tuppers trotting behind for propriety's sake, although she needn't have worried much about the latter. There was rarely anyone about at that unfashionable hour. The *haut ton* partied late and slept later, parading their fashions about the park only late in the afternoon. But the peaceful solace she derived from these rides was like a balm to soothe her after too many restless nights.

Nights plagued with memories of Jamie.

She wasn't sure why Jamie MacIver's presence should still linger in her memory. It wasn't as if she still loved him. His betrayal had taken care of that. Of course, she'd heard it said that love and hate were closely intertwined; but she couldn't even say she hated him. In the beginning, perhaps, when the pain had been fresh. But after that, she'd felt a kind of numbness settle in. Ever of a practical, sensible turn of mind, for which she had Maire's influence to thank, she supposed this was her mind's way of cushioning shock. After all, hadn't she experienced a similar numbness following the news of her parents' deaths? So, why couldn't she dismiss Jamie entirely? It was a puzzle that continued to annoy her. But, again with a sensible turn of mind, she refused to make too much of this. Time, she decided, would eventually take care of everything. She needed only to be patient, and all would be well.

But then came the morning when she found herself rethinking everything. Awakening just after sunrise, as was her custom since the commencement of those early rides, Christina reached into the bowl of fruit left on a stand beside her bed; the fruit served to break her fast when rising so early, obviating the need to awaken Betty when she preferred to be alone in any case. She made short work of a plum and tossed an apple to O'Kelly, who lay in his customary spot across the room, by the fireplace. The wolfhound loved apples and was devouring this one with gusto when Christina glanced at the mantel clock, deciding it was time to dress.

She had just flung back the covers and swung her legs over the side of the bed when she felt the wave of nausea hit. It came without warning, and she barely had time to reach the washstand in her dressing alcove before retching violently into the basin. Behind her she heard the wolfhound whine as if to ask what was wrong. Closing her eyes against a second spasm, Christina wondered the same thing.

After a couple of minutes, she felt somewhat steadier. She dipped the end of a towel into the pitcher of water on the stand and patted it over her face. She took a deep breath and felt better, still.

After locating the cup she kept for washing her teeth, she rinsed out her mouth, then risked a couple of swallows of water. They stayed down. In fact, she felt perfectly fine now.

Wondering if the plum she'd eaten could have been rotten, she wandered back to the bedside stand and eyed the remaining fruit, then dismissed the idea. The fruit in the bowl looked plump and wholesome, and she knew the piece she'd eaten had been the same.

What, then? Was she coming down with something? But then, why did she feel quite recovered now?

With a shrug, she decided to put the mystery behind her and went to her wardrobe to collect some clothes; she would proceed with her ride as usual, barring any further hints of physical distress as she made her toilette.

It was only when she was reaching for a clean shift in one of the drawers of the highboy that awareness struck. There, among stacks of camisoles and other lacy undergarments, lay the pile of flannel cloths she required during her courses.

Courses which she hadn't experienced since leaving the Highlands.

And she'd left over two months ago.

A stillness settled over her as she digested the implications: *she was breeding.*

She carried Jamie MacIver's child! With this realization came a wild leap of joy. It lasted but a split second, but its impact sent her staggering toward a chair.

There was only one thing to account for that reaction, and now she was forced to face it: she was still in love with him.

Dismayed beyond belief, she found herself on the verge of tears. Angrily biting them back, she cursed herself for being ten times a fool. In love with a married man? It was the most hopeless kind of involvement. And stupid! The world's literature was filled with fools like her. She thought of Tristan falling for the married Iseult and collapsed in a fit of wild giggles. At least Iseult had returned that hopeless love! Jamie MacIver had done nothing but trample hers underfoot. And now she carried his babe.

Christina clamped a sudden hand over her mouth, smothering the hysteria. But she felt panic gathering and looked wildly about for something to distract her. Her glance fell on the green velvet riding habit she'd flung across the bed. Taking a deep breath, forcing herself to stay calm, she got up, deciding to finish dressing. The routine would settle her so she could think. She *must think* what to do!

Calm descended as she put herself together. Seeing her dressed, O'Kelly pestered to be off for their ride; so it wasn't until they were cantering in the Park that she settled on a course of action.

It was not a plan that made her comfortable, but she forced herself to accept it because of the child growing inside her. She must be practical—and strong—for the child's sake!

She saw nothing for it but to pass the child off as Aaron's. The thought left a bitter taste in her mouth. It was the most dishonorable thing she'd ever contemplated, but when she considered the alternatives, she knew there was no recourse. If she bore a child out of wedlock, both she and it would be social pariahs. It would not serve.

But to make Aaron believe the child was his, she would need to bed him—and soon. Even then, she'd have the difficulty of explaining a seven-month babe, but she would deal with that later. She had wealth at her disposal, lots of it, and that meant physicians and midwives could be bribed, if necessary. This consideration left a bitter taste, too, but thoughts of the child rallied her.

So, the thing was to seduce Aaron into— She nearly laughed aloud, catching herself just in time, before alerting Tuppers. But, "seduce"? It was such a ridiculous word for what needed doing! "Succumb," yes. Far more apt. But, dear God, how was she ever going to tolerate—

Stop it! Her voice was a ruthless command in her head. *The same way you would have endured him in the marriage bed, you witless ninnyhammer! With courage!*

Digesting this, she turned her mare's head for home. There was an invitation to dine with Lord and Lady Pomfret on Friday. She and Aaron would attend. Then afterward, she would have him take her for a late stroll in Vauxhall Gardens and allow him to coax her into the privacy of the Dark Walk . . .

But as it turned out, Christina never accepted Lady Pomfret's invitation. When she returned home, Townsend greeted her with the news that she had visitors.

"Oh?" queried Christina. It was still inordinately early for visitors and, more than that, she'd seen no carriage out front.

"I took the liberty of asking them to wait in the blue drawing room, milady." The majordomo actually had the suggestion of a smile on his normally expressionless face, making Christina even more curious.

"Well, for heaven's sake, Townsend! Do not keep me at sixes and sevens! Who—"

She got no further. The double doors to her right swung ajar, and a dearly familiar voice cried, "Christmas!"

"Maire!" Christmas (which name she immediately became again in her mind upon hearing it from the Irishwoman) flung her arms about the dark-haired figure who rushed forward, and the two embraced in a frenzy of laughter and tears.

Behind them, O'Kelly began to whine and bark, his tail thumping furiously as he recognized Maire and asked to be included in the reunion.

"Here, you oversized changeling, let ze ladies be!" said a male voice.

"Jacques!" Christmas kept an arm about Maire's shoulders and turned toward him. "Oh, Jacques, I've missed you both!"

There was more embracing while the wolfhound danced about, as happy as the humans. Christmas sent Townsend for tea and led Maire and Jacques into the drawing room.

"So," she said as they settled in chairs beside the fire, "you were wed in Ireland?"

Maire nodded, looking younger and happier than Christmas had ever seen her. "And ye've met Liam, I take it?"

"Yes, or I shouldn't have known where you married."

"Well, I sent a letter as well, but I might've guessed Liam'd be quicker than the mail."

Christmas laughed, and there was a brief discussion of the priest and his visit. Townsend returned with their tea, and while Christmas poured, they filled her in on their journey.

"And when do you sail for America?" she asked when they were finished. "I do hope you'll have time to spend in London before—"

"Ach, lass! 'Tis sorry we are, but we're off t' Liverpool this evenin'." Maire's tone was full of regret.

"So soon?"

"*Oui, ma chère.* Ze deer hounds have already been sent to ze ship, and she sails tomorrow with ze late tide. Ze journey to London took longer than we expected, you see." Jacques made a helpless gesture with his hands.

Christmas nodded. "Then we must make the most of what time we have." It was as much cheer as she could manage.

There followed a few questions about how the hounds were getting on and such; but Maire had seen the sadness in Christmas's eyes and knew she'd been deeply disappointed that they wouldn't be staying on for a while. The Irishwoman met her husband's eyes, and, as if by some prearranged signal, Jacques asked if they would excuse him while he took a stroll with O'Kelly. Soon he was gone, leaving the two women alone.

"Some privacy for us to talk?" Christmas inquired.

"Ach, ye're a quick one, and no mistake!"

"That's just what your cousin said," Christmas replied.

"And speaking of Father Liam, what, exactly, did you tell him about—"

"He's not wed, lass," Maire interrupted in a quiet voice.

Christmas blinked. "Well, of course he's not wed. Everyone knows a Catholic priest—"

"I mean Jamie MacIver, Christmas. He lied t' ye when he told ye he's wed. He's not. He's a widower."

There was silence, except for the ticking of the mahogany tall-case clock in the corner. Christmas stared at Maire, and when, at last, she spoke, the words were delivered in a toneless whisper.

"Lied to me . . ."

"Ach! I fear I shouldn't have put it so baldly. Ye—"

"And why not? 'Baldly' seems to me an admirably suitable means to describe a *baldfaced lie!*"

Maire watched her become conspicuously involved in pouring tea, but not before she caught a flash of raw pain in the gray eyes.

"Macushla . . ." Maire stilled Christmas's hands, making her set the teapot down. When she took them and held them gently in her own, she noticed they were ice-cold.

"Listen t' me, colleen . . . please?"

Had it been anyone but Maire, Christmas would have told her to stuff it and cap it. But as it was, she merely nodded. She was trying desperately not to succumb to tears at this latest perfidy from the sire of her child.

"I think I know how ye must be feelin', lass. And ye've every right t' be bitter after—after what the man's done. But I also think ye deserve t' know somethin' about what made him do it. Will ye listen?"

Another nod, stiff and mechanical.

Maire sighed. "I hardly know where t' begin. 'Twas Jacques he told, not me, so I may not even have all o' the ins and outs of it. What's more, Jacques wasn't at all sure that tellin' ye wouldn't be a breach o' confidence. We finally solved that by agreein' Jacques would disappear fer a while, so as not t' be a party t' tellin' ye directly, ye see . . ."

She went on then to describe the nature of Jamie Mac-Iver's marriage and how it had ended, sparing nothing in rendering what details she was aware of; neither excusing Jamie nor blaming him, she simply let the facts speak for themselves. Christmas was as quick-minded as they came, she thought as the tale wound down. She'd let her sift through the facts and put two and two together. And pray she arrived at the correct answer.

"Now, then, Maire," Christmas said in a tight voice when she'd finished. "Let me see if I have this correct. After leading me to believe there could be something between us, Jamie MacIver wished to extricate himself without causing me too much pain—ah, *difficulty*. He therefore told me he was already wed—but only after I was arrogant enough to propose marriage to him, of course. Oh, yes, I begin to see how much less . . . *difficult* that would render it. He—"

"Christmas—"

"—must have stayed up nights, I should think, forging such an *honorable* solution to those . . . *difficulties.*"

"Christmas, ye must not—"

It was as if Christmas hadn't heard her. "But Mister MacIver is an *honorable* man, is he not? So *honorable*, in fact, that his act of rescuing me from my, ah, difficulty was created out of whole cloth: a lie. The *honorable* gentleman from America, as it turns out, is not wed after all —yet still *in no danger of becoming so*—at least, to *me!*

"Now, then," she finished with a bright, feral glint in her eyes, "have I got it straight?"

Maire looked at the young woman sitting beside her, the child she'd reared like her own, and hardly knew her. There was a brittle quality about Christmas now, almost as if, should someone touch her, she'd shatter and splinter into a million pieces. It made her seem utterly distant and beyond reach.

Still, Maire had to try.

"Lass . . . Christmas, I know he's hurt ye, but—Ach! This is so *hard!*"

"Well, if it's so hard," Christmas said crisply as she resumed pouring tea, "why pursue it? I fear we've worried the topic to death as it is. Sugar?"

Maire heaved an exasperated sigh. "Do ye still love him, lass?"

Christmas paused, then dropped a single sugar lump into Maire's teacup. "You take one sugar, if I recall, Maire." She handed her the tea.

"I asked ye a question, lass."

"So you did. Well, my answer is"—she picked up her own tea, sipped it—"it does not signify."

"Oh, it signifies well enough!" Maire's voice rose in agitation. "Because if ye love him, ye might be willin' t' see his actions in a different light. Ye might see Jamie MacIver as a man so devastated by betrayals from people he trusted in the past, that he's scared t' death t' commit himself t' someone again. *Scared t' death,* Christmas!"

Christmas paled, but said nothing. Maire went on.

"And if ye can see him that way, and ye still love him, ye'll give yer love a *chance.* I say, *go* t' him, *macushla.* Tell him—"

"Go to him? Where?"

Maire sighed. "He—he's here, in London. Jacques got him to agree t' meet us before we all sailed fer America, though he's t' take a different packet."

Christmas's face went paler still. *Jamie in London. Oh, it would be so easy! To run to him, to tell him of the child, and—*

There was a disturbance at the front door and the familiar sound of O'Kelly's bark outside. Maire quickly rose, threw Christmas a hasty glance, and walked to the heavily draped windows that faced the street.

"What is it?" Christmas queried as Maire pulled the draperies aside to peer out one of the windows.

Maire took a deep breath. This was it. But would it work? " 'Tis Jacques," she said. "He's got Jamie waitin' in a carriage outside."

"Jamie!"

"Niver fear, lass. He has no idea whose home this is. He merely thinks he's doin' us a favor and givin' us a lift t' where the post chaise waits t' take us t' Liverpool."

Two spots of vivid color stood out on Christmas's cheeks. "Has he gone so far as to corrupt *you* with lies, as well, Maire? I'd never have believed it of you!"

"Lies?" Maire looked bewildered.

"The *wolfhound!* Tell me Jamie MacIver doesn't know it's I who live here when he sees O'Kelly, clear as day, accompanying Jacques to my door!"

Maire's face collapsed. "Ach! I niver thought—that is, we didn't realize the hound would—"

"Spare me." Christmas's voice was held tightly in check as she marched across the room; then just as Townsend opened the double doors, she continued into the front hall.

Maire hurried after her. "Please believe me, lass! We niver thought—"

"That's just the trouble, Maire. You *didn't* think! But *I've* thought enough about this entire, wretched situation now, and do you know what I've concluded?"

Without waiting for a reply, she gestured for Townsend to fetch the pelisse he'd taken from Maire when she arrived. The majordomo brought it, and she inclined her head in the direction of the door where O'Kelly could be heard, whimpering to be let in.

As Townsend went to open the door, Christmas turned back to Maire.

"I think I shall say goodbye to you now, Maire. *That* is what I've concluded." There was a suspicious brightness to the gray eyes, but her voice was steady.

"Not in anger, lass, I pray. And *niver* thinkin' I betrayed ye in this matter. 'Twas done merely t' give ye a choice, *macushla*. If ye wished t' see him, ye might. If ye didn't, no one was t' be the wiser, ye see. Am I condemned fer hopin' ye might see some advantage in me good wishes fer ye?"

Christmas read the sincerity in the dark eyes and knew she was telling the truth. Blinking back tears, she embraced her old friend fiercely. "Oh, Maire, you dear, foolish woman! Never say so! I *love you!*"

Maire hugged her back. "I love ye, too, *macushla!*"

O'Kelly bounded in, with Jacques a step behind. There were farewells all around. But when Townsend opened the door for the Beaumondes, Christmas had to make a decision: should she turn on her heel now—and avoid even a glimpse of the man in the carriage? It would be the easiest way, surely. On the other hand, this would likely be her last chance to—

At that moment O'Kelly yipped and dashed past her, to follow Jacques and Maire.

"O'Kelly, stay!" Without thinking, Christmas leaped after the hound, catching up with him just outside the portico, where he'd stopped at her command.

"Good dog," she murmured absently. But her eyes were on the man who stood outside the door to the hackney. Filled with him.

He looked older, somehow. Tired. There was a subtle downward cast to his shoulders, despite the erect, military bearing of his posture. And his attire, immaculate and impeccably correct, from the perfectly fitted shoulders of his coat of dark blue superfine, to his gleaming Hessians, seemed out of joint, somehow. Compared to the casual shirts and buckskins she'd been accustomed to seeing him wear in the Highlands, it was just so . . . different. Not the Jamie she remembered.

He was turned toward the driver, saying something she couldn't hear, and she took advantage of the moment to fix him in her mind. This was the man whose child she carried in her womb. The man who'd given her moments of sweet, mindless passion unlike anything she'd ever imagined or would ever experience again. The man she would live with in bittersweet memory until her dying day—the man who'd betrayed her.

Just then, he turned, saw her, and froze. Their eyes met for a brief, clawing moment in time before Christmas turned, called O'Kelly, and went inside.

❖Chapter 21❖

Jamie MacIver stood beside the hackney and watched as the post chaise took the Beaumondes toward Liverpool. He hoped they weren't still feeling guilty about what they'd done. They'd been so full of embarrassed apologies, he'd felt sorry for them. But, as he'd told them, they should have known it would be a useless effort. Christmas and he had no more to say to each other.

And if they hadn't believed it before their visit, they ought to believe it now. That door closing silently on the black-clad figure and the wolfhound was an eloquent testament to where things stood.

She must truly hate him now. Jacques hadn't said, and he hadn't had the heart to ask him when he was so obviously apologetic, but he rather thought they'd told her about him. Not that it mattered. Adulterer or liar, or both, whichever way she saw him, it was reason enough to hate him.

Better this way, he told himself. Easier to put him behind her and go on with her life. With her marriage to that blue-blooded—

Something too close to pain twisted in his gut and Jamie bit out an obscenity. The driver on the box glanced his way, but Jamie ignored him.

She'd been more beautiful than he could remember,

despite the mourning clothes. In contrast to them, the bright hair shone with remembered fire. Her small, heart-shaped face was pale, yet exquisite, against the funereal black gown. A riding habit, actually. Did she ride here in the city, then? Take a turn about the Park with that fiancé of hers?

The echoing recollection of the man she was to marry had him clenching his jaws. The betrothal was still in effect, he knew. He'd taken the time to inquire at the offices of Carruthers and Higgins. Not that there was any reason why he should have suspected otherwise.

He tried not to think of her living here, in this city that seemed such an alien setting for her. Not when, in his dreams, she was always windblown and tartan-clad, laughing against a backdrop of fierce, craggy peaks and storm-tossed skies. He tried not to think of her sitting sedately on a sidesaddle, atop a well-groomed mount. Or nodding to fellow aristocrats as they promenaded along some manicured garden path. Or—

Christ! Was there no end to it? Why the hell wasn't she behind him by now? He knew there was no room in his life for a woman like Christmas MacKenzie—why couldn't his traitorous thoughts cooperate?

But, just seeing her again, even for that brief moment—

Closing his eyes against more pain, Jamie swore a string of expletives that had the hackney driver staring at him, mouth agape.

Setting his jaw, Jamie flung open the carriage door.

"To the hole," he told the man, referring to the London Pool where his ship waited.

He swung himself into the carriage and slammed the door. The whip cracked, and the hackney lurched, carrying its solitary passenger.

It was going to be a long, lonely voyage.

* * *

Christmas's hands trembled as she opened the letter. What if she'd been mistaken? What if Father Liam's words of assurance had been just that, and no more? A whisper of comfort with no real means of help behind them?

The seal parted and she carried the sheet of foolscap to the lamp beside her bed. Adjusting the wick, she sat down to read.

My lady,

Your name was indeed made known to us by Father Killeen. More than that, we received your generous gift and thank you on behalf of the children it will help, in Our Blessed Lord's name.

As to your present request, rest assured there will be no difficulty. Since you will be so generously paying for the means, we have only to await word from you as to the nature of the transportation you wish us to secure for you. Once we have engaged for it, we shall send word as to its exact cost, await a draught in that amount, and send you the details of time and place of departure by return post.

We hope this is to your satisfaction and look forward to meeting with you soon.

> Yours in Christ,
> Sister Mary Michael
> Christian Sisters of Mercy
> London

Christmas let out the breath she hadn't realized she'd been holding. They were going to do it! They were going to help her get away.

The idea had come to her just after Maire and Jacques left. Just after she'd seen Jamie. She'd shut the door behind her, closing out those reminders of the past, both dear and bitter. Only, it hadn't closed them out. Not entirely.

As she'd turned to face what she now realized was a self-imposed prison—her home in England—she'd suddenly found herself unable to bear it. Asking herself why, she'd been startled by the answer. She was vastly unhappy here. Indeed, she hadn't been happy since her return from the Highlands.

The Highlands, where she'd felt vital and free and alive. More alive than ever before in her life. Even when she hadn't known whether the Seadog's Treasure, with all its lure of financial security and comfort, existed.

The Highlands, where she'd learned to do things with her own two hands and had felt the joy of it. Of knowing she could create something of value, be it a loaf of bread or a cleanly swept floor, that would support her own existence; instead of being a parasite who depended on others for it. Like the well-groomed parasites who moved through the assemblies and drawing rooms of London.

And suddenly she'd known that that was what she wanted desperately to feel again. Wanted the child she carried to feel as it lived and grew to adulthood.

So she'd made her decision: she would return to the Highlands to await the birth. And to live. To feel free and alive again, with her son or daughter at her side. And Aaron Crenshawe, and the *ton*, and lying Americans could all go to the devil!

But she'd quickly realized it wouldn't be easy. Aaron had followed her once, and he could again. And this time he knew what he stood to lose. He would try to talk her out of going unless she accomplished two things: she must make the break clean and permanent, and she must depart in secret.

Well, the latter, it seemed, was now possible. Father Liam's people had just agreed to see her safely out of England and back to Inverness-shire.

All that remained was to break with Aaron. And she

knew just how she would do it, too. Smiling, Christmas laid aside Sister Mary Michael's letter, picked up the lamp and carried it to her escritoire. Setting it down atop the writing table, she seated herself, took a sheet of foolscap, and dipped her quill in the ink.

"Dear Aaron," she wrote. "I fear I have a most distressing piece of news . . ."

Christmas allowed herself to relax as the hackney coach made its way along Piccadilly toward the chapel on South Audley Street. O'Kelly rested on the seat across from her, filling it with his massive size.

Everything was in order. She'd left the town house in Townsend's care, with instructions to dismiss all but a skeleton staff, though only after her letters of reference resulted in new positions for those he let go. Letters had been posted to the housekeepers at her country estates with instructions to follow the same procedures there. All were told she was leaving for an extended visit to America, to be the guest of her good friends, the Beaumondes, exact address to follow later. Her solicitors were to be consulted for any problems which might arise in her absence.

Only those solicitors, Carruthers and Higgins, were apprised of her true destination, and they, she knew, would keep her secret. When she reached MacKenzie Manor, she would write to Maire and Jacques, in care of Jacques's New Orleans solicitors, to let them know what was afoot. She would beg them to keep her secret as well, knowing full well they would. After the debacle in front of her town house that morning, how could they not?

So all was in readiness. She was about to become truly independent for the first time in her life. The thought both exhilarated and frightened her.

As she drew closer to the Roman chapel on South Audley, the two conflicting emotions warred with each other. At one moment she could almost taste the freedom, begin to revel in it. Then, she would feel herself trembling violently when she considered the enormity of what she was doing, and she had to clutch one of the leather carriage straps to steady herself.

Would she truly be able to make a new life for herself and the babe? Would her neighbors in the Highlands accept an unwed mother who was also half English? Or would they make her the social outcast the *ton* was sure to make her, if she stayed?

She wondered, too, if the Highlands would remind her too much of Jamie MacIver, then dismissed the notion. Jamie's unwanted presence in her thoughts and dreams was already a fact; in the Highlands, this could hardly grow worse than it already had, she reasoned, and perhaps things just might improve. There was a healing power in the land of her mother's people; she felt it, without knowing how or why. Now, all she had to do was get there.

It was on this positive note that she arrived at the chapel. Her spirits rose even higher when she saw who awaited her there.

"Father Liam!" she exclaimed when she entered the vestibule and saw the familiar, silver-headed figure. "I had no idea you'd returned!"

The priest came forward to clasp her outstretched hands. "Faith, lass, but I had no idea I'd be here meself. How are ye, me lady?"

"I am well, sir. Or I shall be, as soon as I am under way."

Father Liam gave her a penetrating look, but said nothing. He introduced her to a rotund little nun who entered from a side door at that moment, identifying the Sister Mary Michael of her correspondence.

Then, without further ado, things were set in motion for the journey to Scotland. Sister Mary Michael and the priest were both to accompany her, she learned, along with a pair of big-eyed waifs named Jean-Pierre and Gabrielle-Marie.

The children, both under five years of age, had been found in the ruins of a farmhouse outside Laon. They spoke no English, but their dark, expressive eyes told of the terrible things they'd seen. Christmas's heart went out to them. She had a moment to reflect that her problems were as nothing when compared to some. She then resolved that the next time she found herself sinking into self-pity, she would remember these children and carry on.

And so the journey began. Following much the same route she'd traveled with Maire and her little retinue that summer, they made their way northward, stopping at the very inns she'd used before. The chief difference came later, when the main road dwindled to cart tracks and the trappings of civilization disappeared. Then, instead of the farmsteads and crofts mapped out by Angus MacIver, they rested in preestablished havens friendly to the Church. Sometimes these were clerical quarters attached to actual churches or chapels; sometimes nothing more than lofts in barns, as it had been the first trip; and once their shelter even turned out to be the back room of a village pub.

In fact, it wasn't until they were in this last, a rough public house somewhere just south of the Grampians, that Christmas finally told Father Liam her reasons for leaving England. Of course, she knew he suspected them in part, already. There had been too many mornings when a queasy stomach had forced her to skip her breakfast. She'd passed this off as long as she could by pretending that travel had always had the effect of impairing her morning appetite. But even then she'd glanced at the priest on occasion and found his blue eyes studying her with an expression that was keenly assessing, though never unkind.

But on this particular morning, the aroma of frying

bacon had done more than make her queasy; it had sent her running for the back door of the pub to retch helplessly over the side of the stone steps.

When the spasms finally ceased, leaving a patch of ground stained with nothing more than the half cup of weak tea she'd drunk, she heard a footstep behind her.

"Easy, lass, don't lift yer head too suddenly." Father Liam's voice was gentle as he put an arm about her shoulders and handed her a damp cloth.

She accepted it gratefully and blotted her flushed face, wiped the taste of bile from her lips.

"There, now. Raise yer head slowly and lean on me, child . . . That's it . . . Now a deep, cleansin' breath."

She did as he told her, feeling somewhat steadier.

The priest turned her gently by the shoulders, to face him. "Better?"

She nodded, not meeting his eyes.

"How far along are ye, lass?"

Her eyes flew to his face, but she saw no censure there. And there'd been only kindness in his voice.

"A-about three months, I think. Perhaps not quite."

Father Liam nodded. "The good news is that it should pass soon—the mornin' sickness. The bad news is that 'tis unwise t' be makin' such a rough journey with a babe in yer womb. And, as ye well know, the roughest travel is yet t' come. Winter comes early t' the Cairngorms, lass. Still, 'tis not too late t' turn ba—"

"*No!*"

The priest's brows rose at the vehemence of her tone.

"I . . . Father Liam, I cannot turn back now," she pleaded. "There are reasons—this babe must be born at my Highland home, Father. It *must.*"

He searched her face, trying to fathom the cause of her fervency, then nodded toward the door. "Come inside, lass. Sister took the little ones fer a walk with the hound. We'll have privacy, if ye'd care t' tell me about it."

They found a small table by the hearth in the empty

public room. The priest spoke quietly to the ostler, accepting a pot of tea and two mugs when Christmas told him she thought she might be able to keep some down. Then the man disappeared, leaving them alone.

She began hesitantly at first, intending to tell him only of her reasons for wanting to reach the Highlands. But the priest was a compassionate listener, and she soon found the whole story tumbling out. It was the first time she told someone all of it, for even Maire didn't know of the child. And it was as if her mind and heart ached with the need to unburden herself of things too long held inside. When at last she finished, tears were streaming down her face, and she had to blot them away with the snowy linen handkerchief Father Liam handed her.

". . . so you s-see, Father," she added in a watery voice, "I could hold no h-hope for us in England. If *I* was so unhappy there, what hope did I have of r-raising a child there with—with any chance for its own happiness?"

The priest hesitated, then nodded. He knew she was right, as far as it went. The Sassenach *ton* would make her and the child into social pariahs. But he feared the rest of her assumption wasn't necessarily valid; the freedom she sought in the Scottish wilderness was no guarantee of happiness. People tended to carry the seeds of their happiness—or unhappiness—with them, and he told her so.

Christmas met his eyes with a sober look. "You're speaking of my—my feelings for Jamie, aren't you? Saying that I'll carry them with me, that they cannot be erased or softened simply by changing where I live?"

"That will be the largest part of it, lass. The heart has a way o' being indifferent t' time and place." He was silent for a moment. "Well, place, more than time, I suppose. Time may be anither matter. Take the case o' the wee ones we're rescuin'. If I didn't believe time would heal them, I don't suppose I'd be doin' what I am."

Christmas was shaking her head. "You're changing

place, as well, Father. Else you'd not be spiriting them away from the scene of their tragic losses."

I am, he thought, *but you're* returning *to the scene of yours, Christmas MacKenzie.*

But to her he merely smiled, saying, "Ach, lass! I told ye ye're a quick one!"

She smiled with relief, feeling the battle won. "You'll escort me the rest of the way, then?"

"I will," he said, "but before I gather the ithers and we get under way, I do wish t' ask ye one thing more?"

She sipped the last of her tea and set down the mug. "Of course."

He eyed her curiously. "Well, lass, just what was it ye wrote t' yer fiancé t' make him accept yer breakin' o' the engagement?"

"Oh, that!" The gray eyes twinkled, betraying obvious relish over what she would say. "Well, as you know, Father, Britain is suffering an economic depression, now that the war is over and the demand for military supplies has ceased. Continental markets are simply unable to absorb our backlogged inventories of manufactured goods, and prices have fallen drastically."

"Go on," said the priest, showing no sign of surprise that a young, aristocratic Englishwoman should be so well informed on matters that females of her class were supposed to be incapable of understanding.

Christmas couldn't contain her grin. "Well, I simply informed m'lord that I'd invested my entire newfound fortune on 'Change and lost my shirt!"

The priest's grin matched hers and he began to chuckle. "Ach!" he exclaimed through the mirth. "I said ye were a quick one!"

❖Chapter 22❖

The final stages of their journey were hellish. At least, that was the word Christmas most often heard the priest mumble as they made their way across forbidding slopes on barely existent trails. As the cleric had warned, winter came early to the Highlands, bruising a landscape that was already harsh and inhospitable.

Several times, with the advent of snow on the heels of bitter, relentless winds, they'd been forced to turn back and seek shelter at the haven they'd used the night before. Several times, too, the priest begged her to reconsider trying to make it through before spring. And several times, Christmas almost relented. Almost.

But she knew that to wait until spring would mean delaying even longer. The child was due in April, and she could hardly make the rough and difficult journey with a newborn, even in good weather. Moreover, she wanted the child born in the land of her mother's people. It had become important to her in a way she couldn't entirely explain; perhaps it was because of the free and independent nature of the Highland Scots and her longing to have that for her child as well as herself; perhaps it was because the Highlands represented a time and place when she'd glimpsed true happiness, and she could wish no less for the son or daughter she brought into the world.

Then, too, Christmas was encouraged by the abatement of her morning nausea and felt healthier than she had when they left London. And it was this, in the end, which persuaded Father Liam to accede to her wishes and forge on. The lass had pluck and determination, he realized, not to mention a stronger constitution than many men he'd known. So, as long as she was able to take proper nourishment and get adequate rest, he allowed she was in no danger.

But the children were another matter. He insisted that Jean-Pierre and Gabrielle-Marie be left behind in a safe haven. This turned out to be more fortuitous than any of them expected. The middle-aged couple who owned the croft where they offered to pay board for the children for the winter were childless; they'd lost their only son to Napoleon's army two years before, and they longed for children on whom to lavish love and caring. So when Father Liam and Sister Mary Michael made their request for an extended refuge for the orphans, the couple made one in return: might they adopt the bairns themselves?

There was song and laughter in their humble croft that night. To ease the little ones into their new surroundings, it was decided that Sister Mary Michael would remain with them until spring; she was a familiar face by now, and Jean-Pierre and Gabrielle-Marie had grown attached to her.

Then Christmas made their "cup of joy full to overflowing," as the old crofter put it (or, *cup o' jo' fu' t' o'erflowin'*, actually) by bestowing on them a pigeon's-blood ruby the size of an acorn. The wife wept and protested it was too much, but Christmas merely hugged her and laughed. She expected the old Seadog would turn in his grave, she told them, to learn his hard-won booty was going to the support of Catholic orphans!

Then it was back on the trail for Christmas and the cleric. Although they might never have attempted it after all, if it hadn't been for the crofter's two strong nephews

sent along as guides, along with their string of six Highland ponies to ride and use as pack animals.

And so, just a few days before Christmas, Lady Christina St. John, the Laird of Clan MacKenzie at Inverness-
shire, came back to the seat of her ancestors. She was
travel stained and footsore, and exhausted beyond telling.
And, as she told a flabbergasted Mrs. MacLeod who met
them at the door, "never so glad of home in my life."

"Och, lassie!" the housekeeper exclaimed, leading the
half-frozen entourage to the fire. "We thought nae t' see
ye mair. Or certainly no' sae soon! 'Twas t' the kirk ye
were gang—t' wed, we thought!"

Christmas laughed, though in her exhaustion it came
out a croak. "Weel, Mrs. MacLeod," she replied, imitat-
ing the Scots accent perfectly, "I nae made it t' the kirk,
but"—she glanced at the snow-encrusted beard of Father
Liam, meeting his bright blue eyes—"ye cuid say I
brought the kirk wi' me!"

It appeared they'd reached their destination just in time.
That night an unusually fierce winter storm came howling
in from the north, closing all passes through the Cairngorms. It raged and blew for three days, sealing people in
their domiciles, blurring the landscape in a sea of swirling,
churning snow.

When it finally blew itself out, it was Christmas Day,
and the new laird had turned twenty. She hadn't antici-
pated any particular acknowledgment of the occasion, but
Mrs. MacLeod had remembered it was her birthday. So
after the mass Father Liam celebrated—and which Christmas heard, along with Davie and Georgie MacMurry, the
two nephews—there was a surprise in store for her.

She'd suspected nothing, believing only that the roast
goose had been designated to honor the Other whose
birthday it was. So when everyone, from the stableman,
to Mrs. MacLeod, to the guests, gathered at the foot of
the stairs to cheer her when she came down for dinner,

Christmas found herself at a total loss for words. Surprised, deeply warmed, and on the verge of tears, she let them lead her to the dining chamber. There, a silk banner embroidered by the housekeeper proclaimed "Happy Birthday to the Laird" in four-inch letters above the fireplace.

There followed a toast to her health, with champagne brought up from the wine cellar (amid apologies from the small staff, that it had to be her own champagne they drank, for the storm had prevented procurement elsewhere).

Even gifts were not wanting, despite the storm's imposed limitations: an embroidered handkerchief from Mrs. MacLeod, bearing the same inscription as the banner; a blooming miniature rosebud from Mackie, the sometime-stableman sometime-gardener; and an elaborate birthday cake in the exact shape of the manor house from the cook.

But the gift that finally brought the tears that had been threatening was a short poem read to her by Father Liam, but to which, he explained, the entire company had contributed. It read:

> Eyes soft as twilight and
>   lit from within,
> Hair shot with flame, yet as
>   silken as rain,
> Heart of an eagle, despite
>   slender frame,
> This, the young laird, who is
>   finally hame.
> Bless her and hold her,
>   O God Who, this day,
> Shares natal hours with the
>   lady, we pray.
> Guide her, this Christmas,
>   And love let her know

Through all of her days, for
You see, she's our jo'.

Greatly moved, hiccoughing through her tears, Christmas thanked them with a tremendous smile and invited all to join her at table—her staff as well as the guests. And as they all sat, from Mackie the stableman, awkward in his rough woolens, to Cook, red-faced and shy in her apron, Christmas knew with an overwhelming certainty that she'd truly come home.

The new year came with even more feasting, though a haggis replaced the Christmas goose. And when an unusual January thaw melted the snow in the passes, Father Liam decided to chance leaving, along with the MacMurray brothers, who would guide him as far as their home.

"But never say you mean it!" cried Christmas when he told her. "You yourself have said how fickle the weather is in the Highlands. What if another storm should arise out of nowhere, as it did the night we arrived? Father, I beg you to reconsider! I shall be out of my head with worry!"

She spoke the truth, but it went even deeper than that. In the short time she'd known the priest, she'd come to love and respect him enormously. He was more than a guide and kindly companion; he was her friend, a confidant and wise, compassionate father figure whose gentle advice and lack of censure regarding her impending motherhood had given her hope and the courage to carry on. But now he was leaving, and she feared what would happen to her without his strength to lean on. How would she survive?

As if he read her mind, the priest took her hands in his and met her eyes, saying, "I shall be fine, *macushla*. But more importantly, *ye'll* be fine. We meant those words, ye know—'Heart of an eagle.'"

Christmas gave a rueful chuckle. "Some would rather

have credited me with the brains of a sheep, Father, and you know it!"

He laughed, aware that sheep were accounted the stupidest of creatures, then shook his head. "Fer shame, lass! And didn't ye trudge through these wild Scots mountains, in bitter weather, without quittin'? Why, I've heard they've begun composin' songs about it in the village! Ye've become a heroine t' yer folk fer the courage ye've shown—and as we both know," he added with a wink, "they don't know the half of it!"

Christmas laughed despite herself and patted her slightly thickened waistline. "True, but it won't be long before they learn about that half, and then I suppose they'll—"

"They'll be writin' poems about ye as well!" he cut in.

Christmas was shaking her head. "I rather doubt they'll find anything to—"

"Faith, and don't ye believe it!" the priest rejoined. "These Highland Celts prize courage and independence above everythin', lass, and ye've shown them both—in spades!"

"But the babe—"

"Whssht now, darlin'! D'ye fancy they've niver encountered an unwed mother before? Read yer Scots literature, lass, and perhaps ye'll learn somethin' about these fierce, proud people whose blood ye share. I've noticed there's a fine library here at MacKenzie Manor. 'Twould be a grand way t' wait out yer time, I'm thinkin'."

Christmas gave him another rueful smile and nodded. "And a long winter to do it in." She sighed, and the smile faltered. "I'm going to miss you, you know. And I shall worry myself sick until I know you're safe. You'll send word?"

The priest smiled and gave her hands an encouraging squeeze. "From every stop along the way, as I'm able. And prayers, lass. Prayers fer—"

"I know! A safe delivery."

"A safe delivery," he echoed. *And love through all your days, dear lass. Through all your days.*

The winter felt every bit as long as Christmas had predicted. Battered by harsh, bitter winds that could as easily sweep snow from the frozen landscape as pile it yards deep in drifts, the land of her mother's people seemed the very embodiment of that season. It was a time for being indoors; for drawing inward and conserving energy and strength; for biding one's time until the hope of renewal was at hand in the promise that was spring.

For Christmas in particular, with the child growing large in her womb, it was essentially a time of waiting—and perhaps of enduring. She had never taken well to being shut indoors for great lengths of time. Her childhood, with the boys' sports and pastimes with which her parents had indulged her, had been active and peppered with an abundance of time out of doors. Even in London there'd been those rides in the Park to offset the rounds of parties and balls during her Season.

Christina's enforced confinement at MacKenzie Manor made her restless and edgy in a way she couldn't recall experiencing before. Aside from the books in the library, which Father Liam had noted, there was little to occupy her time. Mrs. MacLeod, while gruffly kind and solicitous, especially when Christmas's pregnancy became apparent, was never the conversationalist, and the other servants were even less so. Moreover, they all had their work to occupy them and had been accustomed to doing it without supervision for years.

Only O'Kelly, the young wolfhound, seemed to share her frustration. He might lie at her feet for hours by the fire in the library while she read George Buchanan's *History of Scotland* or Sir Walter Scott, but every so often, when a fierce blast of wind came whistling down the chimney and set sparks dancing, he would raise his great head, rise silently, and move to one of the windows;

there, he would stand for a long time, gazing out over the frozen terrain.

Christmas felt sorry for him and frequently let him out with Mackie when the old man tended the livestock, but it was clear the hound preferred her company. He would make several great dashes about the yard and stables, galloping madly over the packed snow, hurdling high banks where the stableman had piled snow with his shovel; but he always returned to where she stood just under the portico, bundled in her tartans. Then his dark, almond-shaped eyes would meet hers as if to say, "Why won't you come?"

So when the weather cleared for several days in late February, Christmas decided she'd had enough of doing next to nothing, and so had the hound. Bundling herself up in her heaviest tartans and wearing fur-lined boots she'd brought from London, she ignored Mrs. Mac-Leod's protests and set out with O'Kelly for a long walk. It was slow going, despite the clearer weather; snow still covered the ground, and she was able to navigate only through use of a stout blackthorn cane Mackie had insisted she carry.

But O'Kelly loved every mile in their two-hour jaunt. He raced wildly about in circles to either side of her; he plowed through drifts that sometimes came up to his chest; then he would suddenly flop down in front of her, panting, right in the snow, and begin eating it to cool off and quench his thirst. The first time he did this she laughed and called him a mad Irishman, to which the hound barked hearty acknowledgment. Then he lay there, grinning at her as if to say, "Aye, and ye're a mad Scot t' be out here watchin' me do it!"

The mild spell continued into early March, and Christmas took advantage of it. Rising early, she would take a short walk with the hound before breakfast; a longer one followed around midday, but only after she'd rested (upon Mrs. MacLeod's insistence); then, if the skies were still clear, she and the hound would round off their day with a longer hike in the afternoon.

She often thought they must make an odd sight, the two of them: the massive, muscular, yet fleet-footed hound bounding crazily over the snow beside the small, tartan-clad figure who barely managed to shuffle along, thrusting her protruding abdomen before her like a ship with a strange, ponderous prow.

Yet as the milder weather continued, so did these revivifying excursions into the white land. Surrounded by vast, craggy peaks, watching her breath cloud in puffs before her, Christmas had never felt better. Here at last she began to taste some of what she'd come in search of: the sense of being in touch with the land; the knowledge that she moved beneath the vast winter sky under no one's direction but her own; the feeling of being utterly alive in a place where only nature made the rules, and if man acknowledged and respected them, anything was possible.

Each time she came back to the manor, she was physically spent, but smiling. Mrs. MacLeod, who'd initially opposed these excursions, saw how her eyes sparkled, how her cheeks were rosy with health, and held her tongue. The lassie was in the pink and likely to birth a braw, bonnie bairn, she told herself. And most of all, she was *happy*. Let her enjoy her MacKenzie birthright.

And if, in the quiet of the night, the MacKenzie laird awakened to disturbing dreams that testified to the imperfection of that happiness—dreams of deep blue eyes and a man's warm arms about her—there was none but the dreamer to know it.

In the mornings Christmas would arise, wash the telltale trails of dried tears from her face, and begin another day. If she wasn't completely happy in this new life she'd chosen, at least she was content, she reasoned. It was more than many people had, and it would have to do. Somehow, it would have to do.

But then one day something happened which threatened that carefully nurtured contentment. Christmas was out with O'Kelly for the midday walk. And because the sky was almost unnaturally blue and clear for March, she'd taken along some food from the kitchen, planning to travel a little farther than usual. She would picnic on the way, rather than hurry back for luncheon.

She never knew exactly what, but something led her in a different direction that day. Instead of walking south, toward the village, as she usually did, she found herself on the path that led to the MacIver croft.

She realized she must have been daydreaming or otherwise distracted when a sharp bark from O'Kelly brought her up short. The wolfhound was standing some distance ahead of her on the trail, atop a small rise. He barked a second time at something ahead, which she couldn't see, then turned his head to look over his shoulder at her. Then he barked again, as if urging her to hurry to catch up to him.

"O'Kelly? What is it, boy? I don't—"

And then she saw it: a blue-gray curl of smoke winding its way up into the sky above the trees. Chimney smoke. From the MacIver croft. Her heart tripped, and began to hammer in her chest. Without pausing to think, Christmas hurried toward the dog, using the blackthorn for balance as she made her way awkwardly through the trees.

The hound whined softly and wagged his tail as she drew near, and then all at once she was beside him and could see—

Jamie. He was standing at the woodpile where they'd first spied Jacques that day. Bareheaded, coatless, he leaned on an axe that stood propped in front of him, beside a newly split log. But he wasn't looking at the axe or the wood.

He was looking at her.

Christmas gasped as realization struck. He'd obviously

been there, chopping wood, for some time. And the wolfhound had *obviously* been drawn by the sound. Why hadn't she? Or had she heard and denied herself the warning that ought to have sent her back before he saw her?

And now it was too late. She saw his eyes roam over her swollen figure, almost hungrily, she thought. Saw the look of stunned surprise on his face. Saw him drop the axe and take a step toward her—

She turned her back, commanding the hound to "come."

"Christmas, *wait!*"

She froze at the sound of his voice, but didn't turn. O'Kelly whined and nudged her hand, clearly wanting to go back, urging her to do the same.

And the urge within her was stronger than she'd ever have believed. Jamie. His tall, heart-stopping presence as he stood there, sunlight glinting off the dark blond hair and turning it gold. Deep blue eyes meeting hers in silent disbelief. Her every memory of him crystallized, sweeping her back to those brief, fleeting moments when they'd been together—and happy.

But it was over. The distancing, the lies—they'd changed everything. To remember was pain, and she'd had all she could endure of that.

Squaring her shoulders, Christmas gestured to the dog and walked away.

Jamie stood, transfixed, hardly able to credit what he'd seen. Christmas . . . well gone with child. Whose child? His? The Englishman's?

He took a deep breath to steady himself, bent to retrieve the axe. His mind spun with questions, implications. What, in God's name, was she doing here? Especially if she'd married the marquis's heir and carried his—

It made no sense! He knew how those blue-blooded

lords operated. The last thing in the world one of them would do was drag a pregnant wife off to the wilds of Scotland to—

But she hadn't been his wife—at least, not as long ago as last fall. And from the looks of her, she'd have the child fairly soon. She had to have been carrying it already, when he saw her in London.

So, the question was— Hell, there were just too many damned questions!

Jamie heaved a heavy sigh, running his fingers through his hair in agitation. His heart was thudding in his chest, and his breathing hadn't returned to normal since he saw her. She'd been exquisitely, heart-wrenchingly beautiful, despite the body swollen with child. Or maybe because of it. There'd been a softness about her he hadn't seen before. Was this the look the great masters had seen when they'd rendered their famous madonnas?

Even as he asked the question, Jamie felt his fingers itch to test the clay, and he felt a jolt of surprise. He hadn't felt that since—

Grating out an oath, Jamie swung the axe across his shoulder and turned toward the croft. There would be time for what he had in mind, but first, he had to have the answers to some questions.

The village would be a good place to start.

❧Chapter 23❧

Jamie led his pony into the stable, pondering all he'd learned in the village. He'd had no trouble getting people to talk about her. It seemed the new MacKenzie laird was a legend there.

At the blacksmith's he'd learned of her incredible journey back to the Highlands in weather that would have forced most men to turn back. No one thought this foolish. It was seen, instead, as courageous. "Think on it," they'd said. "The wee laird riskin' the high passes i' winter t' see her bairn born where it ought!"

At the inn he'd learned more of her and "the bairn" she carried. That she was admired for holding her head up high, despite the lack of a ring on her finger. (And here he hadn't realized how tense he'd been over the issue until he let out a sigh of relief at the news.) She'd shown the "Sassenach" dandy her heels and come home to birth "a bairn that had nae part of him. 'Twas a Scot she carried, and a Scot she meant t' have . . . Sic a fine, braw lassie, the wee laird!"

And at the cottage of Jeannie MacLaren, where he'd summoned the courage to pay a call when he learned she was the local midwife, he'd gotten a welcome confirmation: "The wee laird? Ach, mon! I dinna ken why ye should wonder, but her bairn's due in late April."

Late April. That meant it had been conceived in late July. The child was his.

Not that he'd really been in much doubt. And once he learned she'd broken with Crenshawe, he'd been certain. Too, somehow he couldn't envision her sharing what they'd had with someone else. *Wouldn't* envision it. Every time he'd come close to doing so, the image had threatened to tear him apart.

Jamie measured a ration of oats into the feed trough and gave the pony a pat on the withers, then headed for the cottage. His head spun with all he'd learned, and he cursed himself for being ten times a fool. Just a few miles away, the woman he loved, more than anything or anyone in the world, sat carrying his child. And he'd driven her away.

He'd driven her away, thinking to spare himself the pain of another Desirée. *Fool!* Why hadn't he seen she was nothing like Desirée? His wife had been so shallow, so self-absorbed, she'd taken her own life in ridding herself of his child. Christmas MacKenzie had risked much to come here, but it was to *keep* the child. A bastard born in England would be an outcast; here, it had a chance.

He didn't doubt that she could have married Crenshawe and passed the babe off as his. There'd been time in which to do it. Yet she'd turned her back on all that— her life in England, the respectability and security the marriage would have guaranteed—to have the child in a place where she could raise it freely. She'd risked everything to come here and have it. *His* child.

He wanted to laugh at the irony of it. He'd been beating himself emotionally for years over his inability to love Desirée. Blaming himself for getting her with child when he'd never loved her. Now, he was steeped in guilt for sending away the one woman he did love, who also carried his child, *who wanted the child,* and he'd made her hate him. He'd rejected her in the cruelest way, after she'd cast aside all pride, *asking him to marry her.* She'd wanted him, loved him, before she could even have known of the child. She'd loved him, and he'd thrown that love back in her face!

Why had it taken him so long to see? He thought back to the moment in London, when he'd been about to board the packet and sail. When he'd been unable to do it. When he'd decided, in a sudden moment of absolute clarity, that there was only one place he could bear to be, now that Christmas MacKenzie was lost to him: here, in the Highlands, where he would at least have the memories to keep him alive.

Jamie stopped before the door of the cottage and looked around him. Late winter twilight was just beginning to soften the edges of the crags and peaks that towered high in the distance. Long purple shadows stretched across the snow in the yard. A bird called from a pine tree near the stable, was answered from somewhere farther away.

It was a wild, free place to be . . . to share a life . . . to raise a son or daughter. But to do that, a man needed a woman by his side. A woman he loved. And he'd thrown her away. Did he dare try to win her back?

With a sigh, Jamie entered the cottage. He was going to try, by God. He was going to try!

Mackie the stableman grumbled to himself as he trudged from the stable to the servants' entrance at the rear of the manor house. He was getting on, he thought, no longer a young man with energy to spare. His bones creaked and his joints ached, especially in the cold. Yet, did anyone care? Certainly not the American, and not Mrs. Mac-Leod, either!

This was the fifth time in as many days he was being shuttled from stable to kitchens and back again, with the results ever the same. Of course, it helped that Angus MacIver's nephew pressed a gold coin into his hand each time he handed him the message he was to deliver. But now Mackie suspected he'd be spending the coins on liniments and simples to ease his aching joints! What was more, he added to himself testily, he was no footman. His responsibilities were the stables and the gardens, and wasn't that enough for an old man?

But here was the American again this morning, note and coin in hand. "Would you kindly see that your mistress receives this?" he always asked. And then, "I'll wait for a reply."

But the only reply that ever came was from Mrs. MacLeod's lips: "Tell the American there is no reply." Hmph! You'd think the laddie would take it for an answer and let be!

Of course, he might be an American, but he was Angus MacIver's kin. And that meant he was at least part Scots.

Mackie's bearded mouth widened in a gap-toothed grin. "Weel, as all men ken," he said aloud, "we Scots cuid no' be mair stubborn if we tried!"

He glanced at the note in his hand, wondering what it said. There hadn't been too many times in his life he regretted not being able to read, but this was one of them. He would give a pretty penny right now to know what was passing between the American and the manor house.

With a sigh, Mackie raised his hand to the latch on the door to the kitchens, only to have the door open ahead of him.

"Another one, I see," said Mrs. MacLeod.

"Aye." Mackie rubbed his hand along his hip joint while handing her the note with the other.

The housekeeper took it, glanced at the bold script that slanted across the foolscap, and sighed. "Well, Mackie," she said, "here's hopin' 'twill be the last time ye'll need t' be draggin' yer tired bones across the yard."

The old man glanced up hopefully as she withdrew a piece of folded foolscap from her pocket.

"This time, Mackie," she pronounced as she handed it to him, "there's a reply written."

The gap-toothed grin appeared as he took the note and nodded. "I'll be takin' it back t' the mon straightaway, Mrs. MacLeod, and be hopin' ye're right that 'tis the last!"

Janet MacLeod sighed as she watched the old servant trudge back through the snow. She supposed, for Mackie's sake, that she ought to wish the mistress's note would put an end to the American's attempts to see her. But for Lady Christina's sake, she wished it were otherwise.

She was fairly certain she had fathomed the connection between her young mistress and this Jamie MacIver: he was the father of the bairn she carried. There were signs that made it all too evident: the way the lassie's face had betrayed her with a host of emotions passing across it, each time Janet handed her another of his messages; the way her hands had trembled just a wee bit when she read each note that came; the clenching of her small jaws as she'd pitched the notes into the dustbin. Och, she tried to hide it, but the lass's face was an open book. Whatever had passed between the two of them, the poor child loved the man, Janet was sure, despite the anger that flashed in those gray eyes. Despite the pain that lurked there, too.

The housekeeper sighed again, wishing she could do something to bring the pair together. No one in the village or at the manor was casting stones at the lass for carrying a bairn without benefit of a trip to the kirk. They'd leave that kind of thing for the Sassanachs. Their laird was their laird, and they'd stand by her till the edge of doom, they would. If she'd chosen not to wed the father, 'twas likely there were reasons.

And Janet had little doubt the choice had been hers—at least in part. It was clear the man pursued her. Imagine, trudging the miles between his croft and the manor, day after day, even now with the weather turning foul again!

Och! Why couldn't the lassie just agree to see him? Janet's curiosity had overcome her sense of propriety and she'd dared to read his notes, God and the mistress forgive her! And they'd seemed so sincere!

"I understand that what I have done is unforgivable, so I do not ask forgiveness. Yet I do request that you at least see me this once and let me try to explain," read the present note as she glanced at it.

Aye, why couldn't she just agree to see him? Perhaps a good airing would clear up what stood between them. After all, if they cared for each other . . .

Besides, Janet added to herself as she thrust the note back in her pocket, a bairn needed a father. At least, if the father was a decent sort, and enough word had come from the village to convince her that Jamie MacIver was that. "A braw, bonnie mon wi' a kindly manner and an honest look aboot him," Jeannie MacLaren, the midwife, had said of the American just the other day.

The housekeeper shook her head and heaved a sigh, then withdrew Jamie's note from her pocket and dropped it in the dustbin. There was no need to show it to the laird. Janet had read the lines on the written reply she'd had waiting for Mackie to take back this morning.

It had read, "The American *widower* is not needed here."

⚜Chapter 24⚜

Jeannie MacLaren grinned tiredly as she watched Janet MacLeod bundle the squalling infant in fine, soft wool. "A braw wee bairn, an' nae mistake, Janet!"

"Aye, an' the look of a Scot aboot him, I'd say!" She touched her fingers lightly to the downy patch of red-gold hair covering the tiny head.

"Mrs. MacLeod?" came a tired voice from the big tester bed. "May I—may I see him?"

"Och!" exclaimed the housekeeper. "Are ye awake, then?" She turned toward the bed and placed the noisy bundle in the slender arms that reached for it.

"A fine Highland bairn fer the MacKenzie clan," the midwife pronounced as she finished washing her hands. "Listen t' him howl!"

Christmas smiled tiredly and accepted Mrs. MacLeod's help in opening the front of the fresh gown she'd dressed her in, after a sponge bath following the delivery. She gazed down at the furious red face of her son as he began to root frantically for her nipple.

There was a collective sigh from all three women as the infant located the source of his nourishment and latched on, plunging the bedchamber into silence.

"I agree, Mrs. MacLaren," Christmas murmured drowsily as she watched her son suckle. "He has the look of a Scot, indeed. I believe I shall call him that, then . . . Scot . . . Scot MacKenzie . . ."

The midwife threw the housekeeper a questioning look as the new mother's eyes closed in sleep. "MacKenzie? 'Tis true, then? She means t' stay on an' raise the bairn as a MacKenzie?"

The housekeeper hesitated, then nodded, unable to avoid thinking of the man who still came daily with messages for poor Mackie to deliver and then return, unread. "Aye, Jeannie, but I fear we've no' heard the end of the matter yet."

But if the housekeeper thought things would continue as they had before the birth of young Scot, she was mistaken. The same day that Jeannie MacLaren brought word to the village that the laird had been delivered of a fine, strong son, the messages that Mackie had come to dread, ceased. Nothing further was heard of Jamie then, but old Annie, the charwoman who came up from the village to dust and clean, mentioned that the handsome American still came to Kingussie for supplies and the like from time to time. And, she said, he'd been at the blacksmith's the day Jeannie MacLaren's news of the bairn had reached them. Asked a lot of questions as well.

It snowed once more, in early May, before the tenacious grip of winter finally released its hold on the Highlands. After that, although sharp, biting winds still blew across the Cairngorms, the weather grew gradually, but perceptibly, milder. Christmas often gazed out the windows, thinking how vastly different a spring they had here, from what she had known in England. Yet she never minded. Nursing her newborn son at her breast, she would watch the winds bending the branches of the trees outside the windows and nod assertively to herself. This was the land of her forebears, she told herself proudly. A harsh, wild land for a fierce, strong people. It was meant to test the mettle of those who would live upon it, and only the strong would endure.

And Christmas MacKenzie St. John meant to endure. No, not merely to endure, but to *thrive*—she, and her son, too. Already, she could feel the strength returning to her body, following the months of carrying the child through the long winter. Her body was taut and firm, despite the pregnancy—a legacy of all those walks through the "hills" with O'Kelly.

And young Scot was strong and healthy, too. He seemed to grow visibly before her eyes. Just watching the strength in his well-formed limbs as he kicked and splashed in his bath, or when his nappies were changed, gave her untold joy in him.

And if that joy was tempered somewhat by the resemblance between his eyes, which were settling into a deep, dark blue, and those of another, she tried not to dwell on it. The messages from the stable had finally stopped, and thank God for it, she told herself. She feared her willpower would be tested enough as she watched her son grow, taking on more and more of the look of the man who'd sired him. God knew it had been all she could do, before the birthing, to reject those messages. But Jamie MacIver belonged to the past, and that was that. It was what her own message had been meant to convey. Her mind was set on it.

She only wondered how long it would take her heart to accept it as well.

The days passed, with the weather at last turning springlike, though never as warm as May in some parts of the world. But Highlanders shed some of their woolen layers and began to spend time out of doors. Christmas longed to take those bracing walks with O'Kelly again, but the mud she encountered across the thawing ground proved more dangerous than the snow she'd trod, so she held off. She would wait until the drier month that June promised to be.

She did stroll about the immediate grounds and gardens, however, often with Scot bundled in her arms as O'Kelly raced and frolicked in mad circles about them. And more than once, during these walks, she found her eyes involuntarily straying in the direction of Jamie's croft, though it was too far to discern if smoke still curled from its chimney.

Yet she knew from talk in the village—cheerfully relayed one day by Annie the charwoman—that someone still lived at the MacIver croft. There was "a fierce bangin' an' hammerin' gang on oop there," Annie told her. "Au manner o' loud noises, fit t' wake the dead."

Christmas nodded, nonchalantly, she hoped, dismissing the charwoman while wondering what it was all about. Was Jamie building something? She recalled his mentioning at one time that the cottage was suitable enough for his needs, though if one were to consider making it a home, it could do with an extra room or two. Was that what he was about? *Was Jamie planning to stay here, at his ancestral home, just as she was?*

The thought jarred her, and she couldn't ignore a sudden, frantic racing of her pulse. She tried to tell herself it didn't make sense, that Jamie had made his choice, and it didn't include her. So, why was he here, and not in America? What did he want?

Too many questions, and she knew she had herself to blame for the lack of answers. All those messages she'd spurned. Then her own, single message, that the *widower* was not needed here.

A rueful, self-deprecating smile crossed her face. It had been her pride speaking then; she'd been bent on letting him know that *she* knew he'd lied, that she knew the truth. But the messages had also spoken of what he'd done as unforgivable, of her *right* in spurning him for it. *Damn* him! How *dare* he assume he knew her mind! Just as he'd assumed *lying* to her, as Maire had explained in London, would *save* her pain in the lõng run. Damn him, damn him, *damn* him.

And now, finally, the messages had stopped. In her anger and pride, she'd put an end to the very thing she now yearned for: answers . . . and perhaps something more.

With a broken sound, Christmas buried her face in her hands and wept.

Mackie let the freshly groomed pony into the paddock, and shut the gate with a sigh of relief. That was the last one, and a good thing, too. It took a great deal of muscle and energy to curry the beasts as they shed their winter coats, and his shoulder and elbow joints ached, despite the mild weather. Och, but he'd be glad of a wee dram of—

The old man paused, squinting against the bright sunshine as he strove to identify the wildly unkempt figure coming toward him.

"Guid God, 'tis the American!" Mackie wondered if his eyes were playing tricks on him as Jamie came toward him. He'd never seen the man like this. He looked beaten and weary, for one thing, this tall man who'd always walked squarely, with the bearing of a soldier. And his clothes! It looked as if he'd slept in them! Wrinkled and dusty, they were, and his face wore what looked like a few days' growth of whiskers. What, in the name of all Scotland—?

"Good morning, ah—Mackie, is it?" the American asked.

"Aye . . ." Mackie noted the tired lines in his face, the red-rimmed eyes. *Has the puir mon taken t' drink, then?*

An all too familiar-looking piece of folded foolscap appeared, along with a tired grin showing through the gold whiskers, and a gold coin in the other hand.

Mackie nearly groaned.

"If I promise there will be only this one message this time, will you take it up for me?" Jamie asked him. "I know I've imposed on your kindness too much already, Mackie, but just one more time . . . Will you?"

The stableman met the tired, hopeful eyes and felt a stirring of pity for the man. If he'd been drinking, there ought to be a reek of it about him, and there was none. Perhaps he'd been ill?

Taking the servant's hesitation for indecision, Jamie pressed his suit. "You won't even need to hurry back with an answer this time, Mackie. Just say you'll deliver it, and I'll be on my way—with thanks."

He held out the note and the coin. Mackie noted the paper trembling slightly in his hand. *Puir mon, whatever's done ye in.*

"Aye," said the old man aloud, accepting coin and note.

"My thanks, Mackie," Jamie replied as he watched the servant trudge toward the manor house.

Jamie sighed, running unsteady fingers through his tangled curls. He knew he should have gotten some sleep, probably bathed and shaved, too, before he came. The poor old Scot had shown out-and-out shock when he saw him.

Still, he'd worked all yesterday and last night to finish it and then there'd been only the one, all-consuming thought: to come here and ask—no, *plead* with her—this last time.

Would she come? Jamie gave a weary shake of the head, then turned for home. *She had to come, dammit—had to!* Because if she didn't, he didn't know what in hell he was going to do.

In her bedchamber at the manor house, Christmas's fingers trembled as she held the folded message and watched the door close behind Mrs. MacLeod. Thinking she needed persuasion to accept it, the housekeeper had launched into a detailed description of how, according to Mackie, Jamie had looked when he met the stableman.

Jamie, looking drawn and wildly unkempt, as if he were ill? Dear God, what if—?

Taking a deep breath, Christmas thrust the unfinished thought aside and unfolded the foolscap. Behind her, Scot stirred in his cradle, and she paused, then went to her son. He was still asleep, but seemed restless. She smiled at this small creature she loved so fiercely, it hurt. She rocked him gently until she saw him relax, a tiny bubble forming on his rosebud mouth.

Still standing beside the cradle, Christmas turned her attention back to the note. Jamie's normally bold, slashing hand looked oddly unsteady, with more than a few wavy lines, but she could easily discern the message: "A forgiving heart is needed here. *Please* come?"

Her heart gave a lurch as she digested the change in his message: he was asking for her forgiveness. Always, before, the notes had spoken of what he'd done as unforgivable, as if he expected none from her. It had gone to the heart of the matter between them in her eyes. Jamie had cut her out of his life in the first place, as she saw it, without ever giving her a chance. *Expecting* her to be as the other had been—his dead wife. Assuming she would betray him as his wife had done.

Then the messages had come. But had they gone beyond that fixation with assumptions about her? No. They'd assumed she had to be unforgiving, and it had hurt. Yes, she had to admit it now. She'd given herself the excuse that it was the lying and the rejection alone that had made her spurn his recent attempts to see her, but she knew now that this simply wasn't true. The lie, the rejection—they'd been bad, true. But, as she'd learned all too well, they hadn't caused her to stop loving him.

But the assumption that she'd not be able to forgive— that had caused a new wound. As if he'd again condemned her without giving her a chance to prove she was other than what he'd have her—a cold, betraying female.

But now this! *A forgiving heart is needed here* . . .

Christmas's hand shook so hard, she could barely turn the handle as she opened her door and ran into the hallway.

"Mrs. MacLeod!" she called, her voice tight with emotion. "Mrs. MacLeod, come quickly, and bring my *tonnag*!"

❧Chapter 25❧

Jamie was standing in the open doorway of the cottage when he saw her. After the bath and grooming he'd promised himself, he'd begun pacing the yard, and then the interior of the cottage, never really sure she'd come. But now she was here, and he froze, hardly able to believe it.

She wore a long, tartan-swathed ensemble exactly like the one he remembered so well from the summer before. The day was mild, but with a steady breeze blowing from across the loch, and she'd draped the plaid over her head in the now familiar manner of the women in the village. Yet her brilliant curls would not be restrained, and they lifted and swirled about her like some bright Highland banner. She carried something wrapped in the folds of tartan and nestled in the crook of her arm, but he couldn't tell what it was. His eyes drank in the sight of her, hungrily scanning the perfect contours of her face, but she was still too far away for him to discern her expression, her mood.

Anxious, hardly daring to believe she'd listen, he forced himself to remain where he was. He would wait until he could read her eyes. Yes, the gray eyes that could flash quicksilver humor or darken like a storm over the loch. Oh, God, had any woman, anywhere, ever been lovelier? She was earth, and wind, and fire itself. Elemental in her beauty, and the very spirit of these wild Highland hills.

And he loved her beyond telling.

Jamie started forward as she reached the yard, then stopped, bracing his hand against the door frame to steady himself. He supposed a man could grow weak from not eating or sleeping for two days, but in this case, he knew the cause was something else.

He was scared to death she'd say no.

Christmas sucked in her breath and drew up short a half dozen yards from the doorway. *Jamie.* Dear God, he looked so strained! No longer unkempt, as Mackie had described, but tired and—

"You needn't look so worried, m'lady. I won't bite." He tried to say it with a smile, but he didn't quite succeed.

Christmas replied without thinking. "I'd ask you not to use that form of address, please. I've given instructions to my solicitors in London to take action to drop the title, and even if they cannot succeed, I've taken to using the name of my mother's people now. I'm—I'm merely Christmas MacKenzie here."

Jamie nodded gravely. "Christmas, then? Or would you rather I—"

"Christmas will be fine . . . Jamie."

A ghost of a smile hovered about his handsome mouth, and he stepped toward her, only to stop short when a small, hiccoughing sound emerged from the bundle she carried tucked in her arm.

He watched Christmas's face grow tender as she glanced down at it. When she looked back at him, he thought her face had a sudden vulnerability to it.

"Your son, Jamie. I—I've brought your son to you. His name is Scot. Would—would you like to see him?"

Jamie closed his eyes as emotion threatened to over-

whelm him. When he opened them again, she was looking at him with that same vulnerable expression in her
eyes. That, and a strong hint of pain.

"Oh, Christmas . . ." he began uncertainly, hardly
knowing where to start. He swallowed the lump in his
throat and began again.

"I *want* to see him, *hold him,* with all my heart, Christmas. I—"

"Well, then!" she replied with a false briskness as she
stepped forward to meet him. "Here."

Jamie looked down at the small figure she unwrapped
and held out to him.

His son. A tiny, beautifully formed face gazing up at
him with fierce blue eyes.

Jamie swallowed hard, trying to dislodge the lump
clogging his throat as she gestured for him to take the
child.

"I—I'm not sure I have the right," he managed
thickly.

Gray eyes met his over the head of their son. They were
every bit as fierce as the babe's. "Of course you have the
right! You're his *father.*"

Again, Jamie closed his eyes. Unfamiliar emotions
threatened to engulf him.

Misreading his reaction, Christmas's eyes grew stormy.
"Never say you question that? Jamie, as God is my wit-
ness, no other man—"

"Christ, *no!*" Jamie's heart was in his eyes as they met
hers. Their look was raw, pleading. "Sweet merciful
heaven, don't *say* that! Don't even *think* it! Of course I
know I'm his father! It's not his parentage I'm doubting,
Christmas, it's the *worthiness* of the parent! After what
I've put you through, I don't think I've the right, don't
you see?"

Christmas was shaking her head, blinking to stop the
tears that had begun to blur her vision. "Why—why did

you ask me here today, Jamie?" she countered in a tremulous voice.

The deep blue of his eyes darkened to the color o
midnight as he answered. "I thought I said it in my note
but you have the right to hear it from my lips as well: I've
been a blind fool, Christmas. I hurt you terribly, and jus
when you'd had the courage to make yourself most vulnerable to me. I hurt you at the very moment I realized
you were the woman I loved. The only woman I'll eve
love. Can you . . . can you ever forgive me?"

A sob tore from her throat before she managed a smile
through her tears. "I—I already have, my darling. And I
love you so much, I could die!"

Jamie released the breath he hadn't realized he'd been
holding. His own eyes were suspiciously bright as he
leaned carefully across the babe, caught her face between
his hands, and captured her lips in a kiss that was achingly
tender and fraught with all the pent-up longing of thei
months of separation.

Christmas closed her eyes, tasting the salt of her tears as
his mouth covered hers. It was a sweet, tender possession
His lips were warm and almost painfully familiar as they
moved unhurriedly over her own. Jamie's lips, Jamie's
warmth, telling her, along with the impossible words
she'd never thought to hear again, that he loved her.

He finally released her mouth, but only to keep his
own hovering close, his hands still capturing her face. His
eyes met hers, held them. They were deep as indigo and
full of an undeniable warmth she'd never thought to see.
Loving. Sweet miracle of miracles, he did love her!

As if to echo the words in her mind, he whispered
hoarsely, "I love you, Christmas MacKenzie. And if the
offer still stands, my answer is yes."

"Y-yes . . . ?" She looked totally bewildered.

Jamie's grin made her heart lurch, and a warm shiver
coursed down her spine. "Yes, I'll *marry* you, you ador-

able goose! You did propose to me last summer, didn't you?"

Christmas managed a smile through tears that began all over again. But before she could say a word, their son suddenly set up a howl that sounded for all the world like a protest.

Jamie released her and threw the infant a mock scowl. "You object? Now, see here, young man! I'm only seeking to make an honest woman of your mother!"

Christmas laughed through her tears and held their son out to him again.

This time Jamie took the swaddled bundle, his face full of wonder as he gazed down at the squalling infant. "He has the MacIver temper, I see."

Christmas grinned. "Maire would likely argue that there's a recognizable MacKenzie strain there."

Jamie laughed, leaning forward to give her a quick kiss, then bent to plant another on Scot's puckered brow.

The infant ceased crying at once and gazed up at his father with a puzzled expression.

"Well, now, young Scot," Jamie said as he smiled down at him, "it appears you know your father loves you, at that. But just in case you doubt it"—his eyes shifted and met Christmas's—"I'm going to spend a lifetime showing you."

Christmas felt as if she were drowning in the deep blue liquid of his gaze.

"A lifetime . . ." she echoed.

When they glanced down at their son again, they saw he'd fallen fast asleep.

"Excellent child," Jamie murmured as he shifted his sleeping son to one arm and caught Christmas's hand. "Knows just when to retreat and allow his mother my full attention. Come, love."

Christmas let him lead her into the cottage, puzzling over the odd intensity in Jamie's voice.

Once inside, she blinked furiously, trying to adjust her

eyes to the dimmer light. Jamie took their son and set him carefully in a large splint basket she and Maire had once used to hold clothes that needed mending. Scot, she noted by his silence, continued to sleep peacefully as Jamie moved the basket a comfortable distance from the fire. Then, as her eyes were finally able to discern other details in the cottage's interior, she swung her gaze to where the trestle table used to be, and she gasped.

There, in place of the table, stood a life-size marble sculpture of a woman holding an infant upon her breast. Its flowing lines were unmistakably maternal . . . arms cradling the tiny babe . . . head bent tenderly over the child . . . face—

The face was her own. Chills coursed over her as she realized she could have been looking at a mirror image, despite the soft whiteness of the marble. She knew it was stone, but she would have sworn that, had she touched it, the statue's skin would have felt warm. In the face she recognized the very echo of her innermost feelings as she'd nursed her child, loving it beyond what words could explain.

But Jamie's hands had explained it. The love . . . the thousand and one complex feelings she'd had even before Scot was born, and then after, when she held him . . . just as the figure in marble held him now.

"How . . . *?"* she breathed, turning to Jamie with questioning eyes. "How did you—" She stopped, unable to put her wonder into words.

But Jamie answered without needing to hear them. "I simply let the things I felt . . . in my heart . . . guide my hands. It was the love I bore you, Christmas, my memories of all that was, and might have been, between us . . . the passion . . . the fire . . . but most of all, the deep, abiding love that wouldn't go away."

He smiled ruefully. "I tried to make it go away, you know. I was so terrified of it, I—" He laughed in self-deprecation. "But it wouldn't go away, my love. It just kept growing stronger and stronger."

"Until—was that when you came back here?"

Jamie nodded. "I felt the clay calling to me. Along with a need to be where the memories were strongest." He laughed, rueful again. "You can imagine my shock when I learned you'd come back, too. And then, when I saw you that day, huge with child . . ."

He came forward and pulled her into his arms, his chin resting on her head as he continued to explain. "Then I knew it had come to me . . . the thing I'd been searching for, for years. Clay was no longer adequate. It had to be the marble . . . marble—strong enough to contain the passion that drove me, the *fire*. And when I began, I knew I was going to find something I'd been trying to reach all my life."

Christmas caught a new, underlying sense of peace in his voice, and she felt something expand and swell inside her. She knew he'd achieved a kind of wholeness which hadn't been there before, and she also knew this had something to do with her, with the love—miracle of miracles, was it really true?—he bore her. That Jamie loved her, that he was committed to her and their child, despite the ghosts of his past, was nearly more than she could take in. It was a wildly heady realization and brought a wealth of emotion that threatened to overflow until she couldn't contain it all.

"It's—it's wonderful, Jamie," she whispered unsteadily against his shoulder. Drawing back within the circle of his arms, she looked up at him. "And I mean that in the truest sense of the words . . . a thing of *wonder* . . . so lifelike, you *must* wonder that it cannot move and breathe."

Jamie smiled down at her. "Perhaps. Still, it is not as wonderful as the woman who inspired it, my love. Without you to turn me around, I'd never have summoned the fire."

"Oh, Jamie," she cried fiercely, "I love you so!"

His smile gave way to a serious look as his eyes coursed over her face and came to rest on her mouth. She felt her breath catch as they darkened, and a new emotion flared. The passion he ignited was instantaneous, catching her unaware, and she felt a giddy weakness steal along her limbs as his mouth descended.

It captured hers as she rose on tiptoe to meet him. Emotions, which already hovered on the surface from all that had transpired, suddenly opened at full throttle.

They clung together, hungrily tasting each other with a passion too long denied. It was madness, almost a dizzying whirlwind of rapture that demanded release.

"Sweet Christ, but I've missed you!" Jamie's words exploded against her ear when at last they broke apart for air. "I thought sometimes I'd go mad if I never held you again!"

Christmas nodded, unable to trust her voice, and the movement sent the tartan sliding from her head.

Jamie caught a handful of the bright curls and brought it to his lips. "Fire . . ." he murmured. "Silk and fire . . ."

His eyes met hers and held them as he began to unwrap the tartan. He moved slowly, deliberately, his gaze never leaving her face, and she knew he was telling her he would undress her completely.

Christmas felt her heart hammering in her chest as his hands moved over her with the familiar sureness. She'd remembered this in her dreams, craved it in her deepest yearnings. His fingers brushed the tips of her breasts, and she gasped, feeling the liquid heat build below. He caressed the smooth line of her hip and thigh, and it was as if her joints melted.

Finally his hands cupped her buttocks, pulling her against him with possessive persuasion before letting the last folds of tartan fall to the floor. Christmas uttered an

ncoherent cry, wrapping her arms about his neck to
bring him closer.

"Ah, love," he breathed, his mouth trailing a path of
fire across her bare neck and shoulders, "here is the real
wonder . . . how very perfect you are!"

His head lowered and he found the throbbing peak of
one breast. He took it into his mouth, suckled where his
son had suckled, but with far different intent. Christmas
felt the familiar rush of sensation below and moaned with
pleasure and increasing need.

Jamie growled something deep in his throat and swung
her up into his arms. "I need you, love," he murmured
thickly, his eyes meeting hers as he carried her to the bed.

Reaching it, he lowered her to the coverlet, his eyes
never leaving her face. "I need you as I've never needed
anyone or anything before, Christmas MacKenzie. And I
want you, love. I want you so damned much, I—"

He gave a low, shaky laugh, and she noticed how unsteady his hands were as they tore away his clothes.
"Look at me. I'm trembling like a schoolboy with his first
crush."

She started to protest that the hard, muscular body he
bared could belong to no schoolboy when he joined her
on the bed. The carved features of his handsome face rose
above hers as he met her eyes. "But you *are* my first,
Christmas. My first love, for all my thirty-odd years of
life, and I find myself so eager, I—" He broke off with
another shaky laugh and caught her to him.

"Oh, love, I want you so damned much, I'm afraid I
can't wait!"

Christmas sucked in her breath as the heat of his body,
of skin on skin, as he crushed her to him, sent a violent
surge of need shuddering through her. "Then why do
you?" she murmured breathlessly. "Jamie, I—I want you,
too! *Please?*"

A tortured groan filled her ears, but he was shaking his
head. "Oh, no," he whispered. "I've wanted this, dreamt

of this, too long to do anything but make it last. Woman'
—he pulled away to meet her eyes—"when we're
through, I promise you're going to have no doubt in
your mind that you've been completely and thoroughly
loved!"

And, mastering every bit of control at his command, he
proceeded to make good his words. Beginning with her
eyes, he placed light, yet exciting, kisses on every inch of
her face, murmuring his wonder at her loveliness, praising
it, honoring it with his touch and his love.

Her mouth, he saved for last, lingering there with kiss
upon kiss, savoring the taste of her with a slow, devastating thoroughness that made her ache. Some of the kisses
were soft and gently probing, teasing . . . featherlight
brushes of his lips against hers . . . gentle nibblings
. . . a heady mingling of his breath with her own. Some
were long and drugging. He captured her mouth completely while placing his fingers through the hair at either
side of her head, holding her still for their sweet, lazy
possession.

But soon they became more demanding; his mouth
parted her lips with greater pressure while his tongue
delved inside, hungry, telling her he wanted more.
Christmas responded in kind, eagerly meeting each careful probe of his questing tongue with her own. She felt
his hands begin to course over her body as the exchange
grew in intensity, caressing, building heat from without
and within.

"Jamie!" she cried when his mouth slid to the corner
of hers and the hot tip of his tongue darted into the
crevice. "Jamie, I can't w—"

But her words disappeared in a rushing inhalation of
breath as she felt his hand slip between her thighs, its
path made easy by the wetness there.

"Easy, love," he murmured. "We've only just begun . . ."

And again, he showed her what he meant, his hands

nd lips taking their time as they began to explore her
lready trembling flesh with slow, deliberate care. Strok-
ng, nibbling, teasing, he covered every inch of her torso,
ust as he had, her face. It seemed no part of her was too
mundane for him to ignore, from the tips of her fingers,
which he nibbled and sucked, to the sensitive skin be-
ween her toes, where his tongue darted, sending deli-
:ious shivers upward, toward the woman's place where
he was growing hot and slick.

Christmas began to writhe and twist beneath him, her
:ries demanding he put an end to this waiting that was
lriving her mad. Jamie almost succumbed. His own con-
rol was nearing the breaking point, tested to its limits by
he sweet flesh he stroked and kissed, by the low moans
and insistent cries of the woman in his arms. The woman
he loved. But he'd made her a promise, and he had every
ntention of keeping it.

So he stilled her with yet more kisses, murmuring her
name and his love for her as his hands continued their
magic. He cupped and caressed her breasts, brushing his
:humbs across tips already peaked and pebble-hard. His
mouth followed the path his fingers had traced, tongue
and teeth gently grazing, leaving her nipples outthrust
and swollen, throbbing with the same desire that pulsed
wetly below.

She was arching against him now, her body a bucking,
frantic thing, and he caught her hips with his hands to
hold her still.

"Not yet, love," he rasped as his mouth scorched a
path across her abdomen and lower, "but soon . . .
soon, I promise . . ."

He had a moment's thought that her belly was as flat as
it had ever been, showing nothing of the swollen contours it had when she'd carried their child, but that it was
lusher somehow, as if motherhood had only served to
complete the promise of before.

But then he had no more time to think. Christmas was

like a wild thing beneath him as he gripped her hips and found the slippery heat between her thighs with his mouth. His hands moved to cup her buttocks, raising her toward him. Then he heard her cry out, first in protest, then in ecstasy, when his lips brushed the tiny nub above her cleft, and again—

The shock of what he was doing had barely registered, and Christmas was trying to push him away, her hands tangled in his short, blond curls when she felt his mouth close over her. She screamed his name as the first, tremulous shudders claimed her, protest dying in the rapture of her climax. Then thought became nothing, as sensation after sensation claimed her.

Jamie moved to wrap her in his arms as her body continued to convulse. Her response was greater than he'd ever imagined, and the heady knowledge of the pleasure he'd brought her was enough to send him to the brink. With a harsh cry, he pulled her beneath him and drove into her, the long minutes of his control at last at an end. She was hot and wet and throbbing as he filled her, and he felt their joining set off a new round—climax giving way to climax, in unbelievable succession. There was nothing to do but pick up the rhythm, and this he did, plunging, thrusting, filling her again and again, until the white-hot furnace of his own pleasure broke, sending him spiraling to completion.

He heard Christmas scream his name as his seed spewed hotly into her, and his own cry was harsh in his ears as their mutual climax rocked them to their bones and flung them to the stars.

Christmas felt the rapid beating of her heart begin to slow and return to normal. She wondered how long it had been, how long she'd lain there, wrapped in Jamie's arms in the aftermath. Beneath her cheek she could feel the rhythm of his heart as well. It matched her own.

She felt him stir and looked up to find him gazing

down at her. A lazy grin tugged at the corners of his mouth, deepening the grooves of those masculine dimples that could make her heart careen madly in her chest.

"That's an awfully smug grin, Jamie MacIver," she accused with a teasing grin of her own.

"Is it, now?" he answered. With his finger, he began to trace the delicate line of her brow. The grin broadened. "Why would that be, do you suppose?"

Christmas put on a look of mock indignation. "Hmph! You know very well why!"

His finger ran along the contour of her cheek and across her lower lip, then lower still, tracing her collarbone and the silken skin of her shoulder.

"Ah, but I'd much rather hear you tell it, love," he insisted. "Why do I seem so smug, hmm?"

Christmas felt herself grow warm. "Because of what we —of what you—" She broke off, unable to say the words. She knew he was thinking of what had gone on between them in their lovemaking. She was, too. How could she help it? She'd never dreamed such intimacy could exist between a man and a woman!

"Of what I did to make you cry your pleasure?" he questioned. A teasing light in his eyes accompanied the grin, and his finger had moved to draw lazy circles around the tip of her breast.

Christmas groaned and buried her face in his shoulder, dismayed at the furious blush she felt heating her cheeks. She was no inexperienced virgin, she reasoned. She'd birthed a child, for heaven's sake!

Jamie's low, delighted chuckle met her ears as he caught her chin with his fingers and raised it, making her meet the deep blue eyes where laughter danced. "I was only doing my duty, love," he drawled.

At her quizzical expression, he went on to explain. "We MacIvers have been serving the lairds of Clan MacKenzie for hundreds of years." He kissed the tip of her nose. "And judging by your cries, I'd guess I served this

MacKenzie laird very well, very well, indeed. I'm only glad we didn't wake the babe. You were certainly loud en—"

"Jamie!"

He laughed, giving her a quick kiss on the mouth. "I loved every sound you made, love," he told her.

Christmas knew she was blushing worse than ever. "I —I had no idea lovemaking could be so—so—"

"Intimate?" His look echoed the word.

She nodded, feeling the blush heighten.

"Ah, darling," he said, smiling, gathering her close. "when two people love each other, such intimacy is the most natural thing in the world. You mustn't be embarrassed by it."

"But—"

He stilled her lips with a light pressure from his thumb. "It's just that you're so new to it, sweetheart. But don't worry. I promise I'll go slowly." His thumb caressed her lower lip.

"S-slowly?" She began to tingle inside.

"Mmm," he replied, "from now on."

"From—from now on? Do you mean there's *more?*"

Jamie pulled away so that he could see her face. He was grinning again. "Oh, yes," he promised. "In fact, we've hardly begun." His thumb drew lazy circles around the tip of one breast.

Christmas felt a familiar curling in the place below her belly as he grinned at her, his eyes heavy-lidded and sensual.

"And—and will you teach me all there is?" she inquired with a shyness that didn't hide the spark of interest in her eyes.

"I can sure as hell try," Jamie murmured as he bent to claim her mouth.

They made love at a leisurely pace this time, the urgency of before replaced by a desire to explore and learn more of each other. As he'd promised, Jamie became her teacher in the ways of love, drawing startled gasps of delight and moans of pleasure from her. And in the end, it was the same as before, their rapturous cries blending in a fierce crescendo of mutual release.

Their son awakened, hungry, soon afterward, earning praise from his father for having the good manners to wait until his parents had appeased their own "appetites." Christmas lay amid the rumpled covers of the bed and nursed him while Jamie looked on, feeling a contentment and peace he'd never known.

"We'll be married as soon as I can arrange it," he told her as she returned their sleeping son to the work basket. "I've met the vicar in the village, and he seems like an accommodating sort. Certainly, there's no need to wait until we reach New Orleans."

Christmas's head snapped up, and she regarded him with incredulous eyes. *"New Orleans?"*

"Well, of course. That's where I—"

"There's no 'of course' here, Jamie. I never said anything about leaving the Highlands, and I have no intention of doing so."

Jamie's eyes narrowed and settled on her face as if trying to gauge her mood—or perhaps something deeper, like her sanity. "New Orleans is where I live, Christmas," he said quietly.

"And the Highlands are where *I* live! I came here to stay, Jamie."

"But that was before we— Surely, now that we're to marry—"

"Marriage won't change the way I feel about these hills." Christmas had begun to draw on her clothes, but suddenly her hands were trembling, making this difficult. She willed them to stop as she turned to face him. "I've come to love this place. It feels more of home to me than all the grand houses and estates I grew up in. I won't—I cannot leave."

Jamie ran a hand haphazardly through his thick curls and heaved a sigh of exasperation. "This is crazy. Just a short while ago we managed to find something neither of us thought we'd ever share." He glanced sharply at her. "Or at least *I* did."

Christmas went white at this last intimation, but Jamie seemed to ignore this and went on.

"I love you, Christmas. I love you, and I want to marry you. I want to make a home for you and our son and share it with you and with the other children we'll have, God willing. I want to share my life with you, grow old with you, love you until I die. Now, in God's name, will you tell me what's wrong with that?"

Tears glistened in Christmas's eyes. "Nothing, my darling. There's—there's nothing wrong with that. It's just about all I could possibly want."

Jamie's face softened and he stepped toward her. "Well, then, I don't see why—"

"But I want it all to be *here.*"

He froze. "Dammit, woman, I have a *life* over there! Thousands of miles and an ocean away! How in hell—"

"You could leave it," she pleaded, her heart in her eyes. "Leave it, as I left England. You said yourself, once, that a man could do worse than lose himself in the majesty of these Highland hills. You said— Oh, stay here, Jamie. *Can't* you?"

"And do what?" he countered, angry now, as much at the pleading in her eyes as at this unforeseen obstacle to the perfect bliss he'd only begun to believe in.

Her eyes traveled from his face to the exquisite sculpture across the room. "You could sculpt," she whispered hopefully.

Jamie's eyes followed hers and his mind spun. Give it all up? Relinquish the life he'd known and— But it was insane to even contemplate it! They had to have the income his plantation produced, even if she believed otherwise. He could never agree to live off her wealth, off the Seadog's Treasure. He was a man, dammit! And a man supported his wife and family, no matter what those blue-blooded English fops she was used to did!

Of course, there were those who became absentee landlords, managing their estates through agents and overseers, but he'd always disdained their ilk. The plantations he'd known at home, when this had been done, never managed to produce as well or run as smoothly as when the owner lived on the property. Their profits, if they didn't slip, were frequently gotten at the expense of other things: buildings were allowed to deteriorate, or the people ill-treated.

No, it simply wouldn't work, not for him. Sadly, he met Christmas's eyes and told her as much, explaining all he'd just run through his mind.

Christmas had completed dressing, though her hands trembled more than ever. *Dear God, we came so close—and now this!* "You're set on this course, then?" she questioned dully. "On going back?"

The strain had returned to Jamie's face, and he felt tired, reminded that he hadn't slept in two days. "Without some meaningful way to support a family, without something of substance to occupy my time"—he gestured at the marble sculpture—"beyond dabbling in something that may, or may not, turn out to be successful —I can't see how I can avoid it."

"I see . . ." Christmas walked to the basket that held their sleeping child, gathered the infant into her arms, and gave Jamie a long, lingering look that was infinitely sad. "Then I suppose we have nothing left to say to each other."

She turned and headed for the open doorway.

Jamie stared in disbelief, unable to credit what was happening. "Christmas, wait! Don't do this. We'll—"

His voice died as he realized his words were having no

effect. Christmas and his son were already halfway across the yard.

With a violent oath, Jamie slammed the door behind them.

❖Chapter 26❖

Christmas returned to the manor with steps that dragged, her thoughts a chaotic jumble. More than once, she let her pace lag to the point of stopping, the urge to run back to Jamie's arms overwhelming. But what would she do when she got there? she asked herself. Tell him she'd do as he wished? Leave this place she'd come to love, and make a new home—again—in a foreign land? Give up what had become a part of herself, just for—

Just for the man she loved so much, he was a part of her, too.

Dear God, it wasn't fair! she wanted to howl. The Highlands and her decision to stay represented far more than making a new home. Her decision had come as a watershed in her life. With it she'd made a conscious choice. A choice that had changed her, changed the way she looked at life, and at herself, forever: she'd taken a long, hard look at the values she'd held—the dispassionate pragmatism and preoccupation with financial security —and determined they were shallow and of little importance. Not when compared to the wonderful feeling of freedom and independence she'd found here. She reveled in the knowledge that she was able to stand on her own two feet, be a person who was true to herself—not a silly copy of the kind of empty-headed female the *ton* prized. Those weeks last summer had been the first time in her life she'd ever felt *useful*. They were the first time she'd ever felt so *alive!*

But, a small voice niggled as she carried her sleeping son back to the manor, *would you have felt so alive without Jamie? Can you ever expect to feel so without him? Especially now, knowing he loves you? Aren't you throwing away your last chance for happiness, and largely out of pride?*

And so her thoughts continued as she made her way home, pulling her this way and that, until she thought she would scream.

If she loved him, she would go with him, no matter what.

If he loved her, he would find a way to stay, no matter what.

She owed her son a life with a loving father.

She owed her son the chance to be free and independent, in the land of his heritage.

She was being courageous, sticking to her newfound values and deepest principles.

She was being a fool.

On and on, the torturous arguments went, chasing her far into the night, keeping her awake. She had thought she could never feel a pain greater than she'd experienced in those days immediately after leaving Scotland last summer. After losing Jamie. But now she knew there was worse. She'd held love in her hands for a brief, ephemeral moment, only to let it slip through her fingers.

And that choice had been hers, too.

Sometime in the early hours before dawn, she gave up trying to sleep and went down to the library, thinking to ease her mind among the books Father Liam had suggested she read. And in the end it was not a native work by Walter Scott or the fashionable Robert Burns that helped her make her decision. It was a book commissioned by a Scottish king, but published in English, two centuries earlier: the King James Bible. Christmas found herself leafing through it for no particular reason, except that it was placed among the Scottish literature, owing to its ties to the Scots-born monarch. But when, in her tiredness, she dropped it at one point and saw where the pages had fallen open, she gasped, taking it for a sign. The words her eyes immediately fell on came from the Book of Ruth: "Whither thou goest, I will go."

Tiredly, Christmas nodded. Like Ruth, she would stay with the one who loved and needed her, in a foreign land, setting her own needs aside. Her eyes were dry as she made her decision, and she forced herself to ignore a dull feeling of dread that had settled somewhere deep inside.

Jamie had fared better than Christmas in the matter of finding sleep. Exhausted from having gone without it for two days, and emotionally drained as well, he'd fallen into a restless slumber soon after Christmas left. Then, when his sleep deepened, it had been troubled by dreams. In one dream he'd seen the face of Desirée, pale and still after taking her own life with that of their unborn child; but the face had changed, the lifeless body rising in front of his eyes while its features became Christmas's, and she'd held young Scot in her arms. Yet when he'd reached for her, she dissolved into Desirée again, and their son became a pale, faceless corpse in her embrace.

In another dream he'd been a twelve-year-old boy again, picking up the yellowed newspaper in the attic of his parents' house. But the painful headline, when he saw it, read: CAPTAIN JAMIE MACIVER COURT-MARTIALED FOR COW-ARDICE: DESERTED WOMAN HE LOVED, RATHER THAN GIVING OF HIMSELF.

And in yet a third dream, and by far the worst, he'd smashed his marble sculpture of the mother and child with a sledgehammer, only to look down, when he finished, to find he'd bludgeoned Christmas and their son instead. He'd awakened screaming at that, sweat pouring down his face, his heart hammering in his chest.

Now, having bathed, shaved, and dressed upon rising, he knew what he would do. But it wasn't until he ran into Robbie MacTavish, who dropped by for a visit, that he knew exactly how he would go about it.

Mackie the stableman had just begun to doze in the late morning sun, his tam pulled down low, over his eyes. His morning's work was done, and the sun felt splendid as it soaked into his aging bones while he sat propped against a mounting block in the stableyard.

"Ah, begging your pardon, Mackie, but I wonder if you'd carry just one more message for me?"

The old man's eyes snapped open under the dark wool of his tam. *Och! Nae, no' agin!* 'Twas the American, come t' test the patience and endurance of the Scots temperament, for certain.

Wondering if God was punishing him for not attending the kirk as often as he ought, the old Highlander sighed, pushing the tam back on his head. And then he gaped.

Standing before him was the American MacIver, well enough. He recognized the face beneath that head of thick, curly hair that was the color of wild honey. Squinting against the sunlight, Mackie took in the handsome features and found them to be much less tired and far healthier looking than the last time MacIver had come. He certainly didn't *look* daft. In fact, the deep blue eyes that met his as MacIver held out an all-too-familiar piece of foolscap and a gold coin had never seemed so untroubled and clear. But the *rest* of him!

Jamie grinned at the old servant as he handed him the note and coin. "No, you're not seeing things, Mackie," he told him. "It's an adjustment that was long overdue. I had the help of a man named Robbie MacTavish, who took me to someone he knew in the village, so I trust it turned out well. Now, would you be so kind as to deliver this message? This *is* the last, I promise."

Grumbling under his breath, Mackie rose and accepted the note and the coin, then headed for the manor house. Robbie MacTavish, was it? Well, that explained it, then. Everyone in Inverness-shire knew the wild clansman for the sly trickster he was. "Puir MacIver," he muttered. "The mon's been taken, fer sure, an' MacTavish is likely a guid many gol' coins the richer!"

Christmas was just giving Mrs. MacLeod some last instructions for Scot's care in her absence when Mackie came to the kitchen door.

"Och, Mackie! No' now," said the housekeeper when she admitted the stableman. "The laird's aboot t' need her pony, sae yer business'll need t' wait whilst ye saddle the beastie."

The stableman shrugged and turned to go, but Christmas caught sight of the piece of foolscap in his hand and her heart gave a leap.

"Mackie, wait!"

The old man turned.

"Is—is that"—she gestured toward the scrap of white fluttering in his hand—"a message for me?"

"Aye, an' him that wrote it waits i' the yard." He handed her the note.

Christmas's fingers trembled as she took it, her eyes drinking in the bold slash of Jamie's familiar hand. She'd been about to leave for the croft, to tell him of her decision, her heart and mind flooded with the bittersweet choice she'd made; she loved these wild free hills, and leaving them would mean leaving a part of herself behind. But she loved Jamie MacIver in the deepest part of her being, and for him, she'd give up the other . . . *Whither thou goest* . . .

Still, it had not been an easy choice, and she'd faced making the trip to the croft with deeply mixed emotions.

But now he'd come to her! He was waiting for her

outside, and whatever that signified, she knew it made her decision easier to accept.

With a glimmer of hope in her eyes, Christmas dashed past the two servants who were suddenly grinning at her and hurried out the door, her skirts flying. Around the corner she ran, brushing against the shiny green leaves of the yew hedge in her haste, yanking on the tartan folds of her *tonnag* with impatience when it caught and she had to pause to free it.

Then she was through the opening in the hedge and racing for the stables, her mind filled with a single refrain: *He came! He came! He came!*

But when she burst into the cobbled yard and finally saw him, his image broke across her mind with the force of a firestorm. He faced her squarely, his military bearing as proud as she'd ever seen it, and correctly arranged over his tall, muscular frame were the colors of *her clan*—the MacKenzie plaid. Christmas's eyes flooded with tears, blurring the deep blue and green squares where the widely spaced, narrow red and white lines intersected them, her head a maelstrom of madly careening thoughts, her heart seized by a wild, fierce joy.

Jamie gave her a smile that was heartbreakingly tender and held out his arms. With a sob, Christmas leaped across the space that separated them and flung herself into his arms.

"Hush, now, darling, hush," Jamie murmured as he stroked her hair. He freed one hand to wipe the tears from her cheeks with gentle fingers. "I know my legs look pretty damned awful in this kilt, but you needn't cry about it," he teased, smiling down at her.

"Y-your legs l-look *wonderful!*" she asserted in a watery stammer, then hugged him fiercely about the neck. "Oh, Jamie, I love you so!"

Closing his eyes, drinking in the fresh, sweet scent of her—like sunshine and heather on the hills—Jamie could only murmur, "My love . . . my love . . ."

When they were finally able to break apart, Christmas plied him with a host of questions that came tumbling out. "Where did you find the tartans? How did you know for certain they were the MacKenzie colors? Who showed you how to wear the brooch on the left shoulder? Where did you manage to get a sporran and a badge with the variegated holly of the MacKenzies on it? How—"

"Whoa! Hold on, there, Your Lairdship!" Jamie laughed. "Robbie MacTavish took me to a weaver in the village. It seems the woman took to whipping up a goodly supply of the MacKenzie tartan, once it had gotten about that the laird was here to stay. I prevailed upon her to part with some when I told her I'd be wedding the laird and that I was here to stay, too."

Christmas began to cry again. "Oh, Jamie, are you s-sure?" she sobbed. "B-because I was—was just on my way to t-tell you I'd go with—*go with you!*"

"Och, lassie! These tears o' yers are gettin' t' be a verra persistent habit!" he teased.

Then his face grew serious, and he tipped her chin up lightly with his knuckles and met her eyes. "I'm sure," he said softly. "And the knowledge that you were willing to make that sacrifice for me merely confirms it. You see, after you left, it took some nightmares and some lonely, terrifying hours for me to realize what's been going on. You've always been the one willing to change, to follow, with courage, your convictions and break out of the mold that held you if it no longer suited. Whether it was turning your soft lady's hands to a maid's labors, or proposing marriage to a man, or deciding to bear your child out of wedlock in a wild and distant land, you were always ready to do what needed doing, no matter how it flaunted convention or how risky it might prove.

"I, on the other hand," he went on as he wiped the latest tears from her face, "have been the one who was trapped by my past. Hurt by betrayals of years long gone, I lacked the courage to commit myself to loving again—

until now, that is. So last night, when I saw myself losing you for the second time, I finally realized what a coward I'd been— No, don't deny it. It's true. In being afraid to love—to trust, and be willing to give more than I might get back, I was being every bit as much a coward as they said my father was. I was running away just like him."

He smiled at her, his eyes a deep, midnight-blue. "Well, I'm done running, Christmas. I'm here to stay . . . if the laird agrees?"

Christmas's smile was dazzling in the sunlight. "Och, mon!" she said. "Dinna ye ken the MacKenzies hae needed the MacIvers fer time out o' memory? 'Tis a link forged i' the bluid an' in our hearts."

Jamie's grin was roguish as he answered her, his eyes moving avidly over her shapely figure. "Aye, lass," he said huskily, "an' if the laird will lead the way, I'm of a mind t' forge it i' the body parts as weel!"

With a laugh, Christmas led him toward the house.

☙ Epilogue ❧

Christmas watched her son race across the high pasture on sturdy legs, O'Kelly at his side. Behind them, Father Liam's latest trio of orphans tried to keep up, but they were no match for Scot and the hound. At five, Scot was a head taller than the seven-year-old twins and the same size as the dark-haired girl who thought she was eight, though she couldn't be sure.

But Scot was all sun-browned muscle, with his father's long legs, and seasons of practice at running and other outdoor activities that develop a child's body. The three youngsters Father Liam had found in an Edinburgh slum had had few decent meals in their young lives, if any, until the priest rescued them from poverty. They'd been pale-faced and nothing but skin and bone when they arrived a fortnight ago, and hardly able to run at all, they were so weak and malnourished.

But after two weeks at MacKenzie Manor they were already filling out. Mrs. MacLeod and Cook considered it their personal responsibility to see that the bands of orphans Christmas and Jamie took in were fed good, wholesome food, and plenty of it. And old Mackie wasn't satisfied until he and Jamie had every youngster astride a pony and able to control it.

But it was young Scot who made the greatest difference in the lives of these often sad, frequently frightened children who sojourned here, usually for months before they were placed in warm, loving homes the priest found for them. A happy, exuberant child, Scot was a natural leader, and he had a way of making the orphans feel at home right from the start. Under his influence, the halls of the manor rang with laughter and the sweet beauty of children's excited voices. Scot was a free spirit, an independent-minded Highlander, through and through, and every time Christmas observed him as he was now, running free and glad against the wild and splendid backdrop of the hills, she knew she'd made the right choice in coming here to live. She shuddered to think of her and Jamie's strong, capable son cooped up in some London drawing room or even a schoolroom on one of her tame estates. Jamie had his share of lessons here—he could already read and write simple sentences—but his proper milieu was the open air and the wild, free beauty of the mountains.

"Wishing you could be racing with them, love?"

Christmas laughed as Jamie's arms wrapped about her from behind, his voice soft in her ear. "If I tried, I'd only manage a waddle at best, and well you know it!"

Jamie's chuckle was a warm breath that ruffled the tendrils of hair at her temple, and he gently patted the rounded abdomen where their second child awaited a birth which was about a month away. "Ha!" he exclaimed, "the way this one moves, she'll be racing Scot as soon as she realizes she has legs!"

Christmas turned and grinned at him, remembering her husband's fascination the first time he'd seen what looked like a tiny foot or elbow poking at him through the wall of her belly as they'd lain in bed together. "She? It might be another son, you know."

Jamie gave her that grin that always made her heart lurch wildly—even now, big-bellied as she was. "It might," he said, "but considering the time she's taken to decide to join this family, I rather suspect it's a young lady."

He was speaking of the fact that Scot had been more than four years old before she'd conceived again, and for a long time they'd thought they might have no more children. They hadn't worried excessively about it because there were always children about, to love, thanks to Father Liam. And Jamie had been fond of reminding her that the best part of her not becoming pregnant was that it provided them with a most delightful task: to keep trying.

"Scot's put an order in for a boy," Christmas replied. "He says Jean-Paul complained that little Kathleen is a pest and can't even throw a ball straight, so he's opted for a brother."

Jean-Paul, four, and Kathleen, who was two and a half, were Jacques and Maire's children. The Beaumondes lived on a plantation near Jamie's in New Orleans, where Jacques managed Thousand Oaks for Jamie as well. The entire family had boarded a packet and visited the MacIvers a few months before, and Scot and Jean-Paul had immediately become fast friends.

"Oh, he has, has he?" Jamie took his hand and lifted a lock of her hair, letting it curl about his fingers as it caught the sunlight. "Well, that young man ought to know that I'm excessively fond of a certain female with hair the color of a newly minted copper and that I rather fancy the idea of a second one about the place, in miniature."

Christmas chuckled. "It will likely turn out a redheaded boy who can't throw a ball straight, and then what will the two of you do?"

Jamie caught her face between his hands and gave her a long, thorough kiss that still had the power to make her toes curl. "We'll love it, my darling," he whispered huskily as he met her eyes. "We'll love it, just as we love its mother."

Christmas flushed, still amazed at the way Jamie could make her want him, even here, standing at the edge of a pasture in broad daylight, and she, eight months along! She glanced over her shoulder, wondering if they were embarrassing the new children (Scot was used to these displays of affection between his parents), but instead of the youngsters, she spied a familiar black-skirted figure coming toward them, and in his wake—

"Good God, Father!" Jamie exclaimed as he caught sight of the priest he'd come to regard as a solid friend. "Where'd you come by that pack of young hounds?"

Puffing from the exertions of climbing the steep path, Liam Killeen eyed the four large, shaggy pups that bounded about his heels. "Ye'll recall I went t' the MacMurchie croft t' pick out a wee kitten fer some gentle companionship on me travels?"

Christmas nodded while Jamie asked if he'd gotten his kitten.

"I did not," said the cleric. "Ye see, on me way t' the MacMurchies, I ran inta this grand old Highlander who asked what I was about. And when I told him, he convinced me I'd fare far better with a fine Irish Wolfhound, what with meself bein' from the Auld Sod, don't ye see . . ."

Jamie took a good look at the hounds and felt sorry for their friend, although he hadn't the heart to tell him why. He was thoroughly acquainted with the heavy bone structure of the world's tallest canine; he'd used O'Kelly as a model for several sculptures, the latest commissioned by a man in Dublin named Hamilton Rowan, who owned an Irish hound.

But the pups frolicking at the priest's feet had none of the bone mass of O'Kelly, even when he was their age. They were Scottish deerhounds, and that was the end of it.

"But Father," Christmas was saying, "how did you

manage to come by *four* hounds? Are they all here on a trial, for you to make your selection, or—"

The priest sighed. "Now, as t' that, darlin', I fear I must own up t' bein' foolish, I'm beginnin' t' think. Faith, but I *began* by selectin' merely one o' the pups from the owner, but . . . Well, now, the Highlander was a highly persuasive man. Perhaps ye know of him?"

Jamie's lips twitched as he struggled to keep a serious face. "Yes," he said, glancing at his wife, who was doing her utmost to maintain a straight face of her own, "I think we might."

Father Liam nodded. "Name's MacTavish . . . Robbie MacTavish, and I niver thought t' ask him if he knew ye, but he did seem interested in learnin' if I'd iver met that Frenchman me cousin wed. Now, why d'ye suppose he wanted t' know about Jacques?"

"Oh," said Christmas, daring her husband, with a look, not to laugh, "I suppose he thought the two of you might . . . have something in common."

For the life of him, the priest was unable to summon a reason why this should produce a guffaw from Jamie MacIver, or why, upon hearing it, his dear friend Christmas should threaten to box her husband's ears.

To the Reader

Although it is one of the great clans of the Scottish Highlands, there was nothing in my research to suggest that Clan MacKenzie had roots in Inverness-shire. This background I invented for *Highland Fire*; it, along with my characters, is purely fictitious. There was a MacKenzie who was an earl—Francis Humbarston MacKenzie, 1st Earl of Seaforth—but this man died in 1815, the end of his line, for his sons had predeceased him.

There is validity to the historical ties between the MacKenzies and the MacIvers, however. Along with about a dozen others, including MacConnachs, MacMurchies, and MacVinishes, the MacIvers have a long history of attachment to Clan MacKenzie. Angus MacIver and his descendants may be invented, but their loyalty to MacKenzie lairds has at least the validity of historical possibility.

My descriptions of the MacKenzie tartan and badge were as accurate as I could make them, although Scottish scholars disagree as to when the various tartans began to become associated with the individual clans which claim them today.

The story of the master who unjustly slew his beloved hunting hound is well-known. In North Wales there is a stone plaque over the grave of this dog—whose name was Gelert—and on the plaque, the story of the thirteenth-century prince who killed his "faithful hound" is told. The place is called Beodgelert.

Finally, a word about my dedication: During the writing of *Highland Fire* I lost two beloved companions. I am speaking of my magnificent Irish Wolfhounds, Finn (Fionn in the Gaelic) and Lacey, the source of inspiration for me, in all my historical romances since *The Bargain*.

Words cannot adequately convey my deeply felt sense of loss, and their steady, comforting presence in my life will never be replaced. Indeed, *Highland Fire* will likely be my last "wolfhound romance" for a while. But, who knows? On April 2, 1992, my birthday, a litter of IW pups was born, and I was helpless to resist taking a "peek" at it. The result was a young scamp who now makes his home with me and my daughter. We've named him Brendan, after the hound in *Sabelle*, and he has brought laughter and joy into our lives. Perhaps his antics will provide a new source of inspiration for a canine character in a novel I've yet to write. Do write to tell me, if you think this is a good idea. (Send a SASE to me c/o St. Martin's Press, 175 Fifth Avenue, New York, NY 10010.)

KATHERINE DEAUXVILLE

DAGGERS OF GOLD

Sequel to the bestselling
BLOOD RED ROSES

When the fierce knight, Simon de Bocage, is ordered to deliver a Saxon beauty as a gift of loyalty to Prince Henry, he takes captive Ingrith, the beautiful granddaughter of a once-powerful Saxon noble. Ingrith has designs to elude her enslavement—but then she feels the heat of Simon's desire, and the awakening of an uncontrollable passion within her....

DAGGERS OF GOLD
Katherine Deauxville
_____ 92857-2 $4.99 U.S./$5.99 Can.